SCABBARD'S SONG

BY KIM HUNTER

The Red Pavilions
Knight's Dawn
Wizard's Funeral
Scabbard's Song

SCABBARD'S SONG

SONG

Book Three of the Red Pavilions

Kim Hunter

www.orbitbooks.net

ORBIT

First published in Great Britain in 2003 by Orbit
This paperback edition published in 2013 by Orbit

A CIP catalogue record for this book
is available from the British Library.

ISBN 978-0-356-50312-7

Typeset in Revival 555 by Palimpsest Book Production Ltd,
Falkirk, Stirlingshire
Printed and bound in Great Britain by CPI Group (UK) Ltd, Croydon CR0 4YY

Papers used by Orbit are from well-managed forests
and other responsible sources.

MIX
Paper from
responsible sources
FSC® C104740

Orbit
An imprint of
Little, Brown Book Group
100 Victoria Embankment
London EC4Y 0DY

An Hachette UK Company
www.hachette.co.uk

www.orbitbooks.net

To Zana Hunter

Chapter One

A strange magic was strewn across the sky. It flowed in livid colours – red, yellow, orange, purple, black – mingling, forming many-hued rivers amongst the placid and seemingly unconcerned clouds. It was like lava from a volcano: a hot, searing magic that burned its passage through the azure heavens. Those who saw it were transfixed in wonder. Those who were not looking skyward at the time soon turned their heads upwards up to behold this amazing sight, for the celestial paints reflected on the ground beneath, the sun imprinting the fantastical marbled tinctures on hill and valley.

'What is that?' asked Soldier of his wife the Princess Layana. 'Is it the weather?'

'You and your weather,' she said, smiling at him. 'The people in the world you come from must be obsessed with weather. We hardly talk about it here, yet you speak of it ten times a day. No, it has nothing to do with rain, wind or sunshine. The young wizard is at last stretching his wings, figuratively speaking of course. He is about to fly the nest.'

Layana spoke as if she were perfectly healthy, but in fact she was suffering from a deep loss of memory. She now knew who she was and what her background had been, but only because those around her had informed her of her past. There were certain intrinsic elements to her which a loss of memory could not erase: she had the bearing, walk and speech of the princess she had always been, along with some of the lofty traits of that rank. A family curse had once left her mad, but now the madness had flown with her memory. Soldier was concerned that once her memory returned, the madness would come back too, and it was a terrible lunacy which would have her trying to murder her husband and suffering horrible nightmares.

'And do battle with OmmullummO, the usurper?'

'Just so,' replied Layana. 'Our witchboy has at last reached maturity.'

The late King Magus had named IxonnoxI as his successor: as the Grand Wizard who managed all the magical forces in the world and kept the balance between good and evil. IxonnoxI however was still a young witchboy when the King Magus had quit his mortal coil and this position of power had been usurped by OmmullummO, IxonnoxI's father. Since then, assisted by Soldier, the witchboy had been in hiding. Now he was grown into a full wizard and ready to do battle with his father, a creature who had been twisted into insanity by centuries of incarceration in a sealed dungeon. This was IxonnoxI's message, this magic flung across the sky, telling the usurper that he was coming for his throne in the Seven Peaks.

Soldier had other problems, however. The head of Queen Vanda, Layana's sister, had been tossed over the walls of Zamerkand just a few days previously. Another usurper, Chancellor Humbold, had executed the queen of the city in defiance of an order to open the gates and admit Soldier. Soldier's army of Carthagans, the Red Pavilions, were now camped at the base of the walls. This was a foreign army, of mercenaries, which had traditionally guarded the wealthy city of Zamerkand from its enemies, the Hannacks, the beast-people and other barbarian creatures of Falyum, Da-tichett and the Unknown Region to the north-west. Soldier's Red Pavilions had just humiliated OmmullummO's hordes of fiends, thus finding revenge for their own defeat. The honour of Carthaga had been restored. For a country whose whole society was founded on its military skill, this had been essential to its existence.

Soldier called a council of war amongst his captains. It was held in one of the huge red tents which normally housed a single regiment of the Carthagan army. Layana had told Soldier she would not be present at the meeting, for it was an internal Carthagan army matter, even though the outcome of the meeting would entirely affect her future. Soldier appreciated her decision. It would have been awkward, having his Guthrumite royal wife listening to the discussion: awkward for him, awkward for her and awkward for any of his captains who wished to voice an opinion.

Velion, the captain of Soldier's old pavilion, the Eagles, was the first to speak.

'Never in the history of Carthaga have its mercenaries entered the city they were protecting in order to interfere in politics. At home our elders would be horrified at even the thought of such a thing. Whether Queen Vanda was the rightful ruler or not, and Humbold, who now calls himself king, is but a jumped-up commoner, it is not our business. Our business is to protect, to defend this city against external enemies. What happens within is to do with Guthrumites, not to do with Carthagans.'

She now sat down amongst the other captains and folded her arms to show that she had spoken. Velion would not be allowed to speak again. Each captain had one chance to voice his approval or disapproval of their general's plan, after which they must hold their peace. This was to prevent long and tedious arguments developing, which went nowhere. You spoke your mind then you shut up and let someone else give an opinion. Next the captain of the Tiger Pavilion stood up. His argument followed much the same lines as Velion's. So did the next captain's.

Soldier fought down the feelings of vexation in his breast. He was annoyed with Velion, a close friend and mentor, for starting this trend. Soldier knew, however, that he had to keep his temper under control. He was a man capable of great outbursts of violence, which earned him praise on the battlefield, but were likely to be his downfall off it. He was a man from another world, having slipped through some window between what was for him reality, and this place of mythical creatures and strange wars. Sometime in his old life he had been wronged, or had wronged someone, enough to create a great bitterness and hatred in his heart. Confusion existed in his head too, for he had forgotten who he was or where he came from, and lived under this pseudonym of Soldier, his only link with the past.

'What?' he said at last. 'Have I not led you to great glory? Have I not helped you vanquish those who had humiliated you in battle? Are these the thanks due my wife, the rightful ruler of Zamerkand now that her sister has been cruelly murdered by Humbold and his minion General Kaff?'

The captain of the Wolf Pavilion stood up with a sigh on his lips. 'You misunderstand us, General. We are eternally grateful for your leadership. You did indeed restore our pride in our army and for that we are yours, hand, head and heart. But what you ask us to do – to enter Zamerkand in arms –

is against all our laws. How would our armies find work in other countries and city states if those who hired them knew that at any time they might be invaded by the very force who had been paid to protect them? It is up to the citizens of Zamerkand to overthrow this upstart king, if they do not want him. We cannot interfere. It would put at risk all Carthagan mercenaries throughout the entire known world.'

'Are you then going to obey the commands of Humbold?' asked Soldier. 'This man is a tyrant, a despot. He holds his place in that city through force – the force of his own Imperial Guard. He has installed himself with the use of fear. Those citizens who might oppose him are put to death or thrown into dungeons and tortured. How can the ordinary citizenship rise up against him when he has the Imperial Guard to protect him? Are you this creature's army now? You saw how he murdered the rightful queen. Surely she was the one who hired you, not him?'

'We are neither Humbold's, nor any other king's army. We belong to the *city*. You could order our withdrawal, General – that is your right as our leader. We could go home and leave Zamerkand and the rest of Guthrum defenceless. Is that what you would wish us to do?'

Soldier was in an agony of frustration. His wife's mortal enemy was smugly and snugly installed behind those walls, which could only be breached with a mighty force of arms. It was clear that his Carthagan army would not follow him over the walls or through the gates. Even if General Kaff – damn his eyes and liver – were to parade outside the walls, the Red Pavilions would do nothing to harm him.

Yet, if Soldier were to withdraw his troops from outside the walls, the Hannacks and the beast-people would be back in their hundred thousands, would swarm over the city and destroy the innocent along with the guilty. It could not happen. He could not leave them defenceless – ordinary men, women and children – open to slaughter from invading barbarians. As general of the Carthagan army he could not even challenge Kaff to a duel, for all the same reasons as those which had been given by the captains here today, in this tent. The situation was intolerable. Now he had to go out and tell Layana that her sister's murderers could not be brought to justice. That they had to be left to their mocking laughter, their sneering from the high walls, and she must bear it all silently.

'I thank you for your patience, Captains,' he told them, once all who wished to speak had spoken. 'You must see I am sorely grieved by the outcome of this meeting, but I realise I cannot persuade you otherwise. It is a bitter blow, but I have to hope that somehow justice is coming, retribution for Humbold and his cronies. Thank you.'

On the way out Captain Velion put her hand on his shoulder, seeking forgiveness with her eyes. Soldier nodded, though a little grimly, and she exited the tent in a sad frame of mind. The two would always be friends. Velion had assisted him in rising from nobody to general. They had saved each other's lives countless times. In war, they were soulmates. In peace, they were comrades. Soldier knew that she would have rather died than go against him in counsel, so he knew that his case was lost.

When they had all gone, he was left alone in the vast ochre-red tent that smelled of goat's cheese and lard-fried grits. A raven flew in through the tent opening and landed at his feet. This creature was the very first being that Soldier had met in this bizarre world, when he had awoken on a warm hill-side. The talking raven was both a pest and a boon. He was like a child, an urchin, in feathers. He *was* a boy in feathers. He was Soldier's ears and eyes in the wider world, but also mocked the general incessantly.

'Well, well. Got your answer did you, General? Ungrateful whelps, aren't they? You give them your all and they kick you in the teeth as a thank you.'

'It's not like that, bird, and you know it,' he replied, as always feeling self-conscious when talking to a member of the animal kingdom. 'They have no choice.'

'Most of them say they would die for you,' muttered the raven, hopping from floor to a perch on a tent pole. 'Humbold and Kaff are having a fine time in there, laughing themselves silly at your antics. You saved them from the barbarian hordes sent by OmmullummO and now you can't touch them. The twins would help you. Why not call on them?'

The raven spoke of the White Prince and the Rose Prince, Sando and Guido, joint rulers of Bhantan, a city which thrived on rituals. The youthful twin princes of the small city state had come with their own army to help the Carthagans defeat the barbarians, but it had been merely a gesture, though a much appreciated one. The Bhantan army was quite small and not at all well equipped or trained. It was only because Soldier had helped them retrieve their kingdom that they were giving of their allegiance.

'I'm sure they would come running,' said Soldier, 'but I could not ask them, bird. They have their own borders to defend, against the Hannacks. If they leave their city state undefended, while the Hannacks are in Da-tichett and not here, they will lose all they own.'

'Well, you're in a pickle then, aren't you, boss? Kaff is going about with a rat screwed to his wrist-socket and tearing out the throats of all those citizens who still oppose Humbold.

Yet you can't do anything about it? Let the bodies pile up, I say. More eyes for me to peck out. Fill the gibbets and the gallows with bodies. Lots of nice pickings for corbies.'

'You stop that, you evil-hearted creature.'

This had come from Layana, who had entered the tent without being heard by the other two. The raven squawked, annoyed at being caught out.

'You should tell that wife of yours that women should remain silent while the men are talking.'

'I might remind you,' Soldier said, 'that you're a bird!'

'I was a man once,' replied the raven, mournfully, 'or at least a boy. I would be a man now, if it weren't for that witch, rot her corpse. Now I have to remain a bird, for only she could change me back again, and she's as dead as a Hannack's brain cells.'

'Sometimes I wish I were a bird,' muttered Soldier, 'then I wouldn't have all these problems to solve.'

'No, then you'd have other problems, like where to find the next meal, how to avoid humans with slingshots, where does a sick raven go when there are no such thing as raven physicians and oh, watch out for that stooping hawk! Ah, Spagg. The one human who smells like a corpse yet is still walking around. Well, I'll be off to the rich pickings in the streets of Zamerkand. I'll keep my eyes and ears open for you.'

The raven flew out of the doorway, narrowly missing the head of a squat hairy man with a patch over one eye. This was Spagg, the trader in hands-of-glory, who had now become a sort of companion to Soldier.

Layana said, 'I swear we'll have that bird for Sunday lunch one day. Husband, I came to tell you that I shall be in my tent,' she still spoke like a spoiled princess sometimes, believing everything to be hers alone, 'if you need me.' She then began to talk of the most intimate of matters, despite the presence of Spagg. Matters which should have been for a husband's ear alone. The trouble was, having had a lifetime with slaves and servants present in every room of her household, Layana did not acknowledge the presence of such lowly creatures as Spagg. As a royal personage, she treated such individuals as if they were not there.

Spagg hummed softly to himself while the princess asked her husband if she should remain awake: if he had any intentions of making love to her. 'My dearest love,' she finished, softly, in a voice pregnant with lust, 'I am yours if you desire me.'

Spagg's involuntary humming got louder.

'Stop that noise, Spagg,' said Soldier, 'you're distracting me. Layana, please! I'm not used to having people present when you speak thus.'

'People?' repeated Layana, raising her eyebrows and adding matter-of-factly, 'Oh, I see. You mean *Spagg*. Well, you know where I am if you need me.'

Layana left. She was not an unkind woman. In fact she had married Soldier not even knowing who he was, simply to save him from execution. She was a lady with a kind heart. But her upbringing had instilled in her certain princessly traits which she could not expunge. They were a natural part of her. So natural she did not know she had them. Soldier loved her to distraction and knew of her virtues, which were without number, but he could still be embarrassed by such outbursts as these.

'What did the raven mean by what he said?' asked Spagg in a hurt voice, once Layana had gone. 'I smell the same as everyone else.'

'We won't get into a debate over that.' Soldier paused, after staring at Spagg's face. 'What happened to you? Or shouldn't I ask?'

Spagg wiped his lips, which were covered in a pink ointment.

'My mouth got burned.'

'Severely burned, by the look of it. Your lips are blistered.' Knowing of Spagg's impatient greed, he added, 'You tried to eat boiling stew!'

'No, I tried to kiss a witch. I *did* kiss a witch.'

Soldier laughed, despite the gravity of the situation he was in.

'Now why would anyone want to kiss a witch? They're the ugliest creatures in Guthrum. Have you a fondness for warts? The seven gods preserve you, Spagg, you never cease to amaze me.'

'It was dark,' cried Spagg, defensively. 'How was I to know she was a witch? It was that damned Gnarlggut. She was sort of lurking around the tents. I thought she was a strumpet looking for customers. So I grabbed her and said, "Here I am, darlin'," and gave her a smacker, right on the lips.' His expression turned sheepish. 'I'd had a few too many drinks. When my lips stuck to hers I thought we was a match made in heaven, till I smelled burnin' flesh – *my* flesh. Then I had to rip away, leavin' some of my skin behind. She laughed, the sow. She cackled like a crow and walked off, licking around her mouth. Bloody witches.'

'This is highly entertaining,' said Soldier. 'I need a little light relief to escape my troubles. So, when did this raging desire for sex with women overcome you? You've always shown remarkable restraint in that direction. Food and drink, yes, you indulge yourself to the full. Money, why that is never safe when you're around. But women have never been a priority with you, so far as I remember.'

'Ah, well, you see, I was with Golgath and some of your captains a while before I saw the witch who I thought was a trollop. They was talking about Captain Cossaona, praising him for being a *two-lamp man*. I'd had a few, as I say, by that time. I was – was jealous of him, this Cossaona. The captains spoke with great envy in their voices. Golgath kept saying that he wished he had Cossaona's stamina, that he was one of the world's greatest lovers. Well, *I* wanted to be a great lover. I wanted men and women to talk about me the way they talked about Cossaona . . .'

'Wait a minute, wait a minute, you've lost me. A two-lamp man? What in Theg's name is that?'

Spagg was, as usual, amazed by Soldier's ignorance of certain matters which Guthrumites took for granted.

'A two-lamp man? Why, you know, some women require their lovers to keep – well, you know, to keep on going until the lamp goes out, before – before . . . you know.'

Spagg was clearly becoming embarrassed, so Soldier helped him out by suggesting, 'Before reaching orgasm themselves?'

'*Orgasm*. I didn't know there was a proper word for it. I only know the rude one. Yes, that's it. You know a woman can do it lots of times, to a man's one time. Well, to satisfy the woman a man needs to keep goin' and goin' for a long time without orgamating. So the woman fills the lamp with oil, lays naked and spread-eagled on the silk pillows like an offering to the gods, and says, "Off you trot, my lovely husky hunk, until the wick dims and the light goes out, then you yourself may orgamate."'

'Climax is the word we normally use. I'm not sure the scribes would approve of orgamate. So, a two-lamp man is one who can keep going for the length of time it takes two lamps, one after the other, to burn through their oil.' Soldier was intrigued. 'What about the size of the lamp?'

'Oh, it's got to be a standard-sized lamp. You can't have 'em coming in with an oil lamp the size of an elephant, can you? I mean, fair's fair. But, you see, all this talk got me going . . .'

'Aroused you.'

'You know all the proper words, don't you? Yes, roused me up, until I thought I had to have a woman. So off I went, looking for one. A *willing* one, o' course. I don't hold with forcing a woman.'

'I should think not – I hang my warriors for that.'

'Yes, and quite right too, General. No, I was looking for a willing partner, and saw this maid lurking around, lookin' under tent flaps, as if calling for custom. She had the right sort of shape to her, so I grabbed her and gave her a kiss. I mean, that's not *forcin'* her, is it?'

'It is certainly taking liberties with a stranger, Spagg, and if that had been a young maid, and not an elderly crone, you might have been in great trouble. As it is, there is no reason why witches can't bring charges for unlawful assault, but since Gnarlggut hasn't brought it to my attention you might get away with it this time. Let this be a strong lesson to you, Spagg, not to attack – yes, it's no good looking at me like that – attack females. Seek their consent first. What if that had been my wife?'

'My head would be on a pointed stick by now?'

'Exactly, decorating my bedpost. Think before you act. You may accost all the cream cakes and beer bottles in the kingdom you like, but do not force unwanted attentions on females young or old, or you'll get more than burned lips.'

'I'm sorry I told you all this now. I didn't want a lecture, I wanted sympathy. I should've said it was hot soup. Well, thanks for nothin', General, I'm off for a walk.' He glanced nervously towards the tent opening. 'I only hope that witch ain't about. She might of got a taste for me. You can't trust witches, you know. They ain't as law-abiding as us real people. An' they're like man-eating tigers – once they get a taste for human flesh . . .'

After his talk with Spagg, Soldier went for a walk himself, to stare at the walls of the city which towered above the red tents of his army. So, it seemed that though the regime inside those walls was not wanted by the citizens who lived there and was perpetrating murder upon its population, he – Soldier – would be unable to intervene. It was not his way. It was not his way at all. To smash down the gates would take but a short time. To pour his warriors into the city, that was his desire. To drag Humbold and Kaff out into the street and behead them, as they had done with the rightful queen, that was Soldier's way. All these damn politics. They got in the way of justice. Yes, he was bursting to behead and quarter those villains, Humbold and Kaff, and scatter their remains over unhallowed ground.

Kaff! Now there was a man he took pleasure in challenging to single mortal combat every day, and would feel no regret in killing when the time came. Kaff, when he had been a captain in the Guthrum Imperial Guard, had been in love with Layana. Was *still* in love with Layana. And Soldier's wife had never completely denied Kaff the right to be in love with her. Oh, she had never reciprocated in full, but had always regarded Captain Kaff – as he had been then – as one of her protectors, as a friend. Well, how much of a friend was he now?

When Soldier had condemned Kaff for decapitating her sister, Layana had said, 'We don't know it was him. He may have tried to prevent it. It was probably Humbold who ordered it.' So she was still clinging to shreds of affection for the man – Soldier's deadly enemy – even though Soldier was in no doubt of his wife's fidelity. He knew she loved her husband fervently, without question. She simply continued to cling to the idea that Kaff was basically a good man, a man she had once considered for marriage. Soldier guessed it was that fact which kept the light burning. Layana could not believe that someone she had once been fond of could be so base and evil, for she had lost her memory and only knew what others told her of her past.

'Oh, the folly of our loyalties,' muttered Soldier, as he stepped around the graves of comrades recently killed in the fighting, 'they will not let us look at the truth.'

Soldier had once cut off the hand of Kaff. Now that man had a mechanical stump into which he screwed various implements, including live animals such as rats and hawks, their rumps removed and silver screw-threaded butts replacing their live rear ends. Kaff now used it as a feature to instil fear in his enemies. Next time I'll cut off his head, thought Soldier, then see if he can screw something in the place of *that*. The idea gave him some satisfaction, until he considered that Kaff might use a tiger's head, or that of an eagle, and the dream turned nightmarish again.

Soldier went to the gates of the city and, as he had done ever since the day of the last battle, called for Kaff to attend him from the other side.

Eventually, after keeping him waiting a long time, the voice of Kaff came through the grille on the gate.

'What is it, the usual?'

'Yes, you coward. Meet me in a neutral place. Single combat.'

Soldier could hear the grinding of teeth. 'I am no coward and well you know it. But a general is not his own man – you know that too. I may no longer risk myself in such games. I have an army to command. I am too valuable, I am told, to throw away my life in duels.'

'I am a general and *I'm* willing to do it. You have no commanders. You make the rules yourself.'

Even as he was speaking Soldier knew he was going to be disappointed yet again. It was true, Kaff was many things, but he was no coward. It must have been agony for him not to rise to Soldier's baiting, especially as Soldier and his men were hurling taunts at those on the walls, day in, night out. Humbold was the only man inside those walls who could forbid Kaff to meet Soldier in combat. He must have done so. To lose Kaff would be to lose his right hand. The false king needed a strong right hand to keep his confidence high. Kaff was that man. Humbold had probably promised Kaff Soldier's head on a platter, one day.

'I'll be back again tomorrow,' said Soldier.

'It will be the same answer.'

'Yet I want to hear it from your own lips.'

Soldier left the gate, still in his quandary.

The magic was beginning to drain from the sky now, along with the light of the day. Soldier wondered whether IxonnoxI would be coming soon, to begin his war. A war between wizards! How was that to be enacted? Was it to be single combat, or would the young IxonnoxI require an army? Would the Carthagans follow Soldier into battle against IxonnoxI's enemy, to install a new King Magus? Soldier believed so. The fate of their own country across the Cerulean Sea was in the same hands. The presence of the King Magus affected the whole world, not just a single country, and it was in every mortal's interest to have a just King Magus.

Flames flared to life in the watchtowers above. In the camp of the Red Pavilions the lamps were lit, the fires were burning, the torches blazing. Night had come to Zamerkand and its surrounds. The scent of tallow, perfumed lamp oil and burning faggots was in the breeze. The aromatic fragrances of the day, coming from the earth, had been put to bed.

As Soldier walked to his own tent, a midge came and whined in his ear. It seemed to be saying something to him and he consciously felt at his side where his singing scabbard – a sheath empty of its sword – hung from his belt. This magical scabbard had saved his life several times, for it sang when he was approached by an enemy. The scabbard's name was Sintra, stitched in gold thread on its leather. There was also another name there, that of Kutrama, the sword. But Soldier could not remember ever having held the sword, nor did he have any inkling where it was. He just knew that Sintra yearned for her male counterpart, and Soldier hoped that one day they would be reunited again.

'I must find my long-lost sword,' Soldier said to Layana, when he reached his tent. 'A midge has told me that now is the time.'

'A midge?' Layana was bathed, powdered and perfumed, and now lay on silk sheets waiting for an amorous husband. Love, fortunately, has no memory to lose and she found she had deep feelings for this man she was told belonged to her. The unwanted interruption to her evening plans was somewhat exasperating. 'What in the name of the Seven Peaks is a midge?'

This brought Soldier up short. 'Oh, of course,' he said, 'I've not seen midges here, in this world. They come from my last. In the summer we were plagued with the devils. That creature which just gave me a message must have come from my previous world – wherever that it.' Things were doubly complicated because Soldier too was suffering from memory loss, but only of his former life in another place and time. 'We're a fine pair, aren't we?' he added jovially, removing his breastplate and kicking off his sandals. 'Both of us with addled minds. I don't know who I am or where I come from, and you have joined me now in this hell of blankness. You, I'm sure we can cure, but I don't want your lunacy to return with your memory, so we've got to do it right. We must take advice before we do anything drastic.'

'Are you coming to bed or not?' groaned the waiting Layana. 'I've had enough of midges and memories for one night. You can go looking for your sword tomorrow. I know just the creature to help you . . .'

The following morning she was as good as her word.

'I was speaking with a local farmer the other day, negotiating for roasting chickens, when he told me of a sword-finder,' Layana said, as she pulled a dress over her head.

Soldier, still lying in bed, mellowed by the previous evening's lovemaking, frowned. 'Why would he do that?'

'Because I asked him. Ever since I met you a few months ago . . .'

'Many years ago.'

'. . . you have been bemoaning the fact that you once owned a sword called Kutrama, which you wanted back.'

'I have the scabbard – she needs her blade.'

'I know how she feels. I was a bit in that way myself, yesterday evening. Anyway, I thought to ask around, for a sword-finder. And I've been told that the best one is amongst the dog-people.'

Soldier went up on his elbows. 'The dog-people!'

'Why so alarmed, my husband?'

'The dog-people – in fact *all* the beast-people tribes, but especially the dog-people – have been sworn enemies of Guthrumites since the dawn of life on this world.'

'They have? Why *especially* the dog-headed people?'

'Because – because . . .' He stood up and stroked her hair, looking into her eyes. 'Because one of them – well, he attacked and – and assaulted you. I killed him, later. I decapitated him with a sword and held his severed head up to ridicule before the armies of the beast-people. They despise all Guthrumites, but they hate *me* with a vengeance. If I went into their territory . . .'

'I see,' she said. 'What if I were to go for you?'

'No – you fought well in the battle the other day, but you are not going to do my work for me.' He made his decision. 'I shall go in, with Golgath and Spagg, if they'll come.'

'Isn't Golgath the brother of General Kaff?'

'Yes, but I am more a brother to him than his own kin – he hates Kaff as much as I do.'

'Never underestimate the power of fraternity, husband.'

'I'll try to remember that, wife.'

Golgath, when he was approached by Soldier, instantly agreed to accompany the general into the dog-head region north of Falyum. Spagg grumbled, asked whether Soldier thought he was mad, argued when Soldier put the case to him, then when Soldier felt he had persuaded enough, finally agreed to manage the pack horses and the cooking. The three mounted men set off in the early dawn. They were riding to the land of dragons, snake-people, horse-people, wolf-people and other such creatures. It was an area where the gods had mixed human features with those of beasts, mostly a human body with an animal's head on its shoulders, and real people were not welcome there. The dog-heads had been amongst the hordes that Soldier and his army had recently crushed under the walls of Zamerkand.

They stopped the first night in the cave of an old warrener, a hunter of rabbits, who sold the meat for the pot and the skins for hats. The old man lived naked as a wild creature, with only his thick, long, greasy grey hair forming a cloak around his body to keep him warm at night. He gave his guests a black-toothed grin before inviting them into the cave.

'Old yellow dragon's cave, eh,' he explained. The walls were blackened by smutty fires. 'Not many of 'em about nowadays. You can see where they used to sharpen their claws, on this piece of gneiss here. Eh? Eh? Wily old bastards, the yellows. Smoke you with their nostrils, so they would.'

'I've killed a few dragons in my time,' boasted Spagg to the old man. 'You can't tell me about dragons.'

'Betcha ain't killed a witch, eh? Eh?'

'Witches? I chaw 'em up and spit 'em out. How about you?'

Golgath rolled his eyes at Soldier, as if to say, we've got a pair of them here.

'Yep. Killed a witch once. Spurlggrot her name was, eh? Chopped her head off when she trapped me in a net made o' gorse. The head bit me then rolled down a rabbit hole. I got sick, o' course, and I burned the body in a fit of pique. That left her head loose, to roam the underground tunnels of rabbits, moles and the like. Lords and peasants out huntin' in this district will tell you they hear her calling, from deep underground. It's said that warreners like myself sometimes get their hands bit, savagely, when they reach down into rabbit holes. Once you get witch-bit, you swell up like a black bladder and burst, if you don't get magic help. Nothin' worse than a witch-bite for turnin' you rotten as last year's plums.'

'I take it you ain't been bitten again?' asked Spagg, impressed in spite of himself.

'I'm the one killed her,' said the old man, proudly. 'She can't touch me no more. It's like some diseases. Once you've had 'em, you can't catch 'em twice. I've already been witch-bit once.'

'And so on, and so forth,' murmured Golgath, unrolling his blanket. He yawned, before saying, 'Now where did I put that bragging stick?'

'Up yer arse,' snapped the old man, before turning the spitted rabbit over the fire.

They slept the night in the cave with the old man, then continued their journey. It was true that in the old days they would have met with many dragons on this route north: yellow, red and green. But now there were so very few. There were rumours of an albino great-dragon, which roamed the Unknown Region to the north-west of the marshes beyond Falyum, but these were unconfirmed. The wingspan of a great-dragon was a hundred yards. They could chase you until you dropped, and their front legs were small and dainty, so they could get their claws into any crevice. The appetite of a great-dragon was voracious, bones, flesh and all, so if you saw one, you didn't usually live to tell of it.

The next day, and the next, they continued north-eastward, into the country of the dog-heads, until they sighted their first beast-person. Once they had been seen, of course, they knew it was only a matter of time before they would be attacked. Sure enough, they were halfway across a plain when a hunting pack of twelve dog-people spotted them and came charging up in a cloud of dust, barking and yelping and waving their spears. It appeared they believed the three men to be ignorant of where they were, until Soldier unfurled the truce-standard, which was blue and white. Even the dog-heads recognised this flag and to a certain extent respected it – at least until they heard what strangers wanted, *then* they killed and ate them.

'What do you want in my country, blue-eyes?' growled the dog-head leader. 'You will go on to my lance and be cut?'

It was not an invitation, this latter question, it was a threat.

'I come to see the dog-warrior called Wo,' said Soldier, 'the sword-finder. My wife the Princess Layana of Zamerkand told me he is the best in the business. I need him to help me find a sword.'

The dog-head's mouth fell open, revealing his rows of fangs. His tongue lolled out as his hairy face took on an expression of incredulity. Then his expression hardened.

'You be the blue-eyed *Soldier*, general of Carthagans, slayer of the noble and dogly Vau, of our canine-peopled nation.'

Soldier's blue eyes were unique in a world of creatures with only brown eyes and he was thus ever known by their colour.

'Vau?' Soldier spat the word. 'May he rot in his grave without his head. Vau was anything but noble. He was *in-famous*. He assaulted my wife – tore her face with his teeth, scarring from brow to jaw down one side. His head was a cheap return for such treatment.'

'You admit to kill Vau?'

'I would do it again, twice over, and laugh.'

The alpha dog-head looked round at his fellows, his tongue lolling out in amusement. They stared back at him and yelped, averting their eyes from their leader, as submissive members of the pack are wont to do.

'We has got the Soldier! Killer of our persons!'

Soldier drew his sword, as did Golgath. Spagg nervously armed himself with a pair of daggers, one in each hand.

'You might kill one of us,' Soldier said to the dog-head, 'but you will all die, every one. You have seen me fight the terrible Vau. You have seen me wreak slaughter on your packs in battle. Golgath here, the brother of my most bitter enemy, General Kaff, is as good a fighter as I am. Spagg there will mop up any wounded or weak among you. Now, do we get to see Wo, or do we chop each other to bits?'

The alpha dog-warrior closed one eye, as if in thought, then wheeled his horse and said, 'You follow.' He went charging off, yelping like a puppy, with his pack following after. Soldier and the other two followed at a more leisurely pace, keeping their guides in sight. Eventually they were led into a valley which was thronging with dog-people. Spagg was absolutely terrified and now regretted joining Soldier and Golgath.

The dozen or so in the hunting pack went charging around, yelping and barking, until the three men were surrounded by hundreds, if not thousands, of dog-heads, all with hostile eyes. Jaws were snapping and the air was hot with the musty breath of hounds. Their hairless bodies, as pale as Soldier's own, seemed incongruous beneath the canine heads. They really were nightmare creatures, with their tall, hairy ears, their drooling mouths full of sharp teeth, and their strong, wiry human bodies.

'What now?' cried Soldier, determined to show no fear to these creatures, who thrived on tearing cringing curs to pieces. 'Will the warrior Wo, finder-of-lost-swords, come forth to speak?'

A tall, willowy creature stepped from the mass.

'I be Wo,' he said. 'What will you with Wo?'

'I am Soldier, Commander-in-Chief of the Carthagan army. I seek a named sword, which has been lost to me for many years.'

'Why will you with Wo? I am enemy of Soldier. All these,' his arm swept over the glaring dog-heads, 'are big enemy of Soldier. You be moon-struck to come here amongst us. You kill many dog-people with you sword. You take head of noble and princely Vau. We tear you to pieces, now you come into our den. I eat you eyes. I eat you liver. I eat you *heart*.'

A great howling followed this speech and some of the younger dog-warriors went scampering around on their knuckles, like real dogs, yelping at the tops of their voices.

'That so?' said Soldier, ready for this eventuality. He swung himself down off his horse. 'Well, I challenge you all to single combat. You cannot refuse. It is one of your unwritten laws that you must accept.'

'What?' cried Wo, stepping back with a surprised look on his face. 'What you say?'

'You heard. I will meet you all, one after another, in single combat, here, today. If the first one kills me, so be it. But I think he will not. I think I will kill at least a hundred of you, if not more, before I tire. You saw me fight Vau? He was your best single fighter, your champion. I slew him with so much ease it made your eyes water to watch me. You dog-warriors, you are fine in packs, but alone you cannot match me. Remember Vau? He was a great braggart, but a poor champion. I took his head from his shoulders and held it up, worked the jaws to make him bark in death, like a puppet. One after the other then, you cannot refuse. Otherwise where is your pride? Where is your code? Where is your *honour*?'

They howled again, this time with a note of despair in their voices.

Soldier drew his sword and made a practice swish at the air.

'And after him,' cried Golgath, also swinging out of the saddle, 'will come me! I too challenge the whole pack to single combat.'

'And,' gulped Spagg, his legs shaking, 'me.'

'Wo first then,' said Soldier.

But a young dog-warrior rushed forward, swinging a club. Soldier stepped aside from the blow aimed at his head, and swiped through the club at the handle. The weapon was in two pieces, the young warrior staring stupidly at the stump gripped in his hands. Then he realised the point of Soldier's sword was at his throat. He whined a death-song, expecting to be run through. Soldier stayed his hand.

'We have not come to kill, we have come to seek a sword. I want no deaths, but I will take them if I have to.'

A large dog-head, surrounded by a retinue of others, barked something at Wo. This was undoubtedly an alpha chieftain, if not a king amongst them. It seemed Wo tried to argue. The bark from the king of dogs came louder and more force-fully. Wo hung his head for a moment, then looked up. He had had his orders. He nodded at Soldier.

'No deaths. You very clever man, to challenge single combat before we swarm all over you. Very clever. If we swarm you, we kill you quick, but we see you fight one-on-one and know you very bad man inside. Very bad. I think you kill too many of us in single fight. Oh yes, in the end you die, but only after many of our pack. How you know we must say yes to single combat challenge? Very clever. I will do finding for you. Then you will go and we will come after you, catch you before border, and cut you down. Wo looks forward to tearing pieces out of Soldier.'

'Thank you.'

Soldier, Golgath and Spagg camped down by a stream, well away from the ground-holes and mud-dwellings of the locals. The first thing Golgath did was go along the bank of the stream and collect aromatic herbs. These he cast liberally around the camp site. This was to counteract the damp odour of dogs, which was powerful enough to drive anyone to distraction, even Spagg, whom no one could accuse of being fragrant. Thankfully they were upwind of the dog-people, but just occasionally the wind felt it necessary to create a back-draught, and the stink that wafted over was unbearable.

Although they kept a guard for the first night, they were not molested. They split the night into three, with Spagg doing the first watch, Golgath the middle and Soldier bringing up the rag end of the small hours. No one bothered them. Watchfires burned in the villages over the rise, filling the heaven with light and blocking out the sharp points of the stars.

Beast-people were not that much interested in what was above their heads. They were, like most animals, ravenous a lot of the time, and if not eating it, out hunting and gathering food. Every so often during the night one nervous bark would set off a whole chorus of them, often ending in group howling, before some organised watch went around the mud dwellings and hammered on the doors with sticks, to restore quiet.

Must be in their dog-nature, thought Soldier. Difficult when you are half-beast, half-man.

In the grey dawn Soldier took a short walk, away from the direction of the dog-men, to get the stiffness out of his limbs. The scenery was scrubland: mostly hard, sandy soil, with the occasional thorn bush or hardy shrub to break the monotony. The beast-people certainly had the poorest land in the region.

No crops would grow out here, in this desert landscape. Any game would consist of small tough birds or the occasional rabbit colony. Such a harsh environment was likely to breed savage and hostile creatures such as the dog-warriors and their animal-headed cousins. Raiding and pillaging was probably their only means of obtaining supplies.

An idea suddenly came to Soldier, which made him stop in his tracks. It was a crazy notion, but he was desperate to get inside Zamerkand. He decided to put the scheme to Golgath and get his reaction.

It was while he was mulling over his latest plan that he saw a snake grappling with a heron. It was a few seconds before he realised that it was the serpent that was in trouble. The heron was attempting to eat the snake. Soldier ran forward, waving his arms, and the bird let go of its prey and took to the air. The snake wriggled away in the dust, finding the shelter of a rock. Why Soldier had reacted thus, he himself had no idea. It was purely a spontaneous gesture. But of course the reptile appreciated it and called out, 'I am beloved of the goddess Kist and your reward for saving me is three single commands, to be used over insects, reptiles or birds. Use them wisely, warrior.' With that the creature was gone, under the stone.

'Well, there you have it,' said Soldier cheerfully to himself. 'You go out for a short walk and come back with a reward.'

He had no idea how or when he would use his commands, but he had no doubt that at some time or another they would be useful to him.

When he got back to the camp he found the raven waiting.

'Oh, there you are. I thought maybe the dog-warriors were cooking bits of you in their old black pots.'

'No, I am well, thank you for asking.'

'A purple heron just told me you stole his breakfast. That's bad. You can't make enemies of us birds, you know. We rule the air. You'll get shat on from here to the Cerulean Sea and back again.'

Soldier ignored this attempt to draw him into an argument.

'How is my wife? What use are you to me if you can't give me news of home?'

'She's well enough. Kaff has been to visit her.'

'You always say that when I'm away.'

'It's true. He came to make love to the Princess Layana, but she sent him away with a flea in his ear.'

Soldier glowered. 'Why didn't someone cut him down?'

'Flag of truce and all that.'

'Damn the flag of truce – I'd have chopped him where he stood.'

'That's why he waited until you were gone, before coming out from behind the walls. He's still saying he's going to have your head on a trencher, before the year's out. Humbold wasn't with him, of course. Humbold was too busy executing Guthrumites. He won't have any citizens left if he goes on like this much longer.'

'We must get inside those walls,' growled Soldier. 'It's imperative we do so soon.' He went over and kicked Spagg lightly awake.

'Whaa . . . ?' cried Spagg, rolling over. 'What was that for?'

'Time to make breakfast. Wo will be here soon.'

Golgath stirred and sat up. He saw the raven. 'That bloody bird here again?'

'Yes, thank you for asking,' said the raven, mimicking the tone Soldier had used with him a few moments previously. 'And how are you, sludge-for-brains?'

'One of these days, bird, I'll pluck you alive.'

Golgath rose and went down to the stream to wash. When Spagg walked upstream to piss in the very same water, Golgath's roar of protest almost took his head off his shoulders. Spagg came back looking confused and ruffled. 'Where's a man supposed to do his business,' he grumbled, 'if not in the stream?'

'If you have to, do it downstream,' said Soldier, 'but why do it in the stream at all?'

'Just seems natural to do it in flowing water.'

The raven said, 'I see you and your merry band of men are still on the best of terms, Soldier. Everything well organised and working efficiently. Who said you were a barbarian? Well, I'm off. If you don't see me, then you know everything's much the same back at the old farmstead. If you do see me, it might not be bad news, but prepare for it anyway.'

With that, the black bird flew off, into the azure sky.

Wo came down to the camp mid-way through the morning.

'I come to talk now,' he said. 'We find you sword.'

He sat cross-legged on the ground, his head looking heavy on his shoulders.

'Bad night?' enquired Golgath.

'I not sleep good,' agreed the dog-warrior. 'Too many howlings. Dog-people nervous with humans nearby. Can smell the stink of human sweat and human breath. Make them uneasy. Then Wo go drink ysip, to make for sleep, but just get waking drunk and not sleepy.'

'You smell *our* stink,' muttered Spagg. 'That's a turn-up.'

'Ysip?' enquired Soldier.

'Fermented cactus juice,' explained Golgath. 'I wonder he's still got a head on his shoulders, drinking that rotgut.'

'Now,' interrupted Wo, 'we get to business. You know name of sword you want find?'

'I do. Its name is Kutrama and this is its sheath, here at my side, which goes by the name of Sintra.'

'Ah, this is good. Name sword easier to find. Give me you scabbard, Soldier.'

Wo held out his hand, but Soldier hesitated before passing over his valuable friend, the singing scabbard, who had saved him from many enemies sneaking up unseen to cut his throat. Finally he handed over the sheath with some reverence. Wo noticed this and commended it.

'Wo understand. Good that you value this Sintra, who is faithful servant to her master. Good that you treat her tenderly. Now, I hold her in my hands and get from her a song . . .'

'She only sings to me,' explained Soldier, 'and then only when I am being attacked unawares – and then only a wizard's song, which no one can underst—' He stopped in mid-word, astonished because Sintra had started singing, a low and throaty song he had never heard before.

Wo had the scabbard resting on the palms of his upward-turned hands and his eyes were closed, his face lifted to the sky. The sheath's song was melodic and lyrical, as always, but the words were less alien than they had been before today. In fact Soldier understood one or two of them. Fascinated, he could see the scabbard vibrating while she was singing. Wo seemed to be concentrating as much on this movement as on the words of the song. Eventually the song ceased and he handed back the scabbard with as much thought and care as that with which it had been given to him.

'There is a cavern,' said the dog-head, 'under the Seven Peaks. In that cave is an underground sea. At the bottom of that icy sea lies Kutrama.'

'So?'

'So, you must make journey, General.'

'I've got a question for Wo,' said Golgath. 'Why did the scabbard tell you, and not any one of us, where the sword lies? Why are you the finder-of-lost-swords? What special powers do you have over forgotten blades?'

Wo's dog-head gave that lopsided look which passed for a smile amongst his kind.

'My father was waylander, a sword-maker – and his father before him, and his mother before him, and her mother before her. My ancestors always have been waylanders, male and female, since our Seven Gods made the world out of cow dung mixed with straw. Wo has special feeling for swords and their sheaths. They speak to him, as a stone speaks to its hill, or a tree to its root-earth. They trust Wo, to find them their right masters.'

'Why would they trust a dog-head?' asked Spagg. 'I wouldn't.'

'That's enough,' snapped Soldier, at Spagg. Then to Wo he said, 'You must forgive the bigot, he knows no better. Now, one last request. Will you come with me to collect what is rightfully mine?'

Wo's head went back sharply, in surprise.

'What? A dog-warrior and the Soldier, to travel together on the same path?'

'Why not?' asked Soldier. 'Perhaps it will send a message to the humans who see us on the road. And to your own people. Why should two creatures of the same earth not travel as companions? We do not have to love one another. We do not even have to like one another. All we need to do is *respect* one another. Already I have enormous respect for you, Wo, and your talents. If you could find it in yourself to trust me, then I see nothing but good coming out of such a venture. What do you say?'

'What about these two?' Wo indicated Golgath and Spagg.

'They will return to Zamerkand.'

Spagg started to protest, but Golgath silenced him with a dark look.

'And what will be my reward for so to do this thing?'

'Once I take Zamerkand from the hands of Chancellor Humbold, who now calls himself king, I shall send engineers to build terraces out of the hillsides around this valley and an irrigation system using the water from streams like this one. When it is all complete, I shall send seed for you to grow corn or whatever crops you feel would suit best. Finally I shall send builders from Zamerkand to erect two huge barns for this valley, in which you can store the grain you grow on your terraced fields. One barn for oats, the other barn for wheat. What do you say?'

Wo's eyes widened. 'At this time we collect wild grain to make our bread. It is hard to find and much coarseness of quality. The texture of the bread is not good to the feel or to the taste. To cultivate our own corn? You would do all this for Wo, just for him to go with you?'

'Kutrama is very important to me. I need him by my side. I would not wish anything to go wrong with the finding of my blade. You are familiar with such searches. You know the geography, probably better than any Guthrumite or Carthagan. I would feel more confident with someone accompanying me who knows what he is doing. Too many times, in this world, I have bumbled through, being lucky. I no longer wish to trust to my luck. I wish to cover all eventualities and take the safe course.'

Wo leapt to his feet, startling the horses.

'If my chief say yes, then I say yes.'

He was off, running like the wind, towards the mud-houses

of the dog-people tribes, to speak to his chief. He came racing back on a piebald pony, yelping his head off. It seemed his chief had said yes, for whatever reason. Maybe he too thought it was time the dog-head clans and the humans got together on something. Or perhaps he was just thinking of the corn fields and the great barns, one for oats, the other for wheat.

(Who knew how a dog's mind worked?)

'Well, you know what *I* think about this,' said Spagg, packing up. 'But then nobody ever takes any notice of me.'

'I too am not sure this is a good idea. Soldier,' Golgath added, quietly, for Soldier's ears only, 'but I know you too well now to argue. What do you want me to do in the meantime?'

'Go back and ask Velion to take charge of the army. I shall give you my token to verify the order came from me. And I ask you to keep an eye on that evil brother of yours. Also – also tell my wife that I love her and will return as soon as I am able. She will understand – I hope.

'Also, Golgath, can you please arrange for my promises to be met. Send carpenters to make the barns for the dog-people, and grain, and several ploughs, along with two farmers to train them in their use. Can you do that for me, please?'

'Consider it done.'

Golgath and Spagg packed up that morning and were on their way south before noon. Soldier and Wo set off at the same time, heading south with the other two at first, but intending to spur off to the south-west when the trail split, one way turning towards Zamerkand, the other towards the Seven Peaks. When they reached the ancient warrener's cave, Wo had great sport using a fishing line to catch the head of the witch the old man had told them about. For bait he put his hook into a venomous toadstool shaped like a human ear.

The witch's head took it at the seventh rabbit hole they tried and the dog-warrior hauled her to the surface. Once back in the light, surrounded by non-magical creatures, the witch's head went berserk, rolling this way and that, snapping with her terrible and deadly jaws, until the toadstool took its effect. The toxin did not kill her, of course, but it rendered her helpless for long enough for Wo to jam her head in the fork of a tree.

She sang songs while she was thus placed, the fungicide hallucinogens causing her to rave about tall black ships on the high seas and climbers scaling mountains of white diamond ice.

'Now you are able to see the world go by,' said Wo, when she came round, 'you can earn your living as a signpost and give travellers wrong directions when they refuse to feed and water you.'

Strangely enough, she did not seem too unhappy with her new station in life, though she did remark that she felt a little vulnerable, jammed as she was in the crutch of the old oak.

'Yet I still have one weapon left to me,' she shrieked, answering her own fears. 'I am still able to spit poison into the eyes of those who short-change me.'

It was at this point in the journey that the two parties went their separate ways. Soldier and Wo struck out towards the Seven Peaks, where the Seven Gods sat and made a muddle of world affairs and the weather. Soldier found it stranger than he had expected, travelling with a dog-person. Their cultures were entirely different, their habits disgusted each other, and their bodily odours revolted one another. Yet they managed to keep open minds, both of them, and fought against their prejudices. Once or twice they felt they had to say something, though they did it without rancour.

Wo, whose grammar improved with every moment he was in Soldier's company, proving him to be quite an intelligent beast, said to Soldier, 'Why do you wear *garments*? The fleece of a dead sheep and the hides of dead cattle? I could not for religious reasons, for they are coats of my brother beasts. But not only that, for being dead the coats easily become filthy within the hour – and yet you carry them around on your body for the rest of the day, sometimes even the next. I find that ugly and loathsome. What do you think you look like, to the rest of nature, with dead skin hanging from your head, shoulders and hips? I shall tell you, you look revolting.'

'It is our way,' said Soldier, shrugging. 'You, I know, would rather freeze to death than wear clothing. Yet you never wash in water. You *lick* yourself clean – *all over*. All that sweaty muck and grime going down your throat. It makes me feel sick even to think of it.'

Yet despite these and other very rare odd exchanges, they seemed to manage to accept one another in the main.

At least he doesn't mark his territory like a beast of the field, thought Soldier. That would be a little too hard to take.

As they came closer to the mountains where the gods sat on their high thrones, so the fantastical side of supernature began to emerge. In this region there were giants and dwarfs, fairies and hobgoblins, sorcerers and marabouts. A flower here was not a flower elsewhere: in place of seeds or scent it might contain darts or poisonous gases. A pretty bird here might sing a song that would kill the listener stone dead. Old men were not what they seemed in this region, for they could run faster than deer and jump higher than antelope. Here winter could fall in the middle of a summer's day as cascading, whirling ice. Winds could spring from nowhere and tear the world apart. Here a sudden deluge could flood a valley in a few seconds and yet an hour later it would be as dry and arid as a central desert. This was the land of things-that-never-were – yet here they were, manifest.

Deeper and deeper the two warriors ventured into the marish-land and woodlands of the warped country beyond the line of reason. A world of nightmares, in which even the dog-headed Wo found it difficult to remain sane, though he had been here many times before. Soldier had visited the region just once before and barely escaped with his life. It was no wonder they moved cautiously, prodding the ground ahead with lances, the horses spooked and ready to bolt at every sprite or wight that popped up from beneath a tuft of grass, happy to do disservice to the invaders. Daylight here was strange, the darkness even stranger. The sun threw out its beams as an oil lamp in a thick fog. The moon and stars glowed but dimly. Pools of water were viscous and stagnant. Fruit rotted on the branches of the trees. Frogs burst in a yellowy pus-spurting manner and let out a putrid stink when stepped upon by a horse's hoof. It was a most alarming place.

Chapter Two

Soldier and Wo camped in a mountainside wood. The snow was thick upon the ground and the branches of the trees were heavy laden. Every once in a while there would be a soft muffled *flop* as a lump of snow fell from a shelf of pine branches to the ground. Fox, wolf, boar and deer tracks were everywhere. Game flourished in this region, guarded from harm as it was by the presence of the gods and the fantastical nature of the area. Not many humans ventured into the magical aura thrown out by the Seven Peaks. Humans tend to like a certain order and predictability about the world. Here there was not chaos, but natural and unnatural spontaneity. Strange things happened just like that, without any real warning, and human visitors tended to be jumpy and wary, having to expect the unexpected.

Wo lit a fire while Soldier went hunting.

Soldier came back with a hare.

'That is the best you can do? In a place thriving with game?' said Wo.

Soldier shrugged. 'The pigs are quick and the deer quicker. Besides, what would we two do with a whole deer or boar? Much of it would be wasted.'

'But a *hare*. Unless we hang it for two or three days it will be tough and stringy.'

'That worries a canine with teeth like yours?'

Wo gave him that lopsided grin. 'True, I can crack open the scapula of an ox with these jaws – but that's not the point. What we discuss here is your ability to hunt.'

'I'm a soldier, not a hunter – don't confuse the two.'

'You can't be both?'

Soldier grimaced. 'As my wife keeps informing me, I'm only a man and therefore can only think of or do one thing at a time. Give me a single task and I'm up to it. At the moment I'm acutely aware of being a warrior and cannot put my whole attention to the skills of hunting.'

The hare actually made a passable stew, being a lazy fat hare in life, having lived high on the hog-grass. Soldier gave the pure white pelt to Wo, who would turn it into a sheath for a knife, or a purse for his loved one. They sat in contentment around the fire, filling their stomachs with the hot stew spiced with herbs. There is something about a camp fire in the woods, amongst the snow, that brings on a sense of well-being in some men. Soldier was one of those. White smoke drifted up through the branches of the trees and into a blackness studded with night's gems. The smell of burning pine branches and needles brought its own feelings of satisfaction.

At midnight some strange creatures came out of holes in the trees. Fairies of a sort, but jet black with small orange eyes that burned like tiny candle flames. Wo told Soldier they were harmless creatures, not like the fairy drots which sucked the blood of mammals. It was the smell of the smoke which had drawn them out of the trunks and they simply flew back and forth on batskin wings through the drifting sparks. Every now and again one of them would fly too low, shrivel and fall into the flames, to go up in a blue-green flare like paper soaked in saltpetre. When Soldier expressed his alarm at this, Wo told him that the creatures only lived for a night in any case, so this premature death was no great loss to the species.

'They are the mayflies of the preternatural world,' said Wo, his human language now well developed, revealing a very sharp intellect. 'They are here and gone in the dark hours. What does it matter, this evanescent life they have, since their souls live for eternity? We are only here to give the soul a chance to embed itself. I sometimes think it would be better if mammals like us were only fleeting creatures. No need for houses, or food, or drink, or *wars*. These are unimportant to a creature with a quick life.'

'You are sure there *is* something beyond life?'

'Absolutely. What would be the point of it all, if not?'

'Well, philosophers have argued over that one for millennia – I don't want to go into it tonight.'

They bedded down, one either side of the fire, and during the night had many more visitors. Mostly these were grey-ghosts, phantom-like beings drifting by in the darkness, but one or two startling forms came right up to the fire, turned the logs with claw, hoof or horn, sniffed the blankets of the sleeping companions, shook the dew out of their leathery wings or whip-long tails, then went on their way again without troubling the newcomers. One weird warty creature actually ate the smouldering charcoal on the edges of the fire, but for the most part they were simply curious mythagos, wandering through the primal woods of a shadowland hollow, neither here nor there. Their world was actually on the edge of dreams and would not exist at all if men simply closed their eyes and thought of nothing from dusk to dawn. These wonderland, nightmarish forms were the product of enlivened unconscious minds, projecting their flimsy shapes into an intangible landscape created by the restless patterns of sleep in the human brain.

The following morning they woke with the first rays of light, and that borderland between reality and fantasy had suddenly moved back, to a horizon far away.

They both went down to a pool to drink and their separate methods emphasised once again the differences between them: Wo lapped, Soldier sucked and drank. They were getting used to each other though.

'Are we close to our destination?' asked Soldier, of the finder-of-lost-swords. 'Or do we still have a way to go?'

'We are virtually there,' replied Wo. 'Over that next ridge, the one bristling with pines, is the cave of Gilchrista and Wilandow, twin dragons who guard its entrance. Within that cave is a crystal cavern and at the bottom of a deep shaft in the cavern is an underground sea. There lies your Kutrama.'

'How do I get past the dragons?'

In the same tone which Soldier had used the previous evening when talking of hunting and soldiering, Wo said, 'I am a finder, not a fetcher. You must devise your own way of passing the dragons. If you will recall, I have never been here myself. It is simply a place I have seen in my vision of the hiding place of your sword. You must find your own way past Gilchrista and Wilandow. I do not even know if they are hostile, but I would expect them to be, or why would they be guarding the entrance to the cave?'

Soldier was a little put out. 'Are there other treasures in the cave?'

'Again, I do not know.'

'Well, a fine help you are.'

'I told you, I find swords, I don't retrieve them. I doubt

the sword would let me in any case. I have seen the hands of thieves and the unworthy burst into flame when taking hold of a named sword. I have seen sword robbers shrivel to nought on touching a magical blade. Not me, Soldier. You must do your own work from now on. I am a spectator.'

'I suppose you're right,' grumbled Soldier. 'Still and all, I would like some assistance, unless you're simply going to turn tail.'

Wo looked grim. 'I have a dog's head, but not its rear end.'

Soldier stared, bemused, then realised what had upset Wo.

'Oh, that – it's just an expression, turning tail. I would say it to another human being too. It isn't meant to be taken literally.'

Wo was mollified. 'All right then. No, I shall not turn and run. I shall accompany you as far as I am able.'

'Good. I appreciate it.'

They travelled that morning to the cave of the twin dragons. When they arrived at the edge of a clearing, there stood the pair, one green, one red, either side of the entrance to the under-earth. They were not leathery dragons, like the little two-legged, red-bellied green dragon who believed itself to be the offspring of Soldier. Soldier had been there at the hatching of this creature and it had imprinted itself on the lost warrior, calling him 'mother' in its own language and following him for a while. Every so often Soldier met with his adopted child and they exchanged simple greetings, delighted to cross paths, before going their separate ways.

These two dragons had a silky sheen to their small tight scales and looked soft and dry to the touch. If dragons had royalty, these would be the princes of dragon-world. Their eyelashes were like velvet brushes, long and curving. Their claws were kept manicured by woodland dwarfs and there were none of the usual blemishes or bruises on their tails, which normal dragons were wont to lash at rocks and trees with. They had tall brows, denoting fine brains, and their ears were like glistening spearpoints: the red dragon's pricked up, the green dragon's bent. They were sister-brothers, these two guardians of the under-earth. Their weapons were their polished and shapely claws, and their long forked tails. There was no fire-breath in their throats, nor terrible teeth, they being herbivores with molars.

'I'll stay here,' said Wo. 'They look gentle enough.'

'Do they?' muttered Soldier, taking a faggot from behind the saddle of his horse. 'Have you looked at their eyes? Everything else about them is soft and warm-looking, but their eyes are like flints. I'm going to get a cold reception.'

'And so you should, until you produce your credentials.'

'Which are?'

'How should I know?' asked Wo. 'That's up to *them*.'

'Oh well, here goes. Have I got my tinder box?'

'Yes, it's there on your belt.'

'Thank you.'

Soldier walked boldly out towards the cave entrance, over which hung a bead curtain, like those which covered the openings to the cooking tents of the Carthagans, to keep out the flies. How strange to have such furnishings out here, in the wilderness, thought Soldier. It was too domestic, in a wild land with wild ways, not to be bizarre. Then his attention was captured by the figure of a hunched old woman, a cowl over her head, sorting through a great pile of bones. She was lining up thigh bones, making what Soldier knew as a pilgrims' path. She took no notice of him whatsoever.

Nearby were more bones, small and large. Piles of round skulls and long skulls; broken rib cages; scapulas; ghastly feet and hands planted like flowers in the ground around the two great dragons. Then a chill went through Soldier as he realised what the bead curtain was made of. Spinal cords! The backbones of warriors who had come to this place and had failed the test. In a pit on the far side of the old woman was a pile of rusting armour, with helmets, breastplates, horse harnesses, chain armour, shields. There were weapons too: many lances and spears, several daggers and swords, a crossbow or two. Here was the graveyard of the unfortunates, with an old woman sexton.

'Mary, Mary, quite contrary, how does your garden grow?' muttered Soldier. 'With finger bones and fleshless toes all planted in a row.'

The old woman looked up, briefly, and cackled, and stared at his chest, his hips, his shoulders.

'Not bad, not bad. But the best, I sell to the fairies,' she said. 'Rib cages to gnome farmers for their harrows. Scapulas to goblins for their spades. Skulls for water carriers. Pelvis bones for flower bowls. Your bones are made of fairy gold, stranger.'

Despite these ugly warning signs – the armour and the bones – Soldier marched up to the dragons. There was little point in pussyfooting around, once he had made up his mind. Dragons would kill you if you were nervous or nerveless, it mattered little to them. At first he thought he was going to be able to stride right between them, without them lifting a claw to stop him. However, just as he was about to do so, they closed together, forming a wall between him and the cave entrance.

'And you are going where?' asked Gilchrista, the red one.

'And for what purpose?' enquired Wilandow, the green.

'I seek my sword,' answered Soldier, 'and was told by the

dog-person, Wo, who is hiding like the coward he is in those trees behind me . . .' a grunt of objection came from the forest fence '. . . that it was here, in this cave.'

'And the name of that sword?' asked Gilchrista.

'Kutrama. I have his scabbard, here.' He touched the sheath at his side. 'Her name is Sintra.'

'Ah,' murmured Wilandow, 'then you would be . . . ?'

'Soldier.'

Gilchrista shook his-her head. 'That is not the name we were given.'

Dismay entered Soldier's heart. 'No, I have forgotten my real name. I was once a knight in another world, in another life. In fact I would appreciate knowing the name I bore then, if you have a mind.'

'Well, we don't have a mind,' said Wilandow. 'We are not permitted to divulge names of people or swords. You'll have to do better than this if you want to walk away whole. What, then, is the name of your bride?'

'You mean the name of my dear wife? Ah, that I can give you,' he replied, eagerly. 'That is the beautiful Princess Layana, of Guthrum's great city Zamerkand.'

'That is not the name we were given,' said Gilchrista. 'The bride we speak of is dead and is buried beneath the snows of another world.'

Despair again. 'Ah, once more I have to fall back on my defence of having no memory of that world, though I do have dreams of her death and those who are responsible.'

'What a pity,' said Wilandow, thrashing his-her tail and raising a dust devil. 'What a great shame.'

The old woman looked up, cackled again, and seemed to be coveting what lay beneath Soldier's flesh.

'Pretty hands,' she said. 'Nice feet.'

Soldier was at a loss. He said, 'How can I convince you?'

Wilandow said, 'You say you are from the other world, the world where your bride rests beneath the snows.'

'My first bride, that is true.'

'And that of course would account for your blue eyes,' stated Gilchrista.

'Yes, there are many in my old world who have eyes of blue, though there are other colours too, including brown.'

'But another came with blue eyes,' said Wilandow.

'And he did not try to enter, so we had to let him go,' added Gilchrista.

Soldier felt anger inside. 'That would be the enemy who has pursued me from the other world into this one and seeks my demise.'

Wilandow said, 'We know something of the customs of this other world you claim to be from – Gilchrista will ask you a question. If you answer it, you may enter. If you make a mistake – any mistake – you will die. Are you ready to stake your life on such a question? Other knights are not. They run away in great fear, though we carol the word *coward* after them, trying to goad them into returning. Are you too a coward, knight? Is that how knights act in this world you are from?'

'Is that the question?'

'Of course not,' growled Gilchrista, 'for there is no proper answer to that one, only one man's opinion.'

'Give him the question, Gilchrista.'

'My question is: can you list for me by rank of noblemen and commoner which bird of prey each is entitled to use when out hunting with eagle, hawk and falcon? Take your time. We've got years if necessary. But you must get the list right. Make no mistake. We are aware of your customs and laws, blue eyes, so if you get it wrong we will know instantly.'

'You mean, for instance,' said Soldier, his heart pounding, 'only a king is permitted to hunt with a gyr falcon?'

'That's what we mean, but you've missed one out. You didn't start at the top of the list as I expected you to. Or if you started at the bottom, you've missed a whole lot of them. I don't know whether that counts as a mistake already,' said the green dragon, turning to the red. 'What do you think, sister-brother? Do we have to kill him now?'

There was a long pause during which Soldier's heart was racing like mad, then the other dragon answered, 'Oh, I think that was just an example – he can start now, from the top of the list, working his way down through it, but with no more errors.'

'Thank you,' murmured Soldier.

'Speak up! Don't mumble,' chorused the dragons.

'Yes, yes, I will. First comes an emperor, who is entitled to an eagle or a vulture.'

'Good,' cried Gilchrista. 'And so on . . .'

'A king with his gyr falcon. Princes, dukes and earls all have the same bird, a peregrine falcon. A knight of course has a saker, while his esquire may carry a lanner on his wrist. The knight's lady will hunt with a merlin. Now, what comes next?' Soldier's mind was in a bit of a whirl. His brain suddenly froze. What came next? Was it a yeoman? He could not remember. It had, after all, been years. A yeoman, yes – yet there seemed to be someone missing. What rank? Surely, below an esquire and a knight's lady was a yeoman? There was no other . . .

'Take your time,' said Wilandow. 'Time has a mellow quality for dragons. We savour it.'

'I think . . . no, wait, yes – next comes *a young man*. He carries a hobby hawk!'

'Excellent!' cried Gilchrista. 'You nearly forgot the young man, didn't you?'

'Yes, I admit it, I did, but then the hobby came to mind and I fitted the hawk to the rank.'

'That's a brilliant way of doing it — but the list is not yet finished,' said Wilandow. 'There are more, of course.'

'Yes there are, for after the young man comes the yeoman, who hunts with a goshawk. Then the priest, whose bird is the sparrowhawk. After him the holy-water clerk, whose permitted raptor is the male of the same species carried by the priest, which we call a musket.'

'Well, there's a piece of information we didn't expect,' said Wilandow.

Gilchrista added, 'No, we weren't aware that the musket was a male sparrowhawk. You learn something every day, don't you? But the list is not yet finished, as I'm sure you know. Continue.'

Soldier's heart started beating again. Surely it was over? As a knight he had not taken a great deal of interest in the ranks and birds below his own station, but he thought he had accounted for them all. Another one? Or two? How frustrating this was. The best thing to do was go through the birds and see what might be missing. He knew his birds better than his people. So, eagle, vulture, gyr, peregrine, saker, lanner, merlin, hobby, goshawk, sparrowhawk, musket . . . what other raptors were there? Harriers, kites, fish hawks like the osprey were not used. Nor were buzzards. There weren't any more, surely?

Even as he was thinking he heard the sound he had heard many times before in his life: a series of *keh-leek* notes, then a repeated *kee-kee-kee*. Soldier had no doubt that it was Wo who was mimicking the calls, from behind the trees, and he went into a cold sweat. Fancy forgetting a *kestrel*. He had almost lost his life because the bird he wanted was such a common sight in his old land that it passed from the mind, like finch or pigeon.

Gilchrista said, '*That* was lucky.'

Wilandow added, '*Very* lucky. I hope you weren't *cheating*, Soldier. Cheats never prosper, you know.'

'You mean that kestrel over there, calling just at the right time. Yes, yes, oh, it was pure luck.' How on earth, or anywhere else, had Wo known that the kestrel was the last on the list? 'So, my dragon guards, the last on the list is the knave or servant, who is permitted to hunt with the kestrel. Have I performed my task satisfactorily? May I now pass into the cave?'

'You have passed the test, you may now enter,' said the red dragon.

'Be our guest,' added the green.

'Oh dear,' groaned the disappointed old woman, cracking open a skull like a coconut, 'all them good bones.'

'Are there any dangers I should be especially aware of, inside the cavern? Or in the underground lake?'

'Who knows?' said Wilandow.

'There's only one way to find out,' added Gilchrista.

'Thanks for nothing,' muttered Soldier. Then came another call from the tree line. It was the cry of an eleonora's falcon – *keya* – a harsher sound than that of a kestrel's call. 'And you too,' he directed back at Wo, thinking it was a good thing Wo had not mimicked the eleonora first, or Soldier might have been lying dead on the ground from a dragon's blow.

Soldier pushed through the curtain of spinal cords and entered the cave. Just inside he unhooked his tinder box from his belt and, striking a light, lit the faggot he carried. This torch enabled him to see into the cavern. There were dancing shadows on the walls, from the flame of the torch, but apart from those nothing moved. Encouraged, Soldier ventured further inside. Right at the back, some twenty yards from the entrance, he found a set of steps cut out of the rock, descending into the lower regions of the earth. Boldly he took this route, hoping it would lead him to the underground sea. No ugly gnomes sprang out from behind stalagmites, nor goblins dropped from overhanging stalactites. It would indeed have been rather unfair if, having got past two formidable dragons, there should be more obstacles in his way.

In fact he made it to the stony, sloping shore of the flat, calm sea without hindrance. He tested the water with his hand. It was icy cold. He began to strip to the waist, wondering how he was going to see to find his sword in the blackness of the lake's depths. Once ready for his dive, he held the torch high above the water. It was clear down to the bottom. There he could see something shiny, a blade definitely, lying on the bottom.

'Why is there no lady of the lake?' he muttered. 'There's usually a lady of the lake who retrieves the sword.'

But for a king, not for some ordinary mean knight. Knights had to get their own swords.

It was then he saw the silvery shadow pass below. A long – very long – lean, serpent-like shape. Perhaps fifty yards in length? But as thick as a man's waist, with powerful swimming muscles. The serpentine form moved away, out of the light, and into the darkness of another part of the lake. A shiver went down Soldier's spine. It was naïve of him to think that there would be no more obstacles, obviously. Here was another. A monstrous water serpent. Only one? Perhaps there were more? Soldier continued to watch, counting the seconds under his breath.

The monster came again, a full minute later. This time Soldier had time to study its head, which seemed to consist of two large eyes and foot-long jaws with rows of teeth. All along the creature's back was a dorsal fin with sharp spines protruding from it. There was a similar fin running the length of its belly. It snaked through the water with ease, turning once it reached the rocky shelf. Then, again, it slid out of sight, into the darkness of the rest of its kingdom.

Soldier watched, timed the visits. There seemed to be only one, which was good. But gauging the depth of the water and the time it took to turn away then reappear again, Soldier guessed he would not be able to retrieve Kutrama and get back to the surface before the monster was on him.

He stared down into the depths of the water. There was a hiding place down there, beneath the shelf of an overhanging rock. If only he could hold his breath long enough for the serpent to come and go, so that he could surface and escape without harm. There was nothing else for it, but to make the attempt. If he failed . . . well, that was not to be thought of. He jammed the torch in between two stalagmites, so that its light fell on the water.

The next time the serpent turned and slid again into the shadowy regions, Soldier dived. It was all he could do not to expel his breath with the shock of the cold. He kicked hard, going downwards, the temperature of the water growing even colder as he did so. It hurt. He hoped his muscles would not seize in such freezing conditions. He used his arms as well as his legs to propel himself downwards. Ten seconds. Fifteen. Was he any closer? His lungs were aching already. Twenty seconds. Twenty-five. Nearer and nearer came the bright blade. It almost seemed to be dancing with excitement down there, on the verge of being owned again.

Another ten seconds and Soldier was now struggling, fighting to stay under while the natural buoyancy pulled the other way. Finally he was there. His hand reached out and grasped the hilt of the sword. He had it in his fingers. Yes, the blade was his! But there was no way he could stay under the water. He had to reach air, and soon, or he would burst. The rock hang was near, but his body could not stand the lack of oxygen. He kicked upwards, heading for that burning light, above the surface. On the way up he sensed the serpent returning, then saw her silvery form above him. Kutrama was in his grasp, though, and if the monster impeded him, he would run the point through the lower jaw and up through the creature's brain. Armed as he was, and so desperate for a breath, he knew he would kill the reptilian undersea creature if it attacked him or got in his way.

But it merely turned at the rocky shore, made its usual manoeuvre sliding past the smooth, stony edge of the cavern floor where it fell into the lake, and out again into the dark side of the water. It was like a captured wild beast, circling its cage, going round and round without any real purpose except to keep moving. Soldier broke the surface and sucked in air, his throat rattling with the effort of drawing in oxygen. Then he was on the shoreline, lying on his back, no longer troubled by the cold, but feeling the warmth of exhilaration. He had succeeded! He had the sword. The word *Kutrama* was etched into the blade. His sword, indeed. It vibrated in his grasp, as if welcoming his grip. They were together again.

He had left the scabbard, Sintra, with Wo in the woodlands. Having dressed again, he made his way out of the cave, snuffing the torch at the exit. The two dragons now took little notice of him. Gilchrista gave him a passing glance, but Wilandow merely sniffed. Soldier felt that he should be given some credit, some praise, for having achieved his goal. But these were dragons who had seen it all before, and would see it all again. Once they had established that he was the bona fide owner of the sword, then their work was finished.

The old woman gave him a little wave, as if to say 'never mind, perhaps next time?' and watched him go down to the forest fence.

Wo was ecstatic. 'You did it? I never thought you would, Soldier. I've sent a good few to this place and never seen hair or tooth of them again.'

'It was your kestrel call that saved me,' admitted Soldier, 'though I could have done without the follow-up – the eleonora's falcon cry.'

Wo looked mystified. Soldier frowned.

'Was that not you? Who made those bird cries?'

'No,' said a voice from above, startling the two companions, 'it was me.'

The raven sat on a branch above the dog-man's head.

'Well,' said the raven, 'you don't think a *man* could mimic a bird that well, do you? I did it perfectly. If it hadn't been perfect, you'd have been stomped to pulp by those dragons out there. They don't like cheats, you know. Your rib cage would be ploughing up a gnome's beet field by next week, if it wasn't for me.'

'I grant you that,' said Soldier, 'but why the eleonora?'

'Just to make you sweat a bit. You know we have this ambivalent relationship. Sometimes I like you, sometimes I hate you. It's one of those things.'

'Shall I leap up and crush that bird in my jaws?' asked Wo, his eyes narrowing. 'I could do it just like that, before it flies.'

'No, no,' answered Soldier, wearily. 'The creature is right – we've both helped each other in the past, and equally, we've both wronged one another at certain times. Leave him be. I must now return my sword to its scabbard . . .' He took Sintra from Wo's hands and, with a feeling of completion, slid Kutrama into her.

Immediately, the scabbard began a song. This was like no other song she had sung before. It was the first time Soldier had understood all her words. Very quickly all present realised what the lyrics were saying. This was no wizard's melody, but the history of a knight. Soldier was being told, at last, who and what he was, and where he came from. The information was startling and unwelcome to Soldier's ears. He had dreamed much of it before, without the names. He was aware of slaughters and massacres. He was aware of great wrongs, but had not known who had perpetrated them and for what reason. The people in the song all seemed to be villains, there being little honour in the protagonists. To his great sorrow he learned that he had a history of which he should be ashamed. Soldier had *felt* this history before now, of course, had known he carried a great hate in his soul, a great enmity, which had come out at times with terrible unstoppable ferocity, such as when he killed Wo's kinsman, the dog-head Vau.

'*You are the knight Valechor*,' sang Sintra, '*and for ever and aye you have fought a feud against your mortal enemies, the Drummonds. Border clans, both, your family and theirs have killed and killed, until one fateful day the Drummonds slew your bride, the lovely Rosalind, and left her bleeding in her bridal gown upon the mountain snows. You, Sir Valechor, went out with your men and hunted the Drummonds down until you had them trapped in a valley, where you slaughtered them without mercy, hate and rage ruling your head.*

'*It was a terrible massacre, one at which you were cursed a thousand times. Blood soaked the white heather and the dog-rose with-*

ered on the vine. Animals now forsake that glen and birds no longer nest in its trees. Yet there was but one who escaped, a Drummond who swore to right the wrongs his clan had suffered under the Valechor blades. This Drummond rose to the right hand of the king, who stood apart from your quarrel and let it fester. Squabbles between knights, the king said, were not the concern of the throne, but to be settled by the combatants themselves. The king would not interfere, no much how much blood was spent.

'There were battles between the knight Drummond and you, the Valechor, and in one such battle the bride of Drummond was slain. An eye for an eye, a bride for a bride. It was an accident, for she wore the armour of a man, and was for all appearance yet another knight. But Drummond was of no mind to accept you, when you asked for forgiveness. Death was all that rested in his mind. Your death. The death of the last Valechor. Or the death of the last Drummond, who shortly after the killing of his wife murdered the king and took his throne. This is how things are now. One seeks the death of the other, even following him into another world.'

'The Drummond is here,' snarled Soldier. 'The Drummond came after me when I was flung from the battle into this world.'

'The Drummond might have been here first and you the one to follow.'

'That's true – but I must find him . . .'

'And seek an end to this terrible feud!' cried Wo. 'Soldier, listen to yourself! You may have been a ferocious enemy to the dog-people, and others in this world, yet you have always fought with honour. Just the one time, with my kinsman Vau, did you overstep the mark, for that unconsciously brought to mind your old antagonism, the old wrong you suffered – the assault of a bride. Vau had scarred the beauty of the woman who was your wife and so you took revenge. All this can be understood, if not approved of. But now it should be over. Two brides dead, two families stripped to the very core, with one member of each left living? That is enough. Forget this Drummond. Live your life now.'

There was great sense in what Wo was telling him, yet Soldier still felt a pull, an urge to plunge his sword into the last Drummond. Surely then it would be all over – and only then? Yet, if he were to reflect on his feelings when other Drummonds had died – something he could do now the memory of his old life had returned – he would admit to feeling no great satisfaction, no settlement of his anger, no sweet sense of revenge. If anything, he had felt more agitated, more angry. Part of that anger was with himself, for being seduced by thoughts of revenge, for allowing rage to control him. Guilt was as heavy a burden as a feeling of injustice – if not heavier. The still, small voice of calm was the only sanctuary from hurt and injustice. Not to forgive or forget, but to stand aside from revenge, to avoid indulgence in destroying the destroyer. To remain aloof from the great violence which fuelled a feud and turned it into a wild fire of torture and death impossible to halt.

'You are coming to the right decision,' said the raven. 'Leave it be, Soldier. Leave it be.'

Soldier's head came up. 'You know what I am thinking?'

'I guess it,' said the bird. 'I can read your facial expressions – they take me on a journey through your head. You humans are very transparent, wouldn't you say so, Wo?'

The dog-headed man nodded, emphatically. 'Yes – easy to read.'

'But the Drummond is here, seeking my death,' groaned Soldier. 'Am I to stand by and let him kill me?'

'If he attacks you, of course you must retaliate,' said Wo,

'but do not be the first to initiate violence. Every man has a right to defend himself. But do not seek him out, goad him, provoke him. Remain conscious of his presence, but otherwise ignore the creature.'

Soldier suddenly felt hypocrisy working. 'This, from a doghead?' he said. 'You plunderers, pillagers, rapists? Why, you live by raiding farms and wayfarers, let alone joining together to attack cities. What right have you to lecture me on violence?'

'What you say is true. There are those among the head clans who follow the Hannack way. The Hannacks cannot help themselves. They have the brains of sewer rats. They have human form but they have the intellect and the mind-set of a low predator like a shark. We, on the other hand, are quite bright in comparison. Yet there are those among us who preach barbarism as the only way of life left open to us. I make no apology for them, or for myself; I only offer advice to someone who – in the last few days – I have come to admire. You once acted in a brutal and bestial manner – do not now return to that way, or I believe you will regret it.'

Soldier sighed and began to pack his horse.

'You are right. You are both right. I still live by the sword, it is true, but it is the honourable sword of a soldier and not that of an assassin or murderer. One must live within rules, within laws, or perish in the mire of the utterly depraved and deviant. I have not finished fighting wars – there is the question of Humbold and Zamerkand to settle – but if I must fight, it should be with reluctance, when all else has failed. I will try to negotiate with those inside the walls of Zamerkand. If they will give up Humbold, I will settle for that. I will not break the laws of two lands and attack the city with the Carthagan army.' He looked up at the raven, then across at the dog-person. 'And I will forget Drummond. He is already dead to me.'

'Good, good,' said Wo, getting up to pack his own mount. 'And so, you have a name now. Valechor – is that what we shall call you?'

Soldier thought about it, then said, 'No, in this world I am known as Soldier.' He grinned. 'Would you have me give up all the hard-found fame which that name gives me in this place and hide behind one that means nothing to the hearer? I have no desire to slip into anonymity – yet. The name of Soldier is respected . . .'

'Feared and hated,' added the raven.

'. . . throughout several kingdoms,' finished Soldier, ignoring the black bird. 'Until IxonnoxI is established as the rightful King Magus, and Zamerkand has got rid of Humbold, I must hold on to all the power that my name in this world gives me.'

The raven flew off, leaving the two companions to finish their packing. When they were ready, the riders set off again, back towards where the tracks forked, one going to Zamerkand, the other to Falyum. On the journey the scabbard, who had not finished her song of the old world to her satisfaction, filled in the rest of Valechor's history. It was during a battle in his old world that he had been flung into this one, to wake on the warm hill's side without his memory, there to kill a snake which had been about to attack a raven, and there to meet a hunter who was to become his wife.

That terrible battle, sang the scabbard, was still in progress. Men had been fighting on that high boggy moor for as many years as Soldier had been in Guthrum. On one side had been the last Valechor, on the other had been the knight Drummond, who had killed the king and made himself monarch, thus giving himself access to greater forces of men-at-arms. With these overwhelming numbers he had marched against knight Valechor, the armies meeting on a high moor covered in peat hags and deep marshy ditches. The fighting had been at its most desperate when the two leaders, both living under a curse, crossed swords. The battle being fought on a magical moor, the spells they were under were invoked and they were flung out of their own world and into another. In that other-world they made their own separate ways, not knowing of the other's presence.

Drummond had landed in the continent of Gwandoland and had retrieved his named sword, and thus his identity, before Valechor. Valechor himself had pitched into Guthrum and had become the Soldier, a man who had risen from condemned malefactor to general of a mercenary army without knowing his real name or where he came from. Both had suffered extraordinary experiences. Now, as in their old world, they had chosen opposite sides. Valechor was for IxonnoxI and Drummond for OmmullummO. It seemed Soldier was destined to battle with his old enemy, if they both survived long enough to cross swords again on the killing fields.

'And what of my poor army in the old world?' he groaned. 'Are they then fighting still?'

'*They are bloody but unbowed,*' sang Sintra. '*Every day they rise from their beds and fling themselves into the fight anew. Many seem lost to the black bog. Many seem to succumb to disease. Some appear to die of mortal wounds. Yet somehow on that magical moor their numbers do not decrease. They strive, as do the more numerous enemy strive, to gain advantage. Both armies have long grown weary of the fighting, and rise from their sleep with a great lethargy of spirit, their limbs like lead, their bodies groaning under the weight of their efforts.*

Their souls have grown grey with age and violent toil and all kneel around the evening watchfires and pray for an end to the fighting, so that they can go home to their families. They age not, nor do their kin, for eternity is become an hour, all time constricted within those sixty minutes during which two clashing armies should settle their differences and the survivors return to their hovels, farms and castles in their homelands.'

'Fighting still?' groaned Soldier. 'How terrible. They must feel they are in hell, and indeed for all eternity. A battle that lasts for ever. What can end it?'

'Only you, and the last Drummond, can end it.'

'How?'

'There are two ways – friendship, or death.'

'The death of both, or the death of one?'

'That is unknown.'

'Then we must put aside our old enmity and become friends,' Soldier said, bitterly. 'It is a hard thing to bear, but it must be done. He will see that. He too has an army, has friends who have been fighting his cause forever-and-a-day. Drummond will want to see an end to this fighting, surely?'

'One would think so,' said Wo, who heard all and was as amazed and appalled by it as Soldier himself. 'One would hope so.'

The face of the sky was mustachioed by a long, thin cloud which drooped at the ends. It seemed peaceful enough up there. Whenever there was trouble between gods, wizards or magi the sky was the place where that trouble was reflected. Things had obviously quietened down since the day the magic colours had been cast over the heavens.

The two creatures, the man and the dog-man, parted at the ways: there was now respect and friendship between them.

Soldier continued back to the Red Pavilions where Layana

was waiting for him. She had been standing on a hilltop, watching the horizon, and rode out to meet him. They embraced, exchanged frivolous love epithets, and were then interrupted by the arrival of others. Spagg came, full of excitement, wanting to hold the sword Kutrama (which Soldier would not allow him to do). Also Velion and some of his friends from amongst his troops. By the look of things, and Velion confirmed this, not a great deal had changed in the time Soldier had been away.

'It's good to hand back command,' said Velion, as they all rode back towards the Red Pavilions. 'I don't enjoy all that responsibility.'

'Can you arrange a meeting with General Kaff?' asked Soldier. 'We need to start discussing peace plans.'

'Peace plans?' Velion, and indeed Layana and the others, were all flabbergasted. 'This is Humbold you're talking about.'

'I know, I know, but up in the Seven Peaks I've had a lot of time to think. The violence has to stop somewhere. Any agreement of course would mean that Humbold would be exiled for life . . .'

That evening, Soldier and Layana were alone for the first time.

'What has happened to you, my husband?' she asked. 'You seem quite different from when you left us.'

'I'm still desperately in love with you, if that is what concerns you,' he replied.

'No, it is not.' She stared into his face. 'I can see the love still burning in your eyes. But you are strangely quiet and thoughtful. And all this talk about peace with Humbold? This has been a sudden turn-about for you. Something has happened. Is it to do with your sword?' She nodded at the weapon which now lay across a stool, within reach.

'Partly, yes. When I returned the sword to the scabbard, Sintra began to sing to me. Now you know she has always sung, when an enemy has been sneaking up on me, as a warning. But before now I have not understood the words. This time I did, and it was not to warn me, but to tell me of my past history in my other life, my other world.'

'Hmm. And now you know who you are? I'm envious.'

'Don't be. I can tell you *your* history and it is full of nothing but self-sacrifice and good. *My* history on the other hand is atrocious. I am a bloodthirsty barbarian – was – in the other world. I pursued a family and drove them into their graves. Oh, yes, they did the same with *my* people, killing my newly wedded bride amongst others, but what does that signify? If I had sued for peace instead of hunting them down and slaughtering them, how different my history might have been.'

'Can you believe the song? After all, the scabbard is surely not a living creature, in the true sense, and may be just repeating the song mechanically, like an automaton.'

'Kutrama and Sintra were once flesh and blood, before they became a weapon – they have souls like you and me.'

'But still, can you believe her song?'

'Yes, because it feels right. Now that the memories have been stirred from the dust of my brains, they are familiar. They make sense of who and what I am today. I am, my darling, a knight called Sir Valechor – a terrible fellow whose blood-rage has been responsible for starting wars. Here, in this world, I have killed, but as a soldier. In my last life I think I might have murdered in cold blood. Certainly it seems I was responsible for the massacre of the Drummonds, the last of whom is here too, having followed me – or I him, it's not certain – yet he is here, to kill me.'

'All this killing talk is doing your spirit no good. Come, sit on this silk cushion at my feet, while I soothe your brow with my cool hands. There, there, my husband.' The stroking of his brow was indeed helping. The hot fever of agitation left him. He relaxed and even took a drink of wine. Layana continued speaking softly to him. 'Sir Valechor? That sounds a noble name. Much nobler than Drummond. Did he come from the same country as you, or was he an enemy from a distant land?'

'We were almost cousins. Certainly we were both from border clans, neither in nor out of two neighbouring countries. Our allegiance was to the greater northern king, though the greater southern might call upon our arms if not our total loyalty in times of crisis. So long as these greater-kings did not fight each other, both Drummond and I might be of the same army. But in my world, border clans are notoriously unsettled, often earning their living by raiding, much as the beast-heads and the Hannacks do here. Our lesser-king knighted both of us, heads of families, hoping this would tame our wildness. It didn't, of course, it simply gave respectability to our savage ways.'

'I understand, but that is in your past now, in a distant place you can't reach even if you wanted to.'

'True. I gain some solace from that. I am no longer the man I was then, I hope.'

'And I shall call you Soldier, not Valechor, for he is nothing to me, and you are everything.'

How well she understood him, this woman, this princess of an alien otherworld. Better than those in his own birth-land.

They lay on the silk sheets of the bed and talked into the early hours of the morning. This was not a time for making love. This was a time for revelations, for speaking truths and discovering meanings. They clasped each other of course, and held hands, and did all those touching-things that new lovers did, for they had been parted many days. When the grey dawn came they fell asleep, to be woken, near to noon, by Velion.

Velion lifted the tent flap and said bluntly, 'Kaff has come.' Then let it fall back into place.

Soldier dressed in his best sandals, put on the gold breastplate that he had been given by the rulers of Carthaga as a symbol of his generalship and command of their northern army. His sword and sheath he left behind, along with his helmet, to show he was not in a mood for war.

Kaff was standing by a water trough, with his retinue of Imperial Guardsmen. His face was like stone. Once or twice, as Soldier walked to meet him with his own retinue, the Guthrumite stared round him as if checking that he was not going to be attacked without warning.

'General Kaff,' said Soldier, stretching out his hand. 'Good of you to come. There is no need for your caution. There will be no ambuscade within these tents, the honour of the Red Pavilions will ensure that, sir.'

'What's all this?' asked Kaff, his eyes narrowing and the hawk he had screwed on to his wrists fluttering her wings. 'I don't trust you.'

'All what?'

'Calling me "General Kaff" and all this smooth talk.'

Soldier said, 'It is time to talk peace. There has been enough killing. I am prepared to offer you open terms. We simply take off from where we left it, over a year ago. The Carthagans will remain as the mercenary troops which protect the outer walls of Zamerkand. The citizens of Zamerkand will throw open their gates again and the siege will end. No one but

Humbold will be brought to book for any crimes. There will be no executions, no imprisonments, only a demand for complete loyalty to the new Queen Layana and a return to the rule of law and the old court.'

'Just like that? No conditions?'

'Only one. Humbold must leave. We will allow him safe passage through our camp and will not pursue him into the wilderness. But go he must. He will give us his word – such as it is – that he will never return. He will also swear not to raise an army, nor join one, which has as its goal the defeat of Zamerkand. I very much doubt whether his word means much, but it would probably satisfy my captains . . .'

At that moment Soldier was interrupted by a shout from the walls of the city, and by another from his own watch-towers. 'A horde is coming!' went up the cry. 'Beast-people!'

There was a sudden flurry amongst the two retinues accompanying the generals, though those two men themselves were curiously unruffled. Both were very experienced warriors and one thing they never indulged in was immediate panic. They took some moments to assess a situation before they gave orders or acted. Soldier was the first to speak. He called up to the nearest watchtower, 'Are they armed?'

'Yes, General.'

'How are they carrying their weapons?' asked Kaff.

'Answer him,' replied Soldier, when there was an indignant pause.

'Trailing them, General – Generals. That is, they are not pricked for war. The swords are sheathed, the lances point to the earth. They come on at a leisurely pace, not urgent, but slow and deliberate.'

'Their numbers?' asked Soldier.

'Perhaps a thousand,' said the man in the watchtower,

experienced at gauging the size of an attacking force. 'Maybe a little more. I see them more clearly now. It is a single clan. The dog-heads.'

Soldier nodded. 'There is no cause for concern. This is a friend of mine, Wo. He has brought all the warriors in his tribe. It might be well to wait until he gets here before you give me your answer, General Kaff. I don't *know* why he's here, but I can guess. Will you wait?'

'Certainly, if only for a flea-bitten dog-head.' Kaff's expression turned harder. 'I'm surprised at you, Soldier. I am your enemy, it is true, but you can have no greater foe than the dog-heads. Why, you have just finished slaughtering the flower of their youth beneath these very walls.'

Soldier did not answer this rebuke. Instead he sent up the word not to attack the dog-heads, but to allow them inside the camp. The Carthagans became nervous at this order and one or two captains arrived hot-foot to argue with their general, but he remained firm, telling them that if the beast-people were going to attack, they would have come with more clans than one, and with their allies, the Hannacks. 'We will admit them,' he ordered.

It was indeed Wo leading the warriors. He barked a greeting from a long way off and requested audience. Soldier called him in. Wo left his clan outside the confines of the tents, which eased the minds of the nervous captains.

'Ah,' said Wo, dismounting and clasping the hand of Soldier. 'Forgive my lolling tongue, it was a thirsty ride.'

'You would like water?'

'Not unless my troops can drink too. Before I say anything else, I thank you for keeping your word. The carpenters have done well and the two great barns are nearing completion – wonderful huge affairs, larger than ten ordinary barns. I am told the horkey boy has already placed a branch in the rafters, as is the custom with barn building in Guthrum. The seed corn has arrived, along with ploughs and two skilled farmers. All is well, my friend, and we are very pleased.'

'I am glad for that. Farming is less glorious than hunting, but more satisfying in the end.'

Soldier ordered that waterskins should be taken out to the dog-clan warriors. To Kaff's disgust, Wo lapped at the water in the algae-green horse trough. Then, with droplets hanging from his jaw-hair, he nodded, taking in the scene around him.

'Have I arrived at a bad time?' he asked Soldier. 'Or a good time? Is this the surrender of the city?'

'It most certainly is not,' growled Kaff.

'Good, because I have come here to solve my friend's problem. General,' he said to Soldier, 'you cannot march on Zamerkand with your Carthagan troops and oust the false king, but there is nothing which says you cannot use another army. My warriors are at your disposal. They are but eleven hundred in number . . .' the guard in the watchtower heard this and nodded with great satisfaction '. . . but under your guidance, for you know the city and its weaknesses, we may force an entry.

'Once inside I have told my warriors to kill only Imperial Guards and to leave the civilian citizens alone.' He sighed. 'This will not be easy for them, for they are used to sacking a captured city, killing all its inhabitants, eating the babies, and setting fire to the libraries, palaces and places of learning. They enjoy a good bonfire, do my warriors. But they have agreed to follow my orders and will only pig-stick those in uniform. A book or two, may go missing, and end up on a camp fire, but for the most part the city will remain whole, and the populace untouched.'

'This is a very generous offer, Wo,' said Soldier. 'I am very touched.'

'Touched in the head,' growled Kaff. 'You must be insane if you think these animals will keep their word.'

'I trust the oath of my friend here and would take it over yours,' snapped Soldier. 'Now, will you convey my message to your leader? If he is to leave it must be tonight. He is allowed to take two people with him, three horses, and baggage. There must be no jewels or treasure. Only clothes, food and water. Otherwise we will attack in the morning.'

Kaff nodded and Soldier sensed resignation in the other general's expression. He hoped he was right. Soldier had no desire to attack the city and did not even know if he could manage to take it with so few warriors. After all, the beast-people and the Hannacks had besieged the city for a year without breaching its walls. It was true that Soldier did know where the weak spots were, and naturally he believed himself a better general than any within the ranks of the beast-people and Hannacks, but still the task was by no means an easy one. Better that Humbold should leave.

The Red Pavilions were a-buzz with the news. The dog-heads were camped just two hundred yards from their own ochre tents! What a very strange state of affairs. Curious Carthagan soldiers wandered out to look across the short divide and were stared at by equally curious dog-warriors. The two had seen each other before, of course, but only in the heat of battle, and only bristling with iron and steel. Yet here they both were, two bitter enemy groups, wandering around quietly eyeing each other. It was a pity there were no children in either camp, or they would have probably met in the middle and played games together, oblivious of the fact that the grown-ups were wary. Children tended to do that, after insulting each other, and getting over the initial shyness of meeting with strangers.

Soldier took Wo back to his tent. Before they got there something occurred to Soldier.

'I want you to meet my wife,' he said, 'but should she react in a hostile way, I hope you will not be offended.'

'My cousin, Vau,' said Wo, nodding. 'I understand.'

But Layana's memory of that terrible attack, when her face was torn half away, had gone from her mind. She was surprised to see the dog-person, it was true, but there was no animosity in her. She offered food and drink, a place to sit and talk, and thanked Wo for helping her husband find his named sword.

'It was nothing,' said Wo. 'I was pleased to be of service – and that word from one such as myself – who is disgusted by the servility of curs and mongrels and their kind when around humans . . .'

'I understand. I never thought of it before, but you must find such behaviour in hounds quite contemptible.'

Wo shrugged. 'They are all-dogs, we are but part.'

'Your use of language is excellent,' Layana praised Wo. 'I had thought that dog-people, and all the beast-people, had difficulty with our tongue.'

'I was with your husband some time. You know, we have good brains, and it did not take me long to gather a considerable vocabulary and learn to use the grammar.'

'Yes, of course. Forgive me. My prejudices are showing. It's just that one of us would not learn as quickly.'

Wo shrugged and gave that lolling smile he used, as if to say, well, there you go, we are superior at some things. He and Layana talked some more. There was supper, of wild fowls and honey, with wine, tea and coffee, then Wo went back to his clan. Soldier gave the dog-men permission to camp and provided them with food and water. Many of the Carthagans, especially recruits newly arrived from their home country, remained curious. They wandered to the edge of their own camp and stared across at these men with the heads of dogs, sitting round their camp fires, erecting tents, and doing much the same chores as they did themselves.

One young Carthagan asked a veteran soldier, 'Do they eat raw meat?'

'Why, sometimes in emergencies, but mostly they eat it cooked. Cooked meat is easier to digest and they of course have human stomachs. And before you ask, yes, they eat vegetables too. And fish. And fowl. And bread. All the things you and I might eat. In most ways they are not so very different.'

'But they howl. I have heard them howl.'

'Yes, and they bark and yip and yelp. But they fight as well as any Carthagan, if a little recklessly. It's their recklessness which is their failing. They have little discipline and throw themselves at the enemy – which is usually us – with abandon. We defeat them because they are an undisciplined horde, not for any reasons of superior fighting skills.'

'They haven't learned to be an army?'

'No, and when they do, by the gods we must hone ourselves.'

While this conversation was taking place, things were happening in the city: momentous things. General Kaff had spoken to his Imperial Guard. He gauged their mood with their king.

Kings and queens, tyrants and despots, had always run things in most countries. There was one small isle, a place called Hellest, where the *people* chose their king, changed him every three years, but such quirky government was not really approved of outside this one tiny state. For the most part kings were born and kings named their heirs and the people got what they were given. However, there were bad kings and there were not-so-bad kings, and Humbold was regarded as one of the former. He overused his power, decreed laws which were unpopular, executed with wild abandon, paid scant attention to good judgements in disputes between citizens, and – the worst king-crime of all – was attempting to have himself made a living god, absolute.

These failings did not endear him to his troops. It was true he gave them special privileges over other citizens, paid them well, and let them do much as they liked in the taverns and inns of the town, but any king would have done as much. The old queen had given them all these favours. Thus when Kaff suggested they send him on his way, most of them agreed at once, and the others took only a little more time. None of them were looking forward to a long siege, with the famine, disease and confinement that sieges bring. When they learned that there would be no punishments, that they would retain all their rights and freedoms, that all they had to do was take one man – a recent upstart usurper – and send him packing – why, soon the whole Imperial Guard was happy to march on the Palace of Birds and exile the king.

Kaff confronted Humbold in his boudoir. The King was in his silk nightgown, clutching the Jewelled Sword of Kingship which he himself had had forged.

'I have the symbol of my office,' he said to Kaff. 'You – you traitor – you must bow before it, bow before me.'

Kaff stepped forward and with his good hand snatched the sword from the old man's grasp.

'Time to go. Lucky for you, with your life. I could strike you down now and no one would weep. Not even these two . . .'

He spoke of the sisters who had been sharing the King's bed. They saw which way the wind was blowing and gathered up their clothes and scuttled from the bedroom. Humbold stood with open mouth, watching them desert him. He had been betrayed. He had been betrayed by his own general and by his army.

'My friends!' he groaned.

'Your friends?' spat the general. 'Your *minions*. The game is over. It's time to go. You may take two servants with you . . .' Kaff explained the terms.

Humbold cried, 'But the Soldier will kill me the moment I step outside the walls. I had his wife's sister beheaded.'

'He has given his word you will go unharmed.'

'His word?' wailed the King. 'What is that worth?'

'Listen,' said Kaff, 'I hate that man with all the force of my being, I loathe him to the very pit of my stomach, but I tell you his word is sacred. If he says you will not be harmed, then you may rest assured. For my part,' Kaff stared out of the window of the palace while the ex-king fumbled with his clothes, pulling on his hose, 'I shall simply turn again to my waiting game. There will come a time when Soldier makes a mistake, either with his wife, with his army, or with the citizens of Zamerkand. I shall be there, ready to kill him when he does.' He turned back again. 'And you, you puffed-up, paunchy old man, had better watch your back. Soldier will not kill you, but remember the twins, Sando and Guido? They are back, ruling the country of Bhantan. And they have sworn to have your head for past wrongs. I would keep looking over my shoulder, if I were you.'

The gates of the city were thrown open the next morning. Humbold left alone, on an ass, the only transport he could beg. He left with nothing, not even the two servants or slaves he was allowed. None would go with him. He was pelted with eggs, fruit and stones as he left, by a population who had come to hate him. Once outside, the Carthagan army protected him as far as the border to the Unknown Region. Soldier did not appear, neither did his wife Layana. They both felt they could not lay eyes on this despicable figure of a man, who had caused them so much pain.

In the city of Bhantan, the king-twins heard of the release. They sent messengers to Soldier berating him for allowing Humbold his freedom and his life. Soldier replied to their notes explaining his reasons. They replied to his replies, saying they did not understand but respected his decision, and that they would be sending out death squads to hunt Humbold down and despatch his life. They would not rest until they had his tongue and his eyes in two separate bottles, one by each of their bedsides.

Princess Layana entered Zamerkand in triumph and was accepted as queen without question, she being next in line for the throne. There was no real opposition. Layana and Vanda's parents had only two children, both of whom were childless, and apart from some very distant cousins there was no one else carrying the blood-right of the royal line. With Soldier, her husband, at her side most believed Queen Layana had everything she wanted. Her madness had been cured, her disfigurement had been magicked away. She was now a mature and beautiful woman with a noble warrior for her consort. Yet she was still without one thing which she sorely desired. Her memory. No one is comfortable without their memory, even those who have been told that their past is not a pleasant thing to behold and best left in the dark.

Chapter Three

Layana had lost her memory in the deserts of Uan Muhuggiag, in the city of the sands, where those who entered remembered nothing of their former life. Taken from the city by a petulant prince, who had since been killed, she was later reunited with her husband, Soldier. It had taken much fortitude and patience for Soldier to woo his wife all over again. To her he was someone new, someone she had never met before, but she did indeed fall in love all over again. Soldier – and others – had told her as much of her former life as they could remember, including the fact that she had suffered terrible bouts of madness which the memory-loss seemed to have cured. Thus she knew who and what she was, but second-hand. She had no primal memory of herself or her old life. She wanted to be able to recall all those past times, terrible and good, which give someone their whole identity. This was brought home to her when she entered the Palace of Wildflowers and two servants she did not know fell on her neck and wept.

'Oh mistress, oh *Your Majesty*,' cried the one known as Ofao, a manservant, 'how we have missed you and prayed to the gods for your deliverance.'

Drissila, the other, sobbed into her ear, 'My lady, we heard you had lost all vestige of memory.'

'And so I have,' she said, gently extricating herself, and warding off any further display of affection. 'I know you not, young woman. Nor you, the other servant,' she said to Ofao. 'Please, I am uncomfortable with this unseemly show of sentiment.'

Ofao looked shocked and fought back his emotions.

'Well,' he said. 'I don't know what to say.' He went off into a corner by himself, upset by this rejection.

Drissila however was made of sterner stuff and collected herself straight away. 'We understand, my lady, and we must work to making you well again. Unless, of course, it would mean your old illness would return . . . then I think it would be better if you remained thus, without your memory, for your former ailment was horrible indeed. You having killed two husbands and attempted to do the same to the third . . .'

'I tried to murder Soldier?' Layana cried in dismay. She had not been told of these dark patches in her past.

'Many times, Your Highness, but he was made of bolder materials than the first two,' Drissila's voice became full of contempt, 'who I have to say went to their deaths with a whimper in their throats.'

Layana's hands fluttered around her face like two pale doves. 'Oh, my lord, what a terrible person I was . . .'

They were in the Green Tower, Layana's favourite building in the gardens of her own palace. The Palace of Wildflowers was where the princess lived, but she was now queen and was entitled – as expected – to live in the Palace of Birds. Yet somehow she had been drawn to the Green Tower by some hidden need within her. Perhaps 'all vestige of memory' had not gone? Something had taken her to this now unfamiliar room.

Soldier entered, having climbed the spiral staircase with his usual annoyance at the number of steps. 'Ah, there you are, my love.'

'My lord, you are home, safe and sound!' Ofao had someone to cling to who remembered him and rushed across the room with open arms. Soldier narrowed one eye and held up a warning hand.

'None of that, Ofao. You know I can't stand that sort of thing.'

Once again, Ofao backed off, sulking. He went out on to the balcony and looked down, to see huge crowds below. They were expecting their new queen and an excited 'Ooooooohhh' went through the waiting multitude. Some of them cheered, automatically. Ofao perked up. He waved. A few confused souls waved back. Then a great roar went up, hats were thrown in the air, men and women blew kisses. Excitement! Ofao threw both arms in the air and was about to dance a jig when he suddenly realised he was not alone. The queen and her consort were out on the balcony too. The cheers had been for them, not for him. He slunk back to the doorway.

'Stop acting the fool, Ofao,' warned Soldier, quietly. 'Gather a little dignity, man.'

For the next half an hour Layana gave herself to her adoring populace, waving and smiling as a queen was expected to do, then Soldier gave a speech, about how the city was going to rise to new greatness under a new great queen, and then they were allowed to go inside again.

'Phew!' said Layana, flopping on to a couch in a very unqueenlike manner. 'Do we have to go through that sort of thing often?'

'No, no, they're excited because Humbold has gone and

you are new to them in the role of queen, that's all. I mean, they're used to seeing you being carried through the streets on your palanquin, but until now it is your sister who has ruled them. Once they settle down you'll only have to show yourself once every few months at state occasions.'

There was to be no coronation. Princess Layana was the sister of the late Queen Vanda. That was enough. But since Humbold had destroyed the whole structure of the former court who governed in her name, new officials had to be appointed to such positions as Lord of the Royal Purse, Lord of the Ladders, Lord of All Sewers and Drains, Chancellor, and various other official offices. All the old members had been executed or poisoned by Humbold. Soldier explained this to his wife, who listened with only the barest understanding. The structure of her court was complicated and complex. Her old mind would have known exactly how it all worked, but to her new mind this was all quite extraordinary and rather confusing.

There was a knock on the door and Ofao went to answer it.

'Go away,' Soldier heard him say coldly. 'You are not wanted here.'

'Who is it, Ofao?' called Layana.

'Your Majesty, it is that ugly worm General Kaff, who presumes to slither into your presence.'

'Let him enter.'

'But Your Majesty . . .'

'Ofao, do as you are told,' growled Soldier, 'or you'll end up selling sprouts in the market to earn your daily bread.'

Ofao sniffed. 'As you wish, sir. Your Majesty, General Kaff, Commander of the Imperial Guard.'

Kaff strode into the room in full armour with his helmet

under his arm. He ignored Soldier and went straight to the couch on which Layana was draped, going down on one knee. There was a dove attached to his right wrist which fluttered and cooed.

'Your Majesty,' he said in a silky voice, 'I am your dedicated servant.'

'Coming it a bit strong,' muttered Soldier. 'You weren't dedicated a couple of days ago.'

'I was addressing the queen,' snapped Kaff, hoping to trade on Layana's old affection for him, 'not her shadow.'

But Layana of course had no memory of her fondness for the treacherous ex-captain of the Imperial Guard.

'You will speak to my husband in a respectful tone,' she said coldly to Kaff. 'He is right. Until recently you were Humbold's creature. You have been General of the Imperial Guard, but my husband has been explaining to me that we are having to build our court from nothing . . .'

Kaff stood up, abruptly, the colour draining from his face.

'I was told by *your husband* that I should retain my position.'

'I gave you no such assurances,' replied Soldier. 'I merely told you that no executions or imprisonments would take place. And none shall. But no one said anything about you keeping your position. It would be impossible for us to leave you as you are, retaining your power over the army. Do you think us insane? You could arrange a military coup at any time you felt dissatisfied with the queen's authority. Do be sensible for once in your life, Kaff. We must have a general who is totally loyal to the queen. It will be my recommendation to Her Majesty that you take up your old post, before the revolution, as captain in the Imperial Guard.'

'Captain?' Kaff was dismayed. 'I am to be demoted so far?'

'You were never promoted in the first instance, not by the proper authority. The rank of general was conferred upon you by a scoundrel and a regicide who had no right to the throne. We have yet to hear who actually cut off Queen Vanda's head, even though under orders from Humbold.'

'It was one of the court executioners. You know the system. I had no personal hand in it.'

Soldier did indeed know the system.

There were twelve court executioners, who on the morning any death sentence was carried out went to a blockhouse with twelve separate rooms. They were men with similar physiques, dressed in black from head to foot and wearing black masks. Already in their disguises they each chose a room at random. At six o'clock soldiers went on to the streets and took the first citizen they found back to the blockhouse. This person, man or woman, then pointed to a room, any room. The executioner in that room was the one who carried out the beheading. He then returned to his room and an hour later all executioners returned to their homes. Thus only the executioner who had carried out the sentence knew who had done the deed. None of his fellow executioners knew who he was. They each knew they had not done it, but so far as they were aware it could have been any one of the other eleven. Anonymity was their protection against future reprisals by any king or queen suddenly remorseful about those they had sentenced to death, and who decided to scapegoat the executioner. Although, of course, it was a false sense of security, for any real tyrant would have the whole twelve of them boiled in oil and have done with it.

'Well, whether you were there or not, it makes no difference to our decision,' said Soldier. 'You are henceforth reduced to captain.'

'I take no orders from *you*!' cried Kaff.

Layana opened her mouth to speak, but a look from her husband made her close it again.

'Listen to me carefully, Captain Kaff,' said Soldier. 'I am the queen's consort. I am the second most powerful person in the kingdom. I have my own authority, separate from that of the queen, and I WILL EXERCISE IT!' Soldier shouted the last four words, but then calmed himself again. 'If you wish to leave the army, you may do so of course. We will accept your resignation without question. You may wish to earn your bread elsewhere. However, if you remain in the Imperial Guard there will be no bias against you earning promotion in the regular way. Should you distinguish yourself, or be recommended by your superiors, I would certainly not block any rise in your fortunes. But you have lost your privileged status with the queen, you will receive no special favours over other officers, and you will – you will look to me as your superior and supreme commander.'

Despite all this, Kaff appeared to be indignant, but now Ofao could not contain himself.

'You, sir,' he spat at Kaff, 'are a filthy traitor! You are lucky to be alive, let alone claiming special status with the queen whose sister you stood by and watched murdered. A general amnesty has saved your treacherous skin, but there are many who would like to see you dead.'

Kaff ignored this outburst by a slave of the royal household and came to attention. He bowed to the queen.

'You may leave us,' she said.

Kaff strode from the room. It was a good two minutes before everyone heaved a sigh of relief. Layana said the air was clearer now that Kaff had gone. 'Did I really regard that man highly?' she asked.

'Yes, you did. You even considered marrying him at one time,' replied Drissila. 'We feared for you. You admired him. Then Soldier came along,' her eyes shone as she regarded her mistress's husband, 'and swept you off your feet.'

'Well, you paint a nice picture, Drissila,' said Soldier, 'but actually it was more pity than love. If you remember, I was about to hang for being a foreigner without a sponsor in a city full of suspicion, which looked for spies and agents in every curtain fold, when your mistress – in her gentle mercy – decided to marry me to save me from the gallows. I was a poor ragged fellow with not a spinza to my name – a despised foreigner, blue-eyed to boot – and she took pity on me. Everyone told her she was a fool for doing so, even you two. But,' he put his arm around his wife's waist, 'she had a heart that would not let a rat drown, let alone a human being.'

'Never test me on that,' laughed Layana.

Drissila said, 'But then she fell deeply in love with you.'

'No, no, not really. She hated the sight of me, in fact. And several times, you will recall, she took a knife to my throat while I was sleeping. I owe my life on those occasions only to my scabbard, which sang out when the lunatic wife entered with a blade in her hand. It took a long while for me to gain her trust, her affection, and finally her love.'

Layana said, 'And now it is as deep as a well.'

'Yet,' interrupted Ofao, 'you did at one time think much of Captain Kaff.'

'I must have been mad.'

No one remarked on this, the reply being obvious.

Later, they were alone together, the queen and her husband, and the raven came in through the open balcony window.

'All's well that ends well,' said the black bird.

'Except that the end has not yet come,' said Soldier, rising from the bed on which he had been resting. 'Did you see the sky this morning?'

'Did I see it? I was up in it. Swathed in magic, you mean. Quite frightening to be flapping through that swirling colour. You can *feel* it, you know. It clings to your wings like attercop webs to a weasel's fur. The magi test each other, I think, and will soon come to blows.'

'Where is IxonnoxI now, bird?'

'In some secret place, which his father is trying to find. Our witchboy grows in strength day by day. The beasts of the field and the birds of the air believe he is already a match for OmmullummO.'

'And the fishes of the sea?'

'Who knows what those cold-brained idiots believe!'

'Keep good watch for me, raven. When the magi stride forth to settle their differences there will be a short unsettled time in the land. After which, I hope we shall see peace of a kind.'

The raven left and Soldier settled back down on the bed.

'Who was that?' asked Layana, drowsily. 'Was I sleeping?'

'You were, my love – it was the urchin bird.'

'Oh, is there news of my memory?'

'No, but now that we have settled the city, at least for the time being, I shall go abroad again, with my sword at my side, to seek that very thing. Tomorrow I shall consult the temple priests and ask them what I must do to find your memory for you.'

'The priests? Will they know?'

'They can find out. That's what they're for. They can consult with the gods. Otherwise, why bother with such creatures?'

The following day Soldier went to see Spagg, who had now

opened a shop on the main thoroughfare through Zamerkand, the path which ran parallel to the covered canal which led to the sea. He was doing good business in hands-of-glory. Many citizens had been hanged by Humbold and they had not all putrefied yet. Some, the last to go, were still in a reasonable condition. Spagg had quickly preserved some of these in vinegar and those who wished to employ the cloak of invisibility bought these hanged men's hands from the trader. They were 'guaranteed' to work.

'Is there any temple priest you respect more than others?' asked Soldier. 'Or are they much the same?'

'There is one man,' said Spagg, scratching at his empty eye socket. 'Cristobel by name. He's in the Temple of Theg.'

Soldier went to the temple in question and took the marble steps two by two, stopping at a table on the top. There sat an old man in a wicker chair, his long beard wrapped several times around his throat for safety reasons. Wrinkled, bent and brittle he may have been, but his eyes twinkled like those of a child. He seemed excited by the way Soldier approached him, and cackled in toothless glee.

'Came up to Cristobel like a bounding gazelle,' he said in a voice like brown paper being crumpled. 'Up, up, he leapt! Look at him, in his prime youth. I was like you once, Soldier. Had a penis like a tent pole. The women went wild for me. All night long I could lust and last. Out of one, into another.' He shrieked with laughter at his own gross humour, slapping his bony knee. 'I loved it. I was strong and virile. Thighs like a canoe. Stomach muscles like stepping stones. I popped a dozen vestal virgins one night. Maidens of the temple. They gave me a good thrashing for that, but it didn't stop me. I was incorrigible.'

'You were a damned rogue, if you ask me, and I cannot

understand how you escaped the dungeons, or worse, if that's what you did. But I am here on serious business . . .'

'What could be more serious than lost youth?' bemoaned the old man. 'Look at these spindly legs now! Look at these rheumy eyes! Who would want to bed a man with a penis like a piece of string?'

'You have a one-track mind and I can see why Spagg comes to you for your prophecies, but I must know something.'

'Fill my heart with pleasure by filling my hand with gold.'

He held out his palm and Soldier placed a bag of money in it.

'This had better be good, old man, or I shall be back for that.'

'I'll have spent it by then,' said the senior citizen with a chuckle, 'on wild women with red lips and pot bellies.'

Soldier was beginning to wonder if this senile old rake could tell him anything of value, but once the question was asked the priest sent for a copper bowl and a charcoal brazier, an astrolabe, a divining rod, and other instruments of conjecture. The astrolabe was consulted with regard to the source of the wind. Then the copper bowl was placed on the fire, substances were put into the bowl and stirred with the divining rod, and green smoke issued forth which contained cryptic messages for the old conjuror to decipher and pass on to this client, the questioning soldier.

'Theg says that to cure your wife, to restore her memory to her *without its companion madness*, you need to go on a quest and gather the following three objects: *the silver container of the song of an eternal prisoner; a golden unborn babe in the house of a stranger; a jade widow who has righteously murdered and devoured her husband*. These are all to be found in the the Unknown Region. Once you have the objects, you must lay them at Theg's altar.'

Soldier was angry at first, with these words from the priest.

'What are these riddles? How can I find objects when I don't understand what they are?'

'They are precisely that, riddles, which you have to solve before you can discover their hiding places. Good Soldier, do you expect it to be easy? You want the gods to place the cure in your lap? No, a knight must *earn* the reward, by using his intelligence, his chivalry, his courage. You must go forth, seek amongst the hidden ways, probe into unknown places of horror, use the goodness of your soul and the brightness of your mind to uncover the truth. Return with the treasures to me and I shall use them to lure your wife's lost memory from the hole in which it hides.'

'How will I find them?'

'Follow the white road.'

Soldier was puzzled. 'Are there roads in the Unknown Region?'

'This one comes and goes,' said the ancient priest, smiling secretly. 'This one is evanescent, transient. Sometimes it's there, sometimes it's not.'

'More damn riddles,' grumbled Soldier.

'Do you want to cure your wife or not? If you don't, stay at home. I don't care. It's nothing to me.'

'Should I take any companion with me?'

'Take the bird, the raven, for it can climb high and see many things which are out of sight to your eyes.'

'Very sensible. I hadn't thought of that.'

'In the meantime, I shall rattle my bones with the contents of this purse and see if I can find a spark of life in these old loins.'

'You are a wicked priest!'

'Yes, I am, aren't I?' cackled the old man.

Soldier returned to the Palace of Wildflowers and told his wife what the priest had said.

'Husband,' she said, taking him in her arms, 'you do not need to do this thing. The place to which that old man has sent you is a dangerous and unnatural land, full of tricks and traps, where even the ordinary needs travel under different guises. There is no stranger you can trust there, and you will find no friend amongst them. It is an isolated, brooding place, where solitary, exiled creatures grow into the landscape. It is full of wild, uncoded magic, uncontrolled and without any sense of order. I am afraid for you. I would spend the rest of my life with a blank history rather than let you wander out into that bleak, desolate region where there are no common rules, where science and philosophy have decayed and fallen into foul hands, to be moulded as they wish into shapes of which you could not dream. Stay here, safe by my side, and we shall make do with less than perfect.'

Soldier sighed. 'That I cannot do, my sweet Layana, for you will always ache for a whole mind. Your whole life has been spent either in the shadow of lunacy or without your memory. We must do all we can to restore you to wholeness, for only then will I know if you truly love me. You must remember who and what I was when I first came to you, and I must tell you the whole of my terrible past history. Then you may decide whether I am worthy to spend the rest of my days sharing your bed, your waking hours, your life. You are the queen of Zamerkand and must ask no less.'

'What rubbish you speak!' she cried. 'I know what I feel in my heart.'

'Zamerkand needs a healthy queen, to put it back on its feet, to restore it to its former greatness as a trading nation.'

They argued thus the whole night long and finally Soldier

won, for there was something in him which drew him forth, to the region of the damned and damnable. There was the sense that he might discover more about himself as well as about his wife. And of course, he was a knight, and what is the *raison d'être* of a knight but to go on a quest for a Holy Grail, or Wonderful Sword, or an otherwise unattainable Truth.

Such marshy, mountainous, treacherous unknown territories were the *princesse lointaine* to knights, drawing them into their cobwebbed regions. And the knight must go. He must. There is the traditional arming of the hero, carried out with great ceremony, with the squire handing the knight those items of armour which must be put on reverently and with solemnity in the right order. Once the knight is armed, cap-a-pie, he says farewell to his lady love, who gives him a favour – a chiffon scarf or a velvet glove – and then his newly groomed charger is brought to him, hoofs clattering on the cobbles of the courtyard, sparks flying from the iron shoes. The saddle is polished and the sheep's fleece that covers it is as soft and pure as the first white rose of spring. High noon sees the knight riding forth, his horse prancing to a chaconne that lives in its head, the pair of them bent on creating mayhem amongst evil and bringing home the desired object.

Thus the vertical sun of the third day saw Soldier attired in his travelling armour, the raven on his shoulder. Half the city was at the walls to watch him go, friends, enemies and neutrals. He struck out north-west, towards the Kermer Pass, which would lead him through Falyum and to the Scalash River. There he would enter the marshes, flanked by two enormous sheer cliff faces, which guarded the border of the Unknown Region. The pass – the crack between the unclimbable cliffs – went from half a mile wide at the outset to just a yard wide at its exit on the other side of the marshes. It was as if a wedge had been taken out of the mountain and had left a soggy triangular stretch of ground covered in quickmud.

They reached the Kermer Pass, an ordinary passage between the first range of mountains, in several days. There they were seen by beast-heads, who dipped and dived behind rocks, but did not attack. Soldier had heard some disturbing reports that Wo had been banished for assisting the enemy of the beast-people in gaining a deadly sword. He hoped this was not true, for the dog-headed Wo did not deserve such punishment. When he returned from his quest Soldier planned to find out for sure what had happened and if at all possible reverse any wrongs.

'You know what you are doing, I suppose?' said the raven, bobbing with the motion of the horse. 'This is certain death.'

'So far every quest I've been on has been certain death to you.'

'Well, this one *definitely* is.'

'So be it, we all have to die sometime. My only regret will be that my wife will be alone in her bed at nights.'

'Maybe not,' said the bird. 'Perhaps Captain Kaff will go on a quest for her and find success where you've found failure.'

Soldier's jaw set grimly. 'In that case, I shall make sure I do not die.'

Eventually they reached the marshy passage which would lead them into the Unknown Region. Soldier walked his charger through very carefully, testing the marish with his lance as they went. As with other border bogs there were stunted figures seen only at twilight which bobbed up suddenly in front of the horse, screeching and shrieking, trying to frighten it. But Soldier's old faithful was not to be intimidated by such wilful creatures, nor by the pungent smell of green marsh gas which puffed from the punctures made by the lance. She was a mare who refused to be impressed by petty magic and obeyed her master's instructions to the last prick of a spur.

Nevertheless, they were unable to cross, finding the sticky way too hazardous, and had to return to the shore.

'What's to do now?' asked the raven. 'Stopped at the first hurdle.'

'We must find some local creature who knows the paths.'

'Can you trust them? I only ask because it is you who will sink to your death in black mire, not me. I, if you haven't noticed, can fly.'

'We will light a fire and hope to attract someone.'

'You might get more than you expect, but who am I to argue?'

The tinder box came out and the fire was lit. Soldier sat back from its flames, keeping partly to the shadow. His ears were tuned to the slightest noise from out of the darkness.

While Soldier dozed, a figure emerged from the trees, drawn by the light of the fire. When Soldier jerked awake, an hour later, he found himself staring into a pair of large brown eyes which looked at him from the other side of the flames. Soldier leapt up, sword in hand, wondering why his scabbard had not sung her warning song.

'Who are you?' he cried. 'By what right do you steal the warmth from my fire?'

His shouts woke the raven, who took off into the night immediately, the bird's philosophy being *get out of danger*, then *find out what's going on*.

'Me Huccarra,' said the creature. 'Me Whin. Name Glokk. No steal. Whin not steal. Only sometimes.'

Soldier stoked the fire with his sword-point, making it flare.

He saw now that the creature was indeed one of the Whin, half-giants from the south of Guthrum. They were strange, muscle-knotted creatures, shaped roughly like men, but twice the size of a normal human and ten times as stocky. Most of them were miners, who worked hard at their profession, but occasionally there was the lazy one, usually a thief of some kind, who sent out jackdaws and jilldaws to steal for them. Soldier had met one called Clokk, a sword-stealer amongst the Whin, and found him to be an amiable creature.

'Glokk? Are you any relation to Clokk?'

'Cousin from me,' said Glokk, eagerly. 'You know me cousin?'

Soldier sheathed Kutrama and sat down. Clearly Sintra had not sensed any danger in the creature, or she would have sung a warning song. 'I've met him. So, what are you doing, a half-giant, this far north?'

'Banishment, for stealing lady Whin.'

Soldier gave him a disapproving look. 'Ah, you took a female by force?'

'Not force. She like me. Her hut-sharer no like me. He important Whin. Tell Glokk he must go away for one year.'

'Well, that'll teach you to poach.'

Glokk hung his head, looking suitably chastised.

'And so, enough about your past crimes, how do you survive here? Do the beast-people bother you at all?'

'No bother. I break their heads.'

'Fair enough. But this is a rocky, inhospitable landscape, with no real vegetation to speak of. How do you live? Do you hunt? Fish?'

'Me go into swamp and take eggs from giant frogs. Very nice.' He rubbed his naked stomach. 'Lots of jelly. Nice black eggs. UmmU no like Glokk steal eggs. UmmU whip with tongue.' The Whin turned and showed Soldier his back. There were the scars of a lash on the thick hairy skin.

'That must have been painful. And UmmU is who?'

'Big toad. Was wizard but now toad. Big teeth.'

The raven had returned now, flapping down to the fire's edge.

'I've heard of this creature,' said the bird. 'He's a natterjack, not a toad, and he'll eat anything.'

Soldier said, 'Nice of you to join us, raven. Tell me about this UmmU.'

'UmmU was once a wizard but is now a hideous, bulbous amphibian with snout and teeth. UmmU is as large as a house.' The raven grimaced, crossing his beak. 'UmmU eats swallows, martins and swifts, using that tongue of his like a fisherman casting for trout. He sends out his fly-tipped fleshy line and the birds dive and are caught. He crunches the struggling creatures in his heavy yellow molars – and another good bird is gone. UmmU will do all in his power to protect the other reptiles and amphibians of the marshes, but he is so heavy he does not move from the small marsh island under which he lives, submerged some of the time, but rising to the surface to eat his fill of the beautiful birds of the air.'

'Hmmmm. I see,' said Soldier. 'A formidable amphibian.' He turned back to Glokk. 'Well now, you know the way across the marsh. That's lucky for us, because we need someone like you as a guide.'

The Whin shook his large-boned, heavy head with an expression of sorrow.

'No, no. Glokk go home tomorrow. Banishing end. Glokk go back Huccarra and be good. Not steal lady Whin no more.'

Soldier was upset. 'But you can stay another day to assist me across the bog?'

'No, no – go home. No go marsh again.'

Knowing of the Whin's fondness for swords and blades of any kind, Soldier offered an incentive. 'What about if I were to give you a shiny dagger?'

Glokk's head perked up. 'What like dagger?'

Besides the one on his belt, which had been given to him by Layana, Soldier had two or three more in his saddlebags. He reached across and took one out: a handsome blade with an obsidian handle which gleamed in the firelight. He took the dagger from its sheath, the flashing blade reflecting the flames. Then he showed the Whin the sheath itself, of black worked leather and decorated with brass studs. Glokk took both the knife and its holder and turned them over in his stubby-fingered hands.

'Nice shiny. Glokk like nice shiny.'

'It's yours, if you take me across there.'

The square-faced half-giant nodded slowly, not taking his eyes from the dagger until Soldier repacked it in the saddlebag. Having found his guide, Soldier relaxed a little. He lay back with his head on a rolled blanket and looked up at the stars. These heavenly bodies had never been much use to him, except for navigational purposes, but they looked quite beautiful on this particular evening. They pierced the sky with unusual clarity, seemingly reaching out to touch each other with their spikes of light.

'Well, you look peaceful enough,' said the bird. 'I wonder you don't consider the fact that this great lumpy fellow might try to murder you and take what he wants, rather than having to wait for it until morning.'

The raven's words disturbed Soldier's tranquillity.

'What do you mean?'

'I mean, what do you know about him? Nothing. He could

have murdered and eaten a hundred like you, for all you know. Just because he says he's been banished for womanising doesn't mean it's true.'

Soldier stared at the half-giant, still sitting on the other side of the fire, seemingly unconcerned by the raven's chatter. Soldier got the impression that the bird spoke too fast for the Whin to understand, and when a half-giant from Huccarra cannot understand something he simply pays no more attention to it. He turns away and hums, or looks vacantly into the middle distance. Glokk was doing this now, his dull eyes blank of expression. He seemed to be counting fireflies, but since the Whin could not count to more than three, this was probably just an impression rather than a fact.

'Look, bird, I have known many Huccarran half-giants — well, one or two anyway — and they have always struck me as being too stupid to be anything but honest. Even my scabbard considers this one unworthy of a warning song.'

'There are always one or two who do not conform. I'm not saying he *is* dangerous. I'm saying he might be. This one looks sly. You can see it in his fidgeting fingers. I tell you, Soldier, you had better not close your eyes with this one around. Sleep with your scabbard in one hand and your sword in the other.'

On the other side of the fire Glokk yawned, giving Soldier a good look at thick square molars that went right back into the creature's throat.

'Tired?' said Soldier. 'You may sleep if you wish — I'll keep guard.'

'Not need. No bad things here. Bad things in swamp. You go sleep. I go sleep. Birdie go sleep. This is best.'

'As you say,' said Soldier, his suspicions beginning to tingle. 'Everyone go sleep.'

The two man-creatures lay down, one either side of the fire. The raven perched on a log. Everyone remained awake for at least two hours after that, the half-giant's eyes on the knight, and the knight's eyes on the Whin, until finally Soldier fell into a doze. He was awoken by the singing of his scabbard and had the impression of someone scuttling away.

Soldier sat bolt upright, sword in hand.

Glokk was standing stock still, awkwardly, as if frozen in motion on the other side of the fire.

'What are you doing?' growled Soldier.

'I go get log,' replied the half-giant, 'for fire.'

'What was that? I saw something move when I woke.'

'He be wildcat I think. Come steal food.'

'There's no new log on the fire – just glowing embers.'

'I not get yet. I get now.'

Soldier watched the creature unfreeze and walk to the log pile. He picked up a huge bough, thicker than a man's leg. It was too large for the fire and Glokk broke it in half over his thigh, just like that. An astonishing feat of strength for any ordinary man. Then he carried the log like a club, at one end, advancing towards the fire – and Soldier.

'That's far enough,' snarled Soldier. 'Throw it on.'

The half-giant stood there, looking innocent of anything but tending to the needs of the camp. He blinked, several times, but still he did not relinquish the log, which remained a lethal weapon to Soldier. Finally, he ambled forward again and tossed the log on the fire. Sparks flew up and the fire was stirred to burst into flame as oxygen went into its roots. Glokk remained on his feet, looking at Soldier. Then finally he sat down, to play with the revitalised fire, encouraging flames to grow. Soldier remained alert and expectant, wondering if Glokk was now safe.

'What did I tell you? Crafty devil, ain't he?'

It was of course the bird who had spoken, in that quick chitter-chatter way that birds have with their beaks and tongues.

'I don't know. I'm still not sure.'

'You – you *don't know*? You're an even bigger fool than we all thought,' said the raven. 'Get a hold of yourself.'

'All right, all right, he's not to be trusted. But I need the sleep.'

'I'll stay awake for you. You get some shut-eye.'

Soldier laid his weary head down, and after a long while, in which his mind turned questions over and over on themselves, he finally fell asleep again. His dreams were fragmented and disturbing: the dreams of a man with an anxiety. When he woke again, it was morning. He still felt ragged, but once he was up and had splashed cold water on his face he felt more able to tackle the day. The black bird was hopping around the fire, fighting with a long and rather thick worm. It appeared for a moment as if the worm were winning, but then it finally started on its journey down the raven's throat, wriggling all the way.

'That's disgusting,' muttered Soldier, without meaning to speak out loud.

'If you think *I'm* disgusting, go round behind that boulder and watch the Huccarran eating a live kicking rabbit.'

Soldier grimaced. 'No thank you.'

The half-giant appeared with blood running down the gullies on the sides of his chin. He seemed unconcerned by the events of the night before. Soldier did not mention them, so they were considered buried. Soldier ate some Carthagan oatcakes that had been soaked in lard and fried. He did not particularly like this army fare, which the Red Pavilion ate while on the march, but he appreciated its energy-giving qualities. Once he had finished and had drunk a hot beverage, to wash down the larded crumbs, he saddled his mare and told the others they should be on their way.

After they struck camp, the trio set out, Glokk heading the way, and Soldier leading his charger by the reins. They picked their way through tall reeds, the swaying tips of which were above Soldier's head. This meant that Glokk could see ahead, but Soldier couldn't, which was a dangerous situation for the human. Soldier ordered the raven into the air, so that he had a spare pair of eyes on the scenery around him.

The reeds were covered with twittering birds, mostly warblers, but many other varieties. While a swamp is a dangerous place for humans and half-giants, it is a great larder for the birds of the air. There are seeds by the hundred-thousand to be gobbled up. A boggy landscape is also a haven to reptiles, many of whom rather enjoy a breakfast of bird's eggs. Insects too abound in such places, along with insect eaters — some of them insects themselves. Thus, as they walked, Soldier was aware of life all around him. One form he did not appreciate, that of a big black mosquito, clouds of which persisted in feasting from his vulnerable skin.

The great cliffs loomed over them on either side, their walls getting closer together as they progressed through the marsh. At noon they rested. Soldier flattened some reeds to make a sort of nest for himself and his horse. The raven came down to eat. Glokk asked to see the dagger about half a dozen times, until Soldier finally refused to show it to him again.

'Glokk not happy,' said the half-giant. 'You give Glokk dagger.'

'You lead us through the marshes and you can have it with pleasure.'

The half-giant became angry. 'Glokk *take* dagger. Glokk very strong. Break Soldier's back with hands.'

The naked, hairy half-giant became menacing, standing up like a bear and setting himself for battle. Soldier leapt to his feet and drew his sword.

'You will do as you promised,' snarled Soldier, 'or your head and body will part company.'

Instead of retreating into whimpering displeasure, as had been the case until now, the half-giant rushed forward. Soldier did not really want to kill the great fellow. Quite apart from the fact that Glokk was so simple it would be like murdering a dumb creature, he would be stuck in the middle of the swamp with only the raven to lead him out. While he trusted the bird on most things, the raven would not be able to recognise a solid path through the mire. At least with Glokk Soldier knew that the half-giant was heavier than he and therefore would be in just as much trouble.

Soldier leapt aside and swiped at one of Glokk's ears.

'Ow, that hurt!' cried the half-giant, reaching up to where Soldier had nicked a slice out of the lobe. Blood poured between the creature's thick, stubby fingers. 'That hurt Glokk bad.'

'Just think how much it will hurt without your head.'

Glokk's hand went to his own throat, imagining just a stump of a neck. But instead of seeing sense, or feeling fear, he had a rush of blood to the head. He became incredibly angry. When a Huccarran half-giant gets angry, he loses all control. Normally passive creatures who toil in the mines, when they go berserk they are impossible to stop with reason.

'You bad man!' cried the half-giant. 'I break you in two bits. I eat you liver. I pop you eyes from you skull.'

He rushed forward again, and again Soldier managed to

evade him, though the space on their small island of reeds was limited. They continued thus for several minutes. Soldier danced this way and that, swinging at Glokk and trying to cut him but not injure him badly. Glokk lumbered back and forth like a crazy bull, head down, huge arms windmilling. The situation was made even more confusing by the raven, squawking like mad and flying around their heads. What the other creatures of the marshes thought of this mêlée was anyone's guess, but the noise did awaken a creature who became very interested in the fight.

This creature rose from the quagmire like a kraken surfacing from a long sleep. It could see a silver thing flashing back and forth above the reeds. The huge silver dragonfly, for that was what it appeared to be, seemed to be attacking an idiot half-giant, who kept flailing at it. The large squamous amphibian that had emerged from the depths was forever hungry. Having been attracted by the silver insect, it decided to do something about it. From the huge wide mouth, from the depths of the cavernous throat, unrolled a long whip-like tongue. It shot out at incredible speed and snatched the silver dragonfly from the air above the half-giant's head. With one swallow it was gone, down the tunnel throat, to lodge there.

Soldier looked stupidly at his empty hand. What had happened to his sword? One moment it had been there, the next, gone.

The vanishing act caught Glokk unawares too. He blinked, thinking he had seen magic at work. A disappearing act. All his anger evaporated. Both creatures, man and half-giant, looked around them, as if expecting to see the sword lying amongst the reeds, or in the shallow water.

'Not there!' squawked the raven. 'Over there, you dolts!'

They glanced up to see which way the raven's beak was pointing.

Glokk saw the problem immediately and groaned in fear.

Soldier had to part the reeds with his hands. When he did he laid eyes on the most monstrous amphibian he had ever seen. As large as a house, it did indeed roughly resemble the shape of a toad, with wide-splayed webbed feet. The green skin on its back and belly were covered with active swellings, which popped every so often, releasing a foul-smelling gas and leaving a splattered scar. Bulbous eyes with horizontal black pupils stared down at the two man-creatures on the reed island. Bulging muscles on its legs and around its neck warned of the amphibian's terrible strength. It was one of the ugliest creatures Soldier had ever beheld and he was astonished by the size of its mouth, which when open split its body in half. Even as he stared, another swelling, like a green balloon, exploded and sent out that awful toxic smell, which killed insects by the hundred.

'UmmU!' cried the raven. 'The toad wizard.'

The bird then wisely dived amongst the reeds, hiding there, rightly fearful of that whip-tongue.

'UmmU,' murmured Glokk.

Soldier was distressed. This plug-ugly giant natterjack had swallowed Kutrama. Having gone to so much trouble to find his sword again, he was not going to let it go without a fight. Arming himself with daggers, Soldier ran out of the reeds, only to find that UmmU was on an unreachable island with a huge patch of quickmud between. One foot on the surface, which created a sucking sound, told him that he needed a hard path to the creature.

'Give me my sword!' Soldier yelled in frustration.

UmmU coughed. The giant natterjack tried to unfurl his

tongue and found that he could not, with a foreign body lodged in his throat. Under normal circumstances he could flay the skin off this intruder with his magnificent tongue, but now he was helpless. He wondered whether to dive back down into the depths of the swamp. Yet that would mean eventual starvation, since he could no longer eat. UmmU was intelligent enough to know that if the sword was not removed, he would waste away. He had to let the man-creature retrieve his property.

The natterjack boomed in the voice of bitterns, calling for the owner of the sword to come and retrieve it.

Then the sword slipped even further down the monster's throat and jammed his mouth open.

'That's easier said than done,' Soldier replied. 'Glokk – can you see a way out to this creature?'

Glokk, still very frightened, stared at the mud between the two of them and the risen frog-wizard.

'No can reach,' he said. 'Glokk go back now.'

'You stay where you are,' growled Soldier. 'And where's that damn raven?'

'Here,' called the urchin bird in a very small voice, 'down in the reeds. I don't like it – there's a lot of snakes down here with shifty eyes.'

'You come up here and see if you can find a path.'

'What about the fisher-frog with his long line?'

Soldier said, 'He can't use his tongue for some reason.'

'You're sure about that?'

'Get up here, bird, now.'

The raven appeared, shaking droplets of water from his feathers. Warily he took off and landed on Soldier's shoulder.

'Can't see a path,' said the bird.

'Fly around, have a good look from all sides.'

The raven stared at the massive warty frog in front of him. He still did not trust Soldier's assumption that the tongue would stay in the creature's mouth.

'No, I don't think so. Look, I've got an idea. Haven't you been given three commands, one over reptiles? Why not use one of those?'

Soldier remembered how he had saved the small snake from the heron and a gift had been given him. Time to try it out. But what should he do? Command UmmU to give him his property? Yet it seemed, from all that was happening now, that UmmU would like nothing better. So what use would it be to order the creature to disgorge Kutrama? None at all.

Then Soldier had another idea. The raven had mentioned snakes. There were indeed thousands of them in the swamp. Mostly they were non-poisonous serpents, which preyed on other swamp creatures. What if he were to command them to make a causeway to the giant frog? It would be similar to laying flattened reeds on the surface of the mud.

Soldier called forth the snakes. Indeed, they answered his call, coming from holes and nests in the reeds in their thousands. They were all lengths, thicknesses and colours – reticulated, plain, patterned, some with hoops and some with stripes, some with collars round their throats and some with rattles on their tails. They came slithering and hissing, their forked tongues darting between their fangs, feeling a way to his feet. Some of them had slim heads, some fat heads, others the flattened diamond shape of the viper's. They gathered around him, tangling together. There were indeed poisonous ones amongst them, one or two so deadly their venom would kill an elephant in two minutes. In normal circumstances, Soldier might believe he was in the throes of a nightmare, but he kept calm, reassured by his knowledge.

Soldier commanded the reptiles to form a bridge.

Incredibly, the snakes did as they were bid, knotting and weaving themselves together, crossing each other's bodies and gradually forming a squirming plaited causeway out to where the squamous UmmU sat. Because they were such versatile and supple creatures, the snakes could render themselves several bodies thick, yet still keep their heads above the mud. Soon the wriggling pathway was ready for Soldier to cross.

'Me no go!' cried Glokk, staring wide-eyed with horror at the moving causeway. 'Me no step.'

'You don't have to,' murmured Soldier. 'I do.'

With his heart in his mouth, Soldier stepped out on to the live bridge of snakes. It moved a little underfoot and he almost slipped into the quickmud. Always good at keeping his balance, Soldier stayed on his feet. After a few steps it became easier, as he grew used to the spongy surface. Those snakes under his feet bore him without protest, sinking a little beneath his weight but rising again with relief. Three feet wide and fifty yards long, the snake-road stretched before the knight. It was constantly moving, constantly shifting, spreading itself where it could, knotting, tangling.

Soldier gradually made his way along it, not slipping now, for snakes are not slimy creatures but soft and velvety. When he reached the centre he felt confident of making the whole journey. So long as they did not part and leave him floundering in the deadly mud, he would achieve his goal.

And so he did, for the command he had been given was an unbreakable one and no reptile would go against it. Soldier finally got to the giant amphibian, who was now in great distress, his mouth jammed open and forming a massive cave for Soldier to climb inside. Before Soldier entered the repulsive open jaws, he would have liked reassurances. But since the creature could not now talk, he had to trust that the toad-wizard would not close its mouth once the sword was removed. Into the fleshy opening with its smell of fetid breath climbed the intrepid knight. It was a most unpleasant experience, the walls, floor and ceiling being slimy. Soldier could see his sword and just beyond it the rolled tongue of the beast. It would take but a cough from UmmU to slam that tongue into Soldier's head.

Soldier reached out and grasped the sword by the hilt.

'I have my hand on it now,' he called, his voice echoing in the bone-dome cavern. 'I shall wrench it free.'

Soldier pulled and the sword came away. The flesh around him pulsed. Clearly the giant wanted to cough, but managed to hold it back until Soldier scrambled free of its jaws. *Then* it let go, the long tongue with its heavy, sticky tip shooting out and destroying a huge patch of reeds. Birds exploded from the spot, going up like pepper-shot into the air. These creatures immediately knew the danger they were in and quickly sought other reed patches in which to hide their gaudy feathered bodies.

'Thank you,' said Soldier, to UmmU. 'I am grateful to be able to reclaim my sword, which has only recently been returned to me after a long absence.'

The giant natterjack said that a knight should never be parted from his blade and bid Soldier hold on to his in future.

'I shall.'

Soldier crossed the causeway of snakes and then bid them dismantle themselves and go about their business. The narrow exit between the two cliffs was now at hand, like a white knife-cut. Glokk would go no further, saying he did not want to enter the Unknown Region. Soldier gave Glokk the dagger he so coveted. The half-giant was immensely pleased with his trophy. He turned it over and over in his large, granite-hard hands, saying, 'This be mine own. This be mine own . . .'

'It certainly be,' mocked the raven. 'So now be off with you.'

And Glokk duly went, back into the marsh mists, travelling the path back to his own side.

Soldier squeezed through the gap in the cliffs and found himself in a foreign land. He advanced further, leading the horse. On looking back just once he failed to find the crack through which they had come. He shrugged, putting it down to sore eyes and tiredness. The journey across the marshes had exhausted both raven and human. When they were able, they made a mossy bed and lay down to sleep. Normally, Soldier would look around first, make sure they were safe in what was after all a strange land, its properties and materials unknown, its populace (supposing it had one) and its wildlife unfamiliar to a stranger such as he. This time, however, the fatigue won. Raven, horse and human slept unguarded.

Soldier woke first, shivering with the cold. It was only because he had covered his mount and himself with fir branches that he had survived sudden winter weather, or he might have frozen to death in his sleep. When he moved the shield of firs, which he had originally placed there to ward off the heat of the noonday sun, he found himself shifting heaps of snow.

This was not so unusual, for winters could come and go within the hour in some places he had known. Yet this time the icy weather was only a hundred yards wide, in a long, hard, glistening white strip which ran like a road over the countryside. Even as he stared at this phenomenon, the snow and ice began to melt into shining drops of water. Icicles which hung from the branches of trees fell with a glassy tinkle to the ground beneath. Great wads of muffled snow dropped from cedar shelves. Yet on either side of this brilliant but frozen path over the landscape the sun had baked the ground hard and grassland withered in the heat.

Soldier woke the bird, which had crawled down a rabbit hole to rest, before the ice-strip thawed.

'I remember half-waking,' said the raven, as surprised and enthralled as the human, 'and feeling intensely cold. When I looked out from my hole, I sensed a huge dark shape passing over us. We seemed to be in the shadow of something that glided – not very high – above and across us. I simply hunched into my wings and fell fast asleep again, convinced I was in a nightmare. Something passed over us, Soldier.'

'Something? A god or goddess, d'you think?'

'I don't know,' replied the raven, shivering, 'but then I'm as familiar with this side of the marshes as you are. No one comes here. No one, bird or beast, has ever entered this hinterland and returned to tell the tale. I don't know why we are here, but I do know I am glad we remained asleep, for some giant raptors find their prey by detecting movement below them, just as hawks see the movement of voles and mice in the grass. Perhaps this one would have stooped and snatched us up, if we had been awake.'

'Well,' replied Soldier, 'here is our *white road*. We must follow it while it lasts,' he looked up, 'which will not be long under this sun.'

Soldier saddled and mounted his charger and soon the trio were on their way again, still heading north-west, seeking a sign that would give Soldier an answer to one of his three riddles. As they followed the icy path, which became a strip of moisture, they came across huge balls of fur and bone that lay by the wayside. The raven recognised these objects.

'When an owl eats a mouse, it regurgitates the fur and bone in a solid wodge. That's what these lumps look like to me. Owl pellets.'

'Yet these are the bones and skins of no mice or voles,' said Soldier, prodding a steaming heap with his sword. 'These are buffalo furs and buffalo bones. Look at the size of that skull. Over there is a deer, for you can see the antlers sticking from the pellet. And yonder must be a wild boar, for the tusks protrude from the mass of tightly bound strips of hide.'

'Perhaps our strange god is an owl?'

'Perhaps. I have an idea that it flies over an area, freezes its prey, then descends and devours it at leisure. We must keep a wary eye open for this monster, which should not be too hard to see.'

They continued on their journey, their eyes constantly flicking heavenwards. Yet no monster appeared in the sky. Finally the rapidly evaporating road led them to a range of mountains, which they crossed using a low, winding pass with tall, steep sides. If there was a monster up there it would surely not be able to drop down into such a narrow gully and they felt safe enough to relax. The black bird chattered the whole way, which Soldier could have done without, but nothing untoward occurred until they emerged on the other side.

There they came to a much wider valley, with pasture land, braided streams and rivers, and what appeared to be orchards, though they were in poor condition. As they proceeded out into this pleasant landscape, Soldier could see that the hill-sides had been cleared and tiered for planting, though the farmers they belonged to had been negligent of late, for the crops had either not been planted or had been left to rot on their roots. Further evidence of neglect could be witnessed in the windmills, their sails tattered and hanging still on their towers.

'We must be wary of the plague,' said Soldier to the bird, 'for there are all the signs of a disease sweeping the land. No hands are in the fields, no one is working the mills. Pestilence is in the air, I think.'

They continued riding down through the foothills, until they opened into a wide, flat plain. When they camped that night, watchfires were visible a little further on. With the dawn came sight of a walled city, with a mounded castle within it. Around the walls of this city were tents, similar to those of the Carthagans, except these were of natural undyed cloth. There were warriors moving around amongst the tents, which were pitched well away from the wall of city. The scene had all the hallmarks of a siege similar to the one Soldier had just ended at Zamerkand.

'I'm not sure we want to get into this,' said the raven, his thoughts on the same lines as the knight's. 'I shall be all right, but you may get dragged away as a spy, or slave, or conscripted as a warrior for one side or the other. Can we not go around?'

Soldier looked for ways to circumnavigate the trouble ahead, but found they were hemmed in at the lower end of a long valley, across which stretched the army that was besieging the city. Wherever he rode he was sure to come across units of that army. It seemed he was going to have to talk his way through. Having made up his mind, and informing the raven of his decision, he urged his charger forward. In an hour they were entering a satellite camp of the besieging army. A peripheral sentry challenged him, spear at the ready, calling for the password.

'I do not know the password,' said Soldier. 'I am a stranger in this land.'

'There are no strangers here,' argued the sentinel. 'Thou art either renegade Plethorite, or Samonite like me. Which is it?'

'I tell you, I come from beyond the marshes which lie at the back of that mountain range. A country called Guthrum, though I am an adopted son of a people called the Carthagans, from across the Cerulean Sea.'

The sentry leaned forward and peered into his face, then let out a startled cry. 'Thou hast the blue eyes of a sorcerer! Watch ho! Here is a creature from the depths of hell, come to visit death upon us . . .'

From a tent nearby poured a band of troops in various stages of dress. Quite clearly they had been interrupted during a meal, or a siesta, and were not expecting an attack. Yet they were armed and though a little bewildered by the sentry's cry, ready for battle. In the front was a captain, who on seeing just one man on a horse, demanded a report from the sentry.

'Here is a dark sortileger of a kind I have never seen before,' said the sentinel, not taking his eyes from Soldier's face. 'See, my captain, he has the eyes of a wolf and a familiar raven sits on his saddle.'

The captain stared and slapped down the man's spear in disgust.

'A wolf has hazel eyes, dolt. This man has the eyes of an angel from the azure-blue world of the sky. Art thou an angel, stranger?'

'No,' replied Soldier. 'I am a traveller, a wayfarer, looking for clues to some puzzles I have to solve. I would be grateful for some fare and safe passage through your army, if that's possible. The bird is just a pet, who travels with me, and has no special powers . . .' the raven gave them a squawk to show that he was just a bird of the crow family, nothing more

'. . . and I mean no harm to any man. I have no magic, I am no sortileger, as your man seems to think. I am merely a knight at arms, seeking.'

The captain stood with hands on hips, surveying the horse and rider for a while, then nodded.

'Come with me. Thou maun eat and tell me a tale, knight. I shall listen with interest. My tent is over there.' He yelled at the rest of the guard, 'And next time there is a call to arms, be much swifter to answer it. We could have been overrun by Plethorites by the time you sluggards were out of that tent flap . . .'

Soldier thought this was a little unfair, since they had come at the run immediately they heard the call, but an officer expects to chastise his men and his men expect to hear such complaints from their captain, so he kept his peace and let the army business run the way it always had.

Dismounting and leading his charger, Soldier followed the handsome captain to his tent. The cool interior was quite lavishly furnished with carpets, silk cushions, tapestries on the walls, and a colourful spread of food and drink on a low table. There were seven young women in the tent, who seemed to have come from the same pod, for they all looked exactly alike in features and dress. Invited to sit, Soldier was then served by the women, who fluttered about him in chiffon and silks, giggled when he looked at them, and hid their faces in shyness.

'You keep a fine tent,' said Soldier, drinking some of the cool and very welcome wine from a golden goblet. 'This is most pleasant. Are you typical of an officer of this army?'

'Me, no,' said the captain, giving the women an irritated glance. 'I'm very rich. Most captains have the bare necessities. My father is the king of our city. I am the eleventh of twelve sons. My brothers are mostly generals and what not. Only my younger brother and I are captains.' He sighed. 'It suits me. I'm not fond of too much responsibility. I prefer a quieter life than that which my older brothers lead. It's rather pleasant to be rich and only have a small troop of soldiers to command. I do not have to spend a huge amount on weapons and armour. Thou shouldst see my eldest brother's uniform bills! Massive. Huge. And the cost of horses, these days! I would much rather spend my money on beef and lamb, and these rare spices thou canst see spread before thee, than puff it away on tight pantaloons and prancers . . . But come, tell me your story,' he said eagerly, sipping his own wine. 'I am all ears. I love a good tale, especially from strange lips.'

Chapter Four

After the meal the women used incense and myrrh to perfume the tent and get rid of the smell of cooked meat. Then they brought both men hookahs. Soldier was not used to smoking but he felt it would be uncharitable to refuse to join the captain, so he did. His head swum for the first few puffs, but after a while he found the activity quite pleasant.

'Before I start on my story,' he said, 'may I know your name?'

'Most certainly. I am Captain Fabulet – a prince of course, but when we are at war we are expected to use our military ranks. And thee?'

Soldier decided he would not go into his full history, only those parts relevant to his quest.

'I am called Soldier . . .'

'You interest me already – a soldier thou art, and Soldier named. Go on.'

'I am the commander-in-chief of the Carthagan Red Pavilions, a mercenary army. Carthaga is a country a long way from this valley, but it is a nation which provides armies for cities and countries who find it difficult to defend themselves . . .'

'A remarkable concept. Go on.'

'The city we are defending at the moment is called Zamerkand, in the country of Guthrum, which lies beyond those mountains that hem your land in and keep it free from all but the most intrepid strangers . . .'

'Such as thyself, Soldier. And more?'

'The long and the short of it is, my wife is the queen of Zamerkand. She was once abducted and taken into a far desert, where she entered a strange city which robbed her of her memory. I have been informed by a priest that the only way to restore it to her is to find three objects, which I am told are available in this land, which we call the Unknown Region.'

'Fascinating,' said Fabulet, puffing away madly. 'What an extraordinary tale. And what are these three objects thou must discover here, in Scintura, happy land of happy people?'

Soldier was rather taken aback by the added description of Scintura, since any country at war with itself was rarely happy.

'Ah, there's the rub,' he said. 'The objects are hidden, disguised as it were, by being wrapped in riddles. I don't know what they are. I shall tell you the riddles and see if you can understand any of them. If you can break all or one of them, I should be eternally grateful.'

'Well,' replied the other, 'I am no scholar, but I shall do my best.'

Soldier told him the riddles. Fabulet, who though quite young had a long silky beard which disappeared into his vest, stroked this river of hair and looked thoughtful.

'No, no – silver container of an eternal prisoner? A golden unborn babe? These are strange phrases in poetic form. Poetry. I have never been good at understanding poetry. It dances back and forth too much and goes from one pole to the next to describe something. Simple philosophies are embroidered beyond recognition in *poetry*. A jade widow who eats husbands?' Now his expression changed. 'Wait. Wait, my friend. I may be just an idle prince, with no liking for books, but there is a gleaming in my head, like that of burnished copper. Someone has polished my brain while I slept. Here, listen to this, is not the locust the colour of jade?'

Soldier frowned. 'A locust? But does the female locust eat her mate?'

Fabulet looked crestfallen. 'No, I do not believe she does . . .'

Then it was the turn of Soldier's brain to shine.

'Not the *locust*, nor even the grasshopper, both jade in colour, but the *praying mantis*. Yes, she eats her mate all right, does she not? *A jade widow who has righteously murdered and devoured her husband.* She is a jade widow. She does eat husbands, and righteously so, for that is how nature has ordained it. I think I have my first object.'

'Thou art a genius!' cried the young Fabulet, slapping his shoulder. 'Here, I have helped thee to thy first light. One small chink in the curtain, allowing a bright beam to fall on the first fragment. Now thou hast a place in which to fit the lever, to prise open the other two riddles, eh? Once the back of the first clock or lock has been opened, and the works viewed, one is aware of the internal workings of *all* clocks or locks. Let us think about the others – is not this tobacco passing good? I love it. It clears my brain of all the dust and dirt of army life. Parades? Bah! Inspections? Phoo! Marching, barking, weapon practice, manoeuvres. They clutter one's mind. Yet this golden harvest, lit with the cleanest of flames, cooled by the clearest of waters, gently blows all that rubbish from the head.'

They sat and pondered on the other two riddles, but after a long time they gave up, admitting to each other that one riddle at a time was enough.

'It hurts the grey matter,' said Fabulet. 'One should not overwork one's brain or one might go into a swoon from which one might never recover.'

'Tell me what is happening here, in your valley,' said Soldier eagerly. 'Why are you camped outside the walls of this city?'

Fabulet's face changed to stone for an instant and Soldier's training instantly told him why.

'Ah,' he said to the prince, 'you think I might be a spy? But look at these blue eyes. They will tell you I serve neither one side nor the other. In fact I am completely ignorant of all that is happening here. I have come over the mountains just this morning, not knowing who lives here, not knowing what to expect. We are told, in my country, that those who enter this region never come out. Some believe it to be heaven and thus those who find their way here do not *want* to return. Others believe it to be hell and say that those who vanish into its interior are not permitted to return.'

Fabulet stared into Soldier's eyes and after a moment he nodded and took a long suck of his hookah.

'I believe thee, Soldier. Well, as a military man thou must have guessed we Samonites are besieging the city of Ut. We are the army of Ged, from the other end of the valley, where our own city is besieged by the army of Plethorites of Ut.'

Soldier blinked. 'Let me get this straight. The army of Ged is besieging Ut while Ut's army is besieging Ged?'

'Correct. We have long been at loggerheads with Ut – they steal our sheep . . .'

A light was beginning to dawn in Soldier's mind, and he interrupted with, 'While you steal their cattle?'

Fabulet frowned. 'Yes, how did you know?'

'I come originally from a borderland. These things are common in border country. But do go on.'

'We began stealing their cattle because they stole our sheep. Of course the herders of Ut say we were the first to rustle their cows, but that is a lie. Anyway, things reached a head one day and we decided to march on Ut and settle the matter once and for all. Unbeknownst to us, Ut had decided to march on Ged, that very same day. Both armies passed unseen by each other on opposite sides of the valley. When we arrived at Ut we found it defended by the city guard and its inhabitants. Word then arrived that Ged was under siege and being defended by our own guard and population. Stalemate. That's how things have been for ten years now.'

'Why does not one army march on the other, to relieve both cities? Why not meet in the middle of the valley and settle things with one decisive battle? War is wearisome. Long wars are doubly wearisome. Long sieges are the most tedious non-activities that war can produce.'

'We men of Ged are convinced that Ut is about to fall. They are starving in there. There is disease amongst them. Soon, soon they will run out of water, they will run out of food, they will be sick of the pestilence that has swept within those walls, and they will open the gates.'

'How long have you been saying that?'

Fabulet shrugged. 'For as long as I can remember.'

'And the army at the other end of the valley are probably saying the same things. Think about your wives and children, in your own city of Ged. Would it not be better to march and procure them relief?'

Fabulet shrugged again. 'I am only my father's son. It is my father who leads the army. He is incensed with those inside the walls, for keeping us out so long. When we enter he says we shall slaughter them to the last child. No one can reason with him. Not even my eldest brother, who has been trying for years now. My father will not leave until the city falls and he is able to get his revenge on those who have kept him waiting.'

'It's an old story,' said Soldier, sighing. 'And in the mean-time your sheep have been depleted to feed the army of Ut, while you eat their cattle? Who are these maidens? Are they hostages?'

'Yes, daughters of the King of Ut. That foul king has mine own sisters in his thrall and will not release them.'

What a mess, thought Soldier, but he did not have time to say so, for the flap of the tent was thrown back and a stout, muscled man strode in. He was dressed in brass armour, with chain mail vest over padded jacket and a helmet that went into a spire at the peak. A massive sword hung from his belt, the tip of the scabbard touching the ground. The expression on his face was thunderous, as he confronted Fabulet.

'Son, what dost thou here, entertaining guests while we are battling for the walls of Ut? Why were thy soldiers not at the ladders this morning? Who is this fellow that keeps thee from thy duties?'

'This is Soldier, Father, from a land beyond the mountains. He leads an army of his own. I am merely providing him with the hospitality for which the city of Ged is so famous.'

'Where is thy army, General?' asked the king, glancing back at the flap of the tent. 'Is it here, in our land?'

'No, sire,' answered Soldier, 'I am here on a private quest.'

The king nodded and frowned, before saying, 'So, you are a commander? Perhaps your knowledge of warfare will be useful to us in crushing these upstart people of Ut. You must have had experience at sieges such as this? What dost thou recommend? The building of a mole? Ramps? Or perhaps tunnels, under the walls? Storming the watchtowers at night? I have tried withdrawing my army, pretending to go home, and leaving a gift of a wooden ox on wheels, the hollow interior carrying armed men who would creep out at night and open the gates to us, but this failed when one of the wheels came off the platform and the whole thing toppled and broke open before they could get it through the gates. Come, you must have some other ideas. Give us the benefit of your vast knowledge.'

'Sire, I have no wish to be embroiled in this fight . . .'

'No *wish*, thou sayest?' cried the king, slapping his thigh with a leather glove. 'Well, sir, it is *my* wish that thee stay and assist us.'

'But Father,' interrupted Prince Fabulet, 'the man is on a sacred quest, to find the antidote to his wife's memory loss. The gods would be angry with us if we diverted him from his purpose.'

'He can spare a few days. The gods won't mind that. He is a commander. He is used to diversions. Look at the man, a warrior from tip to toe. I like thy stance, Soldier. It is a brave one. Dignity. *Authority*. The look of high command is on thy brow. It spells experience of many battles, many wars. Eh? Yes, I do believe I am right. Come, I shall allow thee to review my troops. Let us go and look at the walls of that dastardly city, though for mine own self I am fair sick of the sight of them. Thou shalt remark upon this and that, improve upon our current situation, give us a few pointers of what and what not to do. We have made mistakes, of course. All armies at war do. But thou shalt speak straight language to us, give us the truth of the matter, and I shall be all ears, sir, all ears.'

Soldier saw no way out of the situation for the present, so he had no choice but to go along with the king's request. Indeed, he was able to point out several ways of improving the siege. He did attempt, during the tour of the walls and siege engine stations, to persuade the king that *peace* might be the best option in this war, where both sides held equal advantages and nothing was really to be gained from pressing the issue to its inevitable conclusion.

'It seems to me that all that will happen is that you will burn this city to the ground and they will raze your own city. Why do you not call for a meeting with the king of Ut and agree to both take your armies home and live in peace at either end of the valley?'

'Thou art a spy,' muttered the king, his eyes narrowing, 'or why wouldst thou speak treason to me?'

'I am no spy, I am a complete stranger. I have no interest in Samonite or Plethorite. I am simply speaking as I find, sire.'

'And I thought thou a true warrior,' said the king, with a disgusted look. 'I opened up my heart to thee and this is the thanks I get. Talk of peace! Why, I can get *that* from my son, at any time. I shall forgive thee because thou art new to this land and know not the true nature of this war and its origins, but I tell thee, the man of Ut is a blight on this fair valley. He steals our sheep, he entices our women away from us, he makes war on us without warning . . .' The king went on and on, listing the crimes of the neighbouring city state. Soldier did not feel it wise to point out that the king's own people were guilty of the very same misdemeanours. He was in a precarious position, as a foreigner, and likely to be denounced as an agent of the other side by anyone at any time.

The king continued to rant and rave for a very long time. He was only interrupted by the catapults opening up on both

sides. Fiery balls began descending from the sky and falling
on the tents. Rocks and huge arrow-bolts were shot in the
other direction. For a time the heavens were full of large
missiles. Then a concentrated attack took place on one of the
watchtowers of the walled city, which was repelled by the
other side. Later, it all settled down again and the state of
lethargy that Soldier knew to be the norm in siege camps
overcame the tented army. He knew that the same thing would
be happening within the walls of the city. The injured would
be lining up for treatment, the dead would be buried quickly.
Local shops would trade again, the marketplace would open
like a patch of flowers, the children would run screaming and
playing once again.

In the late afternoon the gates to the city were opened and
a large warrior came striding out.

'Here is Juggarmung,' cried the Plethorite, armed cap-a-
pie. 'Juggarmung challenges the weakling Samonites to single
combat. Should Juggarmung win, food and water will be
placed within reach of the inhabitants of our city. Should he
lose, the gates of Ut will be thrown open for one hour and
the Samonite army invited to enter at their peril.'

Then the warrior stood, leaning on his sword, waiting for
challengers to come forth from amongst the Samonites.

So, thought Soldier, that's how the Plethorites have
managed to survive for so long. Their champion wins and
food is placed within their reach. But what if he loses? The
city will be taken.

He put his thoughts to Fabulet. The young prince said,
'Indeed, we have beaten their champion as many times as
they have ours. But the entrance to Ut is very narrow. We
cannot throw our whole army at the opening, so we always
send in one company of volunteers. They usually manage to

battle their way in after an hour, but once inside they are either chopped down or taken prisoner, and we're back where we started.'

Soldier was never so convinced by the futility of war as in this valley. He remained with Fabulet for the next two or three days, letting the prince's father believe he was staying for good, then slipped away during the night. He had at least broken one of the riddles, so his time in the camp had not been in vain. The raven was well pleased with his efforts in discovering that a praying mantis had to be found, but he asked, was it a *real* insect or one made from jade?

'Looking at the remaining two riddles,' said Soldier, using the valley-edge mountain paths to continue his journey, rather than run into the other army laying siege to Ged, 'I would say that it will be a carving of sorts. The other two riddles speak of silver and gold objects. While green things may be found to be common in nature, gold and silver are not so.'

'What are we looking for then, a treasure house?'

'Possibly, or a temple. You often find carvings of great beauty in temples. We must continue our search and speak with as many locals as do not show hostility towards us.'

'Towards you, you mean. All I have to do is watch for eagles.'

'True. And there's one now, circling overhead.'

There was indeed a mountain eagle gliding on a spiral thermal high above their heads. The raven hunched down into himself. 'They are evil birds, those eagles,' he muttered.

'I imagine that worms must say the same thing about ravens.'

'Worms are not high creatures, they don't count.'

'Tell that to a worm.'

The pair continued to banter with each other, until Soldier

spotted a cabin in a lonely pass that took them over the other end of the mountain range and out of the valley of Ut and Ged. They reached the log dwelling just as the sun was going down. Clearly the place was being used, for smoke was coming from a hole in the roof. Soldier found an area where lush long grass grew and hobbled his horse. Then he went to the door of the cabin and knocked loudly. When he received no answer he opened the door and stepped inside, peering around in the dim light. Finally his eyes fell on an elderly figure hunched over a fire, cooking, in the corner. The occupant of the cabin recognised Soldier almost as quickly as Soldier recognised him. Both let out a gasp of astonishment. Then the other man quickly drew a dagger.

'You followed me here!' he cried. 'It was part of the agreement that I should not be pursued into this godforsaken land.'

'Humbold!' said Soldier, shocked. 'I had no idea.'

'You have come to kill me, despite your oath not to harm me.'

Soldier was sorry for that oath, but in fact he was honour-bound to keep it, no matter how much his hatred for the other man rose like bile to his throat.

'Your presence was unknown to me, or I would not have stopped here,' replied Soldier coldly. 'I have come from the cities of Ut and Ged, in the last valley . . .' Humbold was looking blank. 'You did not see them?' said Soldier. 'Did you not witness two great armies at war?'

'I came along the ridges, between two mountain ranges, and have seen no other human soul – apart from a cloak-and-dagger gang who followed me into the Unknown Region.' Humbold's face turned black with anger. 'Those snivelling brats, Guido and Sando. They sent a death squad after me. I caught one of their cloaked killers in a noose and let him dangle there until he told me what his mission was, then I kicked away the log that held him up. The others? I slit their throats while they slept around their camp fire. Left them like dead bats, their black garments flapping in the night winds. Did those royal brats think they could kill me that easily?'

Soldier was determined not show that he was shocked and ignored this little anecdote. 'We obviously came by different paths. Well, you have reached the hut first. Yet I must have somewhere to shelter the night. You are safe from harm so far as I am concerned. I wish I could feel the same about myself, for I fear I shall have to sleep with one eye open tonight, with a foul fiend like you for a bedfellow.'

Seeing that Soldier was just as surprised to see him as he was to lay eyes on the knight who had caused his downfall, Humbold's courage returned. Clearly Soldier was not chasing him but on a mission of his own. His lip curled in revulsion at having to share his hut with the knight. The ex-chancellor and ex-king began to complain and make claims.

'I found this hut first. You should find another.'

'Impossible, the darkness has fallen and it seems likely it will freeze tonight, here high in the mountains.'

'That's not my fault. And I shall not share my food.'

'I didn't ask you to, and would not. Any food of yours would turn to ashes in my mouth.'

'Good.'

'Yes, good.'

'You will sleep in the woodshed.'

Soldier raised his eyebrows. 'Oh, I will, will I? You have ordered it? By what authority? That of chancellor or that of king? You are a broken man, Humbold. You do not give orders. I, on the other hand, am consort of the queen of Zamerkand.'

'Uppity, aren't we?' sneered Humbold. 'Not out here, you're

not. Here you are just an outcast with ugly blue eyes. I could go out of that door and find ten locals now who would gladly burn you at the stake for a witch. Look at you,' the ex-king sneered, 'half a man, if that! You don't even know who you are, what you are, or where you came from.'

'That's where you're wrong, Humbold,' cried Soldier, unable to stop himself from revealing information which might be useful to his enemy, 'for I am Valechor, knight of a border kingdom between the greater homelands of the Scots and the Angles. I know who I am.'

Humbold glanced down at Soldier's side and sneered again. 'Ah, you found your sword. Your memory returns, piece by piece. You will have remembered Drummond then, your deadly enemy.'

Soldier was astonished. 'You know of Drummond?'

Humbold laughed. 'He visited me – no, not before you arrived, or I would have killed you the instant you entered Zamerkand for the first time. He came to me while you were wandering the deserts of Uan Muhuggiag and I promised him the next time you were in my power I would give you to him. Unhappily, that never happened.'

'Where is the bastard now?' cried Soldier, his memory stirring as he placed his hand on his sword. 'I would have peace with him, but if he will not agree to peace I will fight him any time, any place. Single combat. Just the two of us. Is he such a coward still that he needs to hide from me?' Such were the contradictory feelings that fought for possession of his mind, Soldier was ever and aye switching between peace and war. 'I have such a passion in me when I hear that name,' he groaned, 'I fail to control myself.'

'You know he is no coward. You and he have faced each other in battle many times. He would fight you tomorrow.

But there is a power which keeps you apart, for you are both keys in the destiny of two worlds – the world you both come from and the world you are in now. Only one key fits the lock to the future. Is it you, Soldier? I hope not. I hope and pray to the gods and the magi wizards that it is Drummond.'

'How do you know all this, while I do not?' cried Soldier in anguish. 'You are a mere puppet of this world. A throne-sitter. A man who has fed on his own ambition in one place. I am well travelled . . .'

'Do you know why?'

Soldier was thrown. 'Know why what?'

'Why you are so travelled, you idiot.'

Soldier allowed the insult to pass over him. 'I'm sure you can tell me, you seem to know everything about me.'

'Because you are cursed. You have the wandering curse, placed on you by the witch you killed at the massacre of the Drummond clan. Each time you try to settle down, raise a family, live a happy life, something occurs to send you on a quest. The curing of a scarred wife, the curing of a mad wife, the curing of a wife with amnesia. Haven't you seen it yet, you dolt? You are always off somewhere, roaming in the wilder-ness, never allowed the pleasure of settling, the contentment and peace of a stable existence. Oh what a fool you are, Soldier. I laugh at your simplicity, your stupidity.' Humbold looked down at Soldier's hand. 'Even now you have only just guessed that your sword holds your lost memories. They flowed into it before it flew from your hand into the raging torrent of a river in your last battle in that border kingdom of which you speak. From there your memory, trapped within your sword, was taken by the flowing waters to the resting place of all lost swords, in the underground lake of this world.'

'How is that possible?'

'Why, all the waters of the earth, of all shadow worlds, are joined together in some way – a stream flows into a river, a river into a sea, a sea is part of an ocean. They carry such objects to their destination . . .'

'Not that, not that. How is all of this possible? Wait, listen. You used a phrase there. *Shadow worlds*. What is that?'

'Why, have you never been to school, Soldier? Have you never talked properly with our philosophers and priests? With those who know of the spirit kingdoms? No, of course not. You are a warrior, not a scholar. You would not waste your time with airy-fairy theories of the universe, would you? So many of our young men and women have no interest . . . but that is neither here nor there. Those of us who are wise went to the sages, asked them questions, listened to the answers. I may be, in your eyes, an evil man, Soldier. But I do not lack intelligence. I am a *learned* evil man.'

'You brag, but let us hear the story!'

'Since we are trapped here together, I shall repeat the lesson I learned, when I studied with the priests. The world is one place, like a bright fire in a cave, but it throws shadows on the cave wall, which are worlds themselves, dimmer and some-what different from the original due to the uneven surface of the rock face on which they dance. You live in a shadow world, Soldier.'

'And my old world, that is the true one!' gasped the knight.

Humbold sniggered. 'You are more foolish than I thought. Of course not. That too is a shadow. You and I are mere men. We could not live on the original. Why, it is too bright for our eyes, too hot for our flesh, too fierce for our souls. We would go blind, melt, evaporate on such a place. Even the Seven Gods could not survive there, let alone mere mortals. Perhaps the original is heaven, where only a spirit, a soul, may survive. Some preach that. Others say it is unobtainable, that you have to be another sort of being to exist there, to enjoy its wondrous light and joy.'

'I have it now!' cried Soldier in desperation, wondering at the revelations he was hearing in this simple hut on a hillside in some forest in the middle of nowhere. Revelations from the mouth of a despised enemy, a creature not worth the dirt on the raven's claws. Did he deserve this? Enlightenment from the lips of one who hated him? He looked despairingly at the raven, who had its head cocked to one side, listening, listening. 'You are lying to me to make me feel weak and vulnerable.'

Humbold looked at Soldier in amazement and shook his head in a weary fashion.

The raven said, 'He speaks the truth, Soldier.'

Soldier whirled on the bird. 'You know of these things too?'

'No, but I know when a man is telling the truth.'

Soldier's heart was heavy. He felt he was, after all, no better than Humbold, a man he despised. He too had slaughtered, revenge his only motive. With his hand on his sword, his memory flowed back, *trickled* back, like muddy water into his waiting mind. His first bride, Rosalind, she had been a Drummond too! He had, like a cousin of his, a knight named Lochinvar, fallen in love with one of the enemy. Lochinvar had snatched his bride from the marriage altar and had ridden away with her to a happy life. Not so Valechor. He too had run away with his beloved, but they had been pursued, out into the snowy wastes of the forest, and there she was cut down by a Drummond sword. Her own brother! Ye gods! Her own brother.

And so the ancient family feud had burst forth anew, spewing its blood over the land, Valechor killing Drummond, Drummond killing Valechor, until this knight Valechor had

trapped the whole Drummond clan and wiped them out –
but for one man. He was the one who now pursued him, out
of one world, into the next. Their hatred for each other was
blinding and fierce. Yes, he too had killed a bride, a
Drummond bride, sheathed in armour and unrecognisable as
a woman, and incurred the same uncontrollable hatred from
his enemy. What a field day the gods were having with the
pair of them. They were pawns packed with passion, their
emotions bleeding from their eyes. How terrible.

'Well I want no more of it,' said Soldier, humbly recognising the worthlessness of his soul at this moment. 'If I see
Drummond, I shall pass him by without a word.'

'Ha!' cried Humbold. 'And I have to share a cabin with
this dolt from nowhere.'

'You're welcome to leave. The wind has just risen. I can
hear it howling through the trees. By my reckoning you will
be frozen before you reach the downward path. Off you go,
then!'

'Clever bastard!'

'Yes.'

'Then I shall stab you in your sleep – do not close your
urrgghhh . . .'

Soldier had crossed the room in two bounds. His face had
twisted into fury. Inside he felt such hate for this man it
would take but a spark for him to break Humbold's neck like
a twig. As it was he gripped the man's throat, squeezing. Fear
flowed into Humbold's eyes. His fingers clawed uselessly at
Soldier's iron grip. He knew at that moment he was but a
thread away from death and he was utterly terrified.

'Please!' he managed to gasp, as he tried to prise the strong
fingers from his throat. 'Please!'

Soldier was so enraged he could hardly speak. 'If – if you

– if you take one single step towards my – my bed in the night, I shall crush you like a bug – you understand? You understand?'

Humbold forced a quick and agonising nod.

Soldier let him go, realising that once again he had succumbed to his passions. Humbold fell gasping and choking on to the floorboards. Soldier turned his back on the man and went out to see to his charger. He had to do something to let his anger cool. His horse was in the full force of the blizzard where she was. Soldier led her behind the cabin, but Humbold's ass was in the sheltered lean-to, taking up most of the room. Soldier had no alternative but to take the mare inside the cabin with him. The animal just about squeezed under the doorway and her hoofs clumped on the wooden floor. There was not a great deal of space in the cabin, but the sloping roof rose on the west side and Soldier took her and stood her by the tiny glassless window. There she remained, clearly glad to be out of the storm, and watched the wind battering the trees through the funnelled hole which served as a vent.

Humbold rose from the floor, rubbing his neck. He stumbled to a bunk bed he had made his own and sat on its edge. There he remained, staring at the floor.

'Well, that was an exciting episode, I'm sure. Now I suppose we can all settle for the night?'

These words had been spoken by the raven, who had been perched on the end of Soldier's bunk on the opposite side of the room from Humbold.

'Oh, you,' said Soldier, dully. 'I'd forgotten about you. Do you need feeding? I'm not sure what I can get you – certainly not worms. I'm just about to go out and get some hay for the mare.'

'Nope. I'll eat what you eat, later. You go and get the hay. I'll watch His Majesty over there.'

Humbold looked up and stared hard at the bird.

'Oooops,' said the raven. 'Touched a sore spot.'

Soldier went out into the wind again, which was now raging through the trees and round the eaves of the cabin. He visited the lean-to where the ass stood and pondered on whatever asses think about. The lean-to served as a wood store and corral, having a hollow-log watertrough beneath it and a hayrack fitted to the wall of the cabin. The cabin itself was a wayfarers' resting place, probably for riders, messengers between cities. He took an armful of hay and went back into the cabin, placing the hay on the floor for his mare, who began munching gratefully.

Humbold said, 'The horse has shit on the floor.'

Soldier made no reply. She had indeed. There was a nice steamy pile on the boards behind her, the smell of which had begun to pervade Soldier's frozen nostrils. He took two fire-wood logs and scooped up the mess between them and threw the whole lot through the window.

'Happy now?' he said to Humbold.

'The horse should be outside.'

'You will be the first to leave, not her.'

'Well said,' cried the raven, fluttering his wings. 'Priority to animals and birds, I say. Where's that grub, Soldier?'

'Coming up.' Soldier took his saddlebag to the fire.

'Wash your hands first,' the raven said. 'I don't *mind* the taste of horse shit, but it does give me the runs.'

After the meal they each went to their own side of the cabin. Soldier hung his scabbard over the roughly hewn bedpost, knowing it would wake him if Humbold tried anything in the night. But before they managed to get to

sleep, the raven let out a shriek. Soldier responded immediately, leaping off his bunk and going to the window where the
black bird was looking out into the night.

'What is it?'

'Drots,' said the raven. 'Thousands of them.'

Drots were bloodsucking fairies, not much bigger than a
man's index finger. They were fond of drinking blood. They
liked humans because of the lack of fur and feathers: their
skin was easy to get at. Drots bit into the flesh, or scratched
it with their sharp nails, and then lapped up the blood. A man
so caught in the open might die of bleeding from a thousand
cuts. As it was, they were inside, but needed to block up all
the entrances and exits to prevent the drots from coming in.

'Quickly, the chimney,' said Soldier to Humbold.

There was no argument from his enemy: the pair of them
had to work together now if they were to survive. Humbold
immediately threw water on the fire and began frantically
stuffing rags in the hole in the roof to block it. Soldier did
the same to the window. Then the pair of them began working
on the cracks in the floorboards and round the door jamb.
The activity was feverish, while the bird strutted up and down,
yelling superfluous instructions.

From outside there came a noise like grain falling in a chute:
like hail hammering on a slate rooftop. It came swishing in
on all sides of the cabin and began battering at the door, the
window, the walls. It sounded as if there were a million drots
out there, coming in like a cloud of locusts, their tiny wings
rasping together. Soldier had experienced drots before, but
not in such vast numbers. Down in Guthrum they were
controlled by greater pests, by larger predators – dragons and
such – who ate them in numbers. Here it seemed they bred
uncontrolled. Such a multitude of drots, such a swarm, could

suck a body dry of blood within minutes. They had to keep them out or they would be engulfed.

'Over there, the door! Get something in that crack!'

The drots knew they were in there. They could smell the horse dung and the sweat, and they wanted the blood. They flew at the cabin as if they could batter it down with their tiny bodies. Wave upon wave of them swept into the walls and hit the roof, hoping to force a passage. Others, single drots with a little more intellect, attempted to find holes by which to enter.

'Never before in such numbers,' said Humbold, staring at the roof, on which fairies were landing like arrows from a thousand archers. 'If they get in, we're doomed.'

Then the clattering noise decreased. Suddenly it went quiet outside.

'What's happening?' asked Soldier, tempted to take one of the rags away and peek through a hole. 'What are they doing now? I can't believe they're gone. They must be up to something.'

Almost before the words were out of his mouth there came a creaking sound above the noise of the wind. It sounded like a swaying tree. The noise went back and forth, back and forth. The occupants of the cabin all looked at each other, wondering whether it was the drots who were making that sound, or whether the wind had increased in strength.

'Let me look,' said the raven. 'Just a small hole for me to poke my head outside.'

Soldier looked at Humbold, who nodded. They found a knot hole in one of the walls which had actually been plugged with clay. Soldier took a knife and prised the clay out, until there was a sufficiently large opening for the bird to poke his head through.

'Now watch your eyes,' warned Soldier. 'If any are near, they'll go for your eyes.'

'I'm not daft,' muttered the bird. 'I'll whip my head back in so fast you'll be blinded by the speed . . .'

'You won't believe this,' said the raven.

'What?' chorused the two men.

'The drots – they're all gathered in a thick bunch – like one of those balls of swarming bees. They're right on the tip of a tall pine tree. Uh-uh! The tree is bending towards the cabin . . . bending . . . bending. They're using their combined weight to snap the trunk of the tree so that it comes crashing down on this dwelling, hoping, I suppose, to crush it. Here it comes – here it comes – OH!'

The reason for the bird's last yell became apparent when he withdrew his head from the hole and was seen to have pine needles on and around his beak. The tree had crashed down, narrowly missing the cabin. One of its branches slapped the roof, but failed to dislodge or penetrate the thick turf that covered it. Even should the drots get through this turf, they would still be unable to enter the cabin, for the ceiling was made of solid pine trunks, pegged together and caulked with hard clay.

Before they could close the knot hole in the wall a drot managed to squeeze into it and wriggle through. It whirred around the room like a lone mosquito, looking to draw blood. Soldier swatted at it with a rag, trying to kill or stun it. However, the drot, a silver female (the males being a dark blue, except for the king drots, which were a pastel mauve), finally landed on Humbold's cheek and instantly sank its teeth into his upper lip. Humbold's eyes watered in pain. He slapped at the creature, managing to strike it. The drot flew across the room with a mouthful of torn lip. She hit the wall and bounced down on to the floor, where Humbold trod on her. There was a nasty *crack* like a cockroach being squashed.

Soldier picked up the flattened fairy and studied it. The creature was quite beautiful in many ways, except for its face. It was well formed in its body-shape, much like a slim, fit human. It rested in his right hand, its head on his fingertips and its feet in the hollow of his palm. Close to, Soldier could see the hairline stripe that went lengthways all around its body, going over the head and under the crotch, as if it were an almond nut or bivalve seashell, able to be prised into two perfect halves. There were sharply pointed ears on its head, large glaring eyes, and an expression on its face of utter fury. It was this which made the creature's countenance ugly. It had no malformed features or distorted organs, but the expression of rage and viciousness transformed what might otherwise have been the visage of an angel into the ugliest of beings.

'Such beautiful wings, though,' he murmured, almost to himself. 'Look how they sprout from her back into the most delicate of gossamer appendages – though brittle and shell-like to the touch. Strong too. Your boot has made no impression on them, Humbold. I swear you could use one to slice a hock of ham, they seem so sharp at the edges. Look at the filigree patterns, too, branching out into maps. What a shame these creatures are so hell-bent on blood . . .'

'Yet they are,' growled Humbold, having trouble in staunching the flow from his lip. 'Damned infernal creatures.'

Outside, the attacks on the door were being renewed, as the multitude flew at it repeatedly, trying to force it off its hinges. Then it went ominously quiet again and it seemed apparent they were up to more tricks. The drots' intentions soon became obvious. There was a terrible *thump!* on the roof and the whole cabin shuddered. This was repeated several times, until the ceiling began to bow inwards, clearly under a great weight.

'They're lifting boulders, collectively, and dropping them from a height on to the roof. We must prepare ourselves. There, that birch broom in the corner should do as a weapon,' said Soldier. 'I'll use this frying pan. Bird, you'd better just attack with your own weapons.'

'Beak and claws, never fail.'

At that moment a rock came crashing through the ceiling, narrowly missing the raven, and thudded into the floor planks. Within seconds the drots began pouring through the hole, which was mercifully not too large. Soldier's mare kicked and whinnied, stamping around in one corner as the drots attacked her. She was no slouch at using her own teeth though, snapping at the fairies and biting them in two.

Soldier began swatting the buzzing creatures with the frying pan, while Humbold fought them off with the broom. The raven flew back and forth, snatching them out of the air with its beak and snapping them, letting them drop to the floor.

Even as he was being attacked and bitten, Soldier picked up a three-legged stool and jammed it into the hole in the ceiling, crushing several fairies with the rim as he did so. Then he set about swiping those in the room, batting them with the pan and striking them against the walls and floor. Some lay wriggling there, broken, but still with that same snarling mouth and glaring eyes, never willing to admit defeat. Soldier tramped around, squashing those underfoot, hearing and feeling the sickening crack of their bony forms on the leather of his soles. It was a disgusting battle, which set his teeth on edge and made his stomach churn. This was not something he enjoyed doing, breaking fairies, but it was a matter of life or death. If they did not maim and kill the drots, they would be overwhelmed and their bones stripped cleaner than pale driftwood on a sunbaked beach.

'Help me here!' yelled Humbold, flailing blindly with his witch's broom, as his face became encrusted with snapping drots. 'I can't see — I can't see . . .' He went too near the horse, who was already mad with fear and kicking out with her back hoofs. She trod on Humbold's foot, making him scream in pain as she broke a bone there. It was mayhem and madness, what with the mare, the bird, the men and a roomful of flying rats.

The raven landed on Humbold's head and began pecking away the drots, shaking them like worms, then tossing them aside. Eventually the ex-king's face emerged, covered in blood, but the eyes intact. Humbold had been lucky and had managed to close his lids before being bitten on the eyeballs. One drot was still stuck halfway up one of his nostrils though. Its silvery legs were kicking furiously, hammering against his teeth. Humbold pinched these legs between thumb and forefinger and pulled it out, yelling in pain as several nose hairs were torn away with the fairy. In his anger he bit the drot in two and spat the halves on to the floor.

'We need fire,' growled Soldier, during a respite, 'before they breach our defences again.'

The tinder box was used to light some paper, which in turn was introduced to some faggots, and finally both Soldier and Humbold were wielding blazing torches. The sealed room began to fill with smoke. Soon, though, the stool had been punched through by another well-aimed boulder-bomb, and the smoke poured out through the opening. Thankfully, this slowed any concentrated attack by the drots, who hated fire and smoke and had difficulty breathing once they had entered the hole. They came into the room coughing and spluttering, and Humbold and Soldier were able to shrivel them with the blazing brands before they could recover. The smell of singed fairy-flesh was disgusting and made both men gag. Wings frizzled and frazzled; bodies curled up slowly like those of cooked beetles; heads split and popped like chestnuts on a hot griddle.

'This is the worst fight I've ever been involved in,' complained Soldier. 'It's like being attacked by savage butter-flies.'

But even though they had accounted for hundreds of the determined drots, there were still thousands waiting their chance to get in and engulf the two humans and the bird. They could smell the scarlet fluid now, even over the smoke – that sweet, sickly odour of human blood – and it was driving those on the outside crazy. They were desperate to drink at the well of warm liquid, to lap to their hearts' content on corpuscles. A pack of seven queens, gold with red stripes, went hurtling towards the hole, only to dash themselves on the stool which once again served as a plug to keep them out.

For much of the night the drots continued to try to force an entry, but the occupants of the cabin were determined to keep them out. Then, at about three o'clock, the fairies seemed to go away. At least, it all went quiet outside, followed by a period of intense cold in the cabin. Soldier wondered what had happened, but he was so tired he just fell into a bunk and dropped to sleep straight away. He was awakened once by Sintra, singing out that he was being attacked, to find Humbold halfway to his bed. He drew his sword and threatened the ex-king, who indeed was totally fatigued himself. The pair of them fell back into their beds, exhausted:

Soldier grateful for his scabbard's warning; Humbold cursing that he was so weak.

When morning came Soldier opened the door and stepped outside. He found his feet were crunching on something like thin broken glass. When he looked down he was amazed to see that what cracked under his boots was not ice, but frozen drots. There were thousands of them, frosted into layers all around the cabin, iced into sugary forms that looked good enough to eat. Something had passed through, or over, in the night. Some narrow agent of blizzard and ice-storm, for stretching out before and beyond was the white road which Soldier needed to follow to reach his goal. He kicked at the poor meringued fairy figures that heaped the doorway and called to the black bird that they ought to be on their way, while the road was visible.

'Good bloody riddance!' cried Humbold, limping to the doorway, his face crusted with newly forming scabs. 'Look what you've brought me to! Me, the ex-chancellor of Zamerkand, the dethroned king of Guthrum! To this indignity, this humiliation, this *pain*. I hope you rot, the pair of you, all *three* of you,' he added, remembering the mare. 'I hope you sink in a bog and all traces of you disappear for all time. You have brought me low. I have fallen, plummeted, into the pit of despair. It must make you very happy, Soldier, to see me thus.'

'It does not make me any happier than when I saw Queen Vanda's head flung over the walls of Zamerkand, wrapped in rags. You have a lot of sins to atone for, before you start accusing others of laying you low. You have brought this on yourself. You are a thief and a murderer . . .'

'A king cannot murder. It is called just execution.'

'A thief and a murderer, I say, and lucky to have been

banished rather than hung, drawn and quartered as you should have been.' All the while Soldier was talking he was saddling his horse.

'Bah!' Humbold was disgusted. 'Who can talk to such a creature as you? I shall see the Drummond kill you yet.'

'Perhaps. But I shall die an honourable man.'

'Is there honour in all your deeds?' sneered Humbold, as a parting shot, when Soldier swung himself on to his mare. 'I seem to remember something about massacres and slaughters. Perhaps you've conveniently forgotten again?'

'No, those are my stains and I shall do my utmost to remove them – thank you for reminding me of my own humbleness . . .' Soldier swung his horse round and began to trot along the icy trail that led up into the foothills at the end of the valley. The raven settled on the horse's rump, enjoying the swaying rhythm of the mare's movement.

Soldier turned and looked back once, remembering Humbold's ass for the first time. Its skeleton was propped against the lean-to, still standing, the joints locked in place by the cold. Humbold would have to walk out of this place, for drots had feasted on his transport. Unable to get into the cabin, they had stripped the ass down to the bone. A salutary warning.

Once out of sight of the ex-king, Soldier brooded on the ills of discovering he was the knight Valechor. He too had taken many lives, some of them possibly innocent except in defence of their own kin. Why couldn't he have been a kitchen slave in the last world? How glorious it would have been to find he had been a serf and now risen to the rank of general and consort of a major kingdom! But no, he had been a man of consequence, and not just that, one steeped in the violence of personal wars. Humbold was right: Soldier was no better than the exiled murderer. There was much blood on his hands. It was too late to ask forgiveness of the Drummonds: there was but one left and he a mortal enemy who would never accept the hand of remorse from a Valechor. Soldier had to live with his past and try to make amends in other ways. Perhaps by serving the citizens of Zamerkand to the best of his ability, and being faithful and loving to their queen.

'The second is not so hard to do,' he told himself. 'More the greatest pleasure in the world. The first will take fortitude, for I am a man easily bored by bureaucracy and servitude. There are others more suited to such civilian tasks. But I must do my best not to become impatient, not to look to the horizon, not to scratch the itch in my hand for want of a sword.'

'Going through a bad patch, are we?' asked the raven, its grating voice startling Soldier for a moment. 'Having doubts? Filling the parchment with resolutions? I'm glad I'm a thing of feathers.'

'You are a most *annoying* thing of feathers.'

'Yet here I perch. And I could be your soul, for all you know. Perhaps I am.'

'A dark soul, yes, that is mine.'

'But perhaps not,' continued the raven, 'for there is wit in this feathered form, while your soul . . .'

'Is dull in comparison?'

The raven cackled. 'You said it, Soldier, not I. Oh yes, you love indulgences, don't you? Misery, that's what you enjoy. Wallowing in misery. Maudlin creature! Come out of it. Rise above it. Be determinedly joyful and refuse to follow the lead of your desire. Give you a grey thought and you'll make a cloak of it, aye, and hat and gloves too! Do you want to remain a shadow in your shadowy world?'

'Am I indulgent? Yes, I suppose I am.'

'Then cheer up!'

'Indeed I shall,' cried Soldier stridently. 'You're right, bird, I have no business being miserable. We have a task ahead of us. Humbold said I am cursed, doomed to wander like an itinerant holy man. So I may as well do it cheerfully, of good mind. Once this quest is over, no doubt there'll be another waiting, and another . . .' the reflection was gloomy but Soldier's tone was still positive '. . . but hopefully some time we shall have the witch's curse removed and will be able to settle to an ordinary life.'

'At least it gets you out in the fresh air,' cried the raven, getting into the mood.

'With good company!'

'Aye, that too. And the countryside abounds with game.'

'We shall live like kings.'

'And eagles.'

Soldier was silent for a while, then he said, 'One thing still puzzles me – why was I invited to the wizard's funeral? You remember the wizard's funeral, bird? I was the only human to attend? I have never been able to understand the reason for that.'

'I can answer,' replied the bird. 'He wished to honour you, because you were the only human, apart from IxonnoxI's mother, who was brave enough to support the old King Magus's heir. It was you who protected the witchboy, hid him along with his mother in unknown country, helped him train for King Magushood. That deserved some reward from HouluoH.'

'I'd have preferred gold and jewels,' grumbled the knight, trying to joke with a bird who had a sense of humour, but a strange one. 'Being invited to a funeral isn't my idea of a *reward*.'

'No you wouldn't. You had an experience no one else has ever duplicated, and probably never will.'

'I suppose.'

The pair jogged on, through the wooded countryside, following the snowy road left for them by who knew who or what. Soldier's encounter with Humbold had left a bad taste in his mouth, but it had also unlocked a few more distant memories. Soldier remembered his childhood along the borderland, a place where raiding and thieving was endemic. His father had been a big, bluff man with little patience and rough ways. His mother had died young and he had known her not, though he had an older sister who added gentleness to his upbringing. She had married a Scottish monarch, king of one of the Hebrides, and had thus passed out of his life.

When he was twelve his father took him into his first battle, against the Drummonds of course, and he recalled how terrified he was of the wild clan his family hated. The Drummonds had appeared over the hill, attired in animal skins and armour, with long wild hair flowing from under their helmets, their beards trailing over their shoulders. He had been horrified, and would have run, if his father's bodyguard – the huge and loyal Hamish Haldstack – had not restrained him, out of sight of the elder Valechor.

'They are not worth running from, laddie,' he whispered. 'They may look fierce, but they have rabbit dung for brains . . .'

Still, the Drummonds were impressive to a youth not yet old enough to shave. They had massive barrel chests which seemed to be bursting out of their breastplates. They carried round shields, tards, the size of tabletops. They wielded claymores that dwarfed a sexton's scythe. Their black mouths screamed profanities and obscenities at the Valechors. They raised their kilts and wiggled their genitals to show their contempt for their enemy. They died not with fearful breaths, but yelling with rage at their killers.

He had survived that battle, and many others after it. One day his grizzle-bearded father fell, a Drummond spear in his heart, and on that day he became the leader of the family. Haldstack also died that day, leaving him bereft of a guide and mentor, as well as a protector. He had hardened his heart still further and did as he believed his father would wish him to do: pursued the Drummonds. Eventually this led to the slaughter of the whole Drummond clan but one. He was not at first a baron or anything like, being a blacksmith by trade, but he was as determined as any of the Drummond breed. This Drummond had fought for the king, was knighted, become the king's right-hand man, and eventually the king himself.

Thankfully, for that would have been the end of him, Soldier had been flung into this world, through which he now tramped.

His uncles and cousins had now become hunted outlaws in a country which their enemy ruled as kings. In such feuds there were no winners, no heroes, no honourable men. There was just bloodshed and widows and weeping orphans. Soldier was embittered with himself now, for taking up his father's fight. No one even knew the original reason for the hatred between the two families. A stolen sheep? A slight at a king's banquet? A chance meeting in the middle of a narrow bridge? These family feuds grew out of nothing into never-ending wars. Could it be stopped, even now, by an offer of the hand of friendship? Soldier doubted it, but he had decided he would attempt reconciliation, if it ever became possible.

'Deep in thought,' said the bird, from behind him. 'What's to do, knight?'

'Oh, just indulging in the joys of memory.'

'Sounds like it. I suppose you've noticed that the road has disappeared. Even the dampness has gone. We haven't wandered far away, though. Look, there's one of those giant owl pellets! A packed and steaming pile of skins, horn and bones in the shape of a lozenge. Shall we meet the monster that swallows live cows and lays a road of ice, do you think?'

'I know not. Damn, where has the track gone? I haven't been paying attention. I've just been letting the mare carry us on. Do you think she left the trail?'

'I don't think there's been any trail to leave, not in the last half-hour. I suggest we stop and take our bearings. Have you your astrolabe?'

Soldier dismounted with a grunt. 'Yes, but that'll do us little good out here, where we have no maps, no idea where we're going, and without the road we're supposed to follow.'

Soldier made a fire and then took the crossbow he carried to hunt for food. Despite the abundance of game that the raven had mentioned, he was only able to bag a hare for the pot. To Soldier's disgust the raven pecked out the creature's eyes while it was still warm. Then it complained that the rest of the meat was too tough for a raven's beak, until it had rotted.

'I'll give you the lights in a minute,' said Soldier, 'if you could be patient and wait until I've gutted the beast.'

'Whoa,' cried the raven, looking down the slope which led out of the wood, 'there's carrion down there! I'll have a go at that while I'm waiting.'

The bird flew out of the wood and down the hillside to the carcass of an unidentifiable animal which lay rotting there. The bird began to peck and stab at the putrid flesh, not realising it was violating the territory of another creature, a bird with far more efficient weaponry than the raven possessed. Suddenly, out of the bright blue sky, a thunderbolt appeared and dropped on to the raven, striking it behind the neck. The raven fell away from the cadaver, wounded to the point of death. A golden eagle, the creature on whose kill the raven had been feasting, clutched the carcass of the carrion in its talons and took to the air, heading back to its eyrie.

Soldier had seen the raptor fall from the sky and had witnessed the attack on his feathered companion. He gave a yell and ran down the hillside, sword in hand, but the eagle had risen and was gone into the blue. When he reached the black bird he saw that blood flowed from the wound in the back of its neck, on to the mossy ground. Soldier stemmed the flow easily enough, but realised the raven had taken such a blow as could lead to its death. He carried the pathetic little bundle back to the camp site, placing it on a bed of leaves, wondering what could be done to save its life.

'I have no training in this,' he said. 'What am I to do with you?'

But the bird never regained consciousness. It lay limp and barely breathing, never really stirring for the whole day. Soldier knew that the herb woundwort was good for healing injuries. He found some, boiled it, and applied it to the gash on the raven's neck. There was not much else he could do. The bird was clearly on the threshold of death, its spirit hovering there, ready to fly either one way or the other, the decision not yet made. A fresh breath of wind could win it life. An intemperate night could send it hurtling into the dark-clouded skies of the afterlife of the crow family. There was nothing anyone could do but wait to see which way the scales would tip.

Soldier woke a couple of times during the night. Once he

thought he heard the bird stirring, but it was just the mare, snuffling. He did not dare look at the raven in the dark, in case it had already gone. Such things as death were better viewed in the light of day, rather than in the early hours, when fears of one's own mortality were rife. When morning came, Soldier opened his eyes to stare up at the leafy canopy of the forest and the grey sky above it. Then he rolled over and looked to his erstwhile companion.

Astonishment! Incredulity! Shock!

There lay, not a feathered corpse, but a young boy, an urchin by the look of his rags and dirt, breathing shallowly.

'Wake up! Who are you, lad? Where is my bird?'

The boy, some twelve or thirteen years old, opened his eyes.

'What? My lord?'

Soldier recognised the voice. It was that of the raven. Such nearness to the afterlife, lying on the very borderline between life and death, had removed the curse from the raven's spirit. The dark otherworld of death and the dead had sucked the witch's oath from the heart of the bird, trapping it there, while the soul of the creature had finally slipped back over the threshold, into the world of light. He was a boy again! The bird had become the youth, no younger or older than when first cursed, who now stared up with worried eyes into the face of his saviour.

'Am I thus come back?' said the urchin, lifting his arm to look at the dark skin that covered his human bones. 'Am I *me* again?'

'You are indeed, child,' Soldier said, smiling. 'Your feathers are gone, your beak and claws with them, and you are as good as me.'

'I was as good as you *before*,' snapped the boy, with the

same asperity as the raven would have used. 'I just had a different form.'

'Quite so. I stand abashed and corrected for my prejudice.' He stared at the lice which hopped in the child's thick matted hair. 'We're going to have to clean you up though. Can you rise?'

The boy tried to go up on his elbows, but fell back again. 'I feel giddy.'

'The wound is still affecting you. You must rest. Later, when you have recovered enough, you must get down to that stream and wash away the dirt. I'll find some betony to rub on your head, to get rid of those fleas. Yuck, boy, you smell. And those rags will have to go. I'll sew you a shift from one of the blankets. We can get you some proper clothes later.' He stared at the child and smiled with pleasure. 'Good to meet you at last. You and I are already great friends, through your other self, the raven. What do we call you, lad? Do you have a name?'

'They – they used to call me Ragworm.'

'Ragworm? That's no name for a hero such as you, survivor of many fierce encounters, as well as that last attack by a golden eagle. We shall call you . . .' Soldier paused and gave it thought, before saying, 'Musket – which is a male sparrowhawk. A small but highly spirited bird, quick, with lightning actions. Yes, *Musket*, that's you.'

The boy seemed pleased. He also appeared very tired and eventually closed his eyes and slept. Soldier covered him with a blanket and then set about making him the shift. At noon he woke the child and gave him some hare soup, told him he must drink plenty of water.

'I feel a little better now,' confessed Musket.

'You're not getting up for another two or three days, so

put your mind at rest on that matter, young man.'

'Young man!' marvelled Musket. 'How I have longed to hear someone call me that over the many years. Yet I did enjoy being a raven, sometimes . . .'

'You mean when you picked out the eyes of dead warriors on the battlefield?' joked Soldier.

Musket surprised and shocked him by licking his lips.

Soldier shuddered. 'Clearly there is some residual crow still inside you, lad, which we're going to have to winkle out. We can't have you chewing worms in front of the ladies. In the meantime, eat some more of this delicious soup. I don't want you scavenging on dead creatures behind my back . . .'

Chapter Five

After three days Musket was well enough to be able to travel. He was an engaging young man, a little reluctant to shed his pets and dirt, but eventually Soldier managed to persuade him to clean himself up.

'If you don't, I shall leave without you.'

The boy was terrified of being left alone in the forest and was therefore encouraged to rid himself of his fleas using Soldier's betony, and wash himself thoroughly in a stream with lye-soap. Soldier supplied him with a hand-stitched shift with a leather thong for a belt. Musket was not enthralled with his apparel either, finding it itchy and uncomfortable.

'My feathers didn't feel like this.'

'You can make yourself a cloak of feathers once we return to Zamerkand – in the meantime, you will make do and mend.'

'Who says so?'

'I say so.'

'You're not my father.'

Soldier had to accept this was true. He had no real authority over the boy, apart from the fact of their respective ages. But since Musket wished to travel with him, he said, the child would have to do as he was told. If Musket wanted to leave and go it alone, why that was perfectly acceptable to the knight. Otherwise, he could stay and be Soldier's squire, but if he were to agree to squire for a knight, Musket had to give up his freedom of choice. He had to agree to bondage with that knight, and being bound, was expected to obey in all things.

'If you make me your *son*,' replied the youngling, 'I will *have* to obey you.'

'Crafty, young Musket, but I don't accept the conditions. I want for no son, and when I do, my wife the princess will supply me with one in the normal way. Do you realise what an honour you've been given? How many street urchins are offered the position of squire, a post which is normally open only to boys from high-born families? Very few. It is a position of great responsibility, involving duties of a sacred nature. To carry, on occasions, the knight's weapons. To provide the knight with his vessel of wine before a tourney. To serve his master with all diligence.'

'Those are duties of a sacred nature?' said the boy, incredulous.

'Of course. A knight has a holy task.'

'Well, the knight can stuff it. I'm not lugging weapons around for him, nor fetching his wine. The knight can go and fart into the wind.'

'Can he now?'

'When he likes.'

Soldier foresaw difficulties with this youngster, who had been too long a free-flying bird to be caged. He was exasperated by the child. Of course he could not abandon Musket, not now he was a human boy. He had to make the child see sense. Perhaps, he thought, a threat will do it? No need to carry the threat through. He decided he would just wave a stick at the youngling and tell him to fall in line. He cut a switch and confronted the boy.

'Well, let's see a if a little corporal punishment will bring you round to my way of thinking.'

'You better not touch me with that – I'll peck and scratch you,' warned an alarmed Musket. 'I've got a very poisonous set of claws, I have.'

Soldier advanced, swiping the air menacingly with the switch. Musket lost his healthy pallor and began running down a slope. For the moment he forgot he was not a bird. At the end of the run, where a boulder jutted out over a verdant hollow, he launched himself into the air, flapping his arms, only to come crashing down on the turf. He struggled to his feet, winded but unable to reconcile himself to the fact that he could no longer fly. He had been gliding through the air for so long the idea was lodged in his brain. Once more he attempted to take off, and once more he fell heavily to the mossy ground. Soldier caught up with him and lifted him by the scruff of the neck, so that his feet were windmilling in mid-air.

'Calm down stripling,' growled the warrior. 'Just be still.'

'I won't. I won't,' cried the boy, hot tears of frustration and anger coursing down his cheeks. 'You let me be.'

'I'll let you *be* when you agree to obey me.'

'All right,' replied the boy, sullenly. 'I will be good.'

Soldier put him down on the ground. This time Musket did not run away. He followed Soldier back to where the mare was tethered. Soldier made ready for them to leave. At one point Musket went to pick up Soldier's sword, where it lay resting against a tree.

'Don't touch that,' Soldier snapped, sharply. 'I'll tell you what weapons I want you to carry. The crossbow.'

'Why so touchy about the sword?' said the boy.

Soldier explained, 'It's a named sword. Kutrama.'

'I know that.'

'What you don't know is that you must never touch a named sword. As a raven you weren't interested in it. As a boy its attraction is irresistible. But only its owner is privileged to handle a great sword. The sword might turn on you and cut you down. If you pick it up with your right hand, it might swing and sever your left from your arm.'

'Oh.'

Soldier armed himself, cap-a-pie, and then heaved himself up into the saddle. He offered a hand down. 'Here, come up behind me. That's where you usually ride.'

'I know, but I thought you might make me walk.'

'I'm not a monster,' growled Soldier, put out. 'Come on, boy.'

The youngling swung up behind Soldier's saddle, sitting on the rump of the mare. It felt as if he was there for the first time. There was a wonderful swaying motion to the beast. Its hair was smooth and groomed to a shiny gloss. Musket felt like king of world, sitting up there behind this armed knight, clinging to the back of his saddle. He felt he dwarfed all other creatures in the forest, including the red deer.

'I like this, Soldier,' he said. 'What's the horse's name?'

'She hasn't got one.'

'Your sword has got a name but your charger hasn't? But the horse is flesh and blood!'

Soldier shrugged as they went through the dappled wood, the leafy foliage flickering in the breeze creating dancing shadows.

'I just never thought to give her one. She's not a pet. She's a warhorse with duties to perform. I never gave you a name, did I? Not when you were a raven.'

'Then I shall name her,' cried the boy, delighted to have found a task. 'What shall I call her? He noticed a flower out of the corner of his eye. 'I shall call her Primrose.'

Soldier was shocked. 'You can't call a charger *Primrose*. It doesn't sound right. If you give her a name it has to be one full of blood-and-thunder. Horses called Primrose pull drays and carts, or even ploughs, but they don't carry knights. What am I to say to any giant or evil knight when I cry, "Onward, Primrose!" and they burst out laughing and tell me I am a nurse's bib? How will I hold my head high?'

'Oh, yes. All right, we'll call her Blood-and-thunder, then.'

'Well, that's a bit long. How about shortening it to *Thunder*?'

The boy agreed with a good deal of excitement in his voice.

'Don't forget I was the one who named her,' he said. 'She belongs to me, really, like your sword belongs to you.'

'Then I shall have to ask for a loan of her,' replied Soldier, indulging the boy's fancies.

'Yes you shall, but I shall allow it, since you are a great knight.'

'It would be boasting to agree with you – but yes, I am. I have survived many battles, and one or two wars. Now sit still for the next few hours and try to hold your tongue. We don't want to arouse any malignant creatures in this forest. Once we are out of it and on the windy plains, you may talk as much as you like.'

Musket did as he was told. They continued through the forest, once or twice surprising some eerie and unsettling forest beings, but nothing which was highly dangerous. Goblins sprang from the boles of oaks and gnomes leapt with spraying agility from stagnant pools. These forest creatures had fungi growing from their heads and backs, and moss flourished like mould in their ears and nostrils. Soldier and the boy were allowed to go on their way with perhaps only a few choice oaths flung in their direction. Musket wanted to know the meaning of some of the words a woonkie yelled after them, but Soldier told him he wasn't old enough.

They left the woodland and its creatures behind and went out on to a plain. There before them stretched a purple outland. Soldier had since discovered something about his white road: it left a green one in its wake. Once the snow and ice had melted, the water left behind freshened the greenery beneath it. Thus the grass, the moss and other vegetation was a slightly greener green than its surrounds. It was not the most reliable of roads to follow, but it was the only one they had.

When night came, and they slept beneath the stars, the white road would reappear. Sometimes they found themselves directly on its path and woke shivering with the cold, often covered in snow. Other times they woke outside its swathe, but always within sight of it. Never once did they see what phenomenon made the winter trail, though they did experience dreams of great wide shadows passing slowly overhead.

Even as he was on this quest to cure his wife's loss of memory, Soldier continued to occupy his mind with the fate of his friend, the rightful heir to the position of King Magus. The rogue magus OmmullummO had usurped the throne of the erstwhile witchboy. IxonnoxI had been too young to take his place in the magical order of the universe and the usurper would not now abdicate. IxonnoxI would therefore have little choice but to fight for his place amongst the moons and stars of the mystical world. Soldier was determined to help his friend in any way he could. There was also a fondness in his heart for IxonnoxI's mother, Uthellen. Had things been but slightly different – history moved sideways to the thickness of a shadow – Soldier and Uthellen might have been betrothed to each other. As it was, Soldier was in love with his own beloved and naturally jealous wife, and Uthellen could not be anything more than a dear friend.

But dear she was, and he wondered after her welfare.

Uthellen was at that moment struggling through the mountains of a distant land, on her way to join her son in his fastness hideout. She too had seen the strange magic scattered like coloured moondust over the heavens and knew that her son would soon be engaged in a battle which would see either the making or the disappearance of him.

Wizards do not die easily and IxonnoxI was not only a fully fledged wizard, but a hundred times more powerful than any marabout apart from his father OmmullummO, the present occupant of the seat of King Magus. Any personal struggle between these two highly potent wizards would shake the seven pillars of the earth. Fire, flood, earthquake and eruption would sweep over the world if the pair decided on single combat. It might even lead to the annihilation of the whole human race.

Both sorcerers knew this, and while OmmullummO was not concerned at causing catastrophes and disasters, he did care that the world was peopled. If everyone were to be wiped out he would have dominion over no one and nothing. It is pointless being the most powerful being in the universe if you are the only sentient living thing around. Those who would be kings need subjects, or they are kings of nothing but their own hearths. IxonnoxI *was* concerned about causing mayhem and slaughter, and therein was *his* reason for not throwing himself into a battle of champions.

There was another course for the two great beings to follow.

This would be to have armies of men and women fight their fight for them, in order to keep the world from such destruction as those natural and unnatural disasters would cause. Both would have to agree to abide by the outcome if such armies were employed. A pre-set mechanism for the loser, one which satisfied both wizards, would need to be put into place, a magic spell which automatically went into effect once the battle between the two armies of men was over and the winner declared by the gods. This spell would in fact banish one of the two wizards to the dark and far-flung nether regions of the universe, there to remain until death.

It might seem to the observer that the two wizards had the best of it. They had no need to risk their lives in battle if mortals were to do it for them. Yet their fate, their punishment, for being the loser was too hideous and horrible to contemplate. There were no monsters in those spatial territories to which the loser would be exiled, no terrible storms, no infestations of insects, no swamps or deserts, no devils or demons, no ghosts. There was, in fact, *nothing*. Nothing at all except darkness and dust. A wizard, or indeed any other intelligent creature, sent to such a place would be screaming mad within a short period of time, driven there by pure boredom. Whoever went had to remain there for the whole of their life, and wizards live a long, long, long time in comparison to mortals.

All this was in the mind of Uthellen as she scurried through the mountain passes, hoping to be with her son within the month. She would have been with him now if she had not been sent away – a mere mortal, even if the mother of a great wizard – for her own safety. Yet now she was disturbed by the separation, and wished to be with her son. If it were possible she intended to go with him on his banishment, should he lose the battle against the ruthless and contemptible OmmullummO.

With the night coming on and the wind growing stronger, Uthellen sought shelter. A cave would do. Even a rock hang, out of the wind. But she actually came across a dwelling with a strangely thatched roof, stuck out on a ledge, overlooking a monstrous drop of some two thousand metres. The fall was only frightening if one went to the very edge and looked down. Back on the trail it was simply a direction to be avoided in the darkness.

She went to the doorway of the hut, which had not a wooden door, but the hide of an animal hanging down from a lintel.

'Hello?' she called. 'Anyone there?'

There was no answer from within. She tried calling twice more. Still no one came or replied to her call. Finally she brushed aside the soft skin curtain and entered.

The room was dim within, naturally, for there were no windows. The smell was extremely unpleasant, but not unbearable, certainly not for someone whose only other choice was to spend the night in the open on the side of a bare mountain.

When her eyes became more accustomed to the gloom, Uthellen was able to see that it was sparsely furnished, as was to be expected of a drystone dwelling hanging on the edge of a mountain, unless it were owned by an eccentric sultan or a wealthy merchant turned mad. There were a few animal skins spread about the floor, a bed of stone covered in wood bark in the far left corner, and a fireplace in the centre with the usual hole in the roof for smoke. Very little else was there, apart from bones piled in the opposite corner to the bed. She supposed them to be the bones of animals, for they were too large to be those of fish or birds.

Exhausted by her journeys, Uthellen lay down by the central fireplace, unwilling to take a stranger's bed. If it were that of a shepherd or goatherd, the owner might return soon with his flock and want his own resting place. She had found the hospitality of such men and women to be good, but then she had not taken advantage of them and had showed proper respect for their property before now.

Outside, the wind increased in strength as nightfall followed a dull and dreary grey day. As with all high regions, it whistled and howled through the crevices and passes, creating a wuthering sound. Uthellen was not concerned by mere noise, however unsettling it might be for others.

Only the presence of evil could have alerted her to danger, and she had a good nose for nefarious men. Years of being a fugitive, on the run with her witchboy son, had sharpened her instinct for such creatures – or so she thought.

She fell asleep after chewing a crust of dry bread which had nestled with others of its kind in a deep pocket in her habit.

Uthellen was awaked by a smell in the room. But before she could find her faculties and sort through her muddled thoughts, a hairy creature was upon her, sitting astride her chest, its hands – or claws – around her throat. She struggled, trying to scream, but the hairy fingers of the beast who had her in its thrall would only allow a thin squeal to issue forth. The creature was immensely strong, yet knew its own limits to a fraction. It strangled her only until she fell into unconsciousness, not unto death.

When she came round, she found the fire burning in the room. Squatting behind it was a hideous creature, a naked thing of flesh and hair resembling a man. Lit by the flames of the fire, Uthellen recognised its type. It was one of those creatures that people called a 'wild man'. Wild man of the woods. Wild man of the mountains. Probably only half-human, these solitary quirks which had grown out of the back end of nature — boles on the trunks of humanity, cankers on a branch of beings somewhere between apes and hominids — were found in isolated places. They were often near-mindless eremites, too stupid to be evil — for evil required some contrivance on the part of the individual — but nevertheless as bad to meet as any creature with a black heart and devious mind. Thus the reason why Uthellen had not smelled evil in the hut: the wild man was simply a dangerous beast.

'I kull you,' growled the wild man, seeing she was awake. 'I eating you flersh.'

He licked his lips and stirred the embers with a stick, making them flare. Uthellen tried to rise but found she was bound with strips of bark. Still she did not panic, nor did she speak at first. Secretive passions were best in such perilous circumstances. The wild man then poked her with the stick, which was glowing at the tip. It burned her leg, yet still she did not cry out.

'Red fyrre,' growled the wild man. 'Hurt-hurt. I no lyk fyrre. It hurt-hurt. You no lyk fyrre. I burrn lady and eating her.'

It laughed, revealing two rows of very even teeth, worn down to small stubs in its mouth through chewing on bones.

So, she had discovered two things about her captor, even in the space of a few minutes. One, he was afraid of fire, which he knew could hurt him badly. Two, he ate human flesh. The wild man obviously lived on wayfaring souls, travellers using the paths through the mountains. Peddlers used these trails, as did wise men following stars. So long as they came in ones and twos, even threes, and not in large bands, the wild man was probably prepared to gather them in.

Perhaps he snared them, or dug holes and filled them with spikes? In this case his dinner had walked through the doorway and plonked itself down by his roasting spit. That was most convenient for him. Of course the thrill of the hunt, of finding the prey in a trap, had not occurred, but here was fresh meat anyway.

Groups of bandits, lost armies, he would leave alone to find their way down the fastness into green valleys again. The odd giant might cause him to lick his lips, but though he was stupid, he was not *that* stupid. At a pinch, a mountain goat would sustain him until the next delicious supper on two legs came panting up the narrow trail: a castaway sailor looking for the distant coast; a nun on her way from one convent to another; a caravan driver whose camel had collapsed under him through being driven too hard. There was always the next meal, ready to fall foul of his nooses and pits.

When she looked around her, she realised that the hut was not made of the branches of trees, as she had at first supposed. It was fashioned from human bones. And the ceiling, and roof, comprised skulls with the hair still attached. The hair had been woven into matting, to make the thatch for the roof, leaving the heads to dangle inside. Uthellen knew that human hair continued to grow for some time after the death of its owner and therefore made for an ever-thickening thatch to keep out the rain! Auburn hair, black, blonde, greasy-grey, ginger, mousy – all shades were there. They wove in and out of each other as rivers. The heads to which they were attached, eyeless but not toothless, hung down in grizzled lumps, jostling each other for room on the crowded ceiling, mouths agape, nostrils plugged with dead flies, earholes nests for spiders, beetles and their kind.

The creature got up and tested her fattiness by pinching

her thigh. Uthellen kicked out, viciously, catching him under the chin, sending him reeling back towards the doorway. His eyes went round with fear for a moment, as he caught the edges of the opening, preventing himself from flying through and possibly over that ledge outside which dropped to dark nothingness.

Once his fear had gone he went berserk, leaping around the room like a crazy monkey, throwing stones at her. Fortunately he was too enraged for his aim to be sure and only one or two struck her back. She had rolled into the foetus position, to protect her head and chest. Finally the creature calmed down enough to advance on her and thump her once or twice, though with caution, for he was afraid of being kicked again. Then he retired, muttering, to a corner, to glare at her steadily with red eyes.

Now she felt it was time to try reasoning with the wild man.

'Let me go. I shall send you fat ladies from time to time, up the mountain. You will never want for human flesh again.'

She had no compunction about lying. Her life was at stake. She would say anything to this beast if it meant escape. What she intended to do was tell the next village she came across to send a band of armed men to destroy the creature. But for the moment the important thing was to get out of his clutches.

'You no send,' screamed the wild man, sitting on his haunches. 'You get be etten by me. I pop you eyeballing. I chaw you tong. I sluck you nicey warm bludy lady-liver-kidley. Hek! Hek!'

He then got up again and, carefully avoiding her legs, felt the lush thickness of her hair. His own long, ugly body covering was coarse and brittle by comparison. Uthellen's hair was remarkable, even in a world where women were proud of their thick and luxurious locks. She was exceptionally lucky in having a beautiful, glossy head of hair that, when let free, hung down like a waterfall to her ankles. At the moment it was loosely piled on top of her head, held there by pins. The wild man took the pins out, one by one, very gently now, enthralled by the locks. What a cloak these tresses would make for his back! What a pillow for his head at night!

'Let me go,' she tried again, 'and I will cut off my hair for you before I leave. You may do with it as you wish. I have no use for it. I will grow some more and even come back to provide you with further . . .'

He knocked her head in an annoyed way with his knuckles.

'You no spik. I tyke hair anyways.'

The wild man played with her hair for some time, then found it was long enough for him to take it to his bed, without moving her. He went to his stone resting place in the corner with the end of her locks, stroking his cheek with them, nuzzling them, wrapping them round his head like a silken scarf and giggling, only occasionally glaring daggers at the other end of them, as if daring Uthellen to pull her property out of his reach again. Once he yanked on the long tresses viciously, to see if he could make her eyes water. When he was successful, he laughed, in a guttural fashion. Then, once more wrapping the locks around his head to keeps his ears warm from the wind, he stuck his thumb in his mouth, curled up, and went to sleep.

Uthellen spent an uncomfortable night by the fire. She was able to reach faggots and throw them on, and did so, for the light produced by the flames was comforting. The wild man slept all night, deeply, snoring with loud intent. Uthellen's bonds cut into her hands, but she was determined to act in a kindly way to the creature when he woke, to try to evoke some sort of sympathy from him. He had surely enough man in him to make him vulnerable to emotions? This was her hope, anyway, and when he woke she asked him if he would like her to make some tea.

'Tea?' he repeated, puzzled. 'What for, tea?'

'To drink. I can collect some leaves from the bushes outside. I've seen one or two which would make a nice herbal brew. If you would just loosen these bonds? I promise you I will not try to escape. You can still keep me tied and tethered. Just relax them for me a little.'

'NO!' he shouted at her. 'You no run aways.'

'I will not run away. A nice hot cup of tea . . .'

'Hot?' he went pale at the word. 'You try burrrn we. You try hot-hot to myk hurt. Me kyk you hard, you myk hot in we mouth.'

Ah, she had forgotten about his fear of fire. It obviously went deeper than just flames. It extended to all things hot. She imagined that he was a stupid creature and was always burning himself on his fire. There were scars on his forearms which signified this. It would be better not to mention hot things in the future. She tried another tack.

'Shall I get you some cool water from a stream then? I can be your slave, if you wish it. My name is Uthellen. You can call me by my name if you desire to do so. It is not hard to say my name.'

'No want say. No want it. You no get waters. You stay.'

The creature skipped out then, on all fours, covering the ground like a black hairy spider. She saw him go to the edge of the cliff, just a few yards beyond the doorway. He looked down, surveying the world from his high citadel, feeling no doubt that he had dominion over the earth. Then he came back again, on his knuckles, to scratch her for talking to him when he did not wish it. She was dinner, he told her. Dinner should not talk. Dinner must keep quite until it was ready to be eaten.

'Then you scrim!' he cried, gleefully. 'You scrim and scrim to top of sky. Last people ate scrimmed like gull bird when we strangles him. We puts bits on styk and poke in fire. Then we lets go cold to eat. Cold meat is nicey. We likes cold meat and radishies and bitroot.'

So she got nowhere with him that day. He hopped around, scuttled to and fro, and disappeared mid-afternoon, only to return after dark. He had something with him: a limb of a human. She guessed he was keeping a corpse in a cool place, possibly in a pool in a cave. No doubt he found it necessary to raid this store from time to time. At the moment he wanted to keep her alive, either to fatten her up or to let her hair grow longer. She watched him eat the arm, picking at the skin between the fingers, nibbling under the nails. She withheld her revulsion. Every time he looked at her, she smiled back. Sometimes he growled or snarled in reply. Once he picked up a stick and hit her with it. Uthellen refused to be intimidated, continuing to try to strike up a friendship with her captor.

'My son is a great wizard,' she told him. 'His name is IxonnoxI and he will be the next King Magus. If you let me go he will reward you with whole tribes of people, which you can keep in a corral and use as cattle.' Once again it did not bother her to lie to the creature, for he himself would not know the truth if it kicked him in the teeth. 'If you do *not* let me go, my son will shrivel you to a crisp with the fire from his eyes. My son has great magic at his fingertips and can reach out to every corner of the earth.'

This made the creature blink a little. Thoughts clearly went through the jagged mind inside that huge thick skull. But finally he decided that since he had not already been fried by any distant sorcerer, he was unlikely to be so in the future. He spat at her and raked her with his dirty nails until she screamed at him, shrilly, crying that he would suffer for it. He stopped hurting her but did not let her go.

Seeing that the threats had at least made the wild man wary of her, she continued to let them flow. She told him that if he did not let her go, the hair growing from the heads in the ceiling would engulf him and strangle him while he was asleep. He laughed at this. Then she said she herself was a witch and would call on all the dead people he had eaten to rise up within him and kill him. Uthellen told him the ghosts and souls of his victims were simply waiting for the curse of a witch to release them from hell, whence they intended to come tumbling forth and tear their murderer to pieces.

It was to no avail. The wild man took no notice of such warnings, having heard them many times over. He rejected every friendly advance made towards him. She guessed he had kept others in similar confinement, who had also tried the same wiles. Clearly he was not interested in fattening her or letting her hair grow: he was simply keeping his meat fresh while he finished another carcass. Then she would replace the one in the cave. At least she was able to loosen the cord on her wrists so that it no longer dug into her flesh. It worried her that her bonds would cut off her blood and so deaden her hands, but fortunately that did not happen.

After a week she knew time was running out. She formed a plan. It was not what she wanted to do, but she had to act soon.

He went to sleep every night as he had done the first, with her hair wrapped around his face. The wild man liked the smell of her tresses and the feel of the fine locks on his skin.

That night, once his snores rent the air, she took a burning log from the fire with her feet. Then she wriggled towards the doorway, lying across it. The human bones which made the walls of the hut were not inflammable, so touching them with a brand would not set the place on fire. Uthellen had to try to flick the brand upwards, into the ceiling, so that the hair on the roof would burst into flame.

She lay on her back across the dark exit and flicked with her feet. The brand went up into the hanging skulls above, struck one of them, but failed to lodge there. It fell down upon the wild man's feet. He jumped up instantly, yelling blue murder.

'FIRE!' screamed Uthellen at the top of her voice. 'FIRE! FIRE! FIRE!'

Not waiting to see what was happening, the creature ran towards the door in a great panic. First he wanted to get out, then he would look back and make sure the place was truly on fire. When he reached the doorway, Uthellen hunched her back, making a tump of her body. He tripped over her, went tumbling over his own feet, and rolled towards the edge of the cliff. His nails raked the ground as he tried to save himself from the drop, but he was unable to stop himself falling out into the blackness. His scream of fear was foreshortened when his dead weight came to the end of Uthellen's hair. In his panic he had wrapped the coils of her tresses around his head and throat. This had formed a noose which throttled him as he hung over the precipice.

Uthellen was half dragged through the doorway by his weight, but she gamely jammed herself there. One or two wall-bones cracked and gave way, but the structure had been well built and was solid enough to remain intact. For a moment she felt exhilarated. She had won! She had beaten the mad creature. Then she was alarmed to feel movement in her hair. The wild man was not quite dead! He was climbing up her hair, using it for a rope. She twisted and thrashed, until the weight came back with a wrench. This time her hair stayed taut. She could feel his body swaying in the wind.

The pair remained thus for two hours: Uthellen stuck between the two door posts and the wild man dangling over the lower world. Dawn came in slow and grey, the ghost of yesterday. Uthellen was in a quandary. It was not so much that the weight of the wild man hurt her head, pulling as it was on her hair. It was simply that she could not think of a way out of this impasse. Then, as the ghost of yesterday grew into the golden child of today, revitalised, reformed, she saw the glint of something near at hand. It was a flint scraper kicked by the wild man as he leapt from his bed. It had skidded across the dirt floor and lay between her and the fire. If she could reach it she could cut her hair and let him fall to oblivion.

Dire circumstances produce strength. Uthellen managed to squirm into a position where her heels were one either side of the doorway. Then she pushed out with both legs: legs made strong by much walking during her travels over the landscape with her son. When she was full length, stretched out on her back, she could reach the flint scraper. Using it, she began to cut through her hair, but after only a few strands it went limp. Her movements had caused the wild man to bang against the cliff and thus loosen himself. When she rose and went to look down, she could see the dark and now misshapen figure spreadeagled on some rocks far below. The wild man had murdered and eaten his last wayfarer. His intended final meal had turned out to be the gallows on which he had been executed: poetic justice indeed.

'You poor foul creature,' said Uthellen. 'How sad that an unnatural child of the earth should turn so bad.'

She knew there were many wild men living in the woods, in the mountains, who never turned to human flesh. This one had somehow acquired the taste, perhaps during a harsh winter in which meat was impossible to come by, except on two legs. It was over. Any vestige of its miserable life had been smashed out of it by those black rocks.

Once she had washed herself and tended to her bruises, Uthellen continued down the mountainside track. At the bottom of the trail she came across a village. There she met a fearful people who gathered round her and asked her how she had survived the wild man. They were a gentle folk, not given to wielding weapons, and had been trapped on their side of the mountains for some years now by the presence of the ogre. When she said she had killed the creature, they at first did not believe her. Then she led them to the bottom of the precipice, to where the broken wild man lay. They marvelled at his death and praised her for her courage. Giving her food, they sent her on her way, rejoicing in their deliverance. A young boy went with her, as a guide through their region, and at every village he told the story of how Uthellen had strangled the wild man with her own hair.

Finally she left the territory of the gentle folk and entered a country where the men were severe and kept their women almost as slaves. They asked her why she did not cover her feet and ears, the most ugly parts of the body, they said. They were a tall people, with narrow faces and sharp eyes, and they crowded against her as she used the trails, jostling her, treading on her heels. Finally she rounded on them and told them of her son, threatening them with all kinds of reprisals if they did not leave her alone. These people were not ignorant like the wild man and they knew of the battle between the wizards. They fell back then, frightened by her words, letting her use the paths over their fields without further hindrance.

One night, while in the hills of a place she had never heard of, she saw a light from a cave. Wary through her experience with the wild man, she approached this light ready to run if necessary. In the doorway of the cave, which had the warmth and comforts of a home, stood an elderly man with long silvery hair. He was wearing a red cloak covered in moons and stars and held a carved staff in his right hand. He beckoned her to come in, not to be afraid, for he would shelter her from the coming storm. True enough, the heavens opened up a short while later, and the rain poured forth. Flash floods raced pell-mell down the wadis and lightning cracked against the earth.

Still very wary she accepted the offer of hospitality from the sorcerer, for that was what he proclaimed himself to be.

'But not an evil creature,' he told her. 'Simply one who has a gift for magic, a talent which could not be ignored.'

He made her a hot stew on the fire in the mouth of the cave, giving her bread and water to go with it. All around the cave were the trappings of a man of magic, a marabout. There were wands; shelves carrying bottles full of potions with weird symbols on their labels; there were pointed hats, some jet black, others covered in cryptic letters; there were dried toads, bats, snakes, innards of birds and rodents; there were dusty old books, one a huge tome which lay open on a parson's lectern. In one corner she could see a writing desk, with sheets of parchment spread over it, and various writing implements: styli, reed pens, writing canes, quills, brushes. And scrawled over the parchments themselves was script in

black ink: hieroglyphics and uncials. There was dust everywhere. A kind of uniform dust, as if manufactured in an attic
and spread about evenly for effect. A *clean* dust. It made her
wonder about the wizard.

'I thank you for your hospitality,' she told him. 'I have been
walking long and weary today.'

'Where are you going, my child?'

'I am on my way to meet my son, IxonnoxI, a wizard like
yourself.'

The old man's eyes brightened. 'IxonnoxI? Not like myself.
I am a humble sorcerer alongside such a wizard. I am greatly
honoured to have the mother of such a powerful creature in
my home. Of course, there are probably one or two spells,
family secrets, which I can do and your son could not . . . but
in the main, his magic is far stronger than mine.'

The old wizard beamed at her. Uthellen became a little
suspicious. What if this were some manifestation of an
enemy, sent by OmmullummO? This wizard was too benign
for words. He looked like somebody's lovable grandfather.
But then two shepherds appeared in the doorway of the
cave and asked for shelter for the night. The wizard gave
it willingly.

'Come in, come in,' he chortled. 'The more the merrier. I
shall have no time for my magic, of course, with so many
guests, but there are plenty of nights left for that.' He sighed
and looked up into the starry heavens. ''Tis a horned moon
this evening, see! The portents are good for magic. There,
there, the evening star shines with a special brightness. But
never mind, people are more important than work. I shall
perform my magic tomorrow.'

'What magic is it that you wish to perform?' asked Uthellen.
For a moment the old fellow looked taken aback, then his

expression cleared again. 'Why, the coming harvest, of course. And the lambing.' He nodded to the two shepherds. 'My magic ensures that the crops yield their bounty and that the lambs are healthy and strong.'

'It's true,' interrupted one of the shepherds, a rough-looking man with crossed eyes. 'Youm be a comeling, my lady, but if youm lived here like we have all the time since we was borned, you'd know that here is a great wizard who makes good harvests and good lambing times.'

Their host swelled his chest and beamed at the man.

'But the soil looks good hereabouts, the grass looks green and lush – and I know the climate to be very amiable,' said Uthellen, 'so why *wouldn't* the crops be plentiful and the lambs healthy?'

'Oh,' murmured the other shepherd, a young boy with a sun-burned, star-burned face, 'they wunt be, if twernt for him.'

'There, there,' laughed the elderly wizard, 'that's enough for a modest chap like me. No need to lay it on so thick. I admit the landscape would be in a sorry state if not for my powerful magic, and the rain would have great difficulty in falling, not to say the sunlight appearing, if it were not for my ministrations. It is with great pleasure that I encourage the ministry of frost to appear at the right time, in order to kill all the unwanted insects. Without me, it is true, the dew would not settle on the speartips of the grasses. But hark, I can hear the impatient rumbling of empty stomachs. I would be better turning my skills for magic towards cooking these two hungry fellows a hearty and appetising meal . . .'

He went about this, humming to himself, happy it seemed to have his cave full of unexpected guests. Uthellen was still unsure about him. Something was not quite right here.

It was true that many regions had local wizards, who looked after their own pockets of the kingdom. They did this because they liked to be in control rather than for altruistic reasons, and often local citizens had to put up with a little bullying if they were to have a resident sorcerer. Many farmers, many shepherds, many cottagers with small industries would rather be without one. Local wizards had their disadvantages. They took what they wanted, they sometimes got the magic wrong, and things ended up much worse than before. And they were normally very testy creatures who would turn a boy into a toad on the wrong sort of morning.

Wizards by nature jealously guarded their own territories. They did not like other wizards settling in the same area and trying to take over or carve a slice from the region. They were rather like birds who marked their territories with a twilight song, or mammals who did the same to the periphery of their hunting area with their urine. Wizards threw out invisible boundaries and they knew when they had been violated by another of their kind.

This one did not conform to the usual image of a local wizard. It was true he bragged a lot, as his kind was wont to do, but he was far too cheerful for a sorcerer. Sorcerers generally had little or no sense of humour – Uthellen could attest to that, knowing her own son – and their natures were often twisted and bent so badly they were always ill-tempered. Uthellen had not known a great many local magicians – they were thin on the ground – but enough to know that this one worried her.

'May I know your name?' she asked the wizard, as he stirred a pot. 'I wish to recommend you to my son.'

He seemed startled and about to argue, but changed his mind and replied, 'Certainly, my dear – my name is AmmA.'

'And have you lived here all your life?'

'My, my, what a lot of questions. Yes, yes, I do believe I have.'

'He'm very well known for hundrids of miles around,' said one of the shepherds, tucking into his stew. 'Everbudy know AmmA.'

'Yes, yes, they know me as a very potent sorcerer, a wizard to be reckoned with.'

They finished the meal and AmmA suggested they all get a good night's sleep. One of the shepherds went out to the flocks that grazed around the cave and settled them, before returning. He then, like the other one, unrolled his blanket, laid it in the mouth of the cave and went to sleep. Uthellen wondered if they would be so trusting if this AmmA was not all he protested. If he were a creature of OmmullummO he must have been recently recruited.

Uthellen pretended to go to sleep too, in a dark corner, but kept her eyes open and on the wizard. She saw him fiddle with a few of his potions and dried reptiles, but when he believed everyone was in dreamland he relaxed a little. She watched intently as he went to a chest with some small drawers, each marked with a symbol. He took something bright and shiny from one of these drawers. Then he went to a rather larger cabinet and removed another object: it was sort of egg-shaped and it appeared to be made of a hard material. Finally, he sat on a stool under a lamp and began working with the items in his hands. She saw what he was doing.

AmmA was darning a sock.

The bright thing had been a needle, the other a brook-smoothed darning stone. He hummed under his breath as he worked his magic on the holed woollen sock. The chore was soon finished. He bit off the wool end and held up his work. It was indeed neat. Uthellen had not performed a neater task. AmmA pulled on the sock and stared at it with great satisfaction. Then he blew out the lamp and lay down on a rush mat by the fire.

Whatever he was, Uthellen decided, this man was no good at magic. If he had been, why spend valuable time darning socks? He was a fake. But for what reason? Had he been planted here to trap her? What if these two bumpkins who had arrived later were also spies, or agents for OmmullummO? All things were possible.

She slept lightly, waking in fits and starts and staring about her, wondering if there were enemies inside the cave.

It was a long night, and in the morning she confronted him with a dagger in her hand.

'Your name is not AmmA.'

The fake wizard stared at her, his eyes revealing panic.

The two shepherds, halfway through their porridge, let their gobs fall open to reveal the food within.

'You two, close your mouths,' she ordered, 'and you – tell me your real name, or I will cut out your heart. I have already killed a wild man this last week. I will do the same to you if you do not give me believable answers.'

'My n-n-name is AmmA,' he stuttered. 'B-be very careful, young lady, that I – I do not change that weapon into a d-deadly snake!'

'You couldn't change a baby's nappy,' she snapped. 'Your real name, or I wreak havoc on your home.'

He hung his head. 'Riddelstem. My real name is Riddelstem.'

'And why do you pretend to be a wizard? Have you been offered a reward for my head? Speak up, quickly, man!'

'Your head?' He looked shocked. So did the two men huddled over their bowls of porridge. 'What would I – who – I mean – your *head*?'

'I know you've been told to trap me in some way, stop me from continuing my journey. Let me tell you that once my son gets to hear of this you'll wish you were dead. He will hunt you down with all the power of a King Magus. He will shrivel your souls and send them hurtling down to hell. OmmullummO will not be able to protect you. Whatever that evil creature has promised you, he will not deliver. I know him better than you.'

'OmmullummO? Oh . . .' Riddelstem seemed lost for words. He wrung his hands. The younger of the two shepherds was looking thoroughly frightened. 'Oh, no. I have no truck with him.'

'Then why this charade? What is it all for?' growled Uthellen, certain she was being fooled. 'Quickly, an answer.'

The older of the two shepherds broke down in tears, and sobbed the reply for the pale and trembling Riddelstem. 'We'me done kurtled our gruntle-wizard, for he were a cossen to 'un us. Riddelstem bestack the place on him, to couch other'n come by.'

Uthellen was stunned. 'What are you saying? Riddelstem, you tell me the story, I'm having trouble with that man's dialect. What does *kurtled* mean?'

'We – we did for him,' said Riddelstem. 'We dropped a rock on his head and killed him dead as a nail.' He became defensive then. 'Well, he ruined our crops, the lambs came out all dark and withered, the children would not laugh, the women had trouble with their births. He didn't like us much, he told us so, and his only pleasure was seeing us in pain. This was a miserable region, gloomy as a viper's pit.

Neighbour was against neighbour – he set it up that way – and we had a hell on earth for a life.'

'So you killed him. A rash and illegal act, which I do not condone, but why then take his place?'

'To stop another coming. Any wandering wizards would hear that this region already had a powerful sorcerer, by the name of AmmA, and would pass on by without calling in. When any comelings – strangers – enter the region I rush to this cave, put on the robe, and pretend to be what I am not. Other villagers, such as these two, arrive later to reinforce my pretence.' He paused in his speech and looked a little troubled. 'Of course, if a *real* wizard came, I would be exposed in an instant, but wizards do not like to confront one another, so we really only have to worry about ordinary people, such as you. If they leave our territory believing there is a great sorcerer here, they tell others – and no new wizard comes.'

He hung his head again.

'We are malefactors and must be punished.'

Uthellen said, 'Well, I am not the one to do it.'

She could see that those held in the thrall of a local wizard would have difficulty in ridding themselves of the creature lawfully. No local baron was going to send in an army to get rid of a rogue wizard in such a small region. It would not be worth the lives or the effort. Better to seal off that region and keep the rot contained. It would be down to the people themselves, in the end, and what could one do with a magician? If you stuck him in the local jail he would be out in an instant, breathing fire and seeking revenge. If you tried to banish him he would laugh in your face and turn you into a newt.

'How was it done?'

'From up there,' said Riddelstem, pointing to the cliff above the cave. 'We waited until he came out one morning and let fall a boulder. It squashed him flat, giving him no time to use his magic. What are you going to do? Will you call in the itinerant judges, to bring us to trial?'

'No, I have no time for such things. And I do see what a quandary you were in. But how do you expect to get away with it?'

Riddelstem looked smug. 'We have until now. That was all twenty years ago, when we got rid of AmmA. This works for us. It keeps away the wizards and we live a happy life. Wizards are boils on the backs of mankind,' he spat with some venom. 'They should drown them all at birth then throw the remains on a bonfire.'

'I'll have you remember my son is a wizard.'

Riddelstem's eyes went round. 'He is? I mean, he *really* is? You weren't telling a story?'

'No, he is IxonnoxI, the rightful King Magus.'

'Oh, lordy, you'll tell him and we'll be visited with fire and earthquakes and eruptions and all that sort of thing.'

She smiled at this. 'I will tell him nothing, and even if I did he would not be interested in a small enclave such as this. You go on living in your peaceful way. It is not good to take life, even that of a foul wizard, but I understand you had but little choice.'

The following day Uthellen left the cave and went on into a Dark Region, travelling below the earth. This was a journey which she hoped would save her some hundreds of miles, for it cut through a range of high snow-covered mountains which would have taken an age to cross. Uthellen was aware that there were some strange and savage creatures below ground, but she took it anyway.

* * *

'Come down off there!'

Musket was perched on a low branch, just as if he were still a raven with claws for feet. The boy blinked. He felt comfortable where he was. Why, it was the way he had sat for many years now.

Musket was having great difficulty in changing his habits. The bird brain still commanded him at times. Instinctively he pecked at food. Automatically he skipped when he heard a noise behind him, his brain thinking it was a rival black-bird or crow. Life was not easy for a boy who had recently been a bird.

'Come on off, lad. Down here,' ordered Soldier. 'You must garner hay for the mare.'

'Let her gather her own harvest!'

'She cannot – she's a horse. She relies on me – and I rely on you. Down from that tree and gather the grass while it's dry. I have to groom her. She's not used to the rough hands of an urchin, otherwise I could let you do it. She's a very sensitive and noble beast, quite out of your class.'

Finally the boy did as he was told, grumbling the whole while about the fact that as a bird he had not needed to do chores.

'I was much better off then. Being a youth stinks. You have to jump every time someone a year or two older tells you to. It's not fair. People should do their own work. I only get to ride the rump of the mare, so that's the bit I should take care of. You don't have to feed a rump. Soldier should feed the head while I groom the rump. I don't mind grooming. Grooming's all right. Grooming's . . .'

'Are you going to be quiet or do I have to sew your lips together?'

It was while they were thus engaged in feeding and

grooming the mare that the maker of the white road appeared in the hushed twilight that had spread across the land once the songbirds were roosted.

Soldier saw it first: an enormous white dragon with a wingspan a hundred yards wide. His jaw fell open as he watched the beast glide through the valley below, dramatically but silently. Its immense shadow covered a wide expanse of ground. And where this moving shade of darkness fell, ice and snow formed. Thus as the albino creature glided swiftly across the valley, a road of frost, ice and snow formed below and behind it. The closer she drifted to the ground, the more powerful her shadow seemed to become. This white but opaque dragon was the bringer of intense coldness: an arctic creature with a freezing aura.

Trees, grass, wild flowers: all were frosted as with icing for a cake. Rivers and streams froze into glittering strips, some with drinking deer stuck to their surfaces, others with trapped ducks and geese. Larger animals like bears stopped in their tracks, looked upwards, shivered and trembled in the darkness of the shade. Smaller mammals froze to chunks of ice, their hearts shrivelled to frozen droplets in their breasts. They remained scattered in the grass like small statues awaiting the thaw.

'Icewings!' cried the boy excitedly, and then, as if quoting from a book, 'Icewings, the white she-dragon! Daughter of the thirteen moon dragons. Snow queen of the northern climes. See how she glides like a white kite formed of mountain snow. How beautiful. Her breath is a blast of frost, her form cuts between sun and earth, leaving her shadow to freeze the countryside below. They say her heart is a berg, her soul an arctic wind. Hailstones fly from her nostrils! Her eyes are hard-water crystals!'

'I thought you said you didn't know what made that snowy road,' said Soldier, accusingly.

'Did I? That must have been as a raven. Of course I have heard of Icewings. Every child has. She is the subject of many fairy stories, told to infants. You weren't a boy here, were you? You came as a grown-up.'

'This is true,' muttered the knight. 'Yet she turns and heads this way – look. We must find shelter quickly.'

Even as they spoke the dragon swooped and scooped up a large red stag in her open jaws. She swallowed the creature whole as she stood on an outcrop of rock. Then, a short while later, she seemed to cough and choke, and Soldier thought, she has overstretched herself this time. But it was not that her eyes were bigger than her belly, for she gave one mighty hacking cough, and something flew from her mouth and landed on the turf. It was one of those steaming plugs, or owl pellets, as Musket called them. A wadding of red stag hide, antlers, hooves and bones. All the stuff the dragon could not digest, packed into a boat-shaped quid, and ejected with force. The dragon then made a sound like a satisfied cow after giving birth: a sort of mooning note that went echoing down the valley.

Soldier took the reins of his mare and led her into the shelter of some trees. He and Musket found some thick bushes. They crawled underneath just before the great dragon passed overhead. Something fell from beneath the monster's right wing as she went over, then the icy blast which came from the dragon's shadow took Soldier's breath away. He gasped at the shock. The boy, too, was taken unaware by the severity of the cold. Musket's teeth began chattering so violently he was in danger of chipping them. Then the white reptile of the skies was gone, sliding on a downdraught into a secondary valley, leaving the trail to follow as clear as any road.

'Did she come looking for us, do you think?' mused Soldier. 'I mean, not to harm us, but to show us the way?' Then he turned to Musket. 'How do you know about Icewings? Were you born or raised here, in the Unknown Region?'

'I don't think so.' The child was unsure. 'I think Icewings is just a fairy tale outside this kingdom. I remember someone – maybe it was my mother – they told me about the white dragon. I can't remember whether they believed it themselves. But I don't ever remember being here, on the other side of the wide marshes.'

As they were talking, something scuttled by Soldier's foot. It was a strange-looking monitor lizard, a sort of translucent white, of a variety Soldier had never seen before. He jerked back his leg in alarm as the creature snaked by, a full yard in length. This was the thing which had dropped from the passing dragon. It was obviously one of its creatures, having the same frosty appearance. It left a trail of ice-crystals in its wake.

'What was that?' said Musket. 'One of her babies?'

'More like a parasite,' replied Soldier. 'Just like those you carry on your head, only larger.'

The lizard streaked off, along the white road, seemingly anxious to get back to its host as quickly as possible. Soldier had the idea that perhaps the creature had not fallen from Icewings by accident: after all, it spent its life clinging to the dragon, so why fall now? He called to the monitor and asked it to stop and wait. Sure enough, the creature halted and turned, its throat pulsating in impatience. It remained there, perched on all fours, looking desperately back at the two humans and the horse, willing them, it seemed, to get a move on. Yet Soldier knew the creature would be able to track its host far better than Musket or himself. The white road would disappear soon, under the heat of the sun, and Soldier hoped the monitor lizard would continue along the right track, leading the two humans.

'Thank you,' said Soldier, when they caught up to their guide. 'Lead on, if you please.'

The monitor duly trotted on, with Soldier and Musket on the horse, keeping close behind.

It was a glorious day and the sun soon dismissed the snow trail left by Icewings. Birds were quick to fall in the wet grasses and take advantage of the moisture. In the distance were dark red hills which looked to be fashioned of sandstone. The light fell on these natural domes, forcing them to gleam with a rich ochre rust. Subject to spalling, or shedding their outer layers as a snake sloughs its skin, the hills looked like huge red eggs, with eggshell pieces scattered around them. Soldier and Musket passed between them on the mare, staring at their beauty with quiet minds. They seemed to be natural monuments, like mesas standing above canyons, attesting to the potency of the earth as a moving, almost living creature.

Beyond the red egg hills was a desert. The dragon's parasite started out over this rocky, gritty landscape, looking back occasionally to make sure her charges were in full pursuit. Indeed, Soldier was keeping the lizard in good view, knowing that even if Icewings passed over the desert, her white road would not last long under a sun that beat down like a hammer. The knight paused only long enough to fill their waterskins, before catching up with the inexhaustible reptile, who scuttled ever onwards.

When night came, Soldier ordered the lizard to halt. When

the creature took off in the morning it would not be obligated to wait for the two humans. It had served its time. Soldier therefore determined to wake at first light. He knew that cold-blooded creatures like the monitor had to lie in the sun a while to gain some energy after a cold night. Once the lizard had imbibed enough warm sunshine, it would be off, and Soldier and Musket had to be ready to go with it.

Once the darkness fell, Musket wondered at the heavens. 'Look at the stars, Soldier! They are like diamonds.'

As a raven the boy would have been attentive to jewels, but would have ignored the distant suns which were the stars.

'Many people have made the same observation.'

'Have they?' cried the boy. 'I thought I was the first to say such a thing.'

'No, more like the millionth.'

'Well, I don't care. *I've* never heard it before, so I invented it. Oh, see, there's one flying in an arc across the sky. I shall call that a *shooting star*. I suppose you've heard *that* before, too.'

Soldier smiled and said nothing.

'And the moon is like a cradle tonight. A cradle for a baby. Soldier? I think I shall be a poet when I am grown. I have a natural talent for fresh fantastical images, don't I? Look, a cloud like an elephant is crossing over the moon, so now the moon is a howdah, fit for a rajah or a sultan. I can see a turbaned prince sitting in it. I really can. Oh, no, that too is part of the cloud, but it looked real, didn't it, Soldier? Ahhhh, there is another star shooting like a bolt from a crossbow, leaving its silvery trail like a slithery snail. Oh yes, I am a poet all right, Soldier.'

Soldier sighed. 'We must rejoice.'

'The moon is a ghostly galleon, tossed upon cloudy seas . . .'

Soldier's head came up. 'Hark,' he said, 'that *is* poetical – and so far as I can recall, very original. You could be a poet, Musket, once you learn to shed your clichés. Young rhymer, I salute you. A ghostly galleon, eh? On cloudy seas? Oh very well said, my boy, very well said . . .'

Chapter Six

They came to a great chasm which was impossible to cross without a bridge. The monitor lizard had stopped at its edge and now looked up at Soldier's face. Musket, who had been eating worms again and was feeling sick, also stared at his master. It was obviously now up to the knight to decide what must be done for the party. He stepped forward and looked over the precipice, into the depths of the dark crack in the earth. It was dizzying. Soldier's head swam with the length of the drop. He stepped back again, quickly, experiencing that horrible feeling which overcomes many of us when we stare down from a great height: a sort of urge to jump.

'I must pause here, to think,' he told the boy. He looked around. 'Are there no trees with which we can fashion a crossing?'

There were none. The landscape had been bare for some time now: just rock and dust, with the occasional alpine flower poking from a crevice. They had passed a cataract a short while back, where they had filled their waterskins, but even this tumbling waterfall had not managed to produce trees from the barren ground over which it flew. There seemed to be nothing malleable with which to fashion any kind of bridge.

'Stuck, are we?' said Musket, his skinny arms akimbo. 'Can't think of what to do?'

'Just a temporary setback,' replied Soldier, testily. 'No need for your sarcasm.'

'That wasn't sarcasm, it was just a remark.'

The boy could be too clever by half sometimes.

Soldier sat on a rock and stared at the landscape around him. Granite mountains. Why was it that whenever one went on a quest granite mountains always appeared out of the mist and challenged one? Sunlight shimmered mockingly from the hard walls of the fastness he was attempting to conquer. The mica in the rock glinted with wicked glee. The mountains knew he was in a good deal of trouble here and they were the cause.

He stared up into the hard blue sky. Not a cloud to be seen.

'What we need is a giant roc to descend and carry us over this gaping maw,' he muttered. But there were only one or two small birds darting from rock to rock. Birds. Why would birds be up here, where there were no seeds? Not even fir cones. He watched them dipping and diving below an azure ceiling. Then he realised they were insect eaters. There were indeed insects. They drank the perspiration on his brow. They bothered Thunder so much her tail swished constantly. Even the boy was forever slapping at some part of exposed skin. And on the ground, there were beetles. Beetles of all kinds, scuttling from the shelter of one stone to the shade of the next. They fed on mites, of course, which bred anywhere, even in the most arid and unwholesome places.

Soldier watched as a shiny-backed blue-black coach beetle

scurried past his foot, clearly in a great hurry to reach a boulder's shadow.

'Where are you off to in such a rush?' muttered the knight. 'You have no timetable, I'm sure.'

The beetle stopped and looked up at him.

Soldier was startled by the suddenness of it. Had the insect heard what he had said? Then he remembered. The snake he had saved from the heron had asked the divine Theg to give him dominion over the insects and birds, as well as the reptiles. Birds? He looked up again. There were too few of them to assist him here. But there must have been millions of insects in the air, on the ground. Their hosts were omnipresent yet hardly visible anywhere in the world. Apart from the mosquito and the ubiquitous fly, they were on the whole fairly quiet neighbours.

He stood up and stared at the gap in the earth.

'Uh, uh, something dramatic happening,' said Musket, also standing up. 'Something wily this way comes.'

'Be quiet, boy.' Soldier paused again, then cried out, his voice ringing through the passes as if in a cathedral close, 'Insects of the earth and sky, I command you to make me a bridge of yourselves, over this chasm. I command you to – to knit together as did the reptiles in the swamp, and fashion me a crossing. Do it now!'

For a moment nothing happened. Then they began flying in, or appearing from under stones: millions of glimmering jewels on legs, gems with wings. As word spread they began to come up, from lower down the mountain: cockroaches by the ten thousand, bees, hundreds of varieties of beetle, flies, gnats, midges, mosquitoes, dragonflies, damselflies, crane flies, mayflies, yellow-and-black-striped wasps, orange-and-black-striped hornets. Lacewings came in, bristle-tails, ants, thrips, springtails and – oh ye gods – scorpions. Of course there were moths and butterflies, and lice, and snakeflies and tics and centipedes, some not *true* insects, but either because they did not know it, or did not care to trifle about the difference, they answered the call anyway. Several harvestmen came in on stalk legs, and woodlice and crickets. A whole regiment of leaping grasshoppers. A brigade of earwigs. A squadron of caddis flies. The air was full of humming, hissing, murmuring sounds which fell mellifluously upon the ear.

Soon the crossing began to take shape: a vibrant bridge of small and tiny creatures. It was all waving legs and crisp fluttering wings. Beetle locked into flea, and sawfly into cockchafer. Even a single snail – caught up in the excitement and despite its different status in the chain of being – was wedging itself into a mass of dung beetles. Gradually the bridge thickened as more and more insects came from their holes, their fissures in the rock, their alpine plant abodes, to fit like small jigsaw pieces into the great arch which now spanned the cavity separating Soldier from his continuing path. Finally the living viaduct was complete and awaited the weight of the passengers for which it had formed itself.

'I'm not going over there!' cried the boy, staring with horror at the squirming crossing. 'You can leave me behind.'

Soldier did not reply. Instead he grasped the boy by the collar and heaved him up into the saddle on Thunder's back. The obedient mount was then urged forward by her master, who stroked her nose and kept her far more comforted than the agitated stripling she was carrying.

The lizard ran on ahead, snatching a meal on the way. Soldier watched as the ungrateful monitor crunched a cockroach in its hard jaws, not caring that he was eating all that stood between himself and a drop to death. There was nothing the knight could do to stop it, however, and soon the lizard was over and on the other side.

When the rest of the party was about a third of the way across, danger came in on feathered wings. The birds flocked and descended to make a feast of their favourite food. Here was a banquet, all humped and ready to pick at. They fell in their dozens on the hapless insects, still trying to maintain their status as a bridge. The birds swooped and dived, snatching a stag beetle here, a moon moth there, until the bridge began to lose its stability and wavered in its purpose. Insects fell into the chasm, drifting down past ledges and jutting shoulders to the dark depths below.

'Quickly!' cried Soldier. 'We must cross swiftly now!'

'Use your last command,' cried the terrified Musket, looking down at the rock jaws which waited for his small body to drop inside them. 'Tell the birds to stop.'

'I might need that command yet,' said Soldier, his footing unsteady, his weight suddenly quite important. 'I cannot waste it.'

The bridge bowed in the middle, sagging dangerously as the insects lost key bodies in their locked mass.

'We're going! We're falling!' cried Musket. 'Oh why did I become a boy again? If I were a raven . . .'

'You'd be pecking away at our support like the rest of these pests of the air,' growled Soldier. 'Up, up. Come on, stripling. Don't give up on me now. See, Thunder has a hoof on the edge. Just a few more steps now . . .'

The bridge collapsed. Thunder scrambled on to solid ground, the boy clinging precariously to her mane. She was safe. He was safe. Soldier leapt for the far side as the bridge shattered into a million clicking, humming, whirring pieces.

He managed to clutch at Thunder's ankle, hanging there, over the edge, dangling from a hind leg. The mare, feeling the weight, instinctively stepped forward a few paces, away from the drop, and dragged Soldier with her to safety.

'Wow!' cried a now excited Musket. 'Look at that, will you?'

The bridge was falling into the void. It became a swarm, a multitude of black and coloured dots, some of which flew back up on desperately whirring wings, while others floated gently on the warm updraught of air coming from the volcanic gaseous depths. Thousands upon thousands of them flew out into the sunlight again, glittering, to find safety on both sides of the chasm. Others found homes along the walls of their descent. Some would reach the floor of that deep drop to make new homes in a world of warm toasted rocks and yellow stones. They were resilient creatures, insects, and few would perish outright.

'We did it,' Musket said, his voice now full of confidence. 'We cheated death.' He shook his fist at the birds, still gathering the harvest of cockchafers and midges. 'If I was a raven still I'd come up there and give you a hiding,' he cried. 'Destroyers of bridges! Greedy interferers! Have you no shame? Have you no respect for creation? Oh how I wish the eagles would come and give you a taste of your own foul gluttony.'

Soldier was stroking his mare, telling her quietly what a fine beast she was, what a treasure she was to him. She listened to the sounds, the words, not understanding them, but knowing what they meant. She knew she had done well and was quite happy to imbibe the praise.

At that moment an eerie darkness came in, sweeping across the landscape, to envelop them. It appeared to have texture: black satin it seemed. This strange darkness fell over the travellers, wrapped its silken folds about them, brought with it a

kind of drowsiness, a soporific state which had them dropping to the ground to slide into a deep sleep. How long they
slept, neither of them knew, but when they woke the monitor
was gone. It was light again, with the same scenery around
them, but the lizard was nowhere to be found. Thunder was
there, but no other. Soldier tried calling the lizard, to see if
it had moved further down the track, but it did not appear.
He and the boy searched for some time, but there was no
monitor.

'Something unnatural has happened,' said Soldier, staring
about him. 'Although these look to be the same mountains,
the same rocks, they *feel* different. There is a sharper clarity
to the light, don't you think? Objects like those boulders over
there have a more definite edge to them.'

When they had gathered themselves again, and were calm
and ready for the onward journey, Soldier led Thunder forward
along the narrow trail they had to follow. They had no real
need of the monitor here. They could not get lost for there
was only one path. With a sheer drop down one side and a
sheer face on the other, there was nowhere else to go but on
or back.

Musket grasped Thunder's tail and used her to steady
himself on the uneven trail. Despite all his years as a raven
he found he did not like heights. It was a strange thing.
Without his feathered wings he felt naked and vulnerable up
here in the peaks. One slip and he could plunge into open
space, plummet to his death. It was best to keep his eyes on
the horse's rump, keep a firm grip on her tail, and simply
put one foot in front of the other.

When they reached the snow line, they did not pause for
rest, hoping to cross it in one go. A rather unruly glacier
blocked their way at one point, but Soldier chipped steps in

it with Kutrama, and they crossed gingerly. This ice slide went down thousands of feet to some misty valley below but after the insect bridge earlier in the day the glacier was at least solid, if slippery. There were no mishaps. They all reached the far side.

Then it was a case of going down, out of the colder regions of the mountains, towards flatness and warmth again.

Once down from the mountains the next obstacle they encountered was a raging river. This mighty torrent cascaded from a high force and rushed madly between its banks towards the coast. Its main volume came from melting snows up in the peaks, while rainfall on the western slopes swelled its waistline further. Here the monitor lizard reappeared from behind a boulder. It plunged straight into the flood, managed to swim just a few yards, and was then swept downstream and cast upon the same bank from which it had dived.

'Clearly,' said Soldier, 'we are not going to be able to ford this by wading. And swimming, too, is out of the question. We must try to figure a way to cross without going a hundred miles out of our way.'

The boy was unimpressed.

'Why don't you use that command – the one over the birds. You could get them to take us across.'

Soldier shook his head. 'No, those commands were to be used as a last resort. We must think our way across this time, keeping the last wish in reserve. We have not even started our homeward journey yet. There will be other dangers to be encountered then . . .'

While he was speaking, seven maidens arrived at the bank of the river bearing large jars on their shoulders. They paused at the water's edge and regarded the swift current with frowns and whispers. One or two of them shot a shy glance at Soldier, but they did not attempt to speak to him. They were all of a piece: that is to say, they were similar in looks, and appearance, wearing the same bright-red-coloured loose clothing and having dark hair, dark eyes and countenances of great beauty. Though a kind of curtain fell from their red turbans partly hiding their features, Soldier could see they had flawless complexions. He was almost as shy about approaching them as they were about coming forward to him. However he did now go across and attempt to engage them in conversation.

'Ladies?'

They burst out in a fit of giggles.

'Forgive me for accosting you in this manner . . .'

More laughter and turning away to cover their mouths with their hands.

'. . . but my companions and I wish to cross this river. Do you know of any bridge near here? Or a place where the torrent can be forded?'

One of the women appeared a little older than the others, who could not have been more than seventeen summers. She turned her dark eyes on Soldier. 'Sire,' she said, 'we are the daughters of the seven chieftains of the three plains tribes and four hill tribes. Who are you?'

'I? I am Soldier, consort to Queen Layana of the city of Zamerkand in the country of Guthrum. I am also a knight in my own right and Commander-in-Chief of the Carthagan Red Pavilions, a mercenary force of warriors-at-arms.'

She smiled with the corners of her mouth. 'My, that is a long title. I am Fianda, daughter of the chief of the Ismilate tribe. I learned your language from a traveller in our antique land. He passed through two years ago, when I was their age.'

'Language?' said Soldier, frowning. 'For some reason that disturbs me, but for the moment I can't think why.'

He stared at the seven women. 'Have you no escorts? Are you not afraid of bandits? Or wild beasts? Many women have the skills of warriors, but forgive me, you do not look – any of you – as if you have ever held a sword in your hand. You have not developed the muscle to wield a spear or bear a shield.'

'There are no wild beasts here and no man in this region would dare abuse the seven oldest daughters of the seven chieftains of the seven tribes.'

'Perhaps not, but strangers like myself have no knowledge of your fathers – and why are you out together, if from different clans?'

'Our fathers,' her sweeping arm took in her female companions, who were now staring wide-eyed at their sister as she spoke with this man, 'raise their sons and daughters together, as a group, so that when we are grown – especially the boys who become the leaders – we know each other as friends. This helps to prevent hostilities between us, since it is more difficult to go to war against childhood companions.'

'A very sensible arrangement. Now, my original question . . .'

'You have plenty of time for the answer.'

'I beg pardon, my lady, but I don't understand.'

'We too are waiting to cross the river. When the eventide comes around, the waters will grow calmer and shallower. It you can be patient you will be able to cross the river as the sun goes down.'

'What causes this phenomenon?'

'He who made the rivers.'

He caught the tone of her last words and somehow knew

she was speaking of a monotheistic creator. So far in this world he had encountered only religions which served several gods or were animistic in practice. 'You believe the Creator calms the water with his voice?'

She looked amused. 'I *know* he does. It happens every evening.'

'Then we will wait with you.'

Soldier motioned for Musket to bring the horse nearer to the women. The boy did so but eyed the females with suspicion. He sat with his back to them, staring along the route by which they had come to this place.

'What's in the vessels?' asked Soldier. 'What are you carrying?'

'Olive oil,' replied the woman. 'And wine, and vinegar.'

'Oh – is this the wealth of your tribes?'

'No, *my* tribe lives by raiding. Siska – she's that one there with the largest urn – her tribe are fishermen, and Jess's tribe own the largest flocks of sheep in the region, while Harriam's father . . .' The list went on. Soldier nodded, listening with only half an ear. He was still uneasy. Something was not right here. The knowledge that they worshipped one god only had awakened his suspicions that all was not as it should be. And the woman had spoken of *language*.

At sundown a tidal bore came sweeping up the river against the flow. This wave, or wall of water, must have come from the sea where the tide was higher than the river water and thus produced a wave which forced its way upstream against the current. It served to flatten the surface as it sucked up water on its journey away from its source. Immediately after the bore had passed by, the three women crossed the river, thigh deep. Soldier and Musket followed suit, taking the compliant Thunder with them. Once the bore had run its course, it met with a greater force upriver where the snows were thawing. This ensured it swept back again, creating a flash flood that rushed right back down the river's channel to the sea. Anyone crossing at *that* time would have met with certain drowning.

Now that they were all safely across, the girls went separate ways, some heading west, some south and others north. Fianda began to step out on her own, heading south-west, her oil-filled pot on her right shoulder, steadied by a slim hand. Soldier called after her.

'Wait! Is your home nearby?'

She turned. 'My father's tents are close to that oasis you can see – the date palms, over in that direction . . . You would be welcome to come and meet with him, take tea. We are famed for our hospitality. Please do not feel any fear, for you would be welcome. I shall go in first and inform my father of your presence. He will then come out to greet you like a brother.'

'I would be happy to meet him.'

Musket had said very little since they had emerged from that strange blanket of darkness which had descended upon them in the mountains. He had turned morose and withdrawn. Soldier wondered whether the journey was telling on the boy. They were now in regions far beyond the knowledge of any Guthrumite. No man or woman, if the records were to be believed, had ever come this far north-west of Zamerkand. Perhaps the boy was out of sorts because he realised he was far from home and in a place where the name of their city, their country even, was not recognised. It was understandable. Soldier himself was not comfortable. At any moment he expected a twist or a turn to go against them, put them once more in a hazardous position.

The tents came into view. They were animal-hide yurts, not at all splendid to look at and not of the same design as the red pavilions of the Carthagans, being smaller and having several poles projecting on the corners as well as in the centre. They were not uniform in appearance, being almost arachnid in their shape, as though preparing to walk off on their own. There was smoke coming from a central hole in the roof, but the entrance flaps were thrown wide open as if expecting guests at any moment. Round about the tents were camels, and a pen full of goats, and some sheep grazing on the oasis grasses, and chickens, and dogs and cats slinking between. It was a domestic scene with an understated fierce nomadic touch: weapons ready by the exits and some of the horses already saddled. The owners of those tents could be shepherds or warriors, or both.

A man emerged from the yurt into which Fianda had gone and beckoned to Soldier and Musket to approach. They did, Soldier leading the horse. The man, a large fellow with a barrel chest and a beard which was like a bib covering half his rib cage, threw his arms around Soldier and hugged him. He smelled of goat's cheese and lard, mixed with horse sweat and a few other unidentifiable odours. Musket ducked behind the mare in case he was going to get the same treatment.

'You come in, sir,' said the man. 'You are welcome to my tent. We have sweetmeats and tea. I am Bakbar. My daughter has told you of me? Good. Good. It is not often we get a Christian knight at our table . . .'

A chill went through Soldier.

'What did you say. . . . ?' he began, but was ushered into the dim interior of the yurt before he could finish his sentence. There were cushions scattered on carpets on the floor. Tapestries hung on the walls. A brass kettle was boiling on a brick-surrounded hearth, tended by an old woman. She smiled at Soldier with black teeth. Her face had more creases than a many-folded map, but was full of animation and warmth. In any other circumstances Soldier would have smiled back, but he was too shocked by Bakbar's last words.

'Who are you?' he asked the chieftain when it was polite to do so. 'Who are your people? What country is this?'

Bakbar laughed. 'Lost, are we? Wandering knights, lost on the way home from Jerusalem? This is Maroc and we are Berbers. What, did you think we were Arabs? No. We are of the same faith, of course, but we are not of the same blood. In fact, sad to say, the Arabs and the Berbers do not like each other a great deal.'

Soldier's heart was racing fast. He knew it now. The best had happened at the worst possible time. *Not now*, he thought. Later, when all is settled and done, but not now. Why? How?

He was back in his own world.

'I – I am no crusading knight, sir,' said Soldier. 'I am no Templar or Hospitaller, nor did I follow the standard of knights who went to the Holy Land. To my own way of thinking there were far too many domestic squabbles to settle before starting some with foreigners. I – I am a seafarer, lost on the wrong shore. My squire and I,' he indicated the nervous and clearly bemused Musket, 'and my horse have wandered far from the sandy cove on which we were stranded by a nefarious captain, one who stole my ship from me and set himself on a course of piracy.'

Bakbar stared at Soldier through narrowed eyes. He was clearly having trouble believing him. But then he took in Soldier's armour and weapons, the mode of his dress, and nodded.

'You do not have the look of a Christian knight, that is

certain. Your armour is of a strange design. How far have you travelled? To the Indus? Or beyond? I have heard of a strange country, vast and expansive, called Far Cathay. Is that where you found your armour? They say that if you take a caravan east you will come to this land, a region of great wealth with silk and satin hanging from the trees, and men wearing golden robes.'

Soldier nodded, to save having to lie with his mouth.

'Lions I have seen, sir, and dragons.'

'Lions we have here, but *dragons*! Those I would like to observe, being a scholar as well as a warrior.' Bakbar was impressed. Travellers through his land had spoken of dragons. Sailors had told him stories of sea dragons. Explorers had remarked on land dragons. Yes, Far Cathay was a wondrous place where sightings of these creatures were common, so he had been told. 'Tell me about these dragons . . .'

Soldier began to tuck into the sweetmeats and the wine, which was served by Bakbar's daughter Fianda, who kept glancing at their guest and smiling with white teeth. After a while there was no mistaking her message and this was cause for concern. Soldier did not want an entanglement with a female, especially the daughter of the chief of a savage tribe of Berbers. He smiled back at her, weakly, as if he did not understand the signals and took them to be friendly gestures, the sort of smiles which might be given to any guest to her father's tent.

Then he began to satisfy Bakbar's curiosity by telling him tales of dragons. He began with the story of his own dragon, one of the smaller variety from Falyum, which he had watched break from its egg. This particular dragon now recognised Soldier as its parent and called him Kerroww, the male dragon word for *mother*. Bakbar was fascinated by this narrative, but asked for more. Soldier had a fund of anecdotes regarding dragons with which he regaled his host, ending with the story of Icewings, his latest encounter.

'A pure white dragon,' breathed Bakbar, chewing on a dried stick of goat's meat. 'Its shadow leaving a road of ice! Why this is surely the sultan of all dragons, is it not? And you have seen this creature.'

'We both have,' interrupted Musket, suddenly, peeved at being left out of the tale-telling. 'It was me who saw it first. I knew of this dragon from the fairy tales told me as a child.'

'As a child?' laughed Bakbar. 'And what are you now?'

'I have been a bird, a raven, sir, with black wings, claws and beak.'

He spoke intently as he stared at Bakbar. Soldier was suddenly wary. What if their host took them for sorcerers? He had no idea what Berbers did to magicians or witches. Back in his own land they were burned, or drowned. But he need not have worried. It soon became apparent that Bakbar took the tale at face value and believed, as was the truth, that the boy had been bewitched by an evil marabout. He asked Musket what it had been like, to be a bird, and was fascinated by the urchin's descriptions of soaring through the air, eating grubs and maggots, and nesting in chimneys.

'Such a pair of guests I have tonight!' cried Bakbar. 'In the morning I shall take my quill and parchment, my red, green and black inks, and set this down. These tellings are invaluable to a scholar such as myself, whose writings will one day astound the world. They will bring great glory to the name of Bakbar the Berber and will resound from Alexandria in Egypt to the Indus and beyond.'

Musket whispered to Soldier, 'I do not know these names he keeps speaking about. Where is Egypt? What is the Indus?'

'No matter, I will explain later, Musket – for the moment leave the talking to me.'

'Have you eaten well?' asked Bakbar, his attention taken momentarily by his daughter. 'May I ask you a personal question? How many wives do you have? Oh, I was forgetting. Christians are only allowed one, are they not? Such paucity! But never mind. Do you own a wife?'

'I do not so much own *her*, sir, for she is the ruler of *me*. My wife is the queen of a small distant kingdom, as I explained to your daughter.'

'Ah, ah, but *distant* you say?' He leaned forward, his mouth next to Soldier's ear. 'I will tell you something, stranger. My daughter has taken a shine to you. Yes she has. If this country which contains your queenly wife is so distant, perhaps you might never return to it? In such a case you are short of one wife. She is comely, is she not, my Fianda? A lovely girl with such a sweet nature. Of course you are an infidel and unworthy, but I imagine for such a beauty you might be prepared to renounce your God for ours? Think about it.'

Soldier had to think quickly. He said, 'But sir, you know nothing of me. I might be the worst tyrant in the world. I might be a rogue who lies through his teeth with every word. A murderer or a thief. How can you trust me?'

'This is true,' murmured Bakbar with a frown. 'I am a trusting man. Some say too trusting. But you seem to me to be a man of honour. You have the countenance of one who holds truth to be dear to him.'

'Oh, he is an honourable knight, of that you can be sure,' said Musket with fervour. 'Why, he is the most trusted man in Guthrum.'

'Be quiet, boy,' said Soldier through gritted teeth. 'Do not interrupt your elders.'

'No, no, the boy speaks the truth,' Bakbar said.

'Sir,' sighed Soldier, 'he is my squire, my instrument.' This did not sound convincing enough, so Soldier lied outright. 'He – he is my own adopted son. Of course he believes his father to be the most distinguished and respectable man in the world. What son does not?'

Bakbar frowned again. 'This is also true. My own son . . . well, I am confused. We will leave the subject alone for the moment. Perhaps during the night my dreams will reveal to me what course to take in the matter. For the moment, we shall simply leave it to one side. My daughter will have to be disappointed, for tonight at least.'

Soldier heaved a sigh of relief. He glanced at Fianda, who did indeed look a little disappointed. But no doubt she was thinking that she could persuade her father, before the morning came, that she had found the man of her choice. Soldier had merely worked himself a stay of execution. Not that marrying Fianda seemed a monstrous fate. She was a lovely woman, and as her father had said, she did not seem shrewish or bad-tempered in any way. Had Soldier not already been married he might not have fought against this generous offer with any vigour, but he already had a wife he loved to distraction, and this woman Fianda deserved better than he.

It was said that a sailor had a wife in every port, and here was the chance for Soldier to have a wife in every world!

Soldier then went into a reverie.

Bakbar was talking with Musket, who was regaling their host with stories about Guthrum and the other kingdoms of his own world. The Berber, despite the names that were flung at him, was convinced that this country of which the boy spoke had to be Far Cathay, and so was not surprised by its wonders. The names – Guthrum, Da-tichett, Uan Muhuggiag,

Carthaga, Bhantan – he took to be regions of that country. It was as he had always thought, Far Cathay was a colourful, marvellous place, where people did things differently and where strangenesses – to Bakbar – were commonplace and ordinary to its citizens.

Soldier was trying to decide *why* he had suddenly been thrown back into his own world. Surely there had to be a reason? What was it the Berber had said? He was a scholar as well as a warrior? Well then, since they were in the wise man's tent, why not give him a puzzle to solve?

'Sir,' said Soldier, 'may I ask you a question?'

'Surely,' replied Bakbar, turning his attention back to his main guest. 'Is it of a personal nature?'

'No, no. It is a riddle.'

Bakbar laughed. 'Not the riddle of the Sphinx? What walks first on four legs, then on two legs, and finally on three legs? You surely know the answer to that one? Everyone knows that.'

'Not I?' piped Musket. 'What is it? A demon beast?'

'Some might say so,' Soldier replied. 'It is *man*, of course. He crawls as a baby, walks upright when he is grown, and takes to using a walking stick, his third leg, when he is old.'

'How clever!' cried Musket, clapping. 'Now tell him our riddles, Soldier. Tell him about the unborn babe.'

'Yes, tell me about the unborn babe.'

'Well, sir,' said Soldier, 'there is *a golden unborn babe in the house of a stranger.*'

Bakbar frowned. 'That is *it*? No more?'

'It's all we have,' said Soldier. 'Can you think what it might be?'

Bakbar put his powerful mind to the test.

'It might be,' he said, eventually, 'that the unborn babe is an egg of some kind. The boy might be better placed to say what kind of egg. But as for myself, I cannot think who is the stranger. Or what is his house.'

'An egg!' cried Soldier. 'Yes, I think you have hit on it. But, as you say, who is the stranger?'

'I know not,' sighed Bakbar.

'Never mind, we have part of the riddle solved, perhaps. Shall I give you another? It is the final one of three. Actually, it was the first, but we have solved the last, and the middle one we have already discussed. Here is the third riddle: *the silver container of the song of an eternal prisoner*. Can you apply your learning to solving this mysterious puzzle? I would be most grateful for any help you can give me, sir.'

Bakbar bowed his turbaned head in thought. When he raised it again there was a wisp of a smile on his face. His eyes revealed the inner feeling of triumph.

'Now, this enigma needs first to be examined by looking at the word *song*. What creatures are there that sing? Birds, of course. People. Which of these could be *eternal prisoners*? Both or none. Therefore the singer has to be someone, or something, specific. One of a kind. What other singers are there, who are unique? In nature? The *wind* . . .'

'It is the wind!' cried Musket. 'The wind it is!'

'No,' said Bakbar, indulgently, 'it cannot be the wind, for the wind is free. We even use the term *free as the wind*. It has to be something which is chained, which is bounded and kept within certain walls . . .'

'The *sea*,' murmured Soldier with great satisfaction. 'You are speaking of the ocean.'

Bakbar nodded, smiling. 'Very good. The sea it is. And what object is there, what natural thing contains the song of the sea?'

'A sea shell!' yelled Musket. 'It is a shell.'

'Yes, yes. If you put a shell to your ear you hear the song of the sea, the eternal prisoner. What you must seek is a silver sea shell.'

Soldier reached out and grasped the hand of the Berber and shook it vigorously. 'My dear sir, I thank you for solving my puzzles – one only partly so, it is true, but perhaps there is a cultural barrier to you understanding that one completely. After all, if the *stranger* in that riddle is not known to these shores, then you will have no knowledge of him. I shall ponder on that one myself and am sure to come up with the answer, eventually. Now, sir, I am fatigued. I would be grateful for a bed. The boy . . .'

'Your *son*,' said Musket, significantly.

'Yes, yes, of course – my own *dear* son also looks very tired.'

They were shown corners of the tent on which carpets and mats had been laid to a thickness which made a good bed. Soldier bid Bakbar and his daughter a very good night and thanked them for their generous hospitality. Bakbar told him that Berbers, and indeed the Arabs of this land, could do no less. It was written that travellers, strangers in need, must be given food, drink and a place to rest their heads in safety.

Sleep would not come to Soldier. There were many noises without. He could hear the snuffling of the camels, the restlessness of the dogs. Chickens occasionally clucked on their perches. The breeze was swirling through the palms, whose leaves rustled like stiff parchment. Even the stars seemed to jingle gently in the heavens.

But it was not these sounds which were responsible for his insomnia. It was the fact of being back in the world of his birth. How was he going to return to the world of Guthrum, Carthaga and his dear wife? Surely he would have to retrace his journey to that chasm? And then hope that being there, that bizarre darkness would descend again, enfold him and the boy, and transport them back. His heart was heavy with the dread that it would not work, that he was stuck here on his old earth.

Until another curse or quirk of fate should fling him back again.

He fell asleep.

'Wake up, wake up.'

Soldier opened his eyes. Musket was hovering over him, looking worried.

'What is it?' said Soldier. 'I have only just this instant fallen asleep . . .'

Musket was saying, 'I couldn't wake you. I've been trying for ever so long now, but you wouldn't wake up.'

Soldier sat up and stared about him. He was back at the chasm. The horse was standing quietly just a few yards away. The monitor lizard was basking on a rock in the sun, as he always did in the early morning, to gain the energy he needed to travel. Musket was hopping about, looking very agitated. The boy had lit a fire and a pot of water was boiling on the flames.

'Are we here?' said Soldier, amazed. 'How did we get back?'

'Get back from where?' asked the boy with some irritation. 'We haven't been anywhere.'

'Did we not go down the mountain, after that darkness descended?'

'We went to sleep,' said Musket. 'I woke up and you stayed snoring. You kept talking in your sleep. I couldn't get you up. If you hadn't been chuntering on I would have thought you dead.'

'Asleep,' repeated Soldier, thoroughly relieved to be in this world and not in his old one. 'Then all that – was I dreaming? Was it all a dream? How vivid it was. It was no ordinary dream, that's for sure. Something magical sent me into that sleep. But for what reason?'

Then he remembered. In his dream he had discovered the answer to another of his riddles, and a part-answer to the last of them. Some mountain demi-god, perhaps even a friendly demon, had sent him into that deep sleep. There he had made discoveries. Was Bakbar a real person then? Did he really exist, or was he a figment of Soldier's desire to find answers? Perhaps Soldier had made the discovery for himself, inside his own inner mind. Perhaps he had been capable of solving the riddle but had not trusted his own intellect.

And Fianda? No, if Bakbar was not real then Fianda did not exist either, he thought sadly. Vanity had without doubt produced that lovely woman from the flimsy yearnings of his own mind. Men of a certain age still wonder if they are attractive to beautiful women, if they ever have been, and will go on flights of fancy to appease their vanity. That was where he had been, on one of those flights, telling himself through his dreams that he could still appeal to lovely young females. What, was he not a knight, still ruggedly handsome, still personable? Perhaps, but beautiful young women are attracted to beautiful young men, and he was not one of those any longer. Once, but that beauty had been left behind, happily along with a lot of anxiety and fears. Now he was mature, in body as well as mind. On the surface he was happy to be so, but obviously somewhere deep in his spirit he yearned to be young and appealing again.

'Are you going to just sit there and look stupid all day?' asked Musket, standing with hands on hips. 'Are we going to march?'

'There's no need to be rude,' said Soldier, coming out of his reverie. 'I will teach you some manners else.'

This threat did not impress the boy.

By the time the sun was growing hot enough to dispel the mountain mists, they were on their way down the track to the plains below, following the monitor. Some parts of the journey seemed familiar to Soldier, but he dismissed this with the thought that *many* mountain trails looked much alike. They were all rocky, all dusty, with similar panoramic vistas.

However, the closer he came to the bottom, the more concerned he became. Once there, in the foothills, he saw the river. It thundered down from above, gushing between boulders, tumbling out on to the plain. It was the same river he had seen yesterday, or last night in his dream – the features were identical. When they reached this waterway and saw that it was, of course, impossible to cross in full flood, Soldier became alarmed.

'Why don't we use your last command to get the birds to take us over?' asked Musket.

'We need to reserve that command for emergencies . . .' began Soldier, then realised he was simply repeating history. 'Come, we'll find another way around.'

'There are some women over there,' Musket cried, pointing. 'Seven of them, with jars. They seem to be waiting for something.'

Maddeningly, the monitor lizard was not taking the lead here. It was crouched on all fours, staring at Soldier, as if waiting for his instructions. Its tongue flicked out, cooling its now hot body. Once or twice it looked back over its own shoulder, at the women, but by its stance seemed more inclined to favour the path by the river in the opposite direction.

'Never mind them,' muttered Soldier, darkly. 'Don't look at them. They are witches, every one.'

'They don't look like witches. Witches are ugly and have long noses with warts and drips on the end. These look like pretty maidens to me. They giggle like little girls. There's one smiling at us.'

'What does a boy of your age know of maidens, or witches?'

'It was a witch who changed me to a bird, I might remind you,' snapped Musket. 'I know lots about witches.'

'But nothing of maids. Do not look at them. They have the evil eye. Especially the smiling one. Glare at her, if you will. Show her that her advances are rejected. That we have no interest in her.'

But he himself could not resist a glance, and yes, there was Fianda, smiling sweetly at him. He turned back again, not wishing to be sucked into the vortex. If he went across and spoke to her, he was sure of the circular events that would follow. This was a whirlpool he did not want to enter. It seemed to him that there was a loop from which he must extricate himself. Determinedly he set out in the opposite direction, leading Thunder by the reins. The monitor seemed to approve and went on ahead, occasionally looking back to make sure his charges were in tow. Soldier ignored Musket's pleas to either slow down or change course. He knew the boy was annoyed that they had not made contact with the locals.

'Why didn't you ask them?' grumbled the boy, trotting alongside him. 'You could have *asked* them.'

'Too dangerous.'

'They didn't look dangerous – they were just girls.'

'Women to you, boy. You never can tell though. The female of the species is always deadlier than the male. Look at snakes.'

'What about them?'

Soldier couldn't think. 'Well, all right, look at certain insects. The bee. The male stings once, then dies. The female can sting you as many times as she likes. That's what I mean. Some female insects eat their mates. You can see what I mean? Never trust a strange woman, boy.'

'Oh, I won't. You won't give me the chance.'

'And rightly so. Ah, here – look – a path back up the mountain. A greener path than the other.'

'Not *more* climbing?' grumbled Musket. 'I wish I could fly again.'

Soldier ignored the boy. He felt uncomfortable, recalling the events of the previous night encapsulated by his dream. Not only had he passed back into his birth world; he now remembered that in his dream he had made Musket his own adopted son. He stared at the boy, stumbling along beside him. Not a bad lad, of course, but not the *son* that Soldier had imagined he would one day have. *His* son, his own flesh and blood, would more than likely have features like himself and think like himself.

This ragged urchin looked nothing like the son of any knight, of any prince consort, let alone that of Soldier. He looked like the son of a vagabond or beggar. One or the other was probably the truth. A scruffy young tyke with very few redeeming features. Thin-faced, thin-armed, thin all over. A bitter look to the mouth. A sly and crafty look to the eyes. Oh, without doubt these were the rewards of a starved and desperate early childhood, but they had fashioned the boy into an unappealing creature. Layana would certainly not welcome such a child into the family, would she? Queen of Guthrum? This her child prince, to be doted on? No, the thought was perishable. Theirs would be a golden child, of golden parents.

Yet Layana had still not borne him a child. It was not through want of trying. And they were both growing older. A shocking thought came to Soldier. Was she yet too old to bear young? Perhaps adoption would be the only course left open to them. Then what choices would they have? There were plenty of splendid families with sons and daughters. But of course, most nobles want to keep their progeny, as heirs to their own titles. Perhaps he and Layana would have to settle for a boy or a girl like this? And better the devil you know, as the saying goes.

'I shall ask my wife,' he growled. 'The decision will be hers.'

Musket glanced up at him with a quizzical expression. 'Ask her what?'

'About you,' sighed Soldier, tousling the boy's mop of unruly hair. 'I shall ask about adopting you.'

The bitterness left the child's mouth. The sly, crafty look fled his eyes. All replaced by a wonderful freckled smile.

'You will, Soldier? You will?'

'I said so, didn't I?'

The boy suddenly burst into tears, alarming the knight.

'Here, here, none of that.'

'I am so happy.'

'Well laugh a little then.'

'I am too happy to laugh.'

'All right then, weep if you must.'

The boy sobbed contentedly, the dust drifting up from the path and mingling with his tears, to form a muddy countenance. He gripped Thunder's tail, allowing himself to be half dragged along. There was a sort of glow about him now, which had been absent before. He seemed less of a waif, more of a young man with a purpose. Soldier thought it was amazing, almost a miracle, what transformations a few words could make.

'Are you feeling less melancholy now?'

'Yes, I thank you, Father.'

'Here, I'm not your father yet. We still need Layana's blessing.'

'I know her, sire. She is a kind, generous and gentle lady.'

'Well, yes, she is, but she's a lot of other things beside. You know she tried to kill me several times.'

'But that was when she was a lunatic, influenced by the moon.'

'Influenced by *something*, that much is sure. She can have a foul temper on her, when things do not go right. I have the bruises to prove it. Now, don't get your hopes too high! She may have other plans. What if we arrive home and she already has a son picked out for us?'

'Then I shall call him brother.'

The boy seemed to have an answer for everything. Soldier left it at that. He had to admit he felt good about himself. Imparting happiness had that affect. It filled one with well-being. There was something of vanity in the act of giving too, which did not escape Soldier's attention. But if one could not indulge oneself from time to time, one would be a saint, sure. Now there were two happy people, walking the same path upwards, towards a grotto of a kind. Soldier recognised the type and knew they were nearing their journey's end. He indicated the mound with the earth entrance at each end as they approached it. Sitting in a glade some distance from the grassy mound was the white dragon, the mighty Icewings. She looked composed. Her wings were folded so she cast only a long, lean shadow, from head to long-whip tail. Nevertheless this shadow was as formidable as the silhouette of a raiders' long-ship and was filled with virgin snow.

'A green chapel, boy. You see it?'

'Yes, I see it. The dragon, also.'

'Ignore the presence of the dragon for the moment. She is either the guardian of the green chapel or is there to indicate which end we should take. If she is a guardian we can certainly fool her when we enter, though of course she'll be there when we come out. There will be other guardians to pass. A green knight, possibly, or a dog with three heads. One can never tell. What is certain is that we shall enter the chapel.'

'I see, Father.'

This time he did not correct the boy.

'First we must discover which is the right end to use. Often one entrance leads to a ghastly Otherworld, while the other goes to such places as the treasure halls of mountain kings. We do not want to spend eternity battling with monsters in a world of ice and snow. We need to discover the trove where the jade mantis, the silver shell and a golden egg are to be found.'

'Silver shell? Golden egg?'

'Ah yes, I forgot, you were not really there, were you? It was all a dream. Those three items are on our list, Musket. We must leave here with all of them, or not leave at all. They will help cure the queen.'

'My mother.'

Soldier ground his teeth. 'Not yet, my boy. We must have her agreement to the arrangement before you can say you have come from pauper to prince in one giant leap. Be patient, and try to curb that tongue. I came from humble beginnings . . .'

'The humblest!'

'Yes, and . . .'

'You couldn't have been more humble.'

'All right, all right, but now I discover I have noble blood in my veins, from my last world, so perhaps it was preordained that I become what I am in this world.'

'Who knows what I was, before I became a raven?' said the boy, wistfully.

'A scruffy little hobbledehoy,' snapped Soldier emphatically.

'Yes, but before that? Who knows what kind of baby I was? No one. I could have been a prince put in a reed boat and sent down the river. Or the wetnurse could have changed her own baby for me. Or perhaps I had a twin brother who paid a woodcutter to take me into the forest and lose me. Anything's possible. Look at you. You thought you were just a common thief turned hand-seller's assistant, didn't you? Now you find you're this Sir Valechor, lord of somewhere or other.'

'We're wasting time with this idle chatter,' growled Soldier. 'We must decide which entrance of the green chapel to take.'

Musket frowned. 'We must take the right one, of course.'

'That much is obvious. But which is the right one?'

'Why,' said the boy, 'the one with the rabbit shit, of course.'

Soldier stopped and blinked. He stared at Musket with narrowed eyes.

'Explain.'

'Well, rabbits won't use the hole to hell, will they? They're not silly. They can smell fire and brimstone coming from the wrong entrance and they'll stay clear of that one. To be quite sure we should also look for ducks' feathers. Ducks and rabbits often use the same holes. You stick with me, Father, and I'll lead you to the promised treasure trove.'

Soldier stuck out his jaw. 'Why would rabbits *and* ducks use the entrance to a green chapel at all?'

Musket sighed, as if dealing with a half-wit.

'Why? Because rabbits like to dig into the sides of banks

of soil, rather than go straight down. It's a matter of gently sloping angles and getting rid of the debris, isn't it? Haven't you noticed how rabbit warrens are almost always on hillocks and tumps? The other reason they like mounds is because the soil is soft and easy to move, and they will always go *inside* a larger hole and start from there, because the larger cavern keeps the entrance to the small burrow dry. Wild ducks just use empty rabbit holes for shelter at night and as protection from the foxes while they sleep.'

'I suppose you learned all this as a raven?'

'I never learned it anywhere, it's just so obvious to anyone.'

That remark did not endear the boy to Soldier at all. He tethered Thunder to a tree inside a wooded area, where he hoped the white dragon would not be able to penetrate. The next thing was to discover if Icewings was a guardian or not. It would seem unreasonable of her to act as a guide to the green chapel and then prevent those she had led there from entering, but Soldier took nothing for granted. He kept a wary eye on her as he approached one end of the green chapel. She made no move towards him, made no threatening gestures, and seemed actually to lack any menace whatsoever. Soldier inspected the open end of the chapel, which had a hole as large as a cottage doorway in the shape of a pointed arch. The portal was actually made of moss-covered roughly hewn stone.

'No rabbits' dung this end,' he said to Musket. 'Nor feathers.'

'Then it's the other end.'

They walked the length of the mound, which had much the same features as a long barrow or tumulus. It was turf-covered, with one or two rocks jutting from its roof. There were curious burn marks in the grass on the sides of the mound. Soldier guessed these had been made by the smaller fire-breathing dragons.

Soldier was half hoping there would be no sign of rabbits at the far end, but he was to be disappointed. Rabbit stools were everywhere scattered like dried blackcurrants in the opening. Here and there, a wispy feather. Musket smiled and nodded at his new father. His new father grudgingly acknowledged a superior brain. One more glance at Icewings told them she was not going to impede their entry to the green chapel. They threw her a cheery wave and went into the darkness of the interior.

Soldier said, 'Musket, now listen to me – I have no experience of entering green chapels, but I have met knights who have done so. They tell me that there are things, spirit creatures and earth-lore beings, who will try to accost any intruders. So long as they are ignored we should be safe. Do not acknowledge them. Have no conversation with them. Refuse to be drawn, no matter what they may say or do. Understood?'

'Yes, Father.'

'Good.'

Once past the initial blackness of the entrance, they found their passage along an earth tunnel lit by torches. Wights and wraiths came as flimsy spectres from the walls and attempted to impede them. Imps dropped in their hair like spiders from hidden cobwebs, tweaking the roots, jumping off again when ignored. Duppies tried to spook them by wailing into their faces and gumming their eyelashes. Musket, ducking and weaving to avoid these creatures, was clearly terrified. Soldier took his hand and led him onward; even when a spectre knight in shining white armour stood in their path, Soldier merely strode through him without a hint of awareness.

The pair passed through several empty chambers until they came, finally, to a cavern stacked with treasures.

It was a high, wide dome of rock. The walls glowed with an eerie greenish light, which was reflected by the many hundreds of precious gems, gold ornaments, crowns, jade boxes, ropes of pearls, ruby-handled daggers, jewelled swords, coral necklaces, silver brooches, torcs, and many other precious if not priceless works of art and wealth. Certainly the sight took the breath away. Soldier and Musket simply stood and stared for a full ten minutes, awed by the glister and glitter of the room. It dazzled the eyes and bewildered the brain. Coins were piled in heaps like so much trash. Illuminated books were lying open, their gold-and-silver-leaf illustrations shining brilliantly. Golden bowls full of diamonds lay scattered around the floor area. Sheaves of jewelled staves stood in stacks. Trunks ornamented with mother-of-pearl and semi-precious stones stood gaping, their edges overflowing with heavy gowns inlaid with precious metals.

One object in particular struck Soldier's eyes with great force: a throne fashioned from chalcedony, inlaid with tiger's-eye, amethyst, lapis lazuli, cornelian, topaz and jasper. It defied all laws of taste and elegance, being over-elaborate in design and encrusted with just about every gem the earth could offer. It was the throne of a despot, a tyrant with more wealth than discernment.

'Look at this!' cried Musket, glancing down to find he was ankle-deep in emeralds and sapphires. 'We could be kings of anywhere!'

'We could be, but we are not,' warned Soldier. 'Hard as it is, do not let this display turn your head, son. We must take *only* what we came for, nothing more. If we leave with a grain of gold dust that is not ours, we will suffer horribly for it. A jade mantis, a golden egg and a silver sea shell, that is what we must find, and all else must remain here.'

'Oh,' cried the boy in disappointment. Then he took a step back. 'Something moved,' he whispered, 'in the shadows over there.'

His arm went out and Soldier saw amongst the sparkling treasures a glittering monster: a giant green lizard with scintillating red eyes. Its tongue flashed out between strong-looking jaws. Its claws were like the curved knives of hill bandits. A formidable creature indeed. It stepped out of the shadows and into the light, its throat pulsing, its tail swishing.

'A guardian,' muttered Soldier. 'There had to be one, of course. There may be more. He will watch us as we search for the items we came for. Pay no heed to him. If he attacks, *then* we can defend ourselves. Now, we must seek our objects . . .'

Soldier began to move amongst the treasures. As he did so, the great lizard darted forward. Soldier drew his sword quickly, but the monster was not attacking. It stood on a pile of coins, its tongue flickering. Soldier stared at the creature, wondering if it was poised ready to spring, but it was Musket who first realised what the great lizard was doing.

'See, Father!' he cried. 'By that casket. A golden egg!'

Soldier stared. It was indeed a golden egg. By the gods, he thought, the guarding is *helping* us. It probably wants us to find the items we need, then leave as quickly as possible. We are violating its domain, polluting its home. This was fortunate indeed. It would seem politic to allow the lizard to dictate to them where they should look for their desired objects.

'Get the egg, boy.'

Musket went forward cautiously and picked up the golden egg, which was of the scale of a real wild bird's egg. He weighed it in his hand, as if its heaviness was impressive. Then he looked at the object more closely. He became excited and held it up for Soldier to view.

'Father!' he cried. 'I know the other part of the last riddle now. This is a copy of a cuckoo's egg, for it would be *in the house of a stranger*, wouldn't it? A cuckoo lays her eggs in the nests of strangers, for them to hatch and rear. How clever am I, Father? Very clever?'

Soldier smiled at his newly adopted son. 'Extremely clever.'

The guardian of the treasure led the pair to two more objects: a beautiful jade praying mantis and a silver conch. With these items securely in Soldier's possession, the two mortals began to leave the domain of the giant lizard. However, they had not gone more than ten yards along the tunnel when the lizard came bounding after them, its jaws snapping, its tail thrashing, its tongue lashing.

Soldier took one look at the fury of the beast and then turned to his son.

'What have you stolen?' he cried. 'Did I not tell you?'

Musket reached into his pocket and withdrew a ruby the size of his own fist.

'It is so beautiful,' sobbed the boy. 'I want it. I want it.'

The lizard bounded forward. Soldier snatched the jewel from the child's hand and tossed it towards the green guardian. The lizard caught the ruby in its jaws. It glared at the two mortals, as if daring them to take one more step. After a while it turned on its tail and re-entered the cavern, to spit the gem on to a sparkling pile in one corner, seemingly satisfied that nothing more would be violated.

'Foolish boy,' growled the knight. 'We are lucky to escape with our lives.'

A tear-stained face peered up at him in the flickering torch-light.

'I wanted it.'

'You can't have everything you want.'

'I don't want *everything*,' snapped the boy, angrily. 'I just wanted that ruby.'

'I am gravely disappointed in you.'

Soldier turned away, wondering what possessed the child. He was no real father, in that he had no experience of boys of that age. Of course he remembered his own childhood, but that is seldom any use to a man, for the years between create a mellow past where everything is perfect. *He* would not have stolen the jewel when he was eleven or twelve. *He* would have followed his father's orders. A command was a command. Surely the boy had no right to disobey him. No right at all.

'I don't understand you,' he said, heavily. 'You want to be the son of a queen and her consort, yet you remain a street thief, a guttersnipe.'

Musket started weeping softly again. He said something in a quiet voice which made Soldier stop in his tracks.

'What? Speak up, boy. What was that?'

'I said I wanted it for my new mother. I wanted to give it to Queen Layana, so she would love me. If I gave her a ruby like that, she couldn't turn me away when we go home, could she?'

For a moment Soldier could not speak. When he did, he laid a gentle hand on the boy's shoulder and said, 'Musket, you cannot buy love, my boy – but you can be sure I shall tell her that you risked your life to do so.'

Chapter Seven

In Zamerkand Queen Layana was waiting anxiously for the return of her husband, not caring whether he brought home a cure for her forgetfulness or not, so long as he was safe and well. In the meantime, tended by her faithful servants Ofao and Drissila, Layana attempted to bring some order and stability to Zamerkand. The fact that she could not remember anything about her former life after being abducted and transported to Uan Muhuggiag meant that she had to rely on her servants to assist her in choosing people she could trust for positions of power. There were those who claimed to know her intimately and those who protested that the former queen her sister, and indeed their father before them, had promised them posts in any governing body of the land.

There was nothing wrong with Drissila's memory, and the lady-in-waiting soon weeded out those whom she knew were lying.

In fact, there were few the queen could trust. The brother of Kaff – yet an old and trusted friend of Soldier, a warrior called Golgath – was given charge of the Guthrumite army. Golgath was one of the few Guthrumite soldiers who was utterly loyal to the queen and her husband. Spagg, the trader in hands-of-glory, the severed members of hanged men, to his utter astonishment found himself appointed Keeper of the Royal Purse.

He protested.

'Your Majesty,' Spagg spluttered, 'you can't trust me with a single coin, let alone the purse of the whole kingdom.'

'I trust you, Spagg, and you must trust yourself,' said Layana as the court echoed with the indignant voices of those nobles and courtiers who agreed with the market trader. 'You might run off with a single coin in your pocket, but the wealth of Zamerkand is a little more weighty.'

Thus she left the treasure chests of the great city in the trembling hands of the new Keeper of the Royal Purse. Zamerkand was indeed very wealthy, or had been before Humbold had come to power. It was somewhat diminished now, due to the disruption to trade and industry which had been caused by Humbold's inept government. However, they still had the long covered waterway, the protected canal which led from the heart of the city to the Cerulean Sea. There lay Guthrum port, crammed with trading vessels, which could once again begin to set sail for the nearby continent of Gwandoland and its island, as well as other distant lands where brave ships might venture.

After Spagg had been elevated, far beyond his dreams, a Lord of Thieftakers was appointed, then a new Lady of the Locks, a Lord of the Ladders, and many others. There were none of the old lords or ladies left, Humbold having executed them all when he usurped the throne. A whole new government was formed, some out of nobles and courtiers, some out of people of no former consequence. One or two went, if not from rags to riches, from obscurity to very-important-person overnight. Some were dizzied by the rise. Others, more phlegmatic, took to their new duties as if taking on an apprenticeship to a carpenter or plumber.

Captain Kaff and his henchmen were not enthusiastic about the way the city was developing. Several times the one-handed captain had attempted to see the queen, always to be rejected. She remembered none of her former affection for the captain, only recalled that he had led Humbold's army against her and her husband, and was Humbold's instrument. A message *demanding* audience was returned with the sentence *You are fortunate to be alive* scribbled on the bottom. This had probably been the work of Ofao or Drissila, but Kaff knew that his days of glory were over and he either had to humble himself or leave.

Outside the walls of the city were the mercenary Red Pavilions of Carthaga, a source of comfort to Layana. General Velion was in command in the absence of Soldier and she was a competent and controlled commander-in-chief. Very experienced in the ways of war, especially in Guthrum, she squashed any attacks by the Hannacks or the beast-people before they even reached the borders. She recognised when there was a threat and made pre-emptive strikes on the gathering clans of the barbarians, crushing them within their own regions and territories. Kaff argued that she was violating the rules of war by doing so, but she paid scant attention to anyone trying to tell her how to do her job. She was a seasoned leader.

One morning Captain Kaff had a visitor: a vineyard worker from one of the holdings on the Guthrum border.

'I bring you greetings from the man who was once your friend,' said the worker. 'He is back in Guthrum.'

'Speak plainly, man,' said Kaff. 'Is it Humbold?'

'Yes.'

Captain Kaff was surprised the outlaw had come back.

'Humbold has dared to return? He is outside the law and any man may kill him without reprisal. Having fled to safety I expected him to stay there. What does he have to say to me?'

'He says that he has met Soldier, in the Unknown Region, and that Soldier has made bitter the waters from which he drinks. He will not rest until the blue-eyed stranger has been struck down. He asks that you put aside any recent differences between you. He is willing to forgive and forget, if you will join him in his endeavour to destroy your mutual enemy.'

Kaff laughed, startling the live rat whose torso was screwed into the empty socket of his wrist, making it squirm.

'Ha! And he expects me to do it? Here? He must be mad. Does he know I've tried to kill Soldier in a hundred ways and all have failed before now? Why should the next time be any different? I will not stoop to back-stabbing. I still have *some* honour left. Humbold must work his own miracles, without my help. Tell him to hire himself a murderer to do the assassination, for I will not dirty my hands.'

'No, no,' replied the man, 'no cloak-and-dagger, no shadow killings. Humbold has raised an army in the Unknown Region, from a land called Scintura. They are the Plethorites and the Samonites, from the cities of Ut and Ged. I have seen them for myself. The two cities were at war with one another, but have been promised great riches and spiritual rewards by Humbold and have come together to fight a common enemy. That enemy is Soldier. They sent units to scour the Unknown Region, have placed companies of soldiers on the passes out of the territory, but Humbold does not believe they will get him that way. He believes Soldier has a destiny to fulfil, that he will only be killed in battle.'

The man paused, clearly uncomfortable with his own

speech, which was of great import and uneasy in the mouth of a lowly grape-picker.

'Humbold says,' he continued after being given a sip of wine, 'that there will be a reckoning between the two contenders for the position of King Magus amongst the wizards. OmmullummO and IxonnoxI will not fight themselves, for fear that the sparks of their battle will fire the world and burn it to a cinder. They will rely on the armies of men to do their fighting. Soldier will of course battle for IxonnoxI. It is Humbold's intention to gather together a great army in support of OmmullummO's claim. He wishes you to lead that army, to be its commander-in-chief.'

Kaff was impressed by the scale of the enterprise. Humbold had lost none of his grandeur. And already he had an army?

'Are these good fighting men he has at his beck and call?'

'The warriors from Ut and Ged? Humbold says they are not barbarians, like the Hannacks and beast-people, but seasoned soldiers blooded in many battles. Civilised nations with well-trained troops and engines of war. Humbold reminds Kaff that although Soldier has defeated many armies in battle, they have always consisted of barbarian hordes. Now he and his Red Pavilions will be up against a *real* army.'

Kaff found himself increasingly interested. It would of course be the last throw of the dice. If he failed this time to kill his enemy and take his queen to his own bed, then all would be lost. Kaff had had many chances, many allowances, but Soldier would brook no more. This treachery, if it could be called such, would be the last. He and Humbold, if the offer were accepted, would do better to die on the field if they could not leave it victorious.

'Humbold is confident?' said Kaff, stroking his chin. 'He has a large army?'

'I have seen them myself, sire – a multitude, well armed and with many squadrons of horse. Humbold says that with the beast-people and the Hannacks to use as irregulars, there is no army within five thousand miles which could match the one he leads now. But he needs your generalship. He is no tactician, no strategist, he admits. He is a politician. He has already pledged himself to OmmullummO and wishes you to do the same.'

The half-rat on Kaff's wrist squealed and wriggled. Kaff looked down at the creature and took it to be a sign, a portent that he should accept this offer from Humbold. If he did not and Humbold was victorious without him, he was a dead man anyway. Humbold had not an ounce of forgiveness in his body and would certainly execute any who had stood against him. Kaff could, of course, stand aside from the tumult, but he had never been a man to duck action. He was a doer, not a sit-and-waiter. Especially when he had the opportunity to rid himself of the upstart Soldier, a stranger who had arrived with rags on his back and had risen to become Kaff's ruler.

Oh how sweet the day would be when Kaff could wipe Soldier's blood from his sword! Oh how mellow the mood on the night that Soldier's head was finally thrown to starving wolves!

'Lead the way to Humbold. I am his man.'

The grape-picker smiled nervously, jingling the coins in his pocket.

'There is another with Humbold who may be of assistance to you.'

Kaff stared. 'And who might that be?'

'He calls himself Drummond and is from the same place as Soldier – he is a lifelong foe of Soldier.' The worker's voice dropped and a certain awe came into it. 'He has Soldier's eyes. Blue. They are blue like his. This Drummond says he will not rest until Soldier – he calls him Valechor – is a feast for the worms. This Drummond says he will place himself at the forefront of the battle. He will carve a way through to Soldier himself and cut down the man who killed his clan and slaughtered his bride.' The messenger licked his lips. 'I have seen this Drummond, and he is fierce indeed. His locks and beard are stiffened with cattle dung. He paints his face with strange designs before battle. There are things he calls tattoos, blood-pictures, carved in his arms and on his legs. He wears a bull's skull on his head for a helmet and his cloak is the hide of a bear.'

'He sounds like a barbarian.'

'He *looks* like one, but is not, being the king of a civilised army in that place from which he and Soldier come.'

'A king indeed? And he is happy to leave his kingdom to come seeking a single foe?'

'There is so much bad blood between him and Valechor he said he would relinquish an empire to get at his sworn enemy. Valechor massacred his clan, leaving not one relation alive. He will have no rest until he can smell the death of Valechor in his nostrils. Some say he was flung here, like Soldier, during a battle. Some say that battle was between the two men, who both lived under witches' curses. But whatever the reason for their being here, Drummond will not even attempt to return to his own world until the rotting corpse of the man we call Soldier is fed to crows.'

'I like the sound of this Drummond,' murmured Kaff. 'He shall be the spearhead of my troops.'

As they left the green chapel, Soldier and Musket came across a square chamber which was piled high to the ceiling with human bones. These were they who had attempted to steal from the treasure. Whether it had been the lizard or some other guardian who had stripped the flesh from their bones was not sure. What was certain was that they had been picked clean. There were no rotting corpses, only skeletons white as ivory. There were no rats or cockroaches, nor any clothes or armour. Simply bones.

Skulls were piled in one corner, rib cages in another, leg and arm bones in another, pelvis bones in the last. Spinal columns hung like curtains around the walls. Feet and hands were planted in the floor as if they were expected to grow like flowers. Shades of the old woman at the entrance to the underground lake where Soldier had found his named sword.

Musket shivered. 'I'm glad we didn't see this before we went in, Father.'

'You're not supposed to. The guardians do not care to deter people from stealing. They probably enjoy it when they do.'

Further up the tunnel they came across another room, this time stacked with weapons. There were some formidable arms in that place, but whatever the bearer's skill with them, or his strength, nothing had stopped the guardian from destroying that person. Soldier was glad Musket had had the sense to return the jewel he had taken. He suspected that had his adopted son been older, more of a man, the guardian might not have been so lenient.

Outside the green chapel the air was sweet and cool. Thunder was still quietly grazing on the lush green grass beneath the copse of trees. Icewings had gone, leaving a patch of snow where she had sat. Soldier wondered whether she led all of Theg's supplicants to the green chapel.

Soldier made a fire while Musket was given the crossbow to hunt a rabbit. The boy came back with the game, highly excited with his success. They roasted the meat over a slow fire. While they were eating, the sound of beating wings was heard overhead. Soldier looked up. The white dragon was returning. Down the hill aways, a haggard-looking warrior was trudging along the snowy road she fashioned. The man was tall and handsome, with well-fitting armour, but he looked weary and careworn as he approached the green chapel. Dust was in his hair and on his eyebrows and lashes. More on his sandals. He dragged a sword along the ground which made a snaking mark in the dirt with its point. He smiled wanly at the two eaters.

'A green chapel? Have you been in? Is an onyx horse there?'

Soldier shrugged. 'There is much treasure inside. I saw no carving of a horse, I must admit. But that is not surprising, considering the amount which is piled in the cavern.'

'Still, it could be there?'

'Oh yes.'

'Then I shall enter and seek to find it. Do you know which end?'

'We took that one and were successful,' said Soldier, pointing.

The knight, for such he seemed, was about to enter when he suddenly hesitated on the brink.

Soldier said, 'You don't trust me?'

'Forgive me, sir, but I have met with many strange obstacles on my journey to this place. Theg does not wish to make this easy for me. Seven labours have I had. You just might be the eighth. Tests there have been, almost without number, including a fairy who sought to detain me on a cold hillside with her loving ways and summer wine. That is where I lost my charger and had to proceed on foot.'

'I assure you, sir,' said Soldier, holding up the three items he had come for, 'that these were taken from the chapel just a few minutes ago.'

'He's right,' said Musket. 'We just came out. But if you don't believe us, look for the rabbits' droppings. They wouldn't go into the wrong end, now would they, being able to smell brimstone easy as pie.'

The knight stared around the entrance.

'No, boy, you are right – there are signs of rabbits at this end, which gives your advice credence. I thank you both.'

Before the warrior finally went in, Soldier said, 'You know only to take that which you have come for?'

'Of course, I need nothing else, friend.'

'Good. I just thought to warn you.'

They continued with their meal. Icewings, that fabulous beast of the skies, flew off again. It seemed there was considerable traffic in human visitors and she was a busy dragon. Some time later the warrior came out of the green chapel. To the astonishment of the two diners they saw he was labouring with a huge load: dragging a life-size carving of a horse. It must have taken immense strength to get the statue out of the treasure room and along the tunnels. They went to help him with it the last few yards, setting the beautiful carving on its feet near the trees. It was indeed a wondrous work of art, with attractive patterns flowing through the onyx. The contours – the muscles, the marvellous hoofs, the mane and tail – had been carved and polished by a genius. The eyes were a glistening brown. The mouth, the nose were noble. The ears were pricked and shapely. A blood horse, a racer with fine lines, must have been the model for this statue.

'I thought you meant a *small* carving, like the one we have of the praying mantis,' said Soldier.

'No, no. I meant this one,' said the knight. 'Isn't she a beauty?' He stroked her smooth rump as if she were a real horse. 'I have dreamed of owning this, possessing this – though I mean to exchange it for something – some*one* – better. She has haunted my dreams since I was twelve. Now Theg has granted my prayer and allowed me the quest to her stable. I shall die happy. A man may live for ever and not own such a treasure. Yet – yet,' he looked wistful and yearning, 'I *shall* give her up. Yes, that is my intention, it is true. After all, this is but cold stone and my heart yearns for the warmth of love to touch it, to enter it and possess *me*. For what use are things if one has to live without love? I do intend to give her up, that is certain.'

But his tone indicated he was anything but certain. Soldier could see the pride of ownership in his eye. When Musket went to stroke the neck the knight started, as if to intervene and prevent the boy. He was jealous of anyone else touching the statue, that much was sure.

'May I ask who or what she is for?'

It was Musket who had spoken, otherwise the knight might not have answered. However, he did so with surprising frankness.

'I am charged with taking this to the Sultan of Kurkush, where I intend to ask for his daughter's hand in marriage. The sultan loves his toys and I love his daughter, so we should both be happy. I am to bring this prize – this wonderment, this fantastical horse,' he sighed, as if in longing, 'back to the sultanate. My lord the ruler of Kurkush set this task for all would-be suitors and I am the only one who has not failed. I have to return to Kurkush, of course, but that should be easy now that I have my prize.'

'Toy?' repeated Soldier. 'You mean ornament, of course.'

'No, I mean toy. Watch.'

With his face suffused with the light of joy, the knight swung himself up into the stone saddle. Immediately the horse came to life, kicking out with its hind legs, prancing a little, tossing its mane. The knight walked it round, for the other two to admire its form, then spurred it forth. The charger swept away, gracefully, down the hill, bearing the good knight on its back. At the bottom of the slope it reached such a speed as to enable it to take to the air. There it galloped, climbing high up into the blueness above, the knight waving to the pair below. They watched it go higher and higher, up into the clouds, the knight looking pale and woebegone now that he was ascending to the heavens on his onyx charger. The sun shone brilliantly on the stone's yellowy-white and brown patterns, until it was finally a speck, like some soaring hawk, and they lost sight of it.

'Wow!' cried Musket. 'Why didn't we come and get a horse like that, instead of a silly egg, insect and seashell?'

'We could hop home on the back of the mantis.'

Musket made a face.

'But,' said Soldier, an idle thought entering his mind, 'you could have a good idea there, Musket. Now, put down the golden egg. Do you want to become like that fellow and fall in love with the object instead of the subject?' Soldier mused. 'Did you see his eyes? Avarice was there, as green as that jade mantis and growing fiercer by the second. I'll wager you the sultan's hand never touches that horse. The princess will be palely loitering, lingering by her window, many an hour, a day, a month, waiting for that knight to return and claim her hand. He's off to his own place, to covet his treasure, which Theg will soon take back once she sees his intentions are not pure, his love has turned to greed, his hands are sticky. Mark my words, young Musket, gold is only gold. A lady's love is priceless.'

'Huh!' Musket snorted. 'So you say.'

They struck camp. Soldier then told his newly adopted son what he was about to do. 'You are going to get an earlier wish. I'm going to call on the birds of the air to make a magic flying carpet for us. In this way we do not have to repeat the dangers of the return journey. You and I will travel swiftly and surely over the mountains, valleys, rivers, lakes, forests and swamps, back to Zamerkand. No more chasms or dark dreams for us! No more drot fairies biting through our socks! We are home-ward bound on a raft of feathers.'

'Yes, yes!' cried the boy, putting the golden egg into Soldier's satchel. 'Here we go, through the azure skies, keeping company with clouds.'

Soldier called on the birds of the air.

They flocked to his cry, every manner of feathered crea-ture with wings. When they heard the task, the smaller birds – the robins, tits, finches, blackbirds, thrushes and their kind – begged to be excused. The large birds, they said, would be more suitable for the work. And so it was the herons, swans, cormorants, eagles, falcons, cranes, storks, egrets and their kin who all gathered in one square to make a carpet. On this carpet the two humans lay, arms stretched out, legs akimbo.

Thunder was set free, to graze at will in and around the green chapel, where the grass was luscious and cool, clear becks flowed nearby. Armour was left on the grassy slopes. The only weapon taken was Kutrama, sheathed in Sintra. The precious objects the two had taken from the treasure cavern were safely in the satchel around Soldier's neck. They had to travel light, due to the fact that the birds could not fit tightly together in the middle of the raft. They had to have free air space around them in order to use their wings.

Thus the two humans had to spread themselves and trust to their carriers not to part, or they would fall through the middle.

They rose in the air, climbing on a cool ascent to a height which would carry them over mountain peaks. It was a frightening experience for Soldier and Musket, for their feathered carpet seemed flimsy and fragile beneath them. Yet they distracted themselves with the wonder of the patchwork beneath them. Over green and brown landscape, over blue waters, they flew. The wind lifted their hair and caressed their bodies. The sun warmed their backs. Under and around the pair the wings creaked and swished, the strong swans with slow, deliberate strokes, the falcons quick but powerful in their means.

'Look, Musket!' cried Soldier breathlessly, as they crossed the chasm at a dizzying height. 'I can see the centre of the world down there.'

'I think I'm going to be sick,' was the reply.

They crossed alps with snowy heads and descended lower when these dropped down to the brown plains. It was a fascinating experience, even for the troubled Musket, whose human form had lost its zest for the flying he used to do as a raven. He would remember this journey for the rest of his life and fib a little in the retelling, saying how glorious it all was and how he felt nothing but a great rush of joy coursing through him to be once again swooping and soaring through the blue.

When he was not looking down, the boy stared at the beady eyes of the birds whose faces were closest to his own. He gulped at the hooked beak of the eagle which kept turning its head to gleam wickedly just inches from his nose. Still, the boy knew that this was a unique time. His feathers were gone, but he flew again. Never again would he travel through the air, unless shot from a siege catapult, or thrown from battlements.

When they flew over the large valley which contained the twin cities of Ut and Ged, Soldier was amazed to see it was empty of fighting forces. There were only farmers working out in the countryside rice paddies and a very few people in the streets of the cities. There were no armies down there, battling back and forth. Had the sieges ended? Had the two martial cities of Ut and Ged finally come together and declared a peace? Soldier hoped so. Yet it seemed *eerily* deserted, as if the armies had been snatched up by some force and planted elsewhere in the universe. Had some whirlwind passed through and taken them with it? Or some supernatural power? It was indeed puzzling and Soldier had a bad feeling about it.

Once they had crossed over the marshes which separated the known world from the previously Unknown Region, there was danger. The barbarians of Falyum and Da-tichett, separated from Guthrum by the Kermer Pass and Mount Kkamaramm, were hunters as well as raiders. They lived on the game they could track down. Thus a huge flock of large birds attracted the attention of archers, who fired arrows up at the passing raft of swans, herons, storks and others. The hunters were amazed, of course, to see such a sight, but this didn't stop their mouths from watering or their bow fingers from twitching.

Happily, the raft was too high for the arrows, which fell back down and endangered companions of the archers who had fired them. Eventually they were over Guthrum itself and Zamerkand came into view. Soldier was looking down at familiar sights from an unusual angle; Musket, however, had seen it all before from this viewpoint. This did not prevent him from becoming excited. He pointed things out, saying, 'Look, there's the canal' and 'See how the Green Tower sparkles in the sun from up here.'

The carpet of birds dropped them some miles from the city, fearing more archers, this time crossbowmen with bolts. Soldier and Musket thanked their feathered friends for the ride and set out to complete the journey on foot. They arrived amongst the Red Pavilions at sunset, weary but pleased with themselves. On being informed of their approach by sentries, Velion came out to meet them. She and Soldier gripped one another's arms in greeting and salute.

'Please send a messenger to the queen and tell her that I have returned safely and will join her as soon as I am able.'

Velion left to see this was done and returned a few moments later.

'How have things been in my absence?' asked Soldier.

'Quiet here, but there have been developments elsewhere. I shall bring you up to date soon, but you look as if you need to rest first.'

'All right, so long as they are *distant* problems.'

'Serious, but yes, distant.' General Velion turned her attention to the boy at Soldier's side. 'And who is this tadpole?' she said, smiling at him.

'I am Soldier's son,' said the tadpole. 'Tell her, Soldier.'

Soldier sighed. 'He is correct.'

Velion's eyebrows rose more than a fraction. 'My, my, General, you have been busy up-country, haven't you? How long have you been gone? A decade, I assume, since this stripling is at least ten summers old. And what is the queen to say of this slide from the virtues of matrimony?'

Soldier smiled grimly. 'Yes, very funny, General – but you are in for another piece of startling news. Remember my talking raven?'

Velion groaned. 'How could I forget that blight on the bird world. Is it finally dead? I for one would not be sorry, for its chatter used to drive me to distraction. Now that it has gone, I have to be truthful. I came within a centimetre of strangling the creature myself several times.'

'This is he,' said Soldier, placing a hand on the boy's head. 'His name is now Musket and he is my adopted son.'

Velion went quiet for a few moments and then stated, 'As for myself, there were times when I quite liked the company of that bird.'

'Too late,' said Musket grimly. 'You have offended me.'

'Oh dear. I am desolate.'

Musket folded his arms and turned away from the amused generals, as they regarded him with twitching mouths.

The pair remained in the Red Pavilions' encampment, outside the city walls, until they had washed and changed their clothes. Musket was handed a cut-down robe which Soldier had been given by the senate in Carthaga: a prize taken from a defeated sultan. It was of black silk, a colour the boy was still very much attached to, even though he was no longer a raven. There was a red edge to the robe which gave it a little flare and Musket paraded himself in front of Soldier and Velion, accepting their compliments with easy grace.

'Is it possible to make a prince of this wart?' said Velion. 'He seems almost human now we've removed most of the grime. Of course that snub nose reveals his peasant origins, and those ghastly freckles, but we might be able to disguise these defects with the skilful use of kohl. Once we teach him not to spit or pick his nose we might have something we can parade in public without inviting the disgust of the general population.'

Musket glowered at Velion, who simply laughed.

Later Soldier and Musket wove their way between the watchfires of the sentries and entered the gates of the city. A guard tried to block their entrance, not recognising his ruler's husband. Soldier commended the fellow on his competence, but informed him of who he was. A sergeant-at-arms was called and this man, appointed by Golgath, the new commander of the Imperial Guard, recognised Soldier immediately. He began reprimanding the sentry, but Soldier said the man was to be praised for his attention to duty.

Once inside Zamerkand's walls, Soldier could see these city streets were thriving once again. There were people trading under lamplight, with market stalls everywhere. Soldier looked for Spagg's hand-of-glory stall, which normally stood on the corner of the market square. It was gone, which perturbed him, for Spagg never shut up shop.

The pair walked on, through the hubbub and the thronging shoppers, exiting on the far side of the market. There Soldier almost bumped into his former employer and erstwhile travelling companion. Spagg, not recognising Soldier in the shadows, gave the fellow a haughty look and ordered him and 'the urchin' to step out of the way of an official of the queen, or suffer the consequences. Soldier did so without comment.

The ex-trader flowed past, nose in the air.

Spagg was dressed in a voluminous golden garment with sleeves that hung almost to the ground. On his head was a huge turban fashioned from at least ten yards of green fabric. Imbedded in this turban was a flashing jewel the size of a hen's egg. On his feet were golden slippers, embroidered with silver patterns. They were of eastern design, having toes that curled up and round on themselves, forming a pointed spiral. A dagger encrusted with gems hung from an ornate belt around his thick waist.

Spagg was followed by two young bare-chested men carrying a golden sedan chair upholstered with red velvet. This transport seemed to be there simply in case the great Spagg should weary himself with walking. The truth was, though he liked to travel in the chair, people couldn't see him as well when he was inside it. He wanted everyone to know who he was, what he had been, and how far he had risen.

On the sedan chair, lit by four perfumed-oil lamps, were perched several colourful parrots. A monkey on a silver chain kept poking its chattering head out of the window. The smell of sandalwood and cedarwood was all pervasive. On the shelf in front of the chair sat a carafe of sweet white wine, covered in condensed droplets of chilled water, with a single crystal glass bound about with bands of ivory.

Behind the chair were six well-armed men wearing the livery of the official bodyguard of the Keeper of the Royal Purse.

'Well,' called Soldier after him, 'the hand-of-glory business *must* be good, Master Spagg.'

Spagg, not identifying the voice, whirled round angrily, and the leader of his bodyguards jabbed roughly at Soldier with a spear.

'You are speaking to the Keeper of the Royal Purse – maintain a civil tongue, citizen.'

'Keeper of the Royal Purse? Looks like he's been dipping into it,' said Musket. 'Got a right royal look to him, ain't he?'

'Careful, boy,' Soldier added, 'he might cry "Off with his head" and then where would you be?'

'Headless,' replied the boy, 'but still having more brains than a jumped-up seller of hands-of-glory.'

'How DARE you,' spluttered Spagg. 'You – you – gutter-snipe.'

'Pompous bugger, ain't he?' Musket said. 'And look how he foams at the mouth! Anyone would think that underneath that gold robe he was some sort of *person*. Whereas we know he's just a thief and a liar, a man who has convinced poor gullible shoppers that his wares will make them invisible. It just goes to show you *can* make the keeper of a silk purse out of a sow's ear.'

Spagg was looking unsure of himself now. Why were this man and his boy insulting him in this manner? Were they about to attack him? What had he done to offend them? There was something more to this encounter than met the eye. He looked nervously towards his bodyguards.

'I could order my men to arrest you,' he said.

'Oh,' Soldier answered, 'I don't think they'll do that.'

'And why not?'

'Because they would soon find themselves in the dungeons, that's why not,' snapped Musket. 'I think soldiers who arrest the husband of the queen might even end up being boiled in pig fat, don't you, Father?'

'Very likely, son.'

Spagg stepped forward now and peered into the faces of the two who were insulting him. He did not recognise the boy at all. But when he took one of the sedan chair's lamps and shone it in the face of the man, he gasped and stepped back.

'Soldier!' he said. 'You've come home.'

'As intended.'

Spagg glanced at the boy. 'With a – a – with a child?'

'Not intended, but true.'

'The queen will be most gratified.'

'I certainly hope so. And I see she has elevated you in the world, Spagg, which is both good and rather foolish of her. I shall tell her so. Myself, I think it dangerous to believe that crafty weaselly fellows who love money more than loyalty can ever change, but then I am not a wise queen with a keen insight into human nature. For myself I would have thought once a robber, always a robber. But then here you are, in golden robes, looking as fine as any top civil servant can do. I am pleased for you, Spagg. Do not abuse the trust or I will have your head on a pointed stick.'

The guards had looked away now and were studying the distant stars with avid interest.

'Of course I can be trusted,' spluttered the new official. 'I have sworn my oath to the queen and her court.'

'Spagg, you were always swearing and your oaths were famous for their obscenity, but never mind, I shall see you later.'

'Yes — yes, Soldier. I look forward to it. I — I tried to tell her, you know, that I wasn't a fit person for this job, but she wouldn't listen.'

They left the Keeper of the Royal Purse still holding up the lamp as if he were a member of the watch lost in a reverie.

Soldier now led the way to the Palace of Wildflowers where the queen awaited his return in the obsidian Green Tower. At the gates and within the palace Soldier was instantly recognised. He was led to his wife's bedchamber, where he hesitated on the threshold. It was not that he was not anxious to see his wife, but once upon a time she had been quite mad and he had never got over his concern that his reception might be a nightmarish one. At times Layana had been as sane as the next woman, but on occasion she had been spitting fire, raking the air with her nails, her face twisted into the most hideous mask of hate imaginable. It was the memory of that time which made Soldier nervous of knocking and entering.

However, he did so, and found her looking as entrancing as when he had left her. She was sitting in a chair by the main window, which looked out on to the city gates. It was as if she had been sitting in the same spot the whole time he had been away, watching for him to return through that gate. Sunlight was streaming through the unshuttered window, falling on her hair. A great pang of love and affection went through Soldier's heart. Here was his beloved Layana. True, she was no longer a young woman: like him she had matured, luckily with ease and grace. But there was no denying her loveliness, her extraordinary air of serene beauty.

Yet he cared less for her outward attractiveness than for her inner self. Here was a woman capable of great warmth and mercy, as well as passion, which was well in a queen. There was a primitive savagery in every man and woman, of which most ordinary people were aware and kept under control. Too many absolute monarchs, however, gave vent to their cruelty once they had the power to do so. They displayed the ugly side of their nature and suppressed the good side. There was no one to say them nay. Layana had a temper, it was true. But this manifested itself over small matters. She might battle with some venom when her husband stole too much of the bedsheets at night, but she did not issue proclamations which destroyed the lives of thousands. She was a wise judge, a listener as well as a speaker, and her subjects were growing fonder of her by the day.

Soldier had not realised how much he had missed her until now. When she turned towards him a smile was on her face and passion in her eyes. They kissed, fervently, and whispered in each other's ear. This went on for some time, despite the fact that there was company in the room. Then the queen seemed to notice a young boy hovering by the doorway. She looked over Soldier's shoulder in surprise, then beckoned the child to approach her.

'Have you been sent by the servants for something?'

'Er, no, ma'am.'

'Then what shall you want? Speak up, I'm not a monster. You have no need to look at me as if I was going to . . .'

'Chop off my head? No, ma'am.'

'And stop calling me that.'

'All right, then – Mother.'

Soldier closed his eyes and winced, expecting an explosion from his wife. Layana simply stared at the boy.

'You must have some reason for calling me that name,' she said eventually. 'I take it I shall now learn what it is.'

Soldier answered for him. 'I adopted the boy.'

Layana stared now at her husband. 'Adopted him? Without my agreement?'

'I told the boy he could be regarded as my son. However, I did say that your consent was necessary if he were ever to call you mother.' Soldier sighed, anticipating the flaring temper his wife could fly into when she sensed a personal injustice. 'I cannot now renounce him. I have promised I will be a father to him. But you of course still have the choice as to whether you wish to be his mother.'

'Have I?'

'Yes, my love. I'm sorry to spring this on you, but we were out in the middle of nowhere and unsure whether we would ever return alive. It meant a lot to the child to know he was wanted and that he had a family. This boy was once a crea-ture with feathers who taunted me incessantly – the raven –

who through some magic in the Unknown Region has now reverted to his birth state, that of being a human boy. Despite being a pest the raven saved my life on several occasions, just as I saved his. You will remember that he was the first creature I spoke to on entering this world – I saved him from a poisonous snake with a cudgel. Later, it is true, he betrayed me in the hope that he would become a boy again, but that is forgiven.'

Soldier paused and stared at the boy in his oversized black silk robe and floppy sandals.

'It is true also that he is not a very endearing child. There are some suspect ancestors. The nose, and those sun spots, and the way the hair sprouts in a hundred different directions, may point to first cousins marrying first cousins, at the very least. There is not much of a brow between the eyes and the hairline, but there is a brightness of the mind. If there are inbred dolts in his lineage, then his brain did not pick up the weakness.'

Soldier's expression took on a certain gravity.

'I should also tell you the child risked his life in trying to wrest a huge ruby from a monster. He wanted to give it to you, to buy your love. I told him your love was not for sale, but that you gave it freely to those who deserved it. I have grown quite fond of the youth and plan to turn him into a combat knight, once I find a good man to train him and teach him to ride a horse in a warrior-like manner.'

'Scrivener, philosopher, physician or judge. Not a warrior.'

Soldier stared at her.

Layana shook her head. She had spoken firmly. She now outlined her own plans.

'No son of mine is going to waste a good mind on beating dints into helmets with a heavy piece of metal. I want him

taught by the wisest tutors in the land. I want my son to be
famed for his learning. Anyone can be a warrior.'

'Well, not quite anyone, my love,' said Soldier, stung by this
belittling of his chosen profession. 'It takes a good deal more
than brawn to be a successful knight. But you approve of the
child. That's good. We are both happy, Musket and I. See how
he smiles at you. We will discuss his future later . . .'

'No, he will not be a soldier,' said Layana with even more
firmness than before. 'He will be a man of great wisdom.'

'But we can talk of this . . .'

'Who is queen, you or me?' she flashed.

'Now that isn't fair. You can't keep pulling that card out of
the pack every time we have a domestic discussion.'

'A row.'

'All right, a *disagreement*. I think we ought to come to some
sort of compromise. Let's agree that you can't be queen in
our bedroom, dining room or great hall. After all a farrier
doesn't shoe horses in his own parlour, now does he? You can
be queen anywhere else,' he waved his hand airily, generously
taking in the whole kingdom outside the palace, 'but in these
three places you are my wife. How does that sound?'

'I can be queen anywhere I want to be.'

'Unreasonable! Flagrant misuse of power!'

'Don't care.'

Musket was viewing them with alarm, until they both burst
out laughing, and hugged each other. Then he realised it was
all a game. That his new parents were playing with one
another. Then to his concern and discomfort Layana came
to him and hugged him too. He wasn't ready for *this* kind of
closeness. He wanted to gradually ease himself into relationship feelings, not plunge in with his new mother. She
smelled of face powder and skin cream and alarming scented

things like that. A bird does not have hugging partners and is only intimate with its mate. However, he bore the attack without remonstration and allowed the gladness of the situation to flow through him. He had been accepted. He was in a *family*.

'You squirmed!' accused his mother. 'I felt you wriggle. You'll have to get used to me doing that, you know. I cuddle anyone in sight when the mood comes upon me.'

'I – I shall get used to it, I suppose.'

'Of course you shall. Until then, let me look at you.' She took him by the shoulders and peered at him from arm's length. 'He's not *too* bad when you get over the shock of the hair,' she said, teasingly. 'We can't take him back and exchange him, I suppose? For a raven or something more in the house pet variety? No, then he'll have to do. I'll give him to Drissila to wash and dress. If anyone can make him presentable, she can. I think he'll scrub up nicely with lye soap and some good rough pumice stone.'

The look of alarm returned. 'I've already been washed and dressed and made presentable once.'

'Well, we'll do it again, and this time properly. Well, my young prince – what is your name? Musket? Well, Prince Musket of Zamerkand, what do you think of your new home?'

'I think it is very fine,' said Musket, close to tears with happiness. 'I – I am very proud. Thank you, Mother. Thank you, Father.'

'Drissila?' called Layana. 'Can you come, please?'

The lady-in-waiting appeared a few moments later in the doorway, with Ofao hovering at her shoulder.

'This young man is the new master of the house. He is our adopted son, Prince Musket. My husband and I are very proud of him.'

Drissila's eyes opened wide as she regarded the specimen in front of her.

'He is?' she said in dubious tone. 'You are?'

'Yes, very much so. You must turn him into something resembling a gentleman within forty-eight hours. I'm sure you can do it. Wear out several scrubbing brushes if you have to. And take no notice of tears, screams or wails. Quickly now, the sands are running in the glass.'

'Impossible,' said Drissila, clearly astonished by this turn of events, 'but we shall make a grand effort.'

'You, Ofao, must teach the child to read and write. A little more than forty-eight hours will be necessary for that. I suggest you start by telling him some exciting stories. Tales such as those found in *A Thousand-and-ten Nights*. This will whet his appetite and have him seeking more of the same. You will then teach him to read them for himself. Once he can read, writing will follow naturally, with encouragement of course. After which you can embark on mathematics, astronomy and navigation. All very useful subjects. A little sewing and cooking will also not go amiss. A young man should be able to take care of himself, without his servants, in an emergency.'

'Is that all?' remarked Ofao with a hint of sarcasm in his voice. 'What about stuffing the life cycle of the cockchafer in there as well?'

The queen's eyes narrowed and Ofao bowed quickly, and to Musket's chagrin patted the boy on the head. 'It shall be as you say, Your Majesty. I shall have the infant chanting his times tables within the week. I have always found the rote method the best for arithmetic, especially when accompanied by liberal use of the leather strap.'

'There will be no beating, Ofao.'

Ofao gestured wildly. 'But Your Majesty, it is a necessary part of getting knowledge into a child.'

'There will be no beating. That is my final word.'

In the meantime Musket was looking horrified.

'Mother, I shall burst with all that learning.'

'If you do, you'll be able to sew yourself together again, won't you, once Ofao has shown you how to use the needle. He is very deft with a needle, is our Ofao. Now off you all go. Don't forget to feed and water the prince. He must be hungry. My husband and I will eat in the great hall, where apparently I have no authority as queen and cannot tell him to eat his greens.'

Drissila and Ofao left with the boy, quite used to the frivolity the queen adopted at times when she was full of joy.

Soldier and Layana now spent time over a meal, discussing quite trivial matters, getting to know one another again.

'Now,' said Soldier, over a glass of wine, 'to more serious matters. I have the objects required by the goddess Theg, to put right your memory. With your consent I shall perform the ceremony tomorrow, at the temple. How do you feel?'

'You have gone through great dangers and troubles to bring this cure to me, husband. I would be ungrateful now if I were to reject it. However, I am concerned. What if, when my memory returns, so does my erstwhile madness?'

'I am assured by the priests that will not happen.'

'In that case, we shall go ahead.'

They toasted the morning together.

'Now for my news, husband. I have to tell you that Captain Kaff has left the city with his supporters.'

'Good riddance!'

'But he has gone to join with Humbold and a renegade army.'

Soldier digested this, frowning. 'But I met Humbold in the Unknown Region. We were forced to weather a storm of drots together. He seemed to be heading northwards. Did he then return to the known world, while Musket and I were seeking the three objects?'

The queen nodded. 'Not only did he return, he brought with him the armies of two cities, I am told. Cities called Ut and Ged, who have never ventured this way before because of the dangerous nature of the marshes. From what I have been told, the marshes are moderately dangerous going *into* the Unknown Region, but are infinitely perilous coming out.'

Soldier was mystified. 'Why should this be?'

'Cristobel, Theg's priest, informed me a while ago that those marshes were fashioned as a honey-jar trap. They were placed there by a King Magus called VoommooV long ago. In ancient years the Unknown Region was empty and no one wanted to live there because of mosquitoes, drots and other pests. VoommooV placed the marshes between the known world and the Unknown Region to attract people inside. A rumour began that there was treasure to be had beyond some marshes, which in themselves presented an irresistible challenge to adventurous men and women.

'The marsh, with its mile-high sheer cliffs either side and its ever-narrowing passage, allows a wide, expansive entrance. But the path back is impossible to find. Just as we make honey-jar traps for wasps where the entrance is a funnel. It not difficult for the wasp to enter the jar by means of the wide end of the funnel, but once inside, the winged creature cannot seem to find and negotiate the small end to escape. So it is with the marshes of the Unknown Region, which have an illusional "funnel". This is why I have been worrying so much these past few days. I knew you had to return that way and thought you would perish attempting to find the exit.'

'Damn that priest! He said nothing to me about this,' cried Soldier, annoyed. 'It is well Musket and I had a magic carpet flight over these deadly swamps.' He paused before asking, 'But how did thousands from Ut and Ged finally traverse the barrier which has, until now, kept them contained?'

'OmmullummO removed the funnel.'

Soldier was confounded by such deviousness.

'The wizard moves in crafty ways.'

'The cities of Ut and Ged have standing armies, are martial by nature, and have put aside their own differences in order to assist Humbold. Humbold has pledged himself to OmmullummO in the wizard wars between him and his son, IxonnoxI. We, of course, will be the opposing force and hope to defeat Humbold in his bid.'

Soldier's face was grim. 'Ut and Ged! Why, I met with the leaders of those armies, or some of them. There was a young prince amongst them I quite liked, by the name of Fabulet. It seems the two cities have been at war for years and their fighters are well-trained, experienced warriors. Humbold! He doubled back on his own tracks. What a fool I was to leave him alive. And now he's managed to persuade Ut and Ged to join him. I wonder what he has promised them.'

'The wealth of Zamerkand?'

'Without a doubt.'

Soldier's questioning eyes looked into the middle distance. His wife knew that look and asked what he was thinking.

'Thinking?' he said. 'I was thinking of my oldest enemy, Drummond. I have no doubt he will be with Humbold's new army too, having pursued me here from my old world. Here we have it, all our foes – ancient and contemporary – all in one basket. It is time for a reckoning. However, I must first try to make my peace with Drummond. This much I have sworn. I do not know what will happen, if I fail, for I have done him many wrongs and right is not on my side. His wrongs have been as many, and his righteousness in question also, but one of us must attempt to end this terrible feud. I would fight against our enemies for the general good, rather than in order to settle personal scores. Revenge is not a good motive for a battle: the welfare of the commonweal is a better one.'

As they lay in bed that night, Layana said to her husband, 'So now we have a son?'

'We might have others, of our own, later.'

'It has not happened yet and we are past our prime.'

Soldier hit his pillow with some force. 'We have been cursed, no doubt.'

Layana shrugged and placed a tender hand on her husband's cheek, to stroke it. 'Why, then, the curse has not worked, has it? For we have a son of our very own. I like him, Soldier. I will grow to love him.'

'Certainly he is no oil painting.'

'What? You would have me look for a boy with silken hair and perfect complexion? Shame on you, husband. It is what is *inside* that counts. He is very fond of *you*.'

'Pah!' Soldier tried to brush off the pleasure that remark gave him. 'He is a troublesome brat.'

'He is nothing of the sort. He tries to please. I have seen more mischief in a dainty little golden girl with dimples in her cheeks. Give him time and love and he will make us proud. There is kingship in him.'

'What?' Soldier came up on his elbows, astounded by this observation. 'Kingship? King of the rodents, I would say.'

'Fie, husband! I will not tell you again. He is our son and we will love him and cherish him.'

'Even if it kills us,' muttered Soldier, determined to have the last word.

The next day Soldier went to the Temple of Theg and asked for the ancient and crusty Cristobel.

'Alas, sir, he is dead,' remarked a noviciate. 'We burned his body yesterday and scattered the ashes in the temple gardens.'

'Dead?' cried Soldier. 'What of?'

The young novice blushed and moved his mouth closer to Soldier's ear. 'Why, sir, someone gave the old priest a purse of gold, which he spent on – on *painted ladies*. He was very, very old to be sure – to be doing *that* sort of thing. His ancient wrinkled heart burst in his chest while he was halfway through his pleasure. The young maid – well, to be sure she was neither young nor a maid, sir – she said he was *killed in action*, just as if he were on the battlefield and she the enemy. I – I never heard the like before, sir, and doubtless will not again. His was an unhealthy lust for an elderly priest – always a lewd man with every sin of lechery known to the world. He always said his blood was overheated and that he had only one way to cool it.'

'The old devil!' said Soldier, marvelling at the tale. 'But what am I to do without my priest? Is there another who will perform the rites for the return of the queen's memory? I have artefacts in my possession which are said to guarantee the cure. Who will stand in his stead?'

'Why,' the young man said, 'I will do it, sir.'

'But – but you are young and without experience. If anything should go wrong . . . if my wife were to be harmed in any way . . . I would have to cut off your head.'

'It is a simply ceremony, sir, and can be performed by anyone who has been ordained. I am not afraid.'

'No, but I am.'

'Have no concern. It is the objects which are important, not the priest who performs the rites.'

'Are you a priest yet?'

'Almost.'

Soldier was not convinced, but on asking further of the other priests in the temple, they told him that the novice had studied under Cristobel and was best placed to carry out the ceremony. In the end Soldier decided to trust the youth and placed the precious items in his possession. He was told he need not be a witness to the rites: in fact it were better he was not. As a layman he would not understand what mystical things were going on and might interrupt with questions at a vital time. Better he walked home, through the city, and by the time he reached the Palace of Wildflowers, his wife would be whole again.

'I hope so.'

'There is no question, sir,' said the novice. 'I shall restore her to her former self, with memories of her past. Of course, she will not remember *everything* she has ever done, seen or experienced, for no one does. Nor will all her memories be accurate. We choose to remember some things and forget others. We sometimes alter the truth in our minds, believing that we have the details right when we have not. The queen will recall things as she used to do. Those memories she had before she was ill will come back again, no more, no less. And they will come back in their former clothes, in the way she *used* to remember them, whether that memory was true to the original event or not. Is that satisfactory?'

'It sounds as if it will be as it should be.'

'Yes, sir,' said the earnest young noviciate, '*I* think so.'

Chapter Eight

It was with some trepidation that Soldier made his way home after the rites had been performed. The history of their marriage had not always been smooth – the history of *any* marriage is never smooth unless the two people involved are brain dead – and the bad memories would of course return alongside the good memories. Then, as the noviciate priest had said, there would be incomplete memories, altered memories and false memories as well. On the positive side, Layana always had the ability to surprise him. Look at the way she had received the news that she was now the mother of an adopted boy! Soldier had not expected her to take that rationally. Why should she have done? Yet her reaction had been calm and considered. She had had questions she wanted answered, naturally, but once that had been done, all had been well.

As he hurried along through the streets, pondering on what might be his reception, Soldier ran into the last person he wanted to see while he was in an agitated frame of mind: Spagg. The new Keeper of the Royal Purse was dressed in his finery and accompanied by a retinue. As a very-important-person he was of course entitled to a number of staff, but why they should follow him through the streets was another matter. Many of them would be accountants and scribes: they should be in some room somewhere scribbling away at figures and letters.

'Soldier,' cried Spagg, throwing open his arms, 'how good to see you, my old friend.'

'Is it?' said Soldier, avoiding the embrace with a dancing side-step. 'You will excuse me, I am in a desperate hurry to get to the Palace of Wildflowers.'

'Why,' cried Spagg, deftly managing to link arms with him, 'that is my direction exactly. I have an audience with the queen at noon. We can walk along together and talk about old times.'

Spagg's voice was vulgarly loud. He was trying to impress his retinue. Soldier was famed throughout Guthrum and he had many admirers. Someone who called himself Soldier's friend was also to be revered. Yet many of the weary-looking group who trudged after the Keeper of the Royal Purse had had quite enough of their new master.

Soldier had been quite right: the new Brass Boss (a witty nickname invented by the royal clerks) had dragged them away from their happy scribbling. They should have been tucked away in a quiet room, sitting at a high desk, scratching quill on parchment. It was not a profession many citizens would have chosen, being considered dull and boring. But these people liked the job. It suited their personalities. They were a retiring, introverted set of men and women. To sit in a peaceful back room where the loudest noise was the plop of a split goose's feather plunging into an inkwell was for them a preferred way to pass their working day.

Instead, here they were, hurrying through crowded streets,

carrying armfuls of rolled parchments. They were forced to suffer the noise of rumbling ox-carts, donkeys baying, dogs barking, fishwives shrieking in their ears. There was the heavy smell of animal dung hanging in the air; the constant pestering of the professional beggars, tugging at their gowns; the rats dashing across their feet; the children playing kickball and chase-the-cockroach between their legs. It was all too much for these gentle, meek creatures with their mild manners and sensitive ears. *Horrid* was the word that sprang to their lips. They wanted to be out of it, but their new master had been insistent. He wished them to accompany him to the palace of the queen, and he was not a Brass Boss who liked the word *no*.

Soldier unhooked his arm, saying to Spagg, 'I do not think the queen will wish to see you this morning. I am hurrying home because I believe her to be unwell.'

'Oh?' cried Spagg, looking thoroughly put out. 'But surely the queen would have sent out messengers, earlier in the day? She always does that before cancelling appointments. She wouldn't let us waste our valuable time going to the palace for nothing. The queen is very particular about wasting time. You must be mistaken, Soldier.'

Soldier grabbed Spagg by the sleeve and spun him round.

'Spagg, I am the queen's husband. I ought to know whether she is feeling well or not. When I left her this morning . . .'

'At what time?'

'At cock crow.'

'Well, there you are!' sang Spagg. 'She's probably got better by now. She felt queasy, probably, on waking – but has since taken some salts and has corrected herself. A simple case of *morning sickness?*' Spagg grinned broadly, chuckled and dug Soldier in the ribs with his elbow. 'Eh? Eh? You old dog, you. Will we be hearing happy tidings soon?'

'Spagg, you are the most vulgar, crude man I know.'

Lots of nods from the retinue.

'If you do not watch what you say in the street, or anywhere for that matter, you will kiss goodbye to this new post of yours and find a new one as Keeper of the Dungeon Keys.'

Yes, yes, murmured the retinue. *Please.*

'You jest with me, Soldier.'

'I am deadly serious.'

Spagg said nothing more. His face became quite grim. But he did not falter in his step. He kept pace with Soldier all the way, his retinue scurrying after him. When they came close to the palace Soldier stopped. Spagg halted too, staring at him.

'One more step, Spagg, and I will cut off your head.'

'Here, I say . . .'

Soldier drew his sword.

'But the queen is waiting for me,' pleaded Spagg. 'She sent for me specially. I have an audience with her. The messenger came just a short while ago, just after the bell tolled for late-morning prayers. Urgent, he said. The queen wants you immediately. If I don't go she'll be very angry, Soldier, and you know what she's like when she's angry. I've often said I would not like to be in the queen's boudoir when she's in a rage.'

Soldier ignored the crude remark about the queen's bedroom and stared down at the stunted figure below him.

'Just after the bell?'

'Yes.'

Soldier recalled that the ceremony for the return of the queen's memory had finished just on the bell. She had summoned Spagg immediately afterwards? And now they were here he could see other officials, other courtiers, hurrying up the marble steps to the court. The queen was going to issue a proclamation, that much was obvious. Memories prior to her entering that city in the sands of Uan Muhuggiag had come flooding back, obviously, and a decision had been made.

Now Soldier was really worried. Whatever the queen was about to say, she felt no desire to discuss it first with him. With heavy heart Soldier began to climb the steps to the throne room where the queen held court. Spagg, after a few moments' hesitation, followed him. They trailed others through the entrance hall and into the court. Queen Layana was sitting on her throne, dressed in her robes of office, her face looking small and pale. Prince Musket sat on the steps at her feet, playing with a puppy and a piece of yarn with a rag tied to the end. The room was hushed and waiting.

Soldier remained at the back of the room, in the shadows.

The queen spoke.

'Now that you are all assembled, I shall tell you why you have been called. I have to tell you that we are officially at war.' She dipped her head slightly, then raised it again with a determined expression on her face. 'When I came back from the deserts of Uan Muhuggiag with my husband I had no memory of my life before entering those deserts. When the former queen's head fell at my feet I did not recognise her as a sister and those filial emotions which accompany a death in a family were absent from me. I was told who she was and what she had meant to me, but without my memory it meant nothing more than the death of a stranger.

'Now I have been cured – my beloved husband has risked his life to obtain that cure – and all those remembrances have returned to me.

'I remember how I loved my sister, your former queen, and before her my father and mother. All, including myself, were made mad by the wizard called OmmullummO who has usurped the throne of the King Magus. I can remember how I myself suffered under that lunacy and therefore I know what terrors and horrors the rest of my family went through. OmmullummO hated us because we curbed his excesses and refused to allow him to follow his desire to subject us all to his tyranny. He swore to destroy us.

'The culmination of the enmity which OmmullummO felt towards my family was the turning of Humbold, my sister's chancellor. Humbold murdered my sister, set himself up as despot of this city, and executed and tortured hundreds of innocent citizens. His punishment, while my mind was still vacant of old memories, was banishment. If he had remained in exile he would be outside the wrath of this nation, but he chose to return. Thus any assurances which were given him are now void.

'Humbold is now the instrument of the false wizard. Humbold has gathered an army which will soon march on Zamerkand, to annihilate us. I feel nothing but contempt for this creature, but I have to respect the fact that he has enough warriors to defeat us if things go badly. We have the Red Pavilions of course, who will as always fight to the death to defend Zamerkand. My husband will lead them and as you know he is a seasoned general. He has conquered and will conquer again.

'Until now we have relied almost totally on the Red Pavilions to protect our city. Guthrum's population have been able to go about their civilian business without having to resort to arms, albeit we have kept a small internal force of Imperial Guard to keep order within the walls of Zamerkand and to prevent civil disobedience. However, now there is a need for *all* Zamerkand to join the Red Pavilions in their battle lines. General Golgath will be recruiting every citizen able to fight, training them in the art and science of war, and will form regiments which will stand alongside the mercenary army of Carthaga. We are fighting for our very existence here. If Humbold defeats us, OmmullummO will remain as King Magus and will raze our city to the ground. If that happens, before the century is out we shall be nothing but a faint memory in the minds of travellers passing through the ruins.

'Thus it is my proclamation that all able-bodied citizens between the ages of eighteen and fifty will take up arms. Henceforth every soldier now in the Imperial Guard will be promoted to sergeant-at-arms and will be sent out to gather in the recruits and assign them to battalions. Training will begin as soon as the raw regiments have been formed. That is all.'

The queen then rose and left the court, followed by the prince carrying the puppy in his arms.

Soldier went to the high room in the Green Tower, where he knew his wife would be waiting for him.

'So,' he said, 'you feel a great anger?'

Layana was pacing up and down a very precious rug, with Ofao's protective eyes watching intently for the wear. The queen stopped and stared at her husband. Soldier braced himself for any attack. Instead she ran to him and flung her arms around his neck.

'Oh, my husband, I have wronged you so often! What a terrible thing a memory is, when it recalls such treatment. You have suffered badly under my foul insanity – and did I wound you once or twice?'

'Thrice to be exact,' he said. 'I have the scars from three separate daggers. But that is all in the past and you were ill. You can't be held responsible for your actions while your mind was in such turmoil. The wizard it was who bewitched and bewildered you. He put the violence in your head and turned you from a meek lamb into a savage tiger.'

She gave him a rueful smile while still hanging round his neck.

'I have *never* been a lamb,' she said.

'No, no, I confess I am exaggerating there. But you are not the fierce beast that used to emerge at certain times during the month. That was the demon implanted in you by OmmullummO.' He gently removed her locking arms and held her hands. 'I heard your speech. It was well done. You really do have a determination to destroy that false magus?'

'I am set on it.'

'Good, we are of like mind.' He looked round. 'And where is the boy?'

'Playing with a young dog that he found tied in a sack and thrown by the kitchen waste. It must have been left there by the Keeper of the Royal Hunting Hounds. A breeding bitch had too many puppies I'll warrant. Anyway, husband, I swear if I had known how an animal can entrance a child of that age, I would have asked for one myself as a little girl.'

Soldier was astonished. 'You never had a pet when you were young?'

'A *pet*? The word means nothing.'

'Why, an animal or bird which is there for the purpose of loving and being loved, and no other reason.'

His wife stared at him. Ofao's eyes opened wider and he too looked thoughtful. Even sweet Drissila was making a peculiar face. Soldier shook his head in puzzlement.

'What?' he cried. '*None* of you had pets? I think I see a great fracture between our cultures. Now that I come to think of it, I have seen no one with a pet in Guthrum, or anywhere else in this world. No birds in cages, unless it be the geese on the city walls, to warn of an attack. Dogs and cats in service, yes – cats for ratting and mousing; dogs for hunting deer, for tracking, for rounding up sheep and goats; and horses for riding. Domestic animals which have a purpose other than just being what they are. How could it have escaped me? No wonder most of you are brittle and hard. Did you not know a pet can soften your life?' Something occurred to Soldier. 'Of course! The beast-people. You have a type of creature we do not have in my old world: part-man, part-animal. You have the dog-heads, the snake-heads, the horse-heads, the wolf-heads. Is that why you do not have pets?'

'I am not *brittle and hard*,' argued Layana, hotly. 'I am as soft and sweet as any woman.'

'Any woman in *this* world, yes, but where I come from the women are so soft they melt in the sun.'

He was teasing her now, but she took him seriously.

'Perhaps you'd better go back there,' she said, her little nose pointing haughtily in the air. 'Perhaps you'd better find another wife.'

He took her hands again. 'This one will suit me fine.'

She pulled away. 'No, no, I am as a stick of candy. You had better find one like a satin pillow.'

Soldier laughed, said he was joking with her, and begged her to forgive him for being frivolous. Soon he had her smiling again. But then they had to turn to serious business. An army was to be raised within the walls of the city. Soldier would help with that, even though he was the commander-in-chief of the mercenaries. There was no reason why the Red Pavilions should not help with the training. The Carthagans could not enter the city but the recruits could certainly leave it. They could be as well trained outside the walls as inside. 'I will get some of my sergeants-at-arms in the way of it, tomorrow.'

Thus the hard work began, of raising a citizens' army. It had been done many times before, of course, and with great success in some cases. In Soldier's old world the Athenians had taken up arms at a moment's notice and had repelled the Persian invader. The English, a nation of shopkeepers, had defeated foes. Kings often conscripted armies in order to fight with other kings or against other faiths. In Zamerkand, and Guthrum at large, they took to it with great gusto, having led rather boring lives until now.

Yet for every step taken forward, there is always some agent at work to take a man two steps back again. OmmullummO had his spies in the city and received his reports. He was not about to allow a few shopkeepers and farmers to destroy his plans to rule the world. He acted swiftly.

Soldier was himself training youths a few days later when a dark cloud appeared to the west.

'Look, Father, the rain is coming in!' cried Musket, still obsessed with his hound. 'I must get Catcher under cover.'

'Canines do not wash away in rain,' replied his father, studying the strange cloud. 'But if you wish to return to your mother while I continue attempting to make soldiers of these greensticks, do so.'

The cloud grew alarmingly large, very quickly, until it filled the whole horizon. Finally the youths let fall their wooden training swords and straw shields, to watch the cloud growing ever taller and wider. They saw, as it swept across the landscape and drew closer, that it was fashioned of many colours: a nebulous rainbow on the march. The drops of rain, for they could see now that it consisted of millions and millions of individual driplets, did not seem to be falling on the ground. There was no earthy smell such as precedes a heavy rainstorm; there was no thrumming or pit-a-pat sound as it hit the soil; there was no moistness in the air. Instead, as this multi-hued cloud hit the plains before the city, there was a sort of whirring noise which grew louder and louder, until Soldier cried, 'Run!'

Those who were not caught in idle wonderment at the sight of the richly painted swarm ran and hid inside the red pavilions. The rust tents of the Carthagans, already crammed with mercenary soldiers, were soon bursting at the seams. The tents proved no real protection, however, when the plague of humming-birds hit the encampment. Within a short while they were in shreds, torn to pieces by the sharp beaks of the millions of birds that swept through in a dense tidal wave, stabbing at everything and everyone with their tiny beaks. The birds seemed crazed for fluid, seeking anywhere to dip their small curved beaks. Men and women without armour to protect them were pecked to death, disappearing beneath a throng of tiny aviators with vibrating wings. Those who had some protection had to cover their eyes with one arm while thrashing with the other.

Some, because they were in training, wore full body armour or were thickly padded and wielded bamboo training staves. With visors down they were invulnerable to the plague of birds and swished with bloodied rods at the creatures which attacked them and their companions. Others, when they had gathered their wits, picked up bats, brooms and other broad-bladed instruments and went about beating the clouds of humming-birds, swatting them from comrades, and clearing spaces. As fast as they made holes in the cloud, more tiny birds arrived to fill them. Those partially covered, like Soldier, struggled into full armour, bleeding from a thousand cuts. Once protected, they too battled with the coloured hordes.

Soldier, immediately he was in his armour, swept the winged creatures from his son and rolled the boy in thick canvas. Then he snatched a blazing log from one of the camp fires and set about the enemy. It was a terrible business, scorching small birds, but any way of getting rid of the pests was legitimate. They were killing people by the minute. It took three hours of exhausting work to rid the area of the birds. Gradually people emerged from hiding places to find the ground littered ankle deep in little feathered bodies: corpses that looked innocuous now, except for their numbers. Balls of startlingly coloured fluff, with curved-needle beaks.

Unrolling Musket, he found the boy bleeding but alive; his puppy, all but smothered, was wriggling inside his doublet.

'Stay still, son. We will smear you with ointment. If you move, those cuts will bleed the faster. You are fine, don't worry. Once we get some balm on you, and bandages, I will seek your mother.'

The wounded, and there were many, were treated. The dead lay scattered about. Soldier estimated that one person out of every three who had been caught without protection had died. When he went back to the city he discovered that the same had happened to those caught in the open there. People in their houses who had closed the shutters quickly had survived. Those in the streets, unable to reach shelter, had died. Horses, dogs, cats, rats: carcasses lay everywhere amongst the corpses of humans. Fabric of any kind – balcony shades, stall covers, clothes on washing lines – all were in shreds. Trees, allotments and open stalls had been picked clean of fruit and vegetables, leaves and all. Even the lawns had been stripped of their grass. The wells were choked with humming-bird dead, the drainpipes, drains and gutters clogged with them. Blocked sewers overflowed.

A wailing went up from the citizens as they discovered the raw remains of loved ones caught outside in the storm of birds.

Soldier had his heart in his mouth when he climbed the steps of the Green Tower, only to discover that Layana and her servants had escaped death. The queen had been in the bath when the plague arrived. Some of the humming-birds had come up through the drain holes in the bath, but after the first several had popped into her water, she had quickly decided they were not pretty little creatures to be studied, and beat any more intruders to death with a twisted clout of wet towel. She admitted it was not a pleasant thing to have to do, but had realised that while one or two feathered fairies were a surprise, two dozen and more were a threat. Layana had a few peck-marks on her skin, but for the most part she had avoided being hurt.

'We have lost many citizens,' she said. 'I pity the dead. They died in a horrible fashion. It is OmmullummO who is responsible?'

'Without a doubt,' replied Soldier. 'None of the Seven Gods would send a plague like this. It has to be the rogue magus. His dark soul, or whatever it is that a wizard has in place of such a thing, is rejoicing at the moment, you can be sure. We were caught unawares. It will not happen again. We must be prepared for more plagues. In my world they usually came in tens.'

'Here the old parchments say they come in sevens.'

'Let us hope they stick to your lower figure rather than move up to mine,' said Soldier grimly. 'Now, I shall try to recall what the ancient people of my world had to suffer, what manner of plagues, so that we can prepare ourselves. I believe the first was blood, which filled the rivers and streams and so polluted the drinking waters. Then came lice – or was it frogs? It matters not which way around. I know flies were the fourth plague, followed by livestock, which died where it stood or lay. Then the horrible boils, and behind them the hail. Oh, I remember something like the humming-birds – the locusts – they arrived before a long period of darkness, during which no one could move. Finally, the most terrible of all, unthinkable even, the death of the firstborn, of people and cattle.'

'You were a good student, husband, to remember all those!'

'They were drummed into me by my nurse, who told me I would be visited by such if I were not good for her. She was an evil woman who gave me nightmares. She died of a fever herself, and then I was sorry for her and pitied her, but she made my childhood very dark with her warnings.'

'Fevers!' cried Layana. 'That is one of *our* plagues. We must call forth all the physicians and apothecaries, to make sure they are ready for any illnesses or diseases which sweep through the city. Oh, that foul wizard, he will cull our numbers until we are a feeble force, then send his armies to overwhelm us.'

Soldier said, 'Then we must make sure he does not succeed. We must be ready for the next plague, no matter what it is. Preparation.'

'But how do we prepare for *anything*?'

There was of course no way to plan for a million different insidious attacks on the city. The plague of humming-birds, ugly as it was at the time, was soon behind them. People had taken to killing every last one of the poor little creatures. A hovering thing was soon a dead thing. The feathered bodies were swept from the streets, the human dead were buried and mourned, and life went back to reasonable normality, given that a third of the population had gone. It was a devastating blow. Guthrumites could not withstand plagues of such ferocity if they were to follow in any great number.

Soldier awaited the call from IxonnoxI to gather together his army and march forth to do battle with Humbold.

One day in the month of Huskust, when the tendrils of an early-morning summer sun were curling around the world, Drissila rose and as was her wont went to the kitchens to oversee breakfast for the palace. The kitchen in the Palace of Wildflowers had an invention which was the envy of the whole civilised world: a water pump. There was a well below the stone flags of the kitchen floor which plunged to unfathomable depths, just as there were wells all over the city. A basin of bedrock ensured that Zamerkand never went without water. In fact, on occasion, the city was mildly flooded when the water levels rose too high and overflowed the wells. This had not happened in seventy years, the last time being a period when it had rained for forty days and forty nights: a relentless deluge.

So, on this fine Huskust morning, which seemed to be the prelude for one of the hottest days of the year, Drissila went to the pump to assist the kitchen staff in their daily tasks. She was not a lady-in-waiting who stood on her toes and bawled at the castle minions. Drissila was as beloved below stairs as she was above them, for having once been a slave, she knew what drudgery was and did her best to help alleviate it where she could.

'You get on with the oatcakes,' she told a young man, 'while I pump the water.'

In truth, she enjoyed using the pump. It was such an astonishing innovation it gave her a thrill to use it. She placed a bucket on the hook above the nozzle and began to work the arm up and down. At first the pump was hard to use, as it worked up a strength of suction, but once the liquid began to rise in the pipe it got easier. She listened to the gurgling as she worked with great satisfaction, awaiting that first sparkling gush of clear water cold from the caverns of the earth. Drissila looked forward to a cool drink, for there was nothing quite as refreshing as fresh well water.

But when it came she was totally astonished.

It was not clear at all, but opaque white.

One of the kitchen staff came over. 'Ma'am, it looks like some clay got into the well.'

How disappointing. Not clear at all, but murky.

'It appears to be whiter than kaolin,' said Drissila. 'It looks like *milk*.'

She sniffed the bucket. It *smelled* like milk. What was going on here?

'Shall I taste it?' said one of the girls. 'It is milk, you can see that.'

'No,' replied Drissila, sharply. 'It might be poisoned.'

She was not sure what was going on, but she had learned to be very cautious in a world full of magicians and poisoners. She went first into the gardens and then straight away to the royal boudoir. The royal couple stared, bleary-eyed, at the glass when Drissila presented them with it, wondering why they had been woken at the crack of dawn to view some milk.

'It came from the well,' insisted Drissila. 'There's no water in the palace. I went to the other well, in the gardens, and got a boy to draw me a bucket from there. It was the same. I thought it might be poisoned. You know, we had that plague of humming-birds, and now this.'

Soldier reached out for the glass. 'Here, let me see . . .' but in passing it to him, some was spilled on to the marble floor. One of the palace ratter cats who had accompanied Drissila up from the kitchens dashed forward and lapped at the spilt liquid. It seemed to be enjoying it. They watched in fascinated silence for some time. Once it had finished drinking from the pool on the tiles it began whining for more, looking up with appealing eyes at Soldier, who now held the glass.

Nothing further happened to the cat. It did not suddenly change its expression and roll over in agony, wailing. It did not creep off somewhere, as sick animals often do, to gnaw a bit of grass. There was no slow, lingering, dreamy death either, as one might get with certain numbing poisons that slink through the body and slow the heart to a gentle stop. In fact the cat was most disgusted that no more milk came its way and went off to look elsewhere for more of the same.

And there was plenty elsewhere.

'A plague of milk!' cried Soldier, once he was dressed and about. 'What in the name of the gods does OmmullummO think he's going to achieve with a plague of milk?'

Every well in the city was full of milk. Every basin of water left out overnight had turned to milk. Every drop of water, even sewer water and the canal which came from an underground river and swept down to the sea some miles away, was milk. There was milk to be had by the million gallon, gushing around the city.

At first the citizens were delighted. Here was something for free! A lovely, creamy, rich milk coming from their well. Why, they did not care if they never saw a drop of water again. Milky beverages, milky puddings, milky milk – it tasted nice and was full of life-preserving goodness. They could start selling it, to neighbouring countries, where cows were difficult to pasture. Desert countries, forested countries. Here was another source of wealth for an already wealthy city.

But of course that euphoria was short-lived.

On such a hot summer's day the milk soon turned sour. By noon the city was stinking. People walked the streets with their fingers pinching their noses, or gagged in their own dwellings. There is nothing quite so penetrating and disgusting as the smell of sour milk. And of course it was apparent that there was very little else to drink, so by the end of the first week of the plague of milk, people were separating the curds from the whey in order to drink the latter. Whey is a repellent liquid when one has to drink it straight.

Of course there were at first other sources of drink. There were those who had preserved fruit in jars, who could drink the juice. Those who had bottles of fairly innocuous medicine: placebos if you will. Those who had jars of oil. And, of course, those who had barrels of beer, who were continually drunk on alcohol. As for wine, the citizens of Zamerkand were much addicted to mead, and this fortified wine filled about half the city's cellars. Mead is a treacly drink and does not quench the thirst; it exacerbates it, and there were many who became sick through drinking such thick fluids. It was not long before the city had been drained of anything but whey, and in the process citizens died or became horribly ill. People could not wash, could not keep clean, and disease was rife throughout the land.

In the temples they prayed for rain.

At the end of the second week the rainclouds formed over the distant mountains and dutifully marched towards Zamerkand. The gods were answering hasty orisons with their usual benign alacrity. Storms swept in and drenched the streets. But when the rain came it fell as gentle milk from heaven and the streets were awash with white liquid. It was fresh, so there was drink to be had, but it was still milk. Once the rain had departed, the sun came out again, and the new milk turned as sour as the old.

Even magic is finite, however. One morning, after much suffering, it was water which came from the wells again. OmmullummO's spell over the water had finally dried up and blown away. There was great rejoicing in the streets. Everyone sent up prayers of thankfulness for the water.

'I never thought I'd be glad to see a bucket of water,' said Spagg, who had lived entirely on beer throughout the whole period of the plague. 'I never want to see a glass of ale again in my life.'

Spagg had spent this particular time in a drunken stupor and the whole episode was a haze. Such a condition was not entirely new to him, which was why he had survived. In his youth, now quite distant admittedly, he had followed much the same lifestyle. Now, though, his body ached, and his mouth was like a monkey's armpit. His head throbbed as it had never done before, his eyes feeling as if he had slept on them. He had grown a rough beard, was dishevelled like many through lack of washing, and stank like a hog. When he mentioned this, to Musket, the young prince shrugged and said, 'So, you always look and smell like a pig – don't you?'

'I take great offence at that!' cried Spagg, who despite being elevated in life was entirely jealous of the way a raven he had despised had suddenly changed into a prince. It did not seem fair. Why, the black bird had been a pest. He complained of as much to Soldier. 'Yes, a damn pest, you will admit that, Soldier. You called him such many times in the past. Yet he was raised up far more than I, a loyal friend of yourself and the queen. An upright citizen and a real *person*. Why should the pestilence of a member of the crow family be rewarded?'

'I don't think you're using the word pestilence correctly there, Spagg, but in any case, life is not fair. If it were, you would be sweeping the gutters with a worn broom. As it is, you're the Keeper of the Royal Purse – and by the way, I am calling in independent auditors at the end of the year, so be prepared to be investigated. I hope you're keeping good books.'

Spagg let out a cry of anguish. 'Why me? Why isn't the prince audited?' He went quiet for a moment. 'What does *audited* mean, anyway?'

Soldier told him, and Musket grinned when Spagg turned pale.

'He's been dipping his greasy hoof into the purse,' said the boy. 'Look how white he is around the gills! I told you his tailor's bill is more than Drissila gets for housekeeping – and she has to feed and clothe the whole palace. Oh, Spagg, you are a devil, aren't you?'

'I'm – I'm not feeling very well,' said Spagg. 'You shouldn't mock the afflicted.'

Now that they had had two plagues, the people were prepared for more. And they were not disappointed. OmmullummO was a mad wizard and there was no one more inventive. The next plague that landed on the city was a plague of lewdness. People started tearing off their clothes, walking around naked, and making love in public. Obscene gestures were freely used and spinsters and bachelors thought well beyond such behaviour in years and in status indulged as much as the young. There was no rape, nor involvement of children, nor did the plague affect everyone. It seemed to strike at about one in ten, so there were some to shock and many to be shocked.

Again, at first Soldier thought this was a fairly innocuous plague, one which would not greatly harm the city. But of course it involved people, and such behaviour arouses jealousy. There were many violent scenes on the streets and in the houses. Husbands and lovers were challenging men who accosted women they believed were exclusively theirs. Wives were murdering wayward husbands and lovers. The virgin became a bawd overnight. The shy, timid youth turned from a pleasant young man into a lascivious, leering creature who repelled. Even though only ten per cent of the population was struck with the lewdness plague, they dragged in another twenty to thirty per cent with their unnatural behaviour.

Again, the magic spell wore off, as time passed.

Next came the plague of wind. The wind arrived at night and by morning few could open their doors without letting a hurricane enter their quarters and tear them apart. Trees were uprooted, gibbets were torn from their foundations and carried their caged skeletons with them, night brands were whipped from their holders and thrown on to thatched roofs, which blazed the more when the flames were whipped up. Slates and tiles were stripped from balconies and rooftops and flung like razor-edged missiles to decapitate citizens who ventured out. And those who did go out were lifted from their feet, like dogs and chickens and other animals, and swirled about violently, sometimes to be flung hard against a wall. The air was full of danger – the air *was* the danger – and no one could venture abroad and be sure of returning whole to his or her house again.

'I've always hated the wind,' said Spagg, gloomily, having fought his way through the streets to the palace. 'I can't seen any point in it. Rain, yes, you need that to water the crops and to fill your drinking vessels. Sun? That helps things grow. Darkness is necessary to give the world a rest and let people have time to sleep away their daytime work. Snow and frost help to kill the bugs so the flowers can grow and flourish. But wind? It does nothing but bother you. It's a useless piece of weather.'

'For once we agree,' said Musket. 'You can take the wind and stuff it in a sheep's bladder, for all I care.'

'What about kite flying?' pointed out Soldier. 'What about sailing a ship? What about drying clothes on a washing line? Wind is good for something.'

'Not this kind of wind,' argued Spagg. 'Gentle winds, yes. Winds like this do nothing but destroy things.'

The winds lasted a week, roaring around like wild boys, ripping up fence posts and flinging them like javelins. The straight winds were bad enough, but the corkscrew winds were more destructive. These tornadoes screwed signposts into the ground and warped everything they touched. Spires were left twisted on their foundations. Flagpoles were doubled and whipped and snapped. A man might have his head turned back to front, if caught by one of these fearsome vortex winds.

Next came the plague of poisonous worms. They covered every piece of ground in the city. At first people picked them up to throw them in with the rubbish, but the toxins in them were so potent they were absorbed by the skin and the worms killed their victims that way. Spagg invented a worm picker-upper, like a giant pair of tweezers, and made a lot of money selling them to the frightened populace. The sacks of venomous worms were taken outside the city walls and burned in great wriggling heaps.

The sixth plague was the plague of twelve-headed rats. King rats, some called them. These ferocious creatures began to emerge from the sewers beneath the city and terrorise people in the streets. They were wheels of a dozen rodents, all joined at the rear, and they spun along the pavements and roads, snapping and snarling at everything they met. They would roll from rooftops and fall on the backs of humans or animals, to swiftly gnaw through their necks. They often hid in beds, and once the occupant was fast asleep would creep to the stomach and gnaw through it so quickly that death was sure to follow. Occasionally they managed to get into cupboards and when the door was opened flew into the face of the opener and tore it to shreds before that person could knock the king rat off.

'Here are friends of yours!' said Musket to Spagg. 'You should be able to charm them.'

'Don't be cheeky, boy,' Spagg cried. 'Rats are no friends of mine.'

'No friends, then — relations instead.'

Here at least was a tangible enemy that could be dealt with, however, and citizens soon armed themselves. They went about with blades and clubs, dispatching any king rats they found with savage blows. People were angry and upset and they took it out on the rats. Normally a plague lasted between seven and fourteen days, but the plague of rats was over in four days, the citizens having formed hunting parties and annihilated the rodents.

Having lived through six plagues, the people of Guthrum knew that a seventh would surely follow. Wizards' plagues *always* came in sevens. And the last one was always the worst. It almost always involved grief of some kind. One might, as Soldier had said, lose one's firstborn child. Or all the young mothers of a kingdom would become barren, so no new births were possible. Or young fathers would become sterile. So the people were quite fearful of what the last plague might be. Those who had predicted something awful were right. So were those who said it would be something no one had yet though of, for no one had. Those who hoped for a mild end to the list of plagues were disappointed. It came with horrible vengeance.

Every third citizen woke one morning to find that they were crippled: an essential part of their body, usually necessary to them to earn a living, was damaged in some way.

Musicians had gone deaf overnight.

Archers had gone blind.

The hands of scribes had withered.

The tongues of orators had shrivelled at the root.

Chefs and vintners had lost their sense of taste.

Perfumers their sense of smell.

Great male lovers were horrified to find a piece of seaweed between their legs in place of their previously formidable members.

Warriors had lost their muscle tone.

Slaughterhouse workers had become squeamish.

Actors had lost their charisma.

Seamstresses were all fingers and thumbs.

And so on and so forth.

Spagg arrived at the palace, his face of waxen hue. He took off his hat and wiped his sweaty brow with it. Soldier asked him what the matter was, while Musket sat on a windowsill, staring at Spagg, trying to guess what had changed about him. What, the boy thought, had Spagg ever been good at, anyway? What was necessary to him in his work, first as a hand-seller, and then as Keeper of the Royal Purse? It was a puzzle.

'Me?' squeaked Spagg, clearly out of sorts. 'I do not wish to say.'

'Clearly something has happened to you,' argued Layana. 'You look as if you have lost your nearest and dearest.'

'What about you?' asked Spagg in a husky voice. 'Is everyone here all right?'

The royal family and the servants at the palace had all escaped this latest plague. They did not know it but OmmullummO himself had once lived within its walls, a few hundred years previously when the wizard had been sane and an adviser to one of Layana's great-fathers. OmmullummO had at that time, as any prudent wizard would, erected a magical barrier, to protect himself against spells from other wizards. This barrier had never been removed and all in the palace had thus escaped from this cruel final plague, sent by that same ancient wizard.

'No one here has been touched, so far as we know,' replied Soldier. 'Though one of the gardeners who sleeps at his own home not far from here came to work with his affliction. Every plant he touches turns crisp and brown and dies within the minute. He used to have green fingers, but now they spell death to vegetation of any kind. We have lost our best vine this very morning, several orange bushes in the hothouse, and many other fine plants. Even if the gardener brushes against a single leaf, or touches the bloom of a fruit, the whole plant shrivels and droops to the earth.'

'Oh dear, oh dear,' muttered Spagg, sweating. 'What ever will come next?'

'Nothing, I think,' replied Soldier. 'Yet we still have not heard what ails you, Spagg. Come on, speak up. Are you touched?'

'I am – touched,' replied Spagg, clearly reluctant to speak of his ordeal, but seemingly unable not to.

'And what touches you?' asked Musket. 'Have you lost something we can't see?'

'Yes,' croaked Spagg.

'The mind is in a whirl,' Layana said. 'I'm not sure I want to know what it is, or I might be revolted.'

'The thing is,' whined Spagg, 'I cannot lie. I have lost my ability to swerve from the truth. I have to speak as it is or not at all. Sometimes I have no choice but to speak, and what I say must be truthful. It is quite terrible. This morning I had to tell a woman she was quite ugly, and a man that he had dropped his purse on the ground behind him, and when I passed a tax collector I informed him that I had not paid the proper amount for some thirty years now, and had no intention of paying it.' Spagg gulped and slapped his mouth for betraying him, before adding in a voice full of self-pity, 'Then I called him back and gave him my name and address!' His voice reached a high pitch as the horror of it all came out. 'I do not believe that hanged men's hands will make a body invisible, and what is more, I have been dipping my fingers into the royal purse.'

'There, I told you he had,' cried Musket, clapping in delight. 'See how his chapped lips quiver. Spagg cannot change his spots. He will always be a robber, no matter how high he is elevated. Bad man, Spagg.'

Everyone in the room was quiet for a moment. Ofao had entered during Spagg's speech and he was staring at the Keeper of the Royal Purse with tight lips. The queen hummed to herself, something she did when she was thinking very hard. Layana then waved a hand at her husband.

'Oh, you decide what to do with him,' she said. 'He's your ex-employer.'

Soldier nodded. He was not a vindictive man. At least, not towards anyone in this world. Were Spagg's name Drummond, things would have been different.

'Leave things as they are, for the moment. We have more

serious things to worry about than Spagg's light-fingered exercises. Spagg, you will put back every spinza you have taken. Think yourself lucky that we have a war impending, or you might have ended up on the gibbet . . .'

'All the gibbets were blown away,' pointed out Musket, 'but we still have one or two gallows left.'

'Thank you, son. The gallows then.'

'I'll – I'll try to be good,' said Spagg. 'I don't *want* to be, but I will try to be.'

'It would be better if you were.'

Out in the city the populace had been devastated by the seven plagues. They and the Carthagans had been seriously reduced in numbers of healthy fighting men and women. Soldier hoped that now the plagues had finished they could get down to properly training what was left of the army. He was at his desk, with Golgath and Velion, putting his plans to paper, when an envoy from Humbold arrived. The man was clearly in a state of terror. In this world, as in the last, enemy bearers of bad news often ended up in the wolf pit. This man was not to know that Soldier had never punished a messenger yet.

'You have something to tell me?' asked Soldier. 'Speak up. No harm will come to you. I know you are not the man responsible.'

'Sire,' said the envoy, down on one knee, 'my leader Humbold has the woman Uthellen in his hands. General Kaff captured her as she was making her way through a mountain pass. Lord Humbold wishes you to know that if the tide of the battle goes against him, she will surely die. That is what I have been ordered to tell you.'

Soldier seethed with anger, but hid his rage from the envoy.

He said, casually, 'Does he know that Uthellen is the mother of IxonnoxI, and that if anything happens to her and IxonnoxI becomes King Magus, he will suffer horrible torments for the rest of eternity?'

'He knows, sire, but he feels that once the battle has been lost there is nothing left for him but to take his revenge on the woman.'

'Then what more is there for me to say? The woman is nothing to us. Tell your master he can do with her as he pleases.'

Once the relieved envoy had left, Soldier slammed a mailed right fist down on the desk top, splitting the wood from top to bottom.

'Damn that coward's soul to hell,' he said, now white with fury. 'If I do nothing else in this life I will take his head from his body.'

Layana placed a hand on her husband's shoulder. She knew that he held Uthellen in great affection. Just as at one time, perhaps even now, she herself had had a softness in her soul for Kaff. She knew too that something had to be done to rescue Uthellen. Any distraction like this which took away her husband's focus from the main task was not good. He was the head of the combined forces of Guthrumites and Carthagans. Already they had been cut down to a third of their original size by the plagues. It was important that the commander-in-chief was left free of other concerns.

'We must get her back,' she said to Soldier. 'I will see to it.'

Soldier looked at her over his desk of charts and maps.

'I do not want you going yourself. I know you, Layana. You have a streak of fire in you.'

She smiled. 'I am too old for that sort of thing now. No, we will find someone we can trust. We must locate Uthellen and assist her escape. We need a flier. What about that pet dragon of yours?'

Soldier shook his head. 'We would not get him to understand what was needed. Besides, he is too large. He will be seen. We need a bird of some kind. Do you think there are any magicians in Zamerkand who would change themselves into an eagle or a hawk to carry out the task? Or could command a real bird to do our work?'

At that moment Soldier's scabbard sang out. Now that she had been reunited with Kutrama, her singing was not restricted to the approach of an enemy. She told him that an army was coming from the north-east of Zamerkand, but it was a friendly army. Its numbers were small and it was led by two kings. Soldier knew then that Guido and Sando, the twin kings of Bhantan, were here to join him in his fight. Bhantan and the two kings were beholden to Soldier and they never forsook him.

The youths of yesterday were now the young men of today. Sando entered first. The kings were identical but Soldier knew that Sando was the Rose King while Guido was the White King. Guido came in behind his brother. Both were smiling. They stretched forth their hands, one to shake the left hand of Soldier, the other the right.

'How very good to see you, Soldier,' said Sando.

'Soldier, how very good,' said Guido.

'So, that dastardly Humbold is up to his old tricks. We hated him, you know. He was very rude to us when we were exiles here.'

'Very rude.'

'Such a stupid man.'

'Incredibly stupid.'

'So,' said Sando, 'we have brought our small army to assist you in your battle.'

'Quite small,' said Guido, 'but volunteers all. We would

have come alone, Sando and I, if need be – but the army of Bhantan spoke as if with one voice and swore to accompany us. We could not have turned them back had we another army twice their number. Your good name is legend amongst them, Soldier. They speak it with awe. You are made famous in children's stories. We heard of the plagues that had been visited on this city and how your army had been sorely reduced. Thus we are come, to bolster your numbers with our meagre but willing force.'

Soldier said, 'You are most welcome, both of you – but I must warn you this battle will be a very bloody affair. If we lose . . .'

Sando replied, 'We must not lose – but we shall take precautions. We have drawn straws. Guido will lead our troops in the battle while I remain behind. This way one of us will survive no matter what happens. The rule of Bhantan will not be broken. Should we lose – an unthinkable scenario, given that right and justice is on our side – I shall return to my home country and crown the next twins in line, and thus retire to mourn my brother.'

'Very wise precautions,' said Layana, coming into the conversation. 'We are most grateful to Guido for his generalship.'

'Actually,' confessed Guido with a huge smile, 'I am the better scholar while Sando here is the warrior.' He laughed out loud, before adding, 'But we have drawn the straws. You cannot argue with the straws. The gods mean me to fight and Sando to remain with our people. Perhaps in the thick of the fighting there will be some need for a scholar? Some high encouraging rhetoric from an accomplished poet? A rallying call for our beleaguered troops in iambic pentameter? I am good at spontaneous verse, am I not, Sando? I turn a good rhyme and my work scans reasonably smoothly.'

'Brilliant. Absolutely brilliant, brother. You might wave your sword on high and cry, "My knights! For Sando, Guido and Bhantan, we fought this day and never ran. Within the greatest citadels of fame shall ring your each and every name."'

'That's not bad, Sando, not bad at all.'

'Of course, not as good a poetic rallying cry as you might compose, brother Guido, but thank you all the same.'

Despite the gravity of the overall situation, Soldier and Layana could not help smiling along with these two effervescent young men, whose fizzing, bubbling mood was infectious. Certainly they raised the spirits of all in the room, including the dour Spagg, who was convinced the end of the world was nigh. Musket was staring at them with a frankness which might have discomposed any other men but Sando and Guido.

'And who do we have here?' asked Sando, noticing the stare from the youngster. 'Is this a kitchen whelp?'

'I'm Prince Musket,' replied the boy, glowering. 'You remember me – I used to be dressed in black feathers.'

Guido shook his head. 'We don't remember any boy with a cloak of black feathers, do we, brother?'

'No, not at all.'

Musket said, 'I was the raven.'

Smiles appeared on the faces of the two kings like glass breaking.

Guido said, 'So! The bird? Yes, we remember you.'

Sando added, 'A nuisance bird, I recall. And now you are a nuisance boy?'

Soldier put his arm around Layana and informed the kings, 'Musket is now our adopted son.'

The kings nodded in approval.

'Excellent!'

'Wonderful!'

They playfully tugged an ear on each side of Musket's head, until he could not help grinning at them.

That evening the palace celebrated the arrival of the two kings. The presence of their troops on the battlefield could only be considered symbolic at the most, but Soldier was nevertheless heartened to have them with him. They numbered in the hundreds rather than the thousands, and they were nowhere near as well trained or imaginative as the Carthagans – the high walls of their small city had been their main protection throughout the centuries -- but they were willing. Soldier would rather have one willing warrior than ten coerced men. Many of those fighting for Humbold would not have the motivation of these few, these happy few, who had gathered themselves together and had offered themselves to Soldier in his hour of need.

The feast was not lavish, nor the entertainment spectacular, but everyone enjoyed themselves. It was a time for enjoyment. Soon enough would come the thunder of the captains and the fighting. Tonight there was time for honey cakes, wine and the dulcimer. Soldier gave them a song, slightly off-key, which made his dear wife wince in embarrassment. Guido was indeed brilliant at verse and proceeded to deliver a narrative poem about the journey of a man who set out to find a lost son in the wilderness. It was a sort of homage to Musket and his coming-of-human. When all the music and the poems and the stories ran dry, they talked of more serious matters.

'So,' explained Soldier to the twins, 'we are seeking a magician who can provide us with a hawk or eagle to seek out the whereabouts of Uthellen.'

'Will her son not help her?' asked Guido. 'He is a powerful wizard, after all.'

'IxonnoxI is committed to remaining impartial. He cannot intervene in this struggle and his mother is now part of that struggle. If he interferes, then OmmullummO will have the same right of interference and a war between the wizards will begin. The peripheral damage from such a war would be enough to destroy the whole earth – there would be quakes, floods, wind and fire sufficient to ruin the world and wipe out its population.'

'Well,' said Sando, 'we *may* be able to help you. We have a magician travelling with us, but he is very young.'

'How young?' asked Soldier, eagerly.

'Fifteen or sixteen. He's quite untried at the art of magic and is actually still technically an apprentice. His master died a year ago and he has been struggling with the Spelling Books ever since. A good scholar, one might say, but as a practitioner, who knows?'

'The boy is not a wizard of any kind?'

'Oh, no. Like his master, who died at only eighty-three years of age, he is human. A magician only – not witchboy, not wizard, not even a wixard from the plant world. As I say, a learned human youth, but with much eagerness to become a proper magician. Shall we send for him?'

'Please do,' Layana said. 'We have none left in Zamerkand who would assist us.'

The youth, whose name was Uluzizikia, but whom the twins called Luz, was duly sent for. He entered the room with a fastidious look on his face, but Soldier realised that was because the place smelled like a tavern, with tobacco smoke and alcohol fumes. It is never pleasant for a sober person to arrive clean and bright-minded at the dreg-end of a party.

'Young man,' said Soldier, 'sit with us. That's it, find a cushion. Will you take some wine?'

'I'd rather not, my lord, if you don't mind.'

'Not at all, and you can call me Soldier – everyone does.'

'Yes – Soldier.' The word did not come easily off the boy's tongue.

'Luz – may I call you Luz?'

'Of course.'

'Well then, Luz,' said Soldier, 'we need a magician. We have been told you are at the learning stage, but we have no other to turn to.'

The youth's face suddenly showed great eagerness. He sat bolt upright. His eyes lit up like lamps.

'Yes, sire – Soldier – yes, yes. I am a magician. Pay no heed to the fact that I am still learning. Magicians are learning their whole lives. We never have enough time to absorb all the knowledge of the art. I can assure you I have quite a lot at my disposal – all kinds of different spells – *fee faw fums*, mumbo jumbos, abraxas, love potions,' he glanced quickly at the queen here and added, 'though I see you have no need of the last of those, having a very beautiful wife whom you love to distraction.'

Layana smiled, and murmured, 'Hmmm, a flatterer too.'

'No, not really, Your Majesty, for I can read hearts as well as open books.'

Soldier nodded approvingly. 'The youth is certainly intelligent enough. Well, Luz, I shall tell you what we require. We want a bird of prey which can fly west and spy on Humbold, find out where Uthellen, the mother of IxonnoxI, is being held. Can you produce such a bird?'

'Better than that,' cried Luz, jumping to his feet, 'I can change into one and do the job myself!'

Layana frowned. 'This is a very dangerous quest, Luz.'

'It matters not. I laugh at danger. I spit in danger's eye.'

Guido said, 'He has the fire.'

Sando added, 'He *is* the fire.'

'Willingness is not really enough,' said Soldier, sighing. 'It is important to us that you return with the information we require, perhaps even the person we desire to be set free. You are young and enthusiastic, but we need a cool head here. What sort of bird would you recommend for the mission, supposing we let you go ahead with the transformation?'

'The best of all the birds for such a task – a sparrow,' cried the youth. His face became a little more serious as he viewed the expression around him, and the truth emerged. 'The fact is, I am only able to change myself into a sparrow. It is the only bird spell I have ever managed successfully. Hawks, falcons, eagles. They require a lot of experience. But a sparrow is a bird, after all, and a very tough little bird, with a lot of sand. They have to be, to survive in a world crowded with finches and their kind.'

The crestfallen looks of his audience were enough to tell Luz that he had to expand on this idea.

'Let me explain. Even though it is the only option open to me, it is a very *good* one. Had I the choice of the whole bird kingdom I might still say it was the best. Look, an eagle will arouse suspicion. They will be expecting an eagle. A hawk or falcon, the same. I know it is always wise to send a bird of prey, which can protect itself against other predators. A creature which will not be hunted for its meat. But think how *common* it is, how clichéd, to use a raptor for a spy. Now, a *sparrow*, why, there are so many of them, they blend right into the landscape. A dusty little brown sparrow is anonymous, invisible, dismissed with a blink of the eye. As a sparrow I will be safe from detection, I am sure. I will gather information without arousing suspicion, and return forthwith with the woman.'

'Luz has a point,' said Sando.

'A very keen point,' said Guido.

Soldier was not so sure. 'You are willing to risk your life as a sparrow?' he asked. 'There are sparrowhawks out there.'

'There are many, many sparrows – the world is littered with sparrows. I would be very unlucky to lose my life to a sparrowhawk.'

'So be it,' said Soldier. 'We accept your offer with gratitude.'

Chapter Nine

A sparrow hedgehopped over the landscape. It was a wary little creature, not given to settling for long in any one place, even though it was tired. Exhausted would be a better word. The small bird had been on the wing continually, stopping only for a few moments every now and then, since the break of day. Whenever it fell in with other sparrows they tended to look at it with suspicion, as if it did not belong among their number. Some even tried to squabble with it, though it avoided confrontations where it could.

There were falcons and eagles in the sky, but thankfully no accipiters in the form of sparrowhawks. Luz, for it was he in the disguise of the sparrow, knew what kind of country accipiters preferred, and steered clear of such. This tended to be forested land, or at least land with a goodly cover of trees. Luz went for open country, giving copses and woodland a wide berth. Falcons and eagles were not interested in such small prey as sparrows: they were after hares and even small deer. Luz also knew sparrowhawks by sight: they tended to have rounder wings than buzzards, harriers and kites, and often wore rufous feathers on the underside.

One keen eye, then, on the type of countryside through which he was flying, the other on the lookout for predators.

Once indeed he did have to hole up in the hollow of a blasted oak. A squirrel in residence objected to having him there, but Luz had seen a goshawk, a cousin of the sparrowhawk, and was taking no chances. When the squirrel tried to intimidate him, Luz yelled in the loudest voice his sparrow throat would give him, 'Get away from me, you lunk!' The squirrel had never, of course, heard a bird use a human voice. It almost swallowed its tail in fright and retreated to the back of the hole. Once the goshawk had gone, Luz thanked the squirrel and left it chattering in fear.

One of the problems which Luz had ahead of him was the fact that he only had a vague idea where to look for Uthellen. He knew she would be with a large army of warriors, but the hills and mountains in which those warriors chose to hide were vast. The little bird took several days locating the army, flying into chasms and out of tree-choked gorges, narrowly missing death twice when he ran into goshawks and sparrowhawks.

But nothing daunted, he kept searching, stopping to gain energy on seeds and fruits, and to drink from the mountain streams. On the fifth day of the second week he found them, in a series of valleys to the north of some high crags. On the fringe of the mighty army a soldier was feeding birds with breadcrumbs. By this time Luz was extremely hungry, having eaten nothing for twenty-four hours. He stooped to get amongst the finches that were gobbling up the crumbs.

'Gotcha!' cried the soldier inexplicably.

Suddenly Luz was one of many small birds struggling in the fine meshes of a net. His dusty little wings thrashed and he pecked and clawed at the netting, to little avail. He was well and truly caught. A hand came down and held him, carefully picking him from the folds of his trap. Then he was transferred to a wire cage where a dozen other birds were chattering senselessly, or attacking the thin bars of their prison. Luz was devastated. He had been given a task to do by Soldier and he had failed. Here he was now, in the hands of the enemy, a caged bird, perhaps for life.

The cage was hoisted aloft by a grubby hand.

'Look what I got for supper!'

Several other soldiers were present now.

'That scrawny bunch of finches? They won't even make a decent pie for one man, let alone a dozen.'

'Better than nothing!' argued Luz's captor.

'No, I'd rather eat nothing than a bunch of small splintery bones covered in feathers.'

The soldier took umbrage and went to look elsewhere.

'Would you like to buy these?'

'What for?' asked a burly woman.

'To eat, of course.'

'I wouldn't have 'em if you gave 'em away.'

'Well, for pets then – they make nice pets.'

'Do they? They don't sing, they don't dance, they don't do anything except chatter incessantly. No thanks. Find another fool, this one's busy washing clothes.'

Luz began to hope that he was going to be set free, but a knight with a falcon on his wrist came forward.

'I'll give you two spinza for that bunch.'

The soldier said, 'Only two?'

'More than fair.'

'Oh, all right then.'

The cage was transferred. The new owner of Luz and his

mindless companions strode off swinging his prize. He went into a tent. There, on a perch, was a hunting hawk.

'Supper, Jezebel,' said the knight, showing the hawk the cage full of twittering balls of fluff. 'Nice change from mice, eh?'

Now the other finches went berserk.

A dwarf came into the tent and stared at the cage.

'What have you got there, Rowlf?'

'Some small birds for my hawk.'

'You have to be careful of those,' warned the stocky dwarf, 'they often carry worms. You don't want Jezebel to get worms, do you? She'll be shitting threads by the morning.'

The cage was held aloft again as Rowlf studied the birds darting around madly within.

'Worms?'

'They pick them up from the dirt, sparrows do. Horrid little creatures really,' said the dwarf. 'Always down in the dust amongst the foul things of the earth. I'd hold off on those, if I were you.'

'All right,' growled the disappointed Rowlf, 'I will.'

The hawk began to cry out plaintively now.

'*Leek-keh-leek!*' it cried. '*Keh-keh-leek!*'

'I'm sorry, Jezebel, we don't want to give you tummy ache. Here, Skartt, you take the cage. I'll take Jezebel for a little hunt. Let's see if we can get her some mouse brains for her supper instead.'

The hawk reluctantly went up on to Rowlf's wrist, still eyeing the finches greedily. Rowlf slipped a red velvet hood over her head, tied jesses and bells to her legs, and removed her. Luz and his companions heaved a sigh of relief. Rowlf left the tent, thick glove preventing Jezebel from taking out her disappointment and wrath on his bare skin.

Once the knight and his hawk were out of the tent the dwarf opened the cage door, thrust in a stubby-fingered hand, snatched a finch, and crammed it into his mouth to crunch. He chewed it for some few minutes while Luz looked on in horror. Then he swallowed and the hand came in again to grab Luz. Luz avoided the grubby fingers. Another sparrow wasn't so lucky. He went out squawking blue murder, pecking at the hard-skinned hands of Scartt, only to end up in that red-black hole full of thick, even teeth where his predecessor had gone.

Scartt swallowed the second bird, then delved for a third. A voice called him angrily from outside. Rowlf again. The knight wanted his dwarf to help him into the saddle of his mare. Scartt stopped, eyed the fly of the tent, counted the sparrows, muttering, 'He an't good at arithmetic – he'll never miss those two,' and abandoned the cage to join his master.

The cage door had been left open. Luz flew for it joyfully, but another bird beat him to it, blindly thrashing to get out. The door opened inward and the second bird managed somehow to shut it. A small but determined pin fell into place, locking them all in once more.

'You bloody dolt!' cried Luz at the stupid finch. 'You've got the brains of a cane fly.'

But of course the creature did not answer him. It was actually a dolt with the brains of a bird. Luz went to the door while the others flew hysterically around the cage, fluttering hopelessly at the bars. He did not want to join the first two birds in Scartt's mouth, once the dwarf had helped his master on to his horse. It was important to get out and free before he returned.

Luz squeezed his head through the bars and pecked at the

locking pin. On the third try he managed to get it in his beak. He jerked his head up. The pin flew out. Then he pulled the door open. The birds flew out. Luz flew out. The other birds panicked and spent the next few minutes battering their heads and wings against canvas. Scartt came back and yelled, seeing all his master's birds had been set free. He waved his small thick arms, swatting at them. Luz managed to avoid him and fly out of the tent opening.

Luz flew to a high point on a crag and settled there, his little heart pounding in his chest. Being a sparrow wasn't a great deal of fun. There was a lot of unseen danger around. He stayed where he was, knowing if he perched very still he would not be seen, for he was the same colour as the limestone rocks in which he was nestled. When evening came around he dropped down to a sandy place and changed back into a man.

'Hello, what are you doing here?'

A young female, dusky, big brown eyes with long lashes, regarded him with an amused expression on her face. She seemed to be in the process of removing her bodice.

When in doubt, thought Luz, attack.

'I'm entitled to be here, I think,' he said, haughtily. 'What are *you* doing here?'

'This is where the women wash and change,' she replied, pointing to the pool half-hidden behind the bushes. The cool waters held three other maidens, all of them nude. 'You know that, you naughty look-on. We've caught you watching us, haven't we?'

'Oh?' cried Luz, blushing. 'I – I'm sorry . . .'

'Don't be sorry, sweetheart,' purred the young woman. 'No one can see us, can they, girls?'

'No,' cried the other three, giggling. They splashed him

playfully, one of them adding, 'And my husband would kill you if they could.'

'Oh, oh,' cried Luz. He ran from that place out into the camp, not stopping to answer a gruff cry from a man waiting with a towel in his hands. Luz kept on going, dodging between camp fires, until he had put a good deal of ground between himself and the women's washing pool. Once he felt he was safe he stopped and took his breath.

No one was taking any notice of him. It was twilight and most were lighting lamps or taking meals. The army around him was vast. He wondered how he was going to find Uthellen without arousing suspicions. If he started asking questions he might find himself arrested. It was probably doubtful anyway that the ordinary soldier would know of the existence of Uthellen in the camp. Best just to wander around at first, see what was to be seen, and gauge the opportunities.

Luz did just that, strolling around as if going somewhere specific but not in any hurry to arrive, and taking in the sights. Those around camp fires and outside tents said good evening to him and he replied in kind. It was difficult to realise this was an enemy army, they all seemed so friendly. But then armies everywhere were not formed of bad people. They tended to be misguided, misinformed and misled, but very often no more evil, or good, than those they fought against. The politicians who took them into battle, the leaders, were the ones who carried the moral responsibility. It was they who were evil or good. For the most part the actual fighters would just as soon go home and plough their fields or bake their bread.

Luz came up short when he ran into a man with blue eyes.

The man stared at him, turning the full force of those blue

orbs on to the startled magician. Luz had only ever seen such eyes in the head of Soldier, but these were different. These carried such an intense look of anger and hatred they would have withered grapes on the vine.

'What in dog's hell are you staring at?' growled the man. 'Never seen blue eyes before, eh?'

'No,' gulped Luz.

'Well, now you have, so pass on – you're in my way.'

'Sorry, sir,' Luz said, and got out of his way.

The blue-eyed man, an extremely strong-limbed and powerful-looking individual, walked on. His fists were like large hammers. His head was a boulder with a wide expanse of shining forehead. The nose was heavy and ridged. And finally, those eyes. Luz would have kissed the man's feet had he asked him to, he was in such fear of arousing the other's displeasure. A blow from one of those fists would have crushed Luz's skull like a watermelon. The magician moved on, more quickly than before.

Luz wandered for two hours before he finally heard someone address Humbold by name. Fearfully, Luz remained at the back of the tent, out of sight of the doorway sentry, hoping to hear something to his advantage. But Humbold did not speak of Uthellen and though Luz strained hard to hear, there was no female voice coming from the tent.

Then, about midnight, the front tent flap was thrown open and Humbold stepped out into the moonlight. Luz remained stock still in the shadow of the tent as Humbold drew in some breaths of air. There was a fire in the tent and no doubt his lungs were smoky. Humbold looked up at the stars and ran a grizzled hand through his long grey locks. From his stance he looked aged, bent and weary, but Luz had no sympathy for the tyrant who had killed so many of his own people without compunction or remorse. Tyrants do not mellow with age, they grow more bitter and vicious. They harden in their views and excel themselves at cruelty. This tired old man still had the will to execute and torture. He did not need the strength to wield the axe or the red-hot iron. All he needed to do was whisper into the ears of strong, able men.

Humbold shambled off, in the direction of some caves.

Luz followed him, at a distance. He watched as Humbold entered one particular cave, guarded at the entrance by a dozen thick-set men. Unable to follow him inside, Luz remained where he was until the tyrant emerged again.

Luz had to get into that cave. It was time to take on the form of a sparrow again. He spoke the words which infused the corporeal with powers of transmogrification.

Hopping towards the entrance, he hoped to get past the guards' legs without being seen. He knew if he took to the air and tried to fly in they would be suspicious: sparrows did not fly around at night. If they thought he was a bat they would kill him anyway. Bats were feared creatures, being more often witches than flying rodents. So Luz crept between their legs. A spear was raised just as he was passing beneath the bulky creatures and the butt-end slammed down on the dirt floor. But the guard was not aiming at him. It was simply the restless gesture, one born of frustration, of a sentry who should have been relieved from his post five minutes ago.

Once inside the cave, Luz flew. It was not long before he came to a cavern. There, in this dimly lit chamber, sitting amongst stalagmites, he could see a middle-aged woman whom he guessed was Uthellen. She was alone resting on a blanket under the soft glow of an agate lamp. There was no way out of the cave which did not go past a dozen well-armed men, so there had apparently been no need to shackle her. He changed back into a man in the shadows and then approached her.

'Uthellen?' he said softly. 'Mother of the wizard IxonnoxI?'

'I am she,' replied Uthellen, looking up. 'Who are you?'

'A magician, sent by Soldier. I have flown here as a sparrow, but I did not want to alarm you by appearing before you in that form.'

She seemed amused. 'Alarm *me*? The mother of a wizard?'

He nodded. 'I see what you mean. You must have seen all sorts of magic, far more wonderful than mine. But we must be busy. I have come to rescue you and take you back to Zamerkand. That is, you'll have to get there yourself, but I'll help you. I – I'm afraid I'm not much of a magician . . .'

'You are very young,' she agreed.

'Yes, I am. But,' said Luz, 'I do have the spell of sparrows. I can change us both into that particular type of finch. Finches are not really able to protect themselves, but they are the most numerous family of birds in the world. You can get lost amongst finches. Will you do it?'

'How do I know I can trust you?'

'Oh, yes, as to that I have something to tell you, from Soldier. He said only you and he knew of this. I shall repeat what he said, so that you know I am from him . . .' Luz spoke words which awakened an old memory in the mind of the woman.

She stood up, ready to leave. 'Yes, you are Soldier's magician. Ah, Soldier,' she said, wistfully, 'he has never let me down yet – and how is his wife, the Queen Layana?'

'She is well.'

'Ah, yes – good.'

Luz, being privy to that memory he had just aroused in this lovely mature woman, was vaguely aware that he might hold a secret which would initiate a royal divorce. There was an implication only, which might have had deeper meaning, but in any case Luz as a magician was bound to discretion, to confidentiality. It would be better to consign that knowledge to the dusty regions of his brain, that mental attic where all the junk of childhood was stored.

'Are you ready then, my lady?'

'Do the deed, young man.'

Escape from confinement was always more effective during twilight, when human minds were muddled and moving shadows confused them. The two sparrows flew out of the cave. As bad fortune would have it, Humbold was just entering, coming to check on his prisoner. The sparrows flew over his head. Humbold looked up, and cursed, knowing that something was badly amiss. He called loudly to the camp, to an ancient old witch hunched over a fire. This witch went by the name of Skegnatch and she was the cook in a regiment of witches in Humbold's army. Her comrades were at that moment clustered in covens, awaiting the evening meal of mice brains and lizard's entrails. Skegnatch left her boiling pot.

'I see them, master!' she screeched. 'I am death in feathers!'

Within seconds Skegnatch was a sparrowhawk, vaulting the air after the climbing sparrows. Her troops came out of their tents, shrieking encouragement to their cook. This battalion of witches was an ugly and terrible sight to the two sparrows ascending to the heavens. Luz wondered for one horrible moment whether they were all going to change into hawks and join their cook in the hunt, but it seemed they trusted her to carry out the deed on her own. Knowledge of a witch's pride – for they are vain to the point of blindness – stopped them joining her. Skegnatch was known for her venomous anger and none of them risked it here. Had she called on them, of course, they would have flocked to her immediately. But she would not deign to lower herself by asking for assistance.

Luz and Uthellen saw her coming. They saw the flash of her wings as she came up as if shot from a catapult. There would be no escaping her if they remained clear targets in the blue, so both fell quickly to earth, to be amongst the sparrows that were scattered throughout the rocky valleys and gullies below. The sparrowhawk followed, weaving amongst the tall monoliths, the needles of rock. She kept them in sight, ready to sweep in and strike with talons which could kill with one blow.

'You go on,' said Luz, frantically. 'I'll draw her away.'

Uthellen saw him turn and settle by a mossy stone while she went on to a stream where sparrows were drinking and bathing. She settled amongst the flock. Looking back she saw a single sparrow rise from the ground behind her, only to be struck hard by a thunderbolt bird from the hawk world. The little body fell instantly to the ground, stone dead. Uthellen let out a cry of despair. Poor Luz! He had given his life to save her own. At that moment the flock around her rose in panic. They too had seen the hawk and they were eager to get out of range of its sharp eyes.

Uthellen rose with them, as did other types of finches which covered the bushes and shrubs, the small trees of the mountain valley. The air was full of them, hundreds of darting birds. In came the hawk, now confused by numbers. She swept this way and that, trying to decide which sparrow to strike, finally by necessity fixing on one only. Just as a cheetah needs to pick out one antelope, so a sparrowhawk has to make a choice amongst the confusion of small birds that scatter from the flight path. A bird was struck, the hawk dived with it, hoping for the right kill.

It would have been a lucky sparrowhawk that managed to kill one specific sparrow in hundreds. Uthellen got away safely amongst the zipping finches that sought to put distance between themselves and the rogue hawk. Over open country she flew, staying close to the ground, fearful not only of the witch sent after her, but of other hawks too. She had no time then to grieve for the youth who had saved her, but later the sorrow would come.

When Uthellen finally reached Zamerkand, she flew straight to the Green Tower's window, which she entered. Then she began flying through the palace, looking for Soldier. She was first noticed by Ofao, who was incensed that a bird had got into the building.

'Who left that window open? Was it you, Drissila?' Ofao got hold of a curtain pole and began chasing the sparrow. 'Stay still, little creature, while I flatten you with my stick . . .'

Up and down the stairs went the chase. Drissila then joined in, wielding a broom. The poor beleaguered bird flew along corridors, into rooms, through courtyards, until finally it was exhausted. It settled on a garden wall to catch its breath, while Ofao sneaked up under cover of a fountain and raised his pole.

'Hold there!'

The voice came from the arbour walk, where Soldier and Layana were taking a stroll.

Ofao put a frustrated finger to his lips and pointed to the bird, before raising the pole again.

'I said HOLD!' cried Soldier, striding forward. 'I do not want that bird harmed, Ofao.'

'But it's been in the palace all morning, giving us a merry chase.'

'First let me inspect it.'

Ofao snorted. 'You don't expect it to sit still while you do that, do you?'

But Uthellen did remain immobile. Unfortunately, she could not speak in the way that Luz had spoken when he was a bird, for she was not a magician and had no powers. Nor could she change herself back into a woman again. She simply waited for Soldier to pick her up and stare at her markings.

'This is not Luz,' said Soldier. 'I remember distinctly that he had a dark brown patch on his neck. This bird has no such markings.'

Uthellen felt very vulnerable in Soldier's firm grip. Would he now just squeeze and crush her little form? Who has any use for a sparrow?

Soldier continued to study her, though, as Layana said, 'Perhaps the magician has changed yet again, from bird to human and back again? Who knows whether his identity was discovered by Humbold? Can you speak, bird? If you are Luz, peck the tip of Soldier's thumb.'

Uthellen pecked his thumb, not because she believed she was Luz, but because there would be no second chances. At that moment Sando and Guido entered the courtyard. They went running over to Soldier.

'Is it Luz?' asked Guido.

'Is he back?' said Sando.

Soldier sighed, wearily. 'Well, I think we have the bird, but to what end? He cannot seem to change himself back again. I know of no other magicians in the city who can do it.'

Guido cried, 'We have no more Bhantan magicians to hand.'

Sando added, 'You hold the very last of them in your fingers.'

They were about to retire to the palace with the little bird when a flock of the creatures flew into the courtyard. The sparrows landed on the boxed myrtle bushes that hedged the fountain. They squabbled there, chattering at one another, one or two of them going to the fountain to bathe in the water. Suddenly one of these newcomers detached itself from the others and flew straight at Soldier. It landed first on his shoulder, then flew down to the path at his side. Finally it blossomed into a young man.

'Luz!' cried the twins, simultaneously. 'You are back!'

Soldier stared at the sparrow he held in his fist.

'Ah, fooled again, eh?' he murmured, and tossed the little creature towards the fountain, where it was about to be set on by a dozen of its kind when it too blossomed, but this time into a woman.

'Uthellen?' cried Soldier.

'It is I,' replied the woman. 'Soldier, I am eternally grateful to you, and to Luz, for rescuing me.'

'And to us,' said Sando.

'He was our magician,' continued Guido.

'Yes, thank you all.' She turned and saw Layana, just the other side of the fountain. 'And especially to you,' she added quietly, curtsying to the queen.

Soldier wondered why Uthellen should thank his wife, who had had very little to do with her escape, but guessed it was something to do with the fact that they were both women.

The rest of them, the men, went ahead to order a feast of welcome for the mother of IxonnoxI, while Layana took her to the quarters that had been prepared for her. The two ladies appeared later on, as the men were sitting down, meat already on their plates. They all listened to Luz's story, of how he had flown to Humbold's camp and had narrowly escaped death or detection several times.

'Finally,' said Luz, 'there was our encounter with the witch who had changed herself into a sparrowhawk. I expect Uthellen thought I had been caught there, did you not, my lady?'

'I did indeed,' said Uthellen, smiling. 'I saw you fall.'

''Twas another!' cried Luz, already the worse for the drink, being a youth who had rarely imbibed an alcoholic beverage before. 'Some sacrificial sparrow flew between me and the raptor bird. She struck at him instead and he dropped like a pebble into a well. Saved my life. Poor little bastard. Poor little dusty brown orphan. Saved Luz's life. Dropped like a stone . . .'

Luz started blubbing here, as he grieved for the small finch that had been his saviour, had given its life for his. The young magician, still suffering the trauma of the expedition, fell into a maudlin state. 'This is the greatest sacrifice of all, that one sparrow should give his life for another.' He sobbed again, wiping away his tears with the back of his sleeve.

Then anger followed and he began to rant and rave about witches.

'They ought not to be allowed on the earth!' he yelled at Guido, as if it were the fault of that king that there were such creatures in the world. 'They ought to be drowned at birth like litters of curs.'

'I agree,' said Guido soberly. 'But I have no authority to

carry out these drownings, so please do not clutch at my sleeve, young Luz. Remove your fingers, or I will prise them open with my knife.'

'Yet they live! They cluster together horribly in times of war. They form their ugly regiments . . .'

Sando said, 'Wizards can be ugly too. I once knew . . .'

But Luz would not be deterred from his drunken speech. 'Not like witches, eh, King Guido?' He finally let go of his monarch's sleeve. 'Witches are *despicable*. Witches are the gugliest – the lugliest – well, I tell you, King Sando, they are *horrible*. Horrible. I can honestly say I have never met one nice witch, let alone a regiment of 'em. 'Scuse me.'

The youth then rose majestically from the table, walked unsteadily but regally to the window, and was sick, out and down into the street. Someone yelled up at him from below. He looked down haughtily on his victim and wiped his mouth on his sleeve. 'Pardon!' he said.

'I think someone ought to put the young man to bed,' said Soldier. 'Ofao?'

'Yes, sire.'

'And Ofao . . .'

'Yes, sire?'

'You know, don't you?'

'Yes, sire. I know. I am restraint itself, sire.'

The gentle servant put his arm around the magician and helped him from the room. Luz complained all the way that he was perfectly capable of walking by himself, but when he was let go he fell in a heap on the floor. Ofao helped him regain his legs again and then they were gone, through the doorway and out into the passage. For a few minutes the sound of Luz arguing with Ofao drifted back, then there was silence.

Ofao returned and nodded to the group. 'Sleeping like a babe,' he informed them.

A herald from the Imperial Guard came into the room.

'Your Majesty,' he said, kneeling before the queen, 'an envoy from the beast-people has arrived. He is at the gate. A dog-head.'

Layana's look was cold. 'Send him away.'

'No, wait,' said Soldier. 'Herald, what is the creature's name?'

'He calls himself Wo.'

'Layana,' Soldier said, 'this is the sword-finder who was responsible for the return of Kutrama to my side. I think we should hear what he has to say.'

Layana, the memory of having been savagely attacked and scarred by a dog-head returned, was sorely afraid of the creatures. She not only feared them, she detested the very sight of them. It was true her husband had had dealings with this particular beast-person, but there were precedents.

'No beast-person has ever been within these walls,' she told him. 'It would be against all tradition.'

'Sometimes tradition should be broken.'

Layana said, quite reasonably, 'Why can't one of us go out there to him, rather than let him in here?'

'That would quite ill-mannered,' spake Soldier softly in her ear, 'and not at all in the *tradition* of your family. We must invite him in and treat him with great hospitality, as we would any other envoy. I'm sorry, my darling, for I know you have a great antipathy towards these creatures – and I fully understand why – but it is surely time to begin building bridges. You need say nothing to Wo. I shall do the talking. Perhaps you would like to leave us?'

'No, no. I shall stay. All right, send the dog-head to us. We shall hear what he has to say.'

Uthellen looked approvingly at Soldier.

Sando and Guido simply looked at one another with raised eyebrows.

In a short while a dog-person stood before Layana and her husband, while the rest of the court remained in attendance.

'Yes?' asked Layana, curtly, unable to disguise a tremor in her voice. 'You wished to speak with us?'

Soldier said, getting up and offering his place at the table, 'Would you like to drink before you speak? You must be parched from your journey. Perhaps you would like to eat at the same time?'

'A drink, yes, thank you, Soldier,' said the visitor, his canine jaws forming the words very carefully, his wolfen eyes not leaving the queen. 'The journey has been dusty and I am indeed very thirsty.'

He sat down in Soldier's place next to the queen. There, to the amusement of the rest of the court, he poured some water from a goblet into a shallow dish and proceeded to lap it up with his long dog's tongue. Then he wiped his jaws with the back of his hand. Layana shuddered, violently, and gathered up her voluminous dress around her. The dog-head looked at her again, then around the table, and hung his head in shame, knowing they had been expecting him to drink from the cup.

'I am unable to use these goblet devices,' he said. 'They are not designed for the jaws of a beast.'

'My good friend Wo,' Soldier said, breaking the silence and glaring at the rest of the people present, 'you have no need to explain anything to us. You have your ways, which are as valid as ours. Forgive our bad manners in seeming to stare.

It is simply a fact that we have forgotten how to honour a guest, having been through war and plague. Now that you have quenched your thirst, my dear wife has not yet had the pleasure of meeting you.'

Layana conquered the horror that had been mounting within her.

'No – that is to say – I have not yet had the pleasure.'

'Lady queen,' rumbled Wo, with a friendly growl, 'I am greatly glad to be permitted inside these walls. I know it must be centuries since a barbarian was allowed to enter within, if they ever have at all. We have been enemies for so long. The killing between us has been endless and wasteful of life on both sides. But now your husband has stretched forth his hand across the divide. And I have grasped it. Strange as it may seem, we are now friends. Not master and dog, not alpha leader and human follower, but man and beast-person as equals. Soldier killed one who was close to me in kin, but one who did you a personal harm. I am sorry for both, but all that is now in the past.' He seemed to be coming to the crux of the reason for his visit. 'You are now at war with another, with the enemy from within, Chancellor Humbold. I have heard your numbers have been culled by various methods and I have brought myself, some of my warriors and a plan to assist you in your goal.'

Layana said, 'We would be pleased to hear the plan.'

Wo nodded, then snapped his fingers. Through the doorway came three trolls, ugly little creatures with sickly-white skin, all lumps and bumps. Clearly they were troglodytes, beings whose forms had seen but little of the sun and fresh air. Their heads seemed far too large for their bodies and lolled first this way, then that, as they walked towards the table. Their small, stocky bodies were round, but with muscle not with fat. Unlike Wo, they did not need inviting to the table. They pushed their way on to a bench, and grabbed beakers of wine to swill down, slaking their thirst. Then they looked at Wo and nodded in unison.

'These trolls,' said Wo, 'have a dirt kingdom below our feet. If you did but know it, the whole of Guthrum has passages beneath the surface, with chambers dug out in the fashion of moles. It is there the trolls live and work, bothering no one, eating mostly grubs and worms, drinking from underground streams. They are not refined creatures like you and me,' said Wo, with a flash of an ironic dog-grin, 'but rough-and-ready characters, who take what they need from the subterranean natural world. It is true they sometimes — on feast days — spit-roast a badger, but for the most part they do not bother the other underground creatures, the rabbits, moles and occasional fox. They suck what they can from the soil and leave the rest to its own.'

Layana said, 'We are set to be well disposed towards these trolls, dog-headed Wo, if you would get to the point.'

'Yes, yes, Lady Queen — I'm sorry, I am being lengthy. What I am going to suggest is that our army — I say *our* army, because my warriors and I would wish to join you — can use the tunnels of the trolls to be in any appointed place, then burst forth and surprise the enemy. Thus there would be compensation for our lack of numbers. The foe would be numerous, but confused and divided by our sudden attack. We could come up amongst them, from beneath the very ground on which they tread. We could prevail through the very stunningness of our plan, and conquer, the gods willing.'

Layana looked at Soldier. Soldier felt a great excitement.

'This is a marvellous scheme,' he said. 'Layana, did you know of the existence of the troll underground world?'

'No, my husband. We always believed they lived in caves in the mountains, far from here.'

'Well we did, we did,' said one of the trolls, his mouth full of cake and showering crumbs, 'but we *breed* excessively. We make children faster than rabbits make kittens. We had to expand. Make room. Make room.'

'Expand,' said another, reaching for a sweetmeat. 'We spread out, digging, digging, digging, telling no one.'

'We had to go very deep,' said the third, 'to keep our secret safe from discovery. Otherwise we would have been heard, or your houses would have dropped into our chambers beneath, disturbing our sleep.'

'Interrupting our *breeding*,' giggled the first.

The images this threw up were too much for some of the listeners, who turned away in disgust at the thought of these maggoty creatures making love below the very rooms where they ate, slept and made love themselves.

'And you are willing to let us use your tunnels and chambers?' asked Soldier of the trolls. 'Who is your king? Do we need to formally ask him?'

'Me, I'm the king,' said the first troll, reaching for another cake. 'My name is *Qwooush*, spelt Q-3-0-0-3-q, and I say what's what.'

Soldier said, 'But what do you get out of it? What is your price?'

'You give us your babies for one year,' said King Q3003q, 'and we eat them. Yum, yum.'

'What?' cried Layana.

'Ha!' cried King Q3003q. 'I make the joke!' He grinned widely, revealing two long rows of thick, blunt teeth. 'No, no. Not really. What we wish is this — air shafts. At the present we use the trees, coming up through the hollow

trunks, to hide the air shaft. But we are spreading underground. We need more air shafts and we must come up in
places where there are no trees or rocks to hide the chimneys. You let us come up in other places, guard them so no
one drops things down, or makes a flood, and we help you
fight your battle. This is our price. Simply, the air shafts.
We cannot breathe down there. It is hot and stuffy. We need
more cool air.'

'I think this is a reasonable price to pay,' interrupted Wo.
'For myself and the few warriors I have brought, the cost is
nothing. I wish to fight alongside my friend Soldier. My
warriors have come because I asked them to and I know they
will fight to the death. For the rest of the beast-people, they
still distrust you, and though they will not join with Humbold,
as the Hannacks are doing, they will not fight on your side
either. In time, perhaps, we will all manage to live together
in peace.'

'So?' said King Q3003q. 'Do we have a pact? Air shafts for
free passage underground?'

'I think we can accommodate you,' said Queen Layana,
smiling at her husband. 'Yes, there is a pact between us.'

Afterwards, Soldier took Wo aside, and said, 'Thank you
for coming to our aid – for bringing the trolls.'

'It was nothing.'

'Oh, but it was something. Wo, I am so glad to see you. I
heard you were banished. I was chastising myself for not
finding out more, but the thought of war drove it from my
mind. I am so sorry.'

The dog-head gave him a lopsided grin. 'I was not exiled
– after all, you gave us the barns, the seed grain and the
ploughs; in fact, many secretly confessed they admired me
for what I had done. But publicly I was shunned. Dog-heads

turned away from me when I walked abroad. I was cut wherever I went. Gradually this went away. These things do. Beast-people started speaking to me again.' He grinned a second time. 'Things were almost back to normal when I recruited warriors for this expedition. The gods only know what they will be saying about me back in Falyum now.'

'Good things, I hope. And if not, they are but fools, and who cares what fools think?'

Chapter Ten

Reports had it that Humbold's army was on the move. It seemed to be heading for the south-west coastline of the Cerulean Sea. Soldier spent sleepless nights trying to decide the best place to attack. He wanted the advantage of high ground as well as surprise. But before he committed his army to battle he had to honour his promise to himself. He needed to talk with Drummond and try to heal the terrible wounds they had inflicted on one another in their old world.

A messenger was sent out and Drummond's reply was that he would meet with Soldier in the foothills to the west of Zamerkand. Soldier was to come armed only with a sword (to protect himself against bandits and rogue Hannacks on the journey), which he was to lay down some distance from their exact meeting point. Both parties were to be alone and unarmed at that point, though a bodyguard could be kept a mile distant.

'Since we have never learned to trust one another,' Drummond's message read, 'we must both be prepared for treachery. I have certainly been led over the years to expect such from you, and you must do the same.'

Soldier flared at the implication of dishonourable conduct on his part, but felt it useless to send back counter-arguments. It was best that it all came out at their meeting. He decided to take no bodyguard (against all pleading from his wife and Golgath, who called him mad) and trust to his own persuasive powers of speech. Soldier felt he had to get Drummond to agree to a reconciliation. He, for his part, was full of remorse for all the anguish he had caused the other man and meant to convince him of his sincerity.

Thus he found himself standing unarmed and alone by the needle rock which was to be their meeting place.

Drummond came riding up slowly from the west. When he was still some distance from Soldier, he dismounted and hobbled his charger. Then he strode towards his hated enemy. Soldier waited.

Drummond was a huge man, of immense strength. His blue eyes were set in a broad, tanned face below a wide brow. Dressed in a leather jerkin and a faded kilt, his thick, powerful limbs protruded from both, bare to the knee and to the elbow, covered in tattoos. A shock of greying hair knotted with cow dung fell from his great head about his shoulders. There was a look of pure malice in his expression.

'So,' he said, stopping an arm's length from Soldier, 'we meet face to face.'

'It's been a long time, Drummond. Too many years of blood have flowed between us. I am come to beg your forgiveness for all the wrongs I have done to your family.'

'And so you should. I was the last of my kin. Now I have but a single son, left behind in our old world, who will carry on the name, but that's no thanks to you, slaughterer. You massacred my whole clan that terrible day, Valechor, and I am determined you will answer for it with your own life.'

'You will recall that your clan murdered my bride on our wedding day, left her staining the snows with her blood, even though she was your own kin!' snarled Soldier. Then he remembered he was not here to accuse, but to seek forgiveness. 'But – I am sorry – that is all in the past. I know how you feel and I am ashamed for my acts – especially the battle that killed your own first wife. I knew not that she was a woman in male armour. Drummond, we have each wronged the other in unconscionable ways. It is an unholy mesh of foul deeds, perpertrated on both sides. But my death, or yours, will not set right those wrongs, they will only add to them. Can we not leave them in the old world and start afresh here and now, and beg each other's pardon for our black actions?'

'The knight Valechor is a coward,' spat Drummond. 'Afraid to die.'

'You know that is not true,' Soldier said, patiently. 'I have fought many battles, many single combats, and have proved my courage a hundred times over the course of a lifetime.'

'But old men grow more afraid than young men.'

'This may be true, but neither of us is yet feeble-minded. No, no, I am simply weary of this feud. I do not want your blood on my hands for reasons buried in our past. They are red enough already. I do not know which of us would prevail – you are as good in battle as I and it could go either way – but even if we have to fight in the coming conflict, on opposite sides, I would rather it was not because of the feud. Let it be for the side we take in *this* war, not because we carry over the hate from the last.'

Drummond folded his arms and smiled grimly.

'You mean even if we forgive each other, I can still kill you in the coming fight?'

'If you wish. But here,' Soldier stretched forth his hand, 'say you feel remorse for your old wrongs. I do. I am ashamed for them.'

Drummond looked down at the hand and sneered. 'Is it come to this?' he said. 'That I should touch the vile hand that murthered my kin? I am a king now, my son a royal prince. We prised the monarchy from the last weak line and mean to hold it for our own. We rule that other land you once rode in your arrogant pride. Remember, Valechor, how you trampled on Drummonds as if the clan were nought but tinkers?'

'Cattle thieves and wayside killers!' flashed Soldier, once again overcome by passion where he should have remained calm. 'But — but you force harsh words from my mouth. Words I wish to swallow henceforth and never utter again. Here, take my hand. We need to start afresh.'

After some long hesitation, Drummond reached out and grasped the palm and fingers of his foe. He held them in a powerful grip, staring hard into Soldier's blue eyes. Then, inexplicably, he raised his other arm in the air. Soldier looked at it, puzzled, and tried to pull away, but Drummond held him there, fast to the spot.

Although Soldier had left his sword Kutrama behind, he still wore Sintra, his scabbard. She now sang out with a high, clear note, startling both men. Soldier instinctively turned, thinking someone was coming up behind him to stab him in the back. But there was no one. In the next second he dipped his head, knowing that his scabbard could not lie. Someone, somewhere, was about to try to kill him.

There was a swish, and an arrow struck Soldier high in the chest, just below the left collar bone. A little lower and it would have hit his heart. In the distance he saw through a haze of pain that an archer had risen from a hollow in the ground. This was the would-be assassin.

Drummond's features lit up with pleasure. The erstwhile borderer then drew a hidden dagger from his sock and raised it in expectation of finishing his treachery on Soldier.

'I told you what to expect!' he cried, triumphantly. 'You are a dead man, Valechor.'

Soldier kicked out and caught his adversary in the groin, spoiling his stroke. At the same time he wrenched free of Drummond's grip. Pulling the arrow out of his own shoulder, he used it as a dagger to plunge into Drummond's skull. But the other jerked his head aside. The arrow pierced the joint between shoulder and arm, slicing through muscle and severing a tendon. Drummond yelled in great pain, reactively slashing with his knife. A second arrow from the archer flew past Soldier's hip, missing by fractions. Wounded, Soldier struggled with his adversary, as both fought to stab the other. For a few moments there was stalemate. They heaved back and forth, each trying to pierce the other's heart. Finally Drummond fell on to his back, his dagger flying from his fingers.

Soldier was now weak with loss of blood. He turned and stumbled away. The archer took aim, having a broad back now as a target. However, before he could loose his arrow a hawk suddenly dropped from the sky and tore into his face with its talons. The archer screamed, dropping his bow, his hands going up to try to protect his eyes. It was a hopeless attempt. Now blinded, the hawk still ripping at his features with beak and claw, he ran mindlessly straight into a wall of rock and fell stunned, perhaps dead, at the foot of a cliff.

Luz, thought Soldier. It had to be the magician, who had once more taken on the form of a bird. The young man had obviously followed him, or more likely been told to follow him by Golgath and Layana, to protect him should he need it. Thank the gods he had, for Soldier would otherwise be hugging death to his bosom.

Soldier reached the place where he had tethered his mount. Once on his horse he rode towards Zamerkand. The hawk stayed, to harass Drummond, for though he also had to deal with a wound, it was not so deep nor so wide as Soldier's. There was no blood gushing forth from Drummond's injury. The hawk flew at the blue-eyed warrior time after time, until it was sure Soldier was well on his way back to his own city, then he left Drummond to his own devices.

Soldier reached the city without further hindrance, falling from his horse in a dead faint just outside the gates. He was carried to the court physicians, who immediately stemmed the flow of blood from the artery. Then others were called in, doctors and apothecaries, to assist with his well-being. When he came to he was in a comfortable bed, his dear wife leaning over him, looking grey with worry. Soldier reached up and stroked her hair and drew a smile from her.

'I shall recover,' he said, 'in time to take the life of Drummond on the field of battle.'

'He would not listen?'

'No, he is too full of hate. Where is Luz?'

'Back safe and sound.' She smiled. 'He has finally learned the spell of the hawk as well as the sparrow.'

'Good. Good. I think I must rest . . .' He drifted away again.

Over the next few days he gathered his strength, doing as he was told by the doctors, eating and drinking that which was good for his recovery. In normal times he would have sent them packing, preferring to drag himself back in his own way. But the times were not normal. He had only a short while to make himself battle fit. It was unthinkable that the army should go to war without him. The Red Pavilions would expect him to be in the vanguard and that was where he intended to be. His wife did not argue with him over this matter. The fate of the world depended on victory. There would be no point in recovering if Humbold ruled the earth.

Once he felt able, Soldier began to pore over maps and charts, while listening to the reports of his informants and spies. With Golgath he tracked Humbold's progress. It seemed the enemy were heading for south of the Ancient Forests, near the petrified pools of Yan.

With chilling certainty Soldier realised that the battle would be fought on the very same hill on which he had awoken when he had first found himself in this otherworld. He had come to sensibility without memory of who or what he was, his armour dented and his sword gone, blood on his sandals and kilt. Clearly he had been in some kind of war, but on meeting with Layana, who had been out hunting with her favourite hawk, he had learned that no battle had been fought on that spot for at least a hundred years. It seemed more than co-incidence that the battle looked like taking place in this partic-ular spot, given that it could have been anywhere.

Golgath had spent some time preparing the Guthrumite troops for the coming war. Unknown to Soldier, even Layana had enlisted. She told Golgath that if the allies lost the war she would be wife of no one and queen of nothing, so what would be the point in remaining alive? Golgath had to agree. He had recruited everyone and anyone who was remotely fit and able. Many of them had spent the last few weeks in training. They were far from ready, but time was running short. At any moment the trolls might decide not to let the allies use their underground system and the battle would have to be fought on open ground, putting them at a great disadvantage.

Q3003q took Soldier down the nearest entrance to his kingdom within reach of Zamerkand. It was in the very same woodland that had hidden the witchboy IxonnoxI when he was a callow youth. Q3003q showed Soldier a hollow oak and asked him to squeeze inside the trunk.

'In there?' said Soldier. 'I'll never do it.'

'Oh, you will — just try.'

So Soldier did his best, but it was only because the bark was rotten that he managed it. The shell of the old oak flexed as he squeezed himself into the gap. He then found himself in a narrow, sloping tunnel going down into the earth. He followed this passageway, urged on by Q3003q, who came behind him. There were hairy roots of trees to negotiate, for the trolls had tried to cut their tunnels without harming the denizens of the forest. These white tubers finally formed a knitted ceiling to the passageways and any chambers that appeared on the way. A glowing fungus, nurtured no doubt became of its powers of light, ran the whole way over their heads.

The first thing that Soldier noticed was the musty smell of soil. It was a powerful odour that was omnipresent. Underlying this smell was another less pleasant one of stale sweat and grimy garments. The further he went, the more trolls he encountered, and many of them were none too pleased to see him. Some glared as they got on with their daily chores, others spat in front of him, or growled like animals. He got the impression that though he had descended to this world with the king as an escort, the authority of the monarchy in this underground maze was of no great concern to the troll citizens. It seemed that a king down here was not much more than the head of a village, and the trolls did not all agree with his plans.

'What do you want?' snarled one fat troll, standing in Soldier's way. 'Why don't you go back to the surface where you came from.'

'Now, now, F5555f,' said Q3003q, 'there's no need to be rude. I invited the human down here. There'll be a lot more of them soon, on their way to one of their wars. You know we're getting air shafts in return.'

'I think we've got enough air shafts.'

'Well, what you think or don't think, F5555f, is of little concern to me – just get your fat arse out of the tunnel.'

'Make me!'

'Do you want me to call my thugs?' He turned to Soldier and said, 'What can you expect of someone with no zeros in his name, eh?'

F5555f scowled and eventually stepped aside, but he managed to tread on Soldier's foot as he did so. Soldier winced. He was still a little weak from the wound he had received from Drummond and the extra pain was not at all welcome. He gave F5555f's ear a clip with the back of his hand, saying, 'Do that again and I'll chop that foot off.'

The fat troll wailed and disappeared into a dark chamber.

'Who are the *thugs*?' asked Soldier of Q3003q, once they had a clear passage again. 'Are the letters an acronym for some force of law?'

'No,' replied King Q3003q, candidly. 'Thugs are are trolls who go around beating up other trolls – bullying them just for the sake of it. I use them to keep order down here. Don't you have thugs in the overworld? Generally my subjects don't like violence, but thugs seem to thrive on it, so I harness their viciousness and use it to keep myself in power.'

Soldier blinked, wondering if he actually approved of this king of the trolls. The creature's law enforcement methods were somewhat dubious. Still, it was none of his business, and he tried to ignore the hissing of the female trolls as he passed by their clay homes, and the oaths and missiles of the male trolls who seemed to spend their time blocking passageways.

Q3003q took Soldier all over the underworld. Far from seeming loyal to him, his subjects appeared to regard him as some kind of fool. They jeered at him when he tried to explain what Soldier was doing there. They questioned every sentence that left his mouth. They even leaned on their mops and brooms, blocking his way when he tried to use the tunnels. The king appeared to be entitled to no respect whatsoever from his disloyal subjects.

Finally Q3003q led him to a wide series of chambers and pointed to the earthen ceiling.

'This is the spot,' he said, 'under the hill above the Ancient Forest, by the petrified pools of Yan. Your army can break through here and come up behind the enemy.'

'But,' said Soldier, looking up, 'this seems to be one area of your underground kingdom that is highly regarded. Aren't those fetish dolls hanging from the roots of the ancient trees? Don't your subjects regard this as a holy site?'

'Oh, don't worry about that,' said Q3003q, none too convincingly. 'I'll soon persuade them to agree to ignore the sacrilege. Those dolls have only been up there a thousand years or so. You leave that to me. The air shafts are too important to let things like sacred sites stand in our way. You can feel how hot and stuffy it is down here. We have to get more air in. One breeze is worth violating a dozen temples to Theg.'

'Well, don't you have to get some sort of permission first?'

'Permission?' snorted Q3003q. 'I'm the king.'

'Yes, but the office of king doesn't seem to carry much weight around here.'

'Oh, it'll be all right.'

'I'd like to hear someone else say so.'

Q3003q shrugged and called down the tunnels. Trolls in yellow garments appeared.

'These are priests,' explained the king. 'Look,' he said to the troll priests, 'we're going to smash up the ceiling a bit. That's all right, isn't it? It's for a good cause. It's to get air shafts.'

The priests started wailing at the tops of their voices.

Q3003q waved impatiently for silence. When it came, he said, 'I'll give you the Quartz Crystal Gardens and the Malachite Caves. You can build your temples there.'

There was no more wailing. One of the troll priests mentioned the fact that nothing could replace ancient trees in the eyes of Theg. Ancient trees were a force of nature that had no equal under the gods. They were living proof of the pacifistic nature of the real world. They were strong-limbed, strong-bodied, and symbolic of all that was good and green. The Malachite Caves and the Quartz Crystal Gardens were but poor substitutes for the Tree Temples.

'All right then, I'll throw in the Halls of Garnet too.'

The priests looked at each other and nodded, ambling back into the darkness whence they had come. Soldier was amazed by the avarice of the trolls, but Q3003q said that trolls had always been greedy. They would sell their firstborn for an apple, he told Soldier. They respected nothing, not traditions, not holy sites, not kings, not each other. They treated everything with contempt and were so easy to bribe it was laughable. It was said that if you threw a tiny silver farthing in amongst a crowd of sharp-toothed trolls, they would all go away with a piece of it.

'Do not concern yourself, Soldier – I'll get your army to this place, and there will be ladders ready to burst through to the overworld.'

Soldier returned to Zamerkand. First he visited General Velion, his second-in-command in the coming war. Together they assembled the troops on the hard parade ground outside the city walls.

'Make ready the Red Pavilions,' he cried, addressing his warriors. 'I call on the Wolf Pavilion, the Eagle Pavilion, the Elephant, Lion, Tiger, Hawk – I call on all my Carthagan warriors, for we are about to begin the most important battle of our lives. If we lose, the world will descend into darkness and chaos. If we win, the King Magus usurper will go and the new young King Magus will rule the magic of the earth.'

'Commander,' cried a captain, raising his sword, 'when do we leave?'

'Tomorrow,' was the reply.

Soldier then returned to the city. He spent the night with his wife in one long embrace. Golgath came to fetch him just before dawn.

'Q3003q will meet me and my army at the edge of the woodland – we are leaving now.'

'Good,' said Soldier, dressing as they spoke. He wore a breastplate, sandals and leather kilt only. For the rest, his limbs were bare and his head helmetless. He fought better unencumbered. 'My own Red Pavilions will be ready for me. Wo and his dog-heads are waiting with them, along with Guido and his small force of Bhantans. We have fashioned rafts in the reeds of the Blue River. As you know, the Blue River breaks into three, the Red, the Green and the White

Rivers, just before it reaches the petrified pools of Yan. We will be in three forces, coming down those rivers, arriving just before noon to engage the enemy, who are gathered on the hill above the Ancient Forest. You will burst forth from the ground within the enemy lines precisely at noon. Is that understood?'

'Perfectly.'

They each laid a hand on the other's shoulder, then hugged like men.

'Good,' said Golgath. 'May the Sacred Seven be with us, though I very much doubt they'll even take an interest, stuck up there in their lofty peaks.'

'Oh, you never know, gods are such fickle creatures – they could be taking wagers right now. Spagg is down in the marketplace doing just that, damn his soul. I have heard that the odds are two to one that we'll lose, a hundred to one that we'll prevail.'

Both men laughed.

'One last thing,' said Soldier, buckling his sword. 'You know we may have to kill your brother, Kaff.'

Golgath sighed. 'One hopes that one's family is instilled with honour and good, but unfortunately my brother is empty of both. He is an unworthy vessel. However, if he has to die I pray it will not be by my hand, but that of another. Fratricide is a terrible crime.'

'Hardly murder, Golgath. This is war.' Soldier looked around for his wife, but she had disappeared. Musket was there instead, standing in one of the several doorways.

'Goodbye, son – I shall return as soon as I can.'

'Yes, Father. Will I rule the city while you and Mother are gone?'

'Why, surely your mother . . .' Soldier realised something

and frowned. He turned again to confront Golgath, only to find his friend and general had vanished too. 'Ah, she will be on the battlefield, that little vixen,' he said quietly. Then, to Musket, 'Yes, while we are gone, son, you are in sole charge. Rule Zamerkand wisely.'

'I will, Father.'

Soldier left and joined his troops. He led his army to the river and there they boarded the rafts. They sailed forth, down the waters, towards the sea. Mid-morning they sighted the delta and the rafts split between the three now separate rivers. One raft overturned in a fierce current, but the rest made it to the end of the journey. The Red Pavilions, warriors every one, poured forth on to the shores.

Humbold, Kaff and Drummond were waiting on the hill above the Ancient Forest with their immense army. On seeing the Red Pavilions the captains of their troops became excited. Instead of waiting for the Red Pavilions to ascend the slope, they ran down in great numbers, to fall upon the oncoming allies, despite the recalls of their generals. It is always a hazard with an unwieldy army that communication will break down. So it was with Humbold's army. Yet he, Kaff and Drummond still retained confidence, for they outnumbered the enemy a hundred to one.

Battle was joined.

Soldier's side had no cavalry. The enemy cavalry consisted mainly of Hannacks, those wild, crazy barbarians who wore the skins of flayed men as cloaks and severed bearded human jaws on their bald heads as wigs. The Hannacks charged not in controlled squadrons, but as individuals, as barbarian hordes are wont to do. Their hearing was poor so they heard no commands: they listened to no drum or bugle. They simply thundered in with the joy of bloodlust to chop and hack at their pleasure. Soldier's disciplined regiments of long-spearmen stood fast in determined rows. The long spears broke up the horde into small isolated groups, the swordsmen moved in to drag them from their horses, and they were put to death at the points of weapons. Soon there were few Hannacks left and those that remained were bewildered by the speed at which their comrades had fallen.

The enemy cavalry having been dealt with, Soldier's pavilions did their best to roll up the flanks of the infantry and confuse them by crowding them in together. Soldier found himself fighting hand to hand with someone he had met in the Unknown Territory, Prince Fabulet.

'What are you doing, fighting for that tyrant?' gasped Soldier in the young man's ear. 'Do you not know he will discard you all once you have got him where he wants to be?'

'My father,' replied the prince, miserably. 'I had to obey my father's wishes.'

Then they were parted by the bodyguards of both and found themselves swept to other areas of the battlefield.

As noon approached it seemed that Humbold's army was gaining the initiative. The Red Pavilions were being thinned by the minute. Bullroarers were blaring, trumpets were crowing. The drums beat and the cymbals clashed. Enemy standards were waving proud, while those of the Red Pavilions were wilting. There was an air of anticipation in the foe, who like all who believe they will triumph were enthused. Their success gave them strength. They forced the Red Pavilions on to the back foot. Though none of the allies fled, for Carthagans never run, they were in despair. Humbold stood high on the hill, Kaff at his side, victory in their faces.

Drummond shouldered his way through to the front line and sought out Soldier. The blue-eyed borderer slew several

Carthagans and one or two dog-headed barbarian beast-people
to reach his hated foe. Then he stood before him, broad and
powerful, ready with his sword.

'Now you die, Valechor!'

'Please,' replied Soldier, 'no talk – just fight.'

A mighty struggle began between the pair. Both were not
up to full strength, still nursing their earlier wounds, but they
fought like savage animals. Soldier wielded Kutrama with great
skill, while Sintra now sang inspiring battle songs at the top
of her voice. Her high, clear notes unnerved Drummond, but
still he slashed and thrust with equal skill, using an ancient
claymore which had accompanied him into this world.

In the middle of their struggle the sun reached high noon.

To Soldier it was the hour of the resurrection! The earth
seemed to open in a hundred places, like swollen graves
bursting. All over the battlefield a fresh new army began to
pour forth from the depths. Golgath and the Guthrumites
now came tumbling from below ground to join with the
confused enemy. Soldier saw that the scheme had worked.
The tide was now turning, for Humbold's army had no idea
how many subterranean troops would come from beneath
their feet. All they saw were warriors leaping as if from hell,
flying from dark earthen holes with great energy, screaming
and yelling oaths, hacking, chopping, stabbing. Some of
Humbold's troops were confused and began to panic.

Battlefield rumours flew amongst them.

These newcomers were demons from the lowest fires! They
were devils baked and cooked hard in the ovens of the middle-
earth! They were sons of the volcano, invulnerable and
unstoppable!

The fringes of Humbold's army believed these whispers
and turned to run, leaving the core to continue the fighting.

The smell of gore, blood and sweat filled the hot noon, and underlying these, the horrible odour of fear. Many in the centre of Humbold's army, seeing the edges crumble and run, began to lose their reason. They went berserk, attempting to slash an avenue through their own troops as well as those of the enemy, in order to force themselves an escape route. Soon it was difficult to see who was fighting for Humbold's cause.

Soldier and Drummond remained locked in single combat. They had a bare patch of ground to themselves. Around them was death and chaos as the tide of men rolled back and forth.

A strange thing began to happen.

One moment the pair were fighting in this world; the next they were back in their old land. Soldier saw about him the kingdom of the border country. One second he was wearing a light breastplate and sandals, the next he was in full armour. Both men had been growing more fatigued, their strokes less skilful, their parries less able. Yet this unusual phenomenon invigorated them. They renewed their attacks on one another, each seeking a chink in the other's defences, each hoping to deliver the death blow.

Valechor saw men about him in bright armour and riding battle horses. Their weapons were broadswords and maces. They were fighting in cold green woods and on frost-covered grassy slopes. The conflict was desperate and the sway of battle heaved first one way, and then the other. A stroke from Valechor's sword landed on Drummond's shoulder, the armour dinting but not splitting. Drummond then counter-thrust at his opponent's eyes, but Valechor's helmet protected his head from the blade's sharp point.

Then, just as suddenly, the world was dun-hued dirt ground again, and the fighting men half-naked warriors, with a hot sun burning above them. Short-swords and bossed wooden shields were the weapons here. Soldier battled in the choking dust, trying to find a way through Drummond's guard. A sandal slippery with sweat flew off Soldier's right foot. He kicked the other off to join it, continuing to fight in bare feet. His wooden shield was hacked at the edge, Drummond's blade almost cutting through.

So it went, the pair slipping back and forth, first in this world then in another. They sensed a universal destiny. The victor of one fight, it seemed, was bound to be the hero of the other. Valechor was aware that overall victory depended upon winning both battles. He and Drummond were fighting them as one, and all wrongs and rights were to be settled here on this day, a twin conflict in which only one could prevail.

A regiment of witches were let loose upon the dusty hill in the first world, while a company of trained wolves were unleashed from beneath the greenwood trees in the second. Soldier and Drummond ignored all these distractions, focusing only on a single foe — each other.

Finally the hapless Drummond slipped on an icy patch in the old world and fell forward on Soldier's blade in the new.

Kutrama, the named sword, had triumphed.

Drummond staggered back, the sword protruding from his breast.

'This is not how it should be,' he gasped in pained disbelief. 'I was the one who was wronged.'

'It was an accident,' replied Valechor, who was Soldier. 'You fell on the blade.'

The hate in Drummond's eyes dimmed, to be followed by the glaze that heralded death. He fell forward at Soldier's feet, crashing to the ground in his armour in the old world, then raising the dust in the new. A king, an erstwhile cattle thief and highway robber, had gone to that level ground where his clan had gone before. His despised foe, Valechor, would join him one day, but this was not that day, and victory was Soldier's.

Elsewhere the fight was also coming to an end.

Guido was slain by Kaff's sword.

Wo and his dog-heads chased the remnants of the Hannacks from the field.

Humbold was beheaded by Golgath's axe, his head rolling down amongst the frantic witches, their regiment in disarray.

Layana threw back the visor on her helmet and Captain Kaff, on seeing her beautiful face, went to her.

She stabbed him once in the throat, quick as a viper.

'I loved you,' he said, falling to his knees, the blood gushing forth. 'And you once loved me.'

'Never,' she replied. 'It was but a fancy.'

The enemy army collapsed, their retreat turning to a rout, their heels shown plain and clear to the victorious allies.

Epitaphs

Soldier never again became that splendid but awful and bloody knight Valechor. He remained in Zamerkand until the end of his days, contented. He lived gloriously until he was an elderly man and melted away with a seasonal frost. Layana died within two weeks of Soldier's passing and her adopted son Musket became the new king. The son of Drummond in the old world also held on to kingship, but unlike his father was a peaceful king and brought stability to the borderlands. Spagg outlived Soldier, becoming a toothless, wizened husk, unwilling to release life until it sighed at last from his leathery shell. Some say his remains blew away on the night wind. Uthellen lived for thirty years in Zamerkand as companion to Layana. Her son IxonnoxI ruled for several centuries, playing wisely with the world's magic. OmmullummO retired to a dusty corner of the universe and rotted away. Sando died shortly after hearing of his brother's death, having caught a terrible sadness. Soldier's dragon continued for three hundred years, grieving the only mother he had known when called to his funeral by Wo's mournful barking.

Fractured hearts were mended and whole ones broken anew. That is the nature of the shadow worlds in which we live.